THE
MAGICIAN KING

ALSO BY LEV GROSSMAN

Codex
The Magicians

THE
MAGICIAN KING

A Novel

LEV GROSSMAN

VIKING

VIKING
Published by the Penguin Group
Penguin Group (USA) Inc., 375 Hudson Street, New York, New York 10014, U.S.A.
Penguin Group (Canada), 90 Eglinton Avenue East, Suite 700, Toronto, Ontario,
Canada M4P 2Y3 (a division of Pearson Penguin Canada Inc.)
Penguin Books Ltd, 80 Strand, London WC2R 0RL, England
Penguin Ireland, 25 St. Stephen's Green, Dublin 2, Ireland (a division of Penguin Books Ltd)
Penguin Books Australia Ltd, 250 Camberwell Road, Camberwell, Victoria 3124, Australia
(a division of Pearson Australia Group Pty Ltd)
Penguin Books India Pvt Ltd, 11 Community Centre, Panchsheel Park,
New Delhi – 110 017, India
Penguin Group (NZ), 67 Apollo Drive, Rosedale, Auckland 0632, New Zealand
(a division of Pearson New Zealand Ltd)
Penguin Books (South Africa) (Pty) Ltd, 24 Sturdee Avenue, Rosebank,
Johannesburg 2196, South Africa

Penguin Books Ltd, Registered Offices: 80 Strand, London WC2R 0RL, England

First published in 2011 by Viking Penguin, a member of Penguin Group (USA) Inc.

1 3 5 7 9 10 8 6 4 2

Copyright © Lev Grossman, 2011
All rights reserved

PUBLISHER'S NOTE: This is a work of fiction. Names, characters, places, and incidents either are the
product of the author's imagination or are used fictitiously, and any resemblance to actual persons,
living or dead, business establishments, events, or locales is entirely coincidental.

LIBRARY OF CONGRESS CATALOGING IN PUBLICATION DATA
Grossman, Lev.
The magician king / Lev Grossman.
p. cm.
ISBN 978-0-670-02231-1 (alk. paper)
ISBN 978-0-670-02314-1 (export edition)
1. Magic—Fiction. 2. College graduates—Fiction. I. Title.
PS3557.R6725M28 2011
813'.54—dc22 2011019733

Printed in the United States of America

For Sophie

We shall now seek that which we shall not find.

—Sir Thomas Malory, *Le Morte D'Arthur*

BOOK I

CHAPTER 1

Quentin rode a gray horse with white socks named Dauntless. He wore black leather boots up to his knees, different-colored stockings, and a long navy-blue topcoat that was richly embroidered with seed pearls and silver thread. On his head was a platinum coronet. A glittering side-sword bumped against his leg—not the ceremonial kind, the real kind, the kind that would actually be useful in a fight. It was ten o'clock in the morning on a warm, overcast day in late August. He was everything a king of Fillory should be. He was hunting a magic rabbit.

By King Quentin's side rode a queen: Queen Julia. Up ahead were another queen and another king, Janet and Eliot—the land of Fillory had four rulers in all. They rode along a high-arched forest path littered with yellow leaves, perfect little sprays of them that looked like they could have been cut and placed by a florist. They moved in silence, slowly, together but lost in their separate thoughts, gazing out into the green depths of the late summer woods.

It was an easy silence. Everything was easy. Nothing was hard. The dream had become real.

"Stop!" Eliot said, at the front.

They stopped. Quentin's horse didn't halt when the others' did—Dauntless wandered a little out of line and halfway off the trail before he persuaded her for good and all to quit walking for a damn minute. Two years as a king of Fillory and he was still shit at horseback riding.

"What is it?" he called.

They all sat for another minute. There was no hurry. Dauntless snorted once in the silence: lofty horsey contempt for whatever human enterprise they thought they were pursuing.

"Thought I saw something."

"I'm starting to wonder," Quentin said, "if it's even possible to track a rabbit."

"It's a hare," Eliot said.

"Same difference."

"It isn't, actually. Hares are bigger. And they don't live in burrows, they make nests in open ground."

"Don't start," both Julia and Janet said, in unison.

"Here's my real question," Quentin said. "If this rabbit thing really can see the future won't it know we're trying to catch it?"

"It can see the future," Julia said softly, beside him. "It cannot change it. Did you three argue this much when you were at Brakebills?"

She wore a sepulchral black riding dress and an actual riding hood, also black. She always wore black, like she was in mourning, even though Quentin couldn't think of anyone she should have been in mourning for. Casually, like she was calling over a waiter, Julia summoned a tiny songbird to her wrist and raised it up to her ear. It chipped, chirruped something, and she nodded back and it flew away again.

Nobody noticed, except for Quentin. She was always giving and getting little secret messages from the talking animals. It was like she was on a different wireless network from the rest of them.

"You should have let us bring Jollyby," Janet said. She yawned, holding the back of her hand against her mouth. Jollyby was Master of the Hunt at Castle Whitespire, where they all lived. He usually supervised this kind of excursion.

"Jollyby's great," Quentin said, "but even he couldn't track a hare in the woods. Without dogs. When there's no snow."

"Yes, but Jollyby has very well-developed calf muscles. I like looking at them. He wears those man-tights."

"I wear man-tights," Quentin said, pretending to be affronted. Eliot snorted.

"I imagine he's around here somewhere." Eliot was still scanning the trees. "Discreet distance and all that. Can't keep that man away from a royal hunt."

"Careful what you hunt," Julia said, "lest you catch it."

Janet and Eliot looked at each other: more inscrutable wisdom from Julia. But Quentin frowned. Julia made her own kind of sense.

Quentin hadn't always been a king, of Fillory or anywhere else. None of them had. Quentin had grown up a regular non-magical, non-royal person in Brooklyn, in what he still in spite of everything thought of as the real world. He'd thought Fillory was a fiction, an enchanted land that existed only as the setting of a series of fantasy novels for children. But then he'd learned to do magic, at a secret college called Brakebills, and he and his friends had found out that Fillory was real.

It wasn't what they expected. Fillory was a darker and more dangerous place in real life than it was in the books. Bad things happened there, terrible things. People got hurt and killed and worse. Quentin went back to Earth in disgrace and despair. His hair turned white.

But then he and the others had pulled themselves together again and gone back to Fillory. They faced their fears and their losses and took their places on the four thrones of Castle Whitespire and were made kings and queens. And it was wonderful. Sometimes Quentin couldn't believe that he'd lived through it all when Alice, the girl he loved, had died. It was hard to accept all the good things he had now, when Alice hadn't lived to see them.

But he had to. Otherwise what had she died for? He unslung his bow and stood up in the stirrups and looked around. Bubbles of stiffness popped satisfyingly in his knees. There was no sound except for the hush of falling leaves slipping through other leaves.

A gray-brown bullet flickered across the path a hundred feet in front of them and vanished into the underbrush at full tilt. With a quick fluid motion that had cost him a lot of practice Quentin nocked an arrow and drew. He could have used a magic arrow, but it didn't seem sporting. He aimed for a long moment, straining against the strength of the bow, and released.

The arrow burrowed into the loamy soil up to the feathers, right where the hare's flashing paws had been about five seconds ago.

"Almost," Janet said, deadpan.

There was no way in hell they were going to catch this thing.

"Toy with me, would you?" Eliot shouted. "Yah!"

He put the spurs to his black charger, which whinnied and reared obligingly and hoofed the empty air before lunging off the path into the woods after the hare. The crashing sound of his progress through the trees faded almost immediately. The branches sprang back into place behind him and were still again. Eliot was not shit at horseback riding.

Janet watched him go.

"Hi ho, Silver," she said. "What are we even doing out here?"

It was a fair question. The point wasn't really to catch the hare. The point was—what was the point? What were they looking for? Back at the castle their lives were overflowing with pleasure. There was a whole staff there whose job it was to make sure that every day of their lives was absolutely perfect. It was like being the only guests at a twenty-star hotel that you never had to leave. Eliot was in heaven. It was everything he'd always loved about Brakebills—the wine, the food, the ceremony—with none of the work. Eliot loved being a king.

Quentin loved it too, but he was restless. He was looking for something else. He didn't know what it was. But when the Seeing Hare was spotted in the greater Whitespire metropolitan area, he knew he wanted a day off from doing nothing all day. He wanted to try to catch it.

The Seeing Hare was one of the Unique Beasts of Fillory. There were a dozen of them—the Questing Beast, who had once granted Quentin three wishes, was one of them, as was the Great Bird of Peace, an ungainly flightless bird like a cassowary that could stop a battle by appearing between the two opposing armies. There was only one of each of them, hence the name, and each one had a special gift. The Unseen Monitor was a large lizard who could turn you invisible for a year, if that's what you wanted.

People hardly ever saw them, let alone caught them, so a lot of guff got talked about them. No one knew where they came from, or what the point of them was, if any. They'd always been there, permanent features of Fillory's enchanted landscape. They were apparently immortal. The

Seeing Hare's gift was to predict the future of any person who caught it, or so the legend went. It hadn't been caught for centuries.

Not that the future was a question of towering urgency right now. Quentin figured he had a pretty fair idea of what his future was like, and it wasn't much different from his present. Life was good.

They'd picked up the hare's trail early, when the morning was still bright and dewy, and they rode out singing choruses of "Kill the Wabbit" to the tune of "Ride of the Valkyries" in their best Elmer Fudd voices. Since then it had zigzagged them through the forest for miles, stopping and starting, looping and doubling back, hiding in the bushes and then suddenly zipping across their paths, again and again.

"I do not think he is coming back," Julia said.

She didn't speak much these days. And for some reason she'd mostly given up using contractions.

"Well, if we can't track the hare we can track Eliot anyway." Janet gently urged her mount off the track and into the trees. She wore a low-cut forest-green blouse and men's chaps. Her penchant for mild cross-dressing had been the scandal of the season at court this year.

Julia didn't ride a horse at all but an enormous furry quadruped that she called a civet, which looked like an ordinary civet, long and brown and vaguely feline, with a fluidly curving back, except that it was the size of a horse. Quentin suspected it could talk—its eyes gleamed with a bit more sentience than they should have, and it always seemed to follow their conversations with too much interest.

Dauntless didn't want to follow the civet, which exuded a musky, un-equine odor, but she did as she was told, albeit at a spiteful, stiff-legged walk.

"I haven't seen any dryads," Janet said. "I thought there'd be dryads."

"Me neither," Quentin said. "You never see them in the Queenswood anymore."

It was a shame. He liked the dryads, the mysterious nymphs who watched over oak trees. You really knew you were in a magical fantasy otherworld when a beautiful woman wearing a skimpy dress made of leaves suddenly jumped out of a tree.

"I thought maybe they could help us catch it. Can't you call one or summon one or something, Julia?"

"You can call them all you want. They will not come."

"I spend enough time listening to them bitch about land allocation," Janet said. "And where are they all if they're not here? Is there some cooler, magical-er forest somewhere that they're all off haunting?"

"They are not ghosts," Julia said. "They are spirits."

The horses picked their way carefully over a berm that was too straight to be natural. An old earthwork from an ancient, unrecoverable age.

"Maybe we could make them stay," Janet said. "Legislate some incentives. Or just detain them at the border. It's bullshit that there's not more dryads in the Queenswood."

"Good luck," Julia said. "Dryads fight. Their skin is like wood. And they have staves."

"I've never seen a dryad fight," Quentin said.

"That is because nobody is stupid enough to fight one."

Recognizing a good exit line when it heard one, the civet chose that moment to scurry on ahead. Two sturdy oak trees actually leaned aside to let Julia pass between them. Then they leaned back together again, leaving Janet and Quentin to go the long way around.

"Listen to her," Janet said. "She has so totally gone native! I'm tired of her more-Fillorian-than-thou bullshit. Did you see her talking to that fucking bird?"

"Oh, leave her alone," Quentin said. "She's all right."

But if he was being honest, Quentin was fairly sure that Queen Julia wasn't all right.

Julia hadn't learned her magic the way they had, coming up through the safe, orderly system of Brakebills. She and Quentin had gone to high school together, but she hadn't gotten into Brakebills, so she'd become a hedge witch instead: she'd learned it on her own, on the outside. It wasn't official magic, institutional magic. She was missing huge chapters of lore, and her technique was so sloppy and loopy that sometimes he couldn't believe it even worked at all.

But she also knew things Quentin and the others didn't. She hadn't had the Brakebills faculty standing over her for four years making sure she colored inside the lines. She'd talked to people Quentin never would have talked to, picked up things his professors would never have let him touch. Her magic had sharp, jagged edges on it that had never been filed down.

It was a different kind of education, and it made her different. She talked differently. Brakebills had taught them to be arch and ironic about magic, but Julia took it seriously. She played it fully goth, in a black wedding dress and black eyeliner. Janet and Eliot thought it was funny, but Quentin liked it. He felt drawn to her. She was weird and dark, and Fillory had made the rest of them so damn light, Quentin included. He liked it that she wasn't quite all right and she didn't care who knew it.

The Fillorians liked it too. Julia had a special rapport with them, especially with the more exotic ones, the spirits and elementals and jinnis and even more strange and extreme beings—the fringe element, in the hazy zone between the biological and the entirely magical. She was their witch-queen, and they adored her.

But Julia's education had cost her something, it was hard to put your finger on what, but whatever it was had left its mark on her. She didn't seem to want or need human company anymore. In the middle of a state dinner or a royal ball or even a conversation she would lose interest and wander away. It happened more and more. Sometimes Quentin wondered exactly how expensive her education had been, and how she'd paid for it, but whenever he asked her, she avoided the question. Sometimes he wondered if he was falling in love with her. Again.

A distant bugle sounded—three polished sterling silver notes, muffled by the heavy silence of the woods. Eliot was sounding a recheat, a hunting call.

He was no Jollyby, but it was a perfectly credible recheat. He wasn't much for drafting legislation, but Eliot was meticulous about royal etiquette, which included getting all the Fillorian hunting protocol exactly right. (Though he found any actual killing distasteful, and usually managed to avoid it.) His bugling was good enough for Dauntless. She trembled, electrified, waiting for permission to bolt. Quentin grinned at

Janet, and she grinned back at him. He yelled like a cowboy and kicked and they were off.

It was insanely dangerous, like a full-on land-speeder chase, with ditches opening up in front of you with no warning, and low branches reaching down out of nowhere to try to clobber your head off (not literally of course, though you could never tell for sure with some of these older, more twisted trees). But fuck it, that's what healing magic is for. Dauntless was a thoroughbred. They'd been starting and stopping and dicking around all morning, and she was dying to cut loose.

And how often did he get a chance to put his royal person at risk? When was the last time he even cast a spell? His life wasn't exactly fraught with peril. They lay around on cushions all day and ate and drank their heads off all night. Lately whenever he sat down some unfamiliar inter-action had been happening between his abdomen and his belt buckle. He must have gained fifteen pounds since he took the throne. No won-der kings looked so fat in pictures. One minute you're Prince Valiant, the next you're Henry VIII.

Janet broke trail, guided by more muffled bugle notes. The horses' hooves made satisfyingly solid beats on the packed loam of the forest floor. Everything that was cloying about court life, all the safety and the relentless comfort, went away for a moment. Trunks and spinneys and ditches and old stone walls whipped and blurred past. They dodged in and out of hot sun and cool shade. Their speed froze the falling sprays of yellow leaves in midair. Quentin picked his moment, and when they hit open meadow he swung out wide to the right, and for a long minute they were side by side, coursing wildly along in parallel.

Then all at once Janet pulled up. Quickly as he could Quentin slowed Dauntless to a walk and brought her around, breathing hard. He hoped her horse hadn't pulled up lame. It took him another minute to find his way back to her.

She was sitting still and straight in the saddle, squinting off into the midday gloom of the forest. No more bugle calls.

"What is it?"

"Thought I saw something," she said.

Quentin squinted too. There was something. Shapes.

"Is that Eliot?"

"The hell are they doing?" Janet said.

Quentin dropped down out of the saddle, unslung his bow again and nocked another arrow. Janet led the horses while he walked in front. He could hear her charging up some minor defensive magic, a light ward-and-shield, just in case. He could feel the familiar staticky buzz of it.

"Shit," he said under his breath.

He dropped the bow and ran toward them. Julia was down on one knee, her hand pressed against her chest, either gasping or sobbing, he couldn't tell which. Eliot was bent over talking to her quietly. His cloth-of-gold jacket had been yanked half off his shoulder.

"It's okay," he said, seeing Quentin's white face. "That fucking civet threw her and bolted. I tried to hold it but I couldn't. She's okay, she just got the wind knocked out of her."

"You're all right." That phrase again. Quentin rubbed Julia's back while she took croaking breaths. "You're okay. I always said you should get a regular horse. I never liked that thing."

"Never liked you, either," she managed.

"Look." Eliot pointed off into the twilight. "That's what made it bolt. The hare went in there."

A few yards away a round clearing began, a still pool of grass hidden in the heart of the forest. The trees grew right up to its edge and then stopped, like somebody had cleared it on purpose, nipping out the border precisely. It could have been ruled with a compass. Quentin picked his way toward it. Lush, intensely emerald-green grass grew over lumpy black soil. In the center of the clearing stood a single enormous oak tree with a large round clock set in its trunk.

The clock-trees were the legacy of the Watcherwoman, the legendary—but quite real—time-traveling witch of Fillory. They were a magical folly, benign as far as anyone could tell, and picturesque in a surreal way. There was no reason to get rid of them, assuming you even could. If nothing else they kept perfect time.

But Quentin had never seen one like this. He had to lean back to see its crown. It must have been a hundred feet tall, and it was massively thick, at least fifteen yards around at its base. Its clock was stupendous. The face was taller than Quentin was. The trunk erupted out of the green grass and burst into a mass of wiggly branches, like a kraken sculpted in wood.

And it was moving. Its black, nearly leafless limbs writhed and thrashed against the gray sky. The tree seemed to be caught in the grip of a storm, but Quentin couldn't feel or hear any wind. The day, the day he could perceive with his five senses, was calm. It was an invisible, intangible storm, a secret storm. In its agony the clock-tree had strangled its clock—the wood had clenched it so tightly that the bezel had finally bent, and the crystal had shattered. Brass clockwork spilled out through the clock's busted face and down onto the grass.

"Jesus Christ," Quentin said. "What a monster."

"It's the Big Ben of clock-trees," Janet said behind him.

"I've never seen one like that," Eliot said. "Do you think it was the first one she made?"

Whatever it was, it was a Fillorian wonder, a real one, wild and grand and strange. It was a long time since he'd seen one, or maybe it was just a long time since he'd noticed. He felt a twinge of something he hadn't felt since Ember's Tomb: fear, and something more. Awe. They were looking the mystery in the face. This was the raw stuff, the main line, the old, old magic.

They stood together, strung out along the edge of the meadow. The clock's minute hand poked out at a right angle from the trunk like a broken finger. A yard from its base a little sapling sprouted where the gears had fallen, as if from an acorn, swaying back and forth in the silent gale. A silver pocket watch ticked away in a knot in its slender trunk. A typically cute Fillorian touch.

This was going to be good.

"I'll go first."

Quentin started forward, but Eliot put a hand on his arm.

"I wouldn't."

"I would. Why not?"

"Because clock-trees don't just move like that. And I've never seen a broken one before. I didn't think they *could* break. This isn't a natural place. The hare must have led us here."

"I know, right? It's classic!"

Julia shook her head. She looked pale, and there was a dead leaf in her hair, but she was back on her feet.

"See how regular the clearing is," she said. "It is a perfect circle. Or at least an ellipse. There is a powerful area-effect spell radiating out from the center. Or from the foci," she added quietly, "in the case of an ellipse."

"You go in there, there's no telling where you'll end up," Eliot said.

"Of course there isn't. That's why I'm going."

This, this was what he needed. This was the point—he'd been waiting for it without even knowing it. God, it had been so long. This was an adventure. He couldn't believe the others would even hesitate. Behind him Dauntless whickered in the stillness.

It wasn't a question of courage. It was like they'd forgotten who they were, and where they were, and why. Quentin retrieved his bow and took another arrow from his quiver. As an experiment, he set his stance, drew, and shot at the tree trunk. Before it reached its target the arrow slowed, like it was moving through water instead of air. They watched it float, tumbling a little end over end, backward, in slow motion. Finally it gave up the last of its momentum and just stopped, five feet off the ground.

Then it burst, soundlessly, into white sparks.

"Wow." Quentin laughed. He couldn't help it. "This place is enchanted as *balls!*"

He turned to the others.

"What do you think? This looks like an adventure to me. Remember adventures? Like in the books?"

"Yeah, remember them?" Janet said. She actually looked angry. "Remember Penny? We haven't seen him around lately, have we? I don't want to spend the rest of my queenhood cutting up your food for you."

Remember Alice, she could just as well have said. He remembered Alice. She had died, but they'd lived, and wasn't this what living was about? He bounced on his toes. They tingled and sweated in his boots, six inches from the sharp edge of the enchanted meadow.

He knew the others were right, this place practically reeked of weird magic. It was a trap, a coiled spring that was aching to spring shut on him and snap him up. And he wanted it to. He wanted to stick his finger in it and see what happened. Some story, some quest, started here, and he wanted to go on it. It felt fresh and clean and unsafe, nothing like the heavy warm lard of palace life. The protective plastic wrap had been peeled off.

"You're really not coming?" he said.

Julia just watched him. Eliot shook his head.

"I'm going to play it safe. But I can try to cover you from here."

He began industriously casting a minor reveal designed to suss out any obvious magical threats. Magic crackled and spat around his hands as he worked. Quentin drew his sword. The others made fun of him for carrying it, but he liked the way it felt in his hand. It made him feel like a hero. Or at least it made him look like a hero.

Julia didn't think it was funny. Though she didn't laugh at much of anything anymore. Anyway, he'd just drop it if magic was called for.

"What are you going to do?" Janet said, hands on her hips. "Seriously, what? Climb it?"

"When it's time I'll know what to do." He rolled his shoulders.

"I do not like this, Quentin," Julia said. "This place. This tree. If we attempt this adventure it will mean some great change of our fortunes."

"Maybe a change would do us good."

"Speak for yourself," Janet said.

Eliot finished his spell and made a square out of his thumbs and forefingers. He closed one eye and squinted through it, panning around the clearing.

"I don't *see* anything . . ."

A mournful bonging came from up in the branches. Near its crown the tree had sprouted a pair of enormous swaying bronze church bells. Why not? Eleven strokes: it still kept time, apparently, even though the works were broken. Then the silence filled back in, like water that had been momentarily displaced.

Everybody watched him. The clock-tree's branches creaked in the soundless wind. He didn't move. He thought about Julia's warning: some great change of our fortunes. His fortunes were riding high right now, he had to admit. He had a goddamned castle, full of quiet courtyards and airy towers and golden Fillorian sunlight that poured like hot honey. Suddenly he wasn't sure what he was wagering that against. He could die in there. Alice had died.

And he was a king now. Did he even have the right to go galloping off after every magic bunny that wagged its cottontail at him? That wasn't his job anymore. All at once he felt selfish. The clock-tree was right there in front of him, heaving and thrashing with power and the promise of adventure. But his excitement was slipping away. It was becoming contaminated with doubt. Maybe they were right, his place was here. Maybe this wasn't such a good idea.

The urge to go into the meadow began to wear off, like a drug, leaving him abruptly sober. Who was he kidding? Being king wasn't the beginning of a story, it was the end. He didn't need a magic rabbit to tell him his future, he knew his future because it was already here. This was the happily ever after part. Close the book, put it down, walk away.

Quentin stepped back a pace and replaced his sword in its sheath in one smooth gesture. It was the first thing his fencing master had taught him: two weeks of sheathing and unsheathing before he'd even been allowed to cut the air. Now he was glad he'd done it. Nothing made you look like more of a dick than standing there trying to find the end of your scabbard with the tip of your sword.

He felt a hand on his shoulder. Julia.

"It is all right, Quentin," she said. "This is not your adventure. Follow it no further."

He wanted to lean his head down and rub his cheek back and forth against her hand like a cat.

"I know," he said. He wasn't going to go. "I get it."

"You're really not going?" Janet sounded almost disappointed. Probably she'd wanted to watch him blow up into glitter too.

"Really not."

They were right. Let somebody else be the hero. He'd had his happy ending. Right then he couldn't even have said what he was looking for in there. Nothing worth dying for, anyway.

"Come on, it's almost lunchtime," Eliot said. "Let's find some less exciting meadow to eat in."

"Sure," Quentin said. "Cheers to that."

There was champagne in one of the hampers, staying magically chilled, or something like champagne—they were still working on a Fillorian equivalent. And those hampers, with special leather loops for the bottles and the glasses—they were the kind of thing he remembered seeing in catalogs of expensive, useless things he couldn't afford back in the real world. And now look! He had all the hampers he could ever want. It wasn't champagne, but it was bubbly, and it made you drunk. And Quentin was going to get good and drunk over lunch.

Eliot climbed back into the saddle and swung Julia up behind him. It looked like the civet was gone for good. There was still a large patch of damp black earth on Julia's rump from the fall. Quentin had a foot in Dauntless's stirrup when they heard a shout.

"Hi!"

They all looked around.

"Hi!" It was what Fillorians said instead of "hey."

The Fillorian saying it was a hale, vigorous man in his early thirties. He was striding toward them, right across the circular clearing, practically radiating exuberance. He broke into a jog at the sight of them. He totally ignored the branches of the broken clock-tree that were waving wildly over his head; he couldn't have cared less. Just another day in the magic forest. He had a big blond mane and a big chest, and he'd grown a big blond beard to cover up his somewhat moony round chin.

It was Jollyby, Master of the Hunt. He wore purple-and-yellow striped tights. His legs really were pretty impressive, especially considering that he'd never even been in the same universe as a leg press or a StairMaster or whatever. Eliot was right, he must have been following them the whole time.

"Hi!" Janet shouted back happily. "Now it's a party," she added to the others, sotto voce.

In one huge leather-gloved fist Jollyby held up a large, madly kicking hare by its ears.

"Son of a bitch," Dauntless said. "He caught it."

Dauntless was a talking horse. She just didn't talk much.

"He sure did," Quentin said.

"Lucky thing," Jollyby called out when he was close enough. "I found him sitting up on a rock, happy as you please, not a hundred yards from here. He was busy keeping an eye on you lot, and I got him to bolt the wrong way. Caught him with my bare hands. Would you believe it?"

Quentin would believe it. Though he still didn't think it made sense. How do you sneak up on an animal that can see the future? Maybe it saw other people's but not its own. The hare's eyes rolled wildly in their sockets.

"Poor thing," Eliot said. "Look how pissed off it is."

"Oh, Jolly," Janet said. She crossed her arms in mock outrage. "You should have let us catch it! Now it'll only tell *your* future."

She sounded not at all disappointed by this, but Jollyby—a superb all-around huntsman but no National Merit Scholar—looked vexed. His furry brows furrowed.

"Maybe we could pass it around," Quentin said. "It could do each of us in turn."

"It's not a bong, Quentin," Janet said.

"No," Julia said. "Do not ask it."

But Jollyby was enjoying his moment as the center of royal attention.

"Is that true, you useless animal?" he said. He reversed his grip on the Seeing Hare and hoisted it up so that he and the hare were nose to nose.

It gave up kicking and hung down limp, its eyes blank with panic. It was an impressive beast, three feet long from its twitching nose to its tail, with a fine gray-brown coat the color of dry grass in winter. It wasn't cute. This was not a tame hare, a magician's rabbit. It was a wild animal.

"What do you see then, eh?" Jollyby shook it, as if this were all its idea and therefore its fault. "What do you see?"

The Seeing Hare's eyes focused. It looked directly at Quentin. It bared its huge orange incisors.

"Death," it rasped.

They all stood there for a second. It didn't seem scary so much as inappropriate, like somebody had made a dirty joke at a child's birthday party.

Then Jollyby frowned and licked his lips, and Quentin saw blood in his teeth. He coughed once, experimentally, as if he were just trying it out, and then his head lolled forward. The hare dropped from his nerveless fingers and shot away across the grass like a rocket.

Jollyby's corpse fell forward onto the grass.

"Death and destruction!" the hare called out as it ran, in case it hadn't made itself clear before. "Disappointment and despair!"

CHAPTER 2

There was a special room in Castle Whitespire where the kings and queens met. That was another thing about being a king: everything you had was made specially for you.

It was a marvelous room. It was square, the top of a square tower, with four windows facing in four directions. The tower turned, very slowly, as some of the towers in the castle did—Castle Whitespire was built on complicated foundations of enormous brass clockwork, cleverly designed by the dwarves, who were absolute geniuses at that kind of thing. The tower completed one rotation every day. The movement was almost imperceptible.

In the center of the room was a special square table with four chairs—they were thrones, or thronelike, but made by someone who had the knack, pretty rare in Quentin's experience, of making chairs that looked like thrones but were also reasonably comfortable to sit in. The table was painted with a map of Fillory, sealed under many layers of lacquer, and at each of the four seats, pieced into the wood, were the names of the rulers who'd sat there along with little devices appropriate to said rulers. Quentin got an image of the White Stag, and the vanquished Martin Chatwin, and a deck of playing cards. Eliot's place was the most elaborately embellished, as befitted the High King. It was a square table, but there wasn't any question which side was the head.

The chairs didn't feel comfortable today. The scene of Jollyby's death was still very clear and present in Quentin's mind's eye; in fact it replayed itself more or less constantly, with showings every thirty seconds or so. As Jollyby collapsed Quentin had lurched forward and caught him and eased him to the ground. He groped helplessly at Jollyby's huge chest, as if he'd hidden his life somewhere about his person, in some secret inside pocket, and if Quentin could only find it he could give it back to him. Janet screamed: a full-throated, uncontrollable horror-movie scream that wouldn't stop for a full fifteen seconds until Eliot grasped her shoulders and physically turned her away from Jollyby's corpse.

At the same time the clearing filled with ghostly green light—a bleak, alien spell of Julia's that Quentin still didn't get the details of, or even the broad outlines of, that was intended to reveal any bad actors who might be present. It turned her eyes all black, no whites or iris at all. She was the only one who'd thought to go on the attack. But there was no one to attack.

"All right," Eliot said. "So let's talk about it. What do we think happened today?"

They looked at each other, feeling jittery and shell-shocked. Quentin wanted to do something, or say something, but he didn't know what. The truth was, he hadn't really known Jollyby all that well.

"He was so proud," he said finally. "He thought he'd saved the day."

"It had to be the rabbit," Janet said. Her eyes were red from crying. She swallowed. "Right? Or hare, whatever. That's what killed him. What else?"

"We can't assume that. The hare predicted his death but it may not have caused it. *Post hoc ergo propter hoc.* It's a logical fallacy."

If he'd waited even another second he would have realized that Janet wasn't interested in the Latin name of the logical fallacy that she might or might not have been committing.

"Sorry," he said. "That's my Asperger's flaring up again."

"So it's just a coincidence?" she snapped. "That he died right then, right after it said that about death? Maybe we've got it wrong. Maybe the hare doesn't predict the future, maybe it controls it."

"Perhaps it does not like being caught," Julia said.

"I have a hard time believing that the history of the universe is being written by a talking rabbit," Eliot said. "Though that would explain a lot."

It was five o'clock in the afternoon, their regular meeting time. For the first few months after they'd arrived at Castle Whitespire Eliot had left them to do their own things, on the theory that they'd naturally find their own courses as rulers, and take charge of the things that best suited their various gifts. This had resulted in total chaos, and nothing getting done, and the things that did get done got done twice by two different people in two different ways. So Eliot instituted a daily meeting at which they sorted through whatever business of the realm seemed most pressing as a foursome. The five o'clock meeting was traditionally accompanied by what may have been the most gloriously comprehensive whiskey service ever seen on any of the possibly infinite worlds of the multiverse.

"I told the family we'd take care of the funeral," Quentin said. "It's just his parents. He was an only child."

"I should say something," Eliot said. "He taught me bugling."

"Did you know he was a were-lion?" Janet smiled sadly. "True story. It went on a solar calendar—he changed only at equinoxes and solstices. He said it helped him understand the animals. He was hairy *everywhere*."

"Please," Eliot said. "I would give anything to not know how you know that."

"It helped with lots of things."

"I have a theory," Quentin said quickly. "Maybe the Fenwicks did it. They've been pissed at us ever since we got here."

The Fenwicks were the most senior of the several families who were running things at the time when the Brakebills returned to Fillory. They weren't happy about being kicked out of Castle Whitespire, but they didn't have the political capital to do much about it. So· they satisfied themselves with making mischief around the court.

"Assassination would be a big step up for the Fenwicks," Eliot said. "They're pretty small-time."

"And why would they kill Jollyby?" Janet said. "Everybody loved Jollyby!"

"Maybe they were trying for one of us, not him," Quentin said. "Maybe one of us was supposed to catch the hare. You know they're already trying to put it around that we killed him?"

"But how would they have done it?" Eliot said. "You're saying they sent a rabbit assassin?"

"They could not turn the Seeing Hare," Julia said. "Unique Beasts do not intervene in the affairs of men."

"Maybe it wasn't the Seeing Hare at all, maybe it was a person in hare form. A were-hare. Look, I don't know!"

Quentin rubbed his temples. If only they'd hunted that stupid lizard instead. He was annoyed at himself for forgetting what Fillory was like. He'd let himself believe that things were all better after Alice had killed Martin Chatwin, no more death and despair and disillusionment and whatever else the hare had said. But there was more. It wasn't like the books. There was always more. *Et in Arcadia ego.*

And even though he knew it was crazy, in a childishly elegant way, he couldn't escape a vague feeling that Jollyby's death was his fault, that it wouldn't have happened if he hadn't been tempted by that adventure. Or maybe he wasn't tempted enough? What were the rules? Maybe he should have gone into the clearing after all. Maybe Jollyby's death had been meant for him. He was supposed to go into the meadow and die there, but he didn't, so Jollyby had to instead.

"Maybe there isn't an explanation," he said out loud. "Maybe it's just a mystery. Just another crazy stop on Fillory's magical mystery tour. No reason for it, it just happened. You can't explain it."

This didn't satisfy Eliot. He was still Eliot, the languid lush of Brakebills, but becoming High King had uncovered a dismayingly rigorous streak in him.

"We can't have unexplained deaths in the kingdom," he said. "It won't do." He cleared his throat. "Here's what's going to happen. I'll put the fear of Ember into the Fenwicks, just in case. It won't take much. They're a bunch of pussy dandies. And I say that as a pussy dandy myself."

"And if that doesn't work?" Janet said.

"Then, Janet, you'll go lean on the Lorians." That was Fillory's neigh-

bor to the north. Janet was in charge of relations with foreign powers—
Quentin called her Fillory Clinton. "They're always behind everything
bad in the books. Maybe they were trying to decapitate the leadership.
Stupid pseudo-Viking fuckers. Now for Christ's sake let's talk about
something else for a while."

But they had nothing else to talk about, so they lapsed into silence.
Nobody was especially happy with Eliot's plan, least of all Eliot, but
they didn't have a better one, or even a worse one. Six hours after the
fact Julia's eyes were still flooded with black from the spell she'd cast in
the forest. The effect was disconcerting. She had no pupils. He wondered what she could see that they couldn't.

Eliot shuffled his notes, looking for another item of business, but
business was in short supply these days.

"It is time," Julia said. "We must go to the window."

Every day after the afternoon meeting they went out on the balcony
and waved to the people.

"Damn it," Eliot said. "All right."

"Maybe we shouldn't today," Janet said. "It feels wrong."

Quentin knew what she meant. The thought of standing out there on
the narrow balcony, frozen smiles on their faces, princess-waving at the
Fillorians who gathered for the daily ritual, felt a little off. Still.

"We should to do it," he said. "Today of all days."

"We're accepting congratulations for doing nothing."

"We're reassuring the people of continuity in the face of tragedy."

They filed out onto the narrow balcony. In the castle courtyard far
below, at the bottom of a vertiginous drop, a few hundred Fillorians had
gathered. From this height they looked unreal, like dolls. Quentin
waved.

"I wish we could do something more for them," he said.

"What do you want to do?" Eliot said. "We're the kings and queens
of a magic utopia."

Cheers drifted up from far below, faintly. The sound was tinny and
far away—it had the audio quality of a musical greeting card.

"Some progressive reforms? I want to help somebody with something. If I were a Fillorian I would depose me as an aristocratic parasite."

When Quentin and the others took the thrones, they hadn't known exactly what to expect. The details of what was involved were vague—there would be some ceremonial duties, Quentin supposed, and presumably a lead role in policy making, some responsibility for the welfare of the nation they ruled. But the truth was that there just wasn't much actual work to do.

The weird thing was that Quentin missed it. He'd expected Fillory to be something like medieval England, because it looked like medieval England, at least on casual inspection. He figured he'd just use European history, to the extent that he remembered it, as a crib sheet. He would pursue the standard enlightened humanitarian program, nothing extraordinary, greatest hits only, and go down in history as a force for good.

But Fillory wasn't England. For one thing the population was tiny—there couldn't have been more than ten thousand humans in the whole country, plus that many talking animals and dwarves and spirits and giants and such. So he and the other monarchs—or tetrarchs, whatever—were more like small-town mayors. For another, while magic was very real on Earth, Fillory *was* magical. There was a difference. Magic was part of the ecosystem. It was in the weather and the oceans and the soil, which was wildly fertile. If you wanted your crops to fail you had to work pretty hard at it.

Fillory was a land of hyperabundance. Anything that needed making could be gotten from the dwarves, sooner or later, and they weren't an oppressed industrial proletariat, they actually enjoyed making things. Unless you were an actively despicable tyrant, the way Martin Chatwin had been, there were just too many resources and too few people to create anything much in the way of civil strife. The only shortage that the Fillorian economy suffered from was a chronic shortage of shortages.

As a result whenever any of the Brakebills—as they were called, even though Julia had never even been to Brakebills, as she wasn't slow to point out—tried to get serious about something, there turned out not to be much to be serious about. It was all ritual and pomp and circumstance. Even money was just for show. It was toy money. Monopoly money. The others had all but given up on trying to make themselves useful, but Quentin couldn't quite let it go. Maybe that was what had been nagging at him, as he stood on the edge of that meadow in the woods. There must be something real somewhere out there, but he could never quite seem to get his hands on it.

"All right," he said. "What next?"

"Well," Eliot said, as they filed back inside. "There is this situation with the Outer Island."

"The where?"

"The Outer Island." He picked up some royal-looking documents. "That's what it says. I'm king of it, and even I don't know where it is."

Janet snorted. "Outer is off the east coast. Way off, a couple of days' sail. God, I can't believe they even let you be king. It's the easternmost point in the Fillorian Empire. I think."

Eliot peered at the map painted on the table. "I don't see it."

Quentin studied the map too. On his first visit to Fillory he'd sailed deep into the Western Sea, on the other side of the Fillorian continent, but his knowledge of the east was pretty sketchy.

"It's not big enough." She pointed to Julia's lap. "That's where it would be if we had a bigger table."

Quentin tried to imagine it: a little slip of white tropical sand, embellished with a decorative palm tree, embedded in an ocean of blue-green calm.

"Have you been there?" Eliot said.

"No one's ever been there. It's just a dot on the map. Somebody started a fishing colony there after his ship collided with it like a million years ago. Why are we talking about the Outer Island?"

Eliot went back to his papers. "Looks like they haven't paid their taxes in a couple of years."

"So?" Janet said. "Probably that's because they don't have any money."

"Send them a telegram," Quentin said. "DEAR OUTER ISLANDERS STOP SEND MONEY STOP IF YOU HAVE NO MONEY THEN DO NOT SEND MONEY STOP."

The meeting flagged while Eliot and Janet tried to outdo each other in composing the most useless possible telegram to the Outer Islanders.

"All right," Eliot said. The turning tower had rotated to where the flaming Fillorian sunset lit up the sky behind him. Ladders of pink cloud were stacked up above his shoulders. "I'll lean on the Fenwicks about Jollyby. Janet will speak to the Lorians." He waved vaguely. "And somebody will do something about the Outer Island. Who wants scotch?"

"I'll go," Quentin said.

"It's just there on the sideboard."

"No, I mean to the Outer Island. I'll go there. I'll see about the taxes."

"What?" Eliot sounded annoyed by the idea. "Why? It's the ass end of nowhere. And anyway, it's a treasury matter. We'll send an emissary. That's what emissaries are for."

"Send me instead."

Quentin couldn't have said what the impulse was exactly, he just knew that he had to do something. He thought of the circular meadow and the broken clock-tree and the film clip of Jollyby dying started up again. What was the point of all this when you could just drop dead, just like that? That's what he wanted to know. What was even the fuck-ing point?

"You know," Janet said, "we're not invading it. We don't need to send a king to the Outer Island. They haven't paid their taxes, which by the way is like eight fish. They're not exactly powering the whole economy."

"I'll be back before you know it." He could already tell he'd gotten it right. The tension inside him broke as soon as he said it. Relief was flooding through him, at what he didn't even know. "Who knows, maybe I'll learn something."

This would be his quest: collecting taxes from a bunch of backwater yokels. He had skipped the adventure of the broken tree, and that was fine. He would have this one instead.

"Could look weak, with the Jollyby thing." Eliot fingered his royal chin. "You taking off at the first sign of trouble."

"I'm a king. It's not like they're going to not re-elect me."

"Wait," Janet said. "You didn't kill Jollyby, did you? Is that what this is about?"

"Janet!" Eliot said.

"No, really. It would all fit together—"

"I didn't kill Jollyby," Quentin said.

"All right. Fine. Great." Eliot ticked the item off on his agenda. "Outer Island, check. That's it then."

"Well, I hope you're not going alone," Janet said. "God knows what they're like out there. It could be Captain Cook all over again."

"I'll be fine," Quentin said. "Julia's coming with me. Right, Julia?"

Eliot and Janet both stared at him. How long had it been since he surprised those two? Or anybody? He must be on to something. He smiled at Julia, and she looked back at him, though with her all-black pupils her expression was unreadable.

"Of course I am," was all she said.

That night Eliot paid Quentin a visit in his bedroom.

When he first found it the room had been stuffed with an appalling amount of hideous quasi-medieval junk. It had been literally centuries since all four of Whitespire's thrones had been filled at the same time, and in the meantime the extra royal suites had been invaded and occupied by creeping armies of superfluous candelabras, defunct chandeliers listing and deflated like beached jellyfish, unplayable musical instruments, unreturnable diplomatic gifts, chairs and tables so piteously ornamental they would break if you looked at them, or even if you didn't, dead animals ruthlessly stuffed in the very act of begging for mercy, urns and ewers and other even less easily identifiable vessels that you didn't know whether to drink out of or go to the bathroom in.

Quentin had had the room cleared out to the bare walls. Everything must go. He left the bed, one table, two chairs, a few of the better rugs, and some pleasing and/or politically expedient tapestries, that was all. He liked one tapestry in particular that depicted a marvelously appointed griffin frozen in the act of putting a company of foot soldiers to flight. It was supposed to symbolize the triumph of some group of long-dead people over some other group of long-dead people whom nobody had liked, but for some reason the griffin had cocked its head to one side in the midst of its rampage and was gazing directly out of its woven universe at the viewer as if to say, yes, granted, I'm good at this. But is it really the best use of my time?

When it was finally empty the room had grown by three times its size. It could breathe again. You could think in it. It turned out to be about as big as a basketball court, with a smooth stone floor, towering timbered ceilings where light got lost in the upper reaches and made interesting shadows, and soaring Gothic lead-glass windows a few little panels of which actually opened. It was so gloriously still and empty that when you scuffed your foot on the stone it echoed. It had the kind of hushed stillness that on Earth you saw only from a distance, on the other side of a velvet rope. It was the stillness of a closed museum, or a cathedral at night.

There was some murmuring among the upper servants that such a spartan chamber was not entirely suitable for a king of Fillory, but Quentin had decided that one of the good things about being a king of Fillory was that you got to decide what's suitable for a king of Fillory.

And anyway, if it was high royal style they wanted, the High King was their man. Eliot had a bottomless appetite for it. His bedroom was the gilded, diamond-studded, pearl-encrusted rococo lair of a god-king. Whatever else it was, it was entirely suitable.

"You know in the Fillory books you could actually get into the tapestries?" It was late, after midnight, and Eliot was standing eye-to-eye with the woven griffin and sipping from a tumbler of something amber.

"I know." Quentin was stretched out on the bed, wearing silk pajamas. "Believe me, I've tried. If they really did it I have no idea how they did it. They just look like ordinary tapestries to me. They don't even move like in Harry Potter."

Eliot had brought a tumbler for Quentin too. Quentin hadn't drunk any yet, but he hadn't ruled out the possibility either. At any rate he wasn't going to let Eliot drink it, which he would inevitably try to do when he was done with his own. Quentin made a nest for the tumbler in the blankets next to him.

"I'm not sure I'd want to get into this one," Eliot said.

"I know. Sometimes I wonder if he's trying to get out."

"Now this fellow," he said, moving on to a full-length portrait of a knight in armor. "I wouldn't mind getting into his tapestry, if you get what I mean."

"I get what you mean."

"Pull that sword out of its scabbard."

"I get it."

Eliot was building up to something, but there was no rushing him. Though if he took much longer Quentin was going to fall asleep.

"Do you think if I did you'd see a little tapestry version of me running around in there? I don't know how I'd feel about that."

Quentin waited. Since he'd made the decision to go to the Outer Island he felt calmer than he had in ages. The windows were open, to the extent that they could be opened, and warm night air flowed in, smelling like late summer grass and the sea, which wasn't far off.

"So about this trip of yours," Eliot said finally.

"About it."

"I don't understand why you're doing this."

"Do you have to?"

"Something about quests and adventures and whatever. Sailing beyond the sunset. It doesn't matter. We don't need you here for the Jollyby thing. One of us really should go out there anyway, they probably don't even know they have kings and queens again. Just pass along any prurient details as a matter of state security."

"Will do."

"But I want to talk to you about Julia."

"Oh." Whiskey time. Trying to drink lying down, Quentin took a bigger swallow than he meant to, and it ignited a brush fire in his guts. He suppressed a cough. "Look, you're only High King," he gasped, "you're not my dad. I'll figure it out."

"Don't get defensive, I just want to make sure you know what you're doing."

"And what if I don't?"

"Did I ever tell you," Eliot said, sitting on one of the two chairs, "how Julia and I met?"

"Well, sure." Had he? The exact particulars were fuzzy. "I mean, not in granular detail."

The truth was that they hardly ever talked about that time. They talked around it. No good memories there for anybody. It was after the big disaster in Ember's Tomb. Quentin had been half-dead and had to be left in the care of some irritating but ultimately very medically effective centaurs while Eliot and Janet and the others returned to the real world. Quentin had spent a year recovering in Fillory, then he went back to Earth and gave up magic. He spent another six months working in an office in Manhattan until Janet and Eliot and Julia finally came and got him. If they hadn't he'd probably still be there. He was grateful, and he always would be.

Eliot stared out the window into the black moonless night, like an oriental potentate in his dressing gown, which looked too heavily embroidered to be comfortable.

"You know Janet and I were in pretty rough shape when we left Fillory?"

"Yes. Though at least Martin Chatwin hadn't chewed you practically in half."

"It's not a contest, but yes, that is true. But we were shaken up. We loved Alice, too, you know, in our way. Even Janet did. And we thought we'd lost you as well as her. We were well and truly done with Fillory and all its goods and chattels, I can tell you.

"Josh went home to his parents in New Hampshire, and Richard and Anaïs went off somewhere to do whatever it was they'd been doing before they went to Fillory. Not big mourners, those two. I couldn't face New York again, nor could I face my grotesque so-called family in Oregon, so I went home with Janet to L.A.

"That turned out to be an excellent decision. You know her parents are lawyers? Entertainment lawyers. Fantastically rich, huge house in Brentwood, working all the time, no discernible emotional life whatsoever. So we sucked around Brentwood for a week or two until Janet's parents got tired of the sight of our post-traumatic faces shuffling off to bed as they were getting up for a predawn squash match. They packed us off to a fancy spa in Wyoming for a couple of weeks.

"You wouldn't have heard of it, it was that kind of place. Impossible to get into and ludicrously expensive, but money means nothing to these people, and I wasn't about to argue. Janet practically grew up there—the staff all knew her from when she was a little girl. Imagine that—our Janet, a little girl! She and I had a bungalow to ourselves and positively legions of people to wait on us. I think Janet had a manicurist for every nail.

"And they did a thing with mud and hot stones—I swear to you there was magic in it. Nothing feels that good without magic.

"Of course, the terrible secret of places like that is that they're horrifically boring. You have no idea the extremes we were driven to. I played tennis. Me! They got *very* scoldy when it came to drinking on the court, I can tell you. I told them it's just part of my form. You can't relearn technique, not at my age.

"Well, by the third day Janet and I were considering having sex with each other just to relieve the tedium. And then, like a dark angel of mercy come to safeguard my virtue, Julia appeared.

"It was like one of those Poirot mysteries set at a posh country seat. There was some accident down by the pool—I was never clear on the details, but an enormous fuss was made. I suppose that's one of the things you pay for: first-class fuss. At any rate the first time I laid eyes on our Julia she was being carried through the lobby strapped to a backboard, soaking wet and cursing a blue streak and insisting that she was fine, absolutely fine. Take your paws off me, you damned dirty apes.

"The next day I came down to the bar around three or four in the afternoon and there she was again, drinking alone, all in black. Vodka gimlets I believe. The mysterious lady. It was painfully obvious that she didn't belong at the spa. Her hair was a rat's nest, you literally can't imagine. Worse than now even. Her cuticles were bitten down to the quick. Shoulders hunched. Nervous stutter. And then she had no grasp of how things worked. She tried to tip the staff. She pronounced the names of French wines with an actual French accent.

"Of course I was drawn to her at once. I figured she must be Russian. Daughter of a jailed oligarch, that sort of thing. No one but a Russian could afford to stay there and still have hair that bad. Janet thought she was just out of rehab and from the looks of it headed right back in. Either way we fell upon her like starving people.

"The approach was subtle. The trick was not setting off her alarms, which were all obviously set to a hair trigger. It was Janet, that mistress of seduction, who cracked her in the end—she planted herself in a public lounge and complained loudly about a rather involved computer issue. You could watch our Julia wrestle with herself, but it was a fait accompli.

"After that—well, you know how it is on those vacations. As soon as you learn another person's name they become inescapable. We ran into each other everywhere. You wouldn't think a place like that was her style, would you? But there she was, up to her neck in mud, with cucumber slices over her eyes. She was constantly plunging in and out of baths and things. Once Janet tried to go in a steam bath with her, but she'd turned it up so high everybody else had to flee. Probably she had them thrash her with birch twigs. It was like she was trying to rid herself of some stubborn taint.

"It came out that she had a weakness for cards, so we spent hours just drinking and playing three-handed bridge. Not talking. We didn't know she was a magician, of course. How could we? But you could tell she was bursting with some terrible secret. And she had those things that one likes about magicians: she was disgustingly bright and rather sad and slightly askew. To tell you the truth I think one of the things we liked about her was that she reminded us of you.

"Well, you know how in the Poirot books he always goes on vacation to get away from it all, the mysteries and whatever else, only to have a murder committed on the very island he's fled to for peace and quiet and some civilized gastronomy? It was exactly like that, except that we were fleeing magic. One night I wandered over to her bungalow around ten or eleven at night. Janet and I had had a fight, and I was looking for someone to complain about her to.

"When I passed Julia's window I saw that she was building a fire. That was odd to begin with. The fireplaces were absolutely enormous in those bungalows, but it was the middle of summer and nobody in their right mind was using them. But Julia had a roaring blaze going. She was building it very methodically, placing the logs very carefully. She marked each log before she put it on—scraped away some of the bark with a little silver knife.

"And then as I watched . . . I don't know how to describe it so you'll understand. She kneeled down in front of the fire and began putting things in it. Some of the things were obviously valuable—a rare shell, an old book, a handful of gold dust. Some of them must just have been precious to her. A piece of costume jewelry. An old photograph. Each time she put one in she'd stop and wait a minute, but nothing happened, except that whatever it was burned or melted and gave off a nasty smell. I don't know what she was waiting for, but whatever it was it never came. Meanwhile she got more and more agitated.

"I felt utterly tawdry spying on her, but I couldn't look away. Finally she ran out of precious things, and then she started crying, and then she put herself into the fire. She crawled over the hearth and collapsed, half in and half out of the flames, sobbing her little heart out. Her legs were sticking out. It was awful to see. Her clothes went up right away, of course, and her face got black with soot, but the fire never touched her skin. She was absolutely sobbing. Her shoulders shook and shook . . ."

Eliot stood up and went to the window. He struggled with one of the little panes for a second, then he must have found a catch Quentin had never noticed because he pulled the whole window open. Quentin couldn't see how he did it. He put his glass on the sill.

"I don't know if you're falling in love with her or if you just think you are or what it is you're doing," he said. "I suppose I can't blame you, you always did like to make things as hard as possible on yourself. But just listen to what I'm telling you.

"That was how it all started, how we knew she was one of us. The spell was something very strong. I could hear the hum of it even over the fire, and the light in the room had gone a funny color. But so much of her magic is just impossible to parse. I knew right away she'd never been to Brakebills, because it sounded like gibberish to me, and I couldn't get within a thousand miles of how it worked or what she was trying to do, and she never said, and I never asked.

"But if I absolutely had to guess I'd say she was attempting a summoning. I'd say she was trying to bring back something that she'd lost, or that was taken away from her, something that was very precious to her indeed. And if I had another guess, I'd have to say that it wasn't working."

CHAPTER 3

The next morning, Quentin rode down to the docks in a black carriage with velvet curtains and plushly padded velvet seats. It was safe and musty inside, like a living room on wheels. Next to him, swaying loosely with the rocking of the carriage, sat Queen Julia. Across from them, their knees practically touching, was the admiral of the Fillorian navy.

Quentin had decided that if he was going on a trip to the island at the ass end of the universe, he should do it properly. He should make preparations. There were rules for this kind of thing. Such as: if you were going on a journey you needed a stout vessel.

All ships were available to the crown, in theory, but most of the ones they kept just lying around on call were warships, and those turned out to be scarily spartan on the inside. Rows of hammocks and racks of hard pallets. Not a stateroom in sight. Not really suitable at all for the Voyage of King Kwentin, as Eliot liked to spell Quentin's name in official documents. So they were going down to the docks to find a ship that was suitable.

Quentin was feeling good. He was full of energy and a determination that he hadn't felt for long time. This is what he'd been waiting for. The admiral was an almost alarmingly short man named Lacker with a thin gray face that looked like it had been hollowed out of schist by the action of fifty years of wind and spray.

It wasn't that Quentin couldn't have said what he was looking for, it's just that he didn't want to, because if he did it would have been embarrassing. What he was looking for was a ship from one of the Fillory novels, specifically the *Swift*, which figured in the fourth book, *The Secret Sea*. Pursued by the Watcherwoman, Jane and Rupert—he could have explained to Admiral Lacker, but didn't—had stowed away on the *Swift*, which turned out to be run by pirates, except they were only pretending to be pirates. They were really a party of Fillorian noblemen, wrongly accused, who were seeking to clear their names. You never got a particularly nautically rigorous look at the *Swift*, but you nonetheless came away with a powerful impression of it: it was a plucky but cozy little vessel, elegant to look at but game in a fight, with sleek lines and glowing yellow portholes through which one glimpsed snug, shipshape cabins.

Of course if this were a Fillory novel the ship he needed would already be tied up at the docks, awaiting his command, just like that. But this wasn't a Fillory novel. This was Fillory. So it was up to him.

"I need something not too big and not too small," he said. "Medium-sized. And it should be comfortable. And quick. And sturdy."

"I see. Will you require guns?"

"No guns. Well, maybe a few guns. A few guns."

"A few guns."

"If you please, Admiral, don't be a cock. I'll know it when I see it, and if for some reason I don't, you tell me. All right?"

Admiral Lacker inclined his head almost imperceptibly to indicate that they had a deal. He would endeavor to be as little of a cock as possible.

Whitespire stood on the shore of a wide, curving bay of oddly pale green sea. It was almost too perfect: it could have been carved out of the coastline on purpose by some divine being who took a benevolent interest in mortals having somewhere to put their ships when they weren't using them. For all Quentin knew it had been. He had the driver drop them at one end of the waterfront. They clambered out, all three of them, blinking in the early morning sun after the swaying dimness of the carriage.

The air was ripe with the smell of salt and wood and tar. It was intoxicating, like huffing pure oxygen.

"All right," Quentin said. "Let's do this." He clapped his hands together.

They walked, slowly, all the way from one end of the docks to the other, stepping over taut guy ropes and squashed and dried fish carcasses and weaving their way around massive stanchions and windlasses and through labyrinths of stacked crates. The waterfront was home to an astounding variety of vessels from all points in the Fillorian Empire and beyond. There was a gargantuan dreadnought made of black wood, with nine masts and a bounding panther for a figurehead, and a square-snouted junk with a brick-red sail crimped into sections by battens. There were sloops and cutters, galleons and schooners, menacing corvettes and tiny darting caravels. It was like a bathtub full of expensive bath toys.

It took an hour to reach the far end. Quentin turned to Admiral Lacker.

"So what did you think?"

"I think the *Hatchet,* the *Mayfly,* or the *Morgan Downs* would suffice."

"Probably. I'm sure you're right. Julia?"

Julia had said almost nothing the entire time. She was detached, like she was sleepwalking. He thought about what Eliot had told him last night. He wondered if Julia had found whatever it was she'd been looking for. Maybe she was hoping she'd find it on the Outer Island.

"It does not matter. They are all fine, Quentin. It makes no difference."

They were both right, of course. There were plenty of decent-looking ships. Beautiful even. But they weren't the *Swift.* Quentin folded his arms and squinted down the length of the docks in the late-morning glare. He looked out at the ships floating in the bay.

"What about those ones out there?"

Lacker pursed his lips. Julia looked too. Her eyes were still black from the day before, and she didn't have to shade them against the sun. She looked right into it.

"They are at your disposal as well, Your Highness," Lacker said. "Of course."

Julia walked out along the nearest pier, straight-backed and sure-footed, to where a humble fishing smack was tied up. She jumped the gap neatly and began untying it.

"Come on," she called.

Lacker gestured to Quentin to precede him.

"Sometimes you just have to do things, Quentin," Julia said, as he climbed on board after her. "You spend too much of your time waiting."

It was good to get out on the open water, but there wasn't much wind, and as it warmed up the smack began to smell. Amazingly its owner emerged from belowdecks, where he must have been asleep. He was a sun- and windburned man with a gray beard, wearing overalls with nothing obviously on underneath them. Lacker addressed him in a language Quentin didn't recognize. He didn't seem at all put out or even surprised to discover that his boat had been commandeered by two monarchs and an admiral.

As for Lacker, he looked unfairly comfortable in the heat in his full dress uniform as they toured an even greater variety of inappropriate vessels. Most of them were out there because their drafts were too deep to anchor any farther in: a great bruiser of a ship of the line, some nobleman's bloated party yacht, a fat, butter-colored merchant tub.

"What about that one?" Quentin said. He pointed.

"I beg your indulgence, Your Highness, my eyesight has suffered in the service of our great nation. You do not mean—"

"I do." Enough with the period drama. "That one. There."

A flat sandbar projected from one of the horns of Whitespire's great bay. A ship lay near it in a few feet of water. The low tide had laid it gently down on one side on the sandy bottom, its underbelly exposed like a beached whale.

"That ship, Your Highness, has not left the bay for a very long time."

"Nevertheless."

It was partly out of thoroughness, partly out of a perverse desire to pay the admiral back for being, his promise notwithstanding, a little bit of a cock. The owner of the smack exchanged a long look with Admiral Lacker: this man, the look said, lubs his land.

"Let us return to the *Morgan Downs*."

"And we will," Julia said. "But King Quentin wishes to see that ship first."

It took ten minutes to tack over to it, the sails flapping as the fisherman gamely worked his way upwind. Quentin reminded himself to pay the man something for this after. They circled the wreck listlessly in the shallow water. Its hull had been painted white, but the paint had been weathered and blasted down to the gray wood. There was something odd about its lines—something curiously swoopy about them. It finished in a long slender bowsprit that had been snapped off halfway.

He liked it. It was neither harsh and blocky like a warship, nor soft and too pretty like a yacht. It was elegant, but it meant business. Too bad it was a carcass and not a ship. Maybe if he'd gotten here fifty years earlier.

"What do you think?"

The smack's keel scraped the sandy bottom loudly in the stillness. Admiral Lacker regarded the horizon line. He cleared his throat.

"I think," he said, "that that ship has seen better days."

"What do you think it was?"

"Workhorse," the smack's owner piped up huskily. "Deer Class. Ran the route between here and Longfall."

Quentin hadn't even realized he spoke English.

"It looks nice," Quentin said. "Or it looked nice."

"That was," Admiral Lacker said solemnly, "one of the most beautiful ships that was ever made."

He couldn't tell if Lacker was joking or not. Except that it was pretty obvious that he never joked.

"Really?" Quentin said.

"Nothing moved like the Deer Class," Lacker said. "They were built to carry bergspar from Longfall, then coldspice on the way back. Fast and tough. You could ride them to hell and back."

"Huh. So why aren't there more of them?"

"Longfall ran out of bergspar," the fisherman said. Now he'd gone all chatty. "So we stopped sending them coldspice. That was the end of the Deer Class. Most were broken up for the clockwood in them, sold for scrap. It was the Lorians built them. Every shipwright in Fillory tried to copy them, but there was a trick to it. Trick's been lost."

"My first command," Lacker said, "was a Very Fast Picket out of Hartheim. Nothing in the service could have caught us, but I saw a Deer Class blow by me once on its way north. We had studding sails set on both sides. Made us look like we were standing still."

Quentin nodded. He stood up in the boat. A halo of little birds lifted off from the ship's blasted hull, stalled for a moment on a puff of wind, and then settled back down again. The smack had come around to the far side, and they could see the deck, which was stove in in at least two places. The ship's name was painted across the stern: MUNTJAC.

This wasn't a Fillory novel. If it were, this was the kind of boat he'd have.

"Well, I think that settles it," he said. "Take us back to the *Morgan Downs*, please."

"The *Morgan Downs*, Highness."

"And when we get there tell the captain of the *Morgan Downs* to get his floating rattrap over here and haul that thing"—he pointed at the *Muntjac*—"into dry dock. We're taking it."

That felt good. Some things it was never too late for.

Getting the *Muntjac*—it turned out to be the name of a species of deer—into anything like seaworthy condition was going to take a couple of weeks, even if Quentin exercised his royal prerogatives and press-ganged all the best shipwrights in the city, which he did. But that was fine. It gave him time for more preparations.

He'd been sitting on his nervous energy for so long, it was good to have something to do with it, and he was discovering how much of it he had. He could have powered a small city with it. The next day Quentin had an announcement posted in every town square in the country. He was going to hold a tournament.

In all honesty Quentin had only a very vague idea of how tournaments worked, or even what they were, except that they were something kings used to do at some point between when Jesus was alive and when Shakespeare was alive, which was as close as Quentin could get to placing when the Middle Ages had actually happened. He knew that tournaments were supposed to involve jousting, and he also knew that he wasn't interested in jousting. Too weird and phallic, plus it was hard on the horses.

Sword fighting, though, that was interesting. Not fencing, or not just fencing—he didn't want anything that formal. He had in mind something more like mixed martial arts. Ultimate fighting. He wanted to know who the best swordsman in the realm was: the no-buts, fuck-you, all-Fillory champion of sword fighting. So he put the word out: a week from now anyone who thought he could handle a blade should turn up at Castle Whitespire and start whacking till there was no one left to whack. Winner gets a small but very choice castle in the Fillorian boondocks and the honor of guarding the king's royal person on his upcoming journey to an undisclosed location.

Eliot walked in while Quentin was clearing the grand banquet hall. A column of footmen was filing out, carrying a chair each.

"Pardon me, Your Highness," Eliot said, "but what the hell are you doing?"

"Sorry. It's the only room that was big enough for the matches."

"This is the part where I'm supposed to say, 'Matches, what matches?'"

"For the tournament. Sword fighting. You didn't see the posters? The table goes too," Quentin said to the housekeeper who was directing the move. "Just put it in the hall. I'm having a tournament to find the best swordsman in Fillory."

"Well, can't you have it outside?"

"What if it rains?"

"What if I want to eat something?"

"I told them to serve dinner in your receiving room. So you'll have to do your receiving somewhere else. Maybe you can do that outside."

A man was on his hands and knees on the floor ruling out the piste with a lump of chalk.

"Quentin," Eliot said, "I just heard from someone in the shipwrights' guild. Do you have any idea what that ship of yours is costing us? The *Jackalope* or whatever it is?"

"No. The *Muntjac*."

"About twenty years' worth of Outer Island taxes, that's how much it's costing us," Eliot said, answering his own question. "Just in case you were curious how much it's costing us."

"I wasn't that curious."

"But you do see the irony."

Quentin considered this.

"I do. But it's not about the money."

"What's it about then?"

"It's about observing good form," Quentin said. "You of all people know all about that."

Eliot sighed.

"I suppose I can see that," he said.

"And I need this. That's all I can tell you."

Eliot nodded. "I can see that too."

Contestants began trickling into the city a few days later. They were a bizarre menagerie: men and women, tall and short, haunted and feral, scarred and branded and shaved and tattooed. There was an ambulatory skeleton and an animated suit of armor. They carried swords that glowed and buzzed and burned and sang. A handsome pair of conjoined twins offered to enter individually and, in the event that they vanquished the field, gallantly declared themselves willing to fight each other. An intelligent sword arrived, borne on a silk pillow, and explained that it wished to enter, it merely required somebody willing to wield it.

On the first day of the tournament there were so many pairings that some of the bouts had to be held outside after all, on wooden stages set up in the courtyards. A circus atmosphere prevailed. The weather was just turning—it was the first cold morning of the year—and the fighters' breath smoked in the dawn air. They performed all kinds of weird stretches and warm-ups on the wet grass.

It was everything Quentin had hoped for. He couldn't sit still long enough to watch a whole match, there was always something unmissable going on in the next ring over. Shouts and clashes and weird war cries and even less easily identifiable noises broke the early morning calm. It was like being in a battle, but minus all the death and suffering.

It was three full days before the contestants worked their way through the draw to the final pairing. There were a few incidents and explosions along the way, where forbidden weaponry or major magic overpowered the safeguards they'd put in place, but no one was hurt too badly, thank God. Before it started he'd had a romantic idea about entering the tournament himself in disguise, but he could see now what a disaster that would have been. He wouldn't have lasted thirty seconds.

Quentin oversaw the final match himself. Eliot and Janet condescended to attend, though such grunting, sweaty exercises were beneath Queen Julia's notice. Various barons and other court grandees and hangers-on sat in a row against the walls of the banquet hall, which looked woefully unmartial—he wished he'd done it outside after all. The last two fighters entered together, side by side but not speaking.

After all that they looked oddly alike: a man and a woman, both slender, both of average height, nothing outwardly extraordinary about either of them. They were cool and serious, and they showed no obvious animosity for each other. They were professionals, drawn from the upper tiers of the mercenaries' guild. They were just here to transact business. Whatever violence they had stored up in their lean, compact bodies was still latent for the time being, fissile but inactive. The woman was called Aral. The man's name, absurdly enough, was Bingle.

Aral fought veiled and tightly swathed, like a ninja. She had a reputation as an elegant fighter who made a fetish of her technique. Nobody had been able to break her form, let alone touch her. Her sword was an oddity: it was curved slightly and then recurved, in the form of an elongated letter *S*. Pretty but a pain to carry around, Quentin thought. You couldn't fit it in a scabbard.

Bingle was an olive-colored man with hooded eyes that gave him a permanently melancholy look. He wore what might once have been an officer's uniform from which the bars and trim had been snipped, and he fought with a thin, flexible, whiplike blade with a complicated basket hilt that didn't look Fillorian. Though he'd won all his matches, the buzz on him was that he'd managed it without doing a lot of actual fighting. One infamous duel started in the morning and ran almost till sundown while Bingle engaged in an endless series of feints and evasions. The whole tournament was held up while they waited for the bracket to be filled.

In another match Bingle's opponent waited till the opening bell had rung and then calmly stepped over the chalk line out of bounds for an automatic forfeit. Apparently they'd met before, and once had been enough. Quentin was looking forward to watching somebody make Bingle actually stand and fight.

Quentin nodded to the Master of Sword to start the match. Aral began a sequence of highly stylized movements, drawing fluid shapes in the air with her recurved blade. She didn't approach her opponent. She seemed to be lost in concentration, practicing some ritualized, almost abstract martial art. Bingle watched her for a little bit, flicking the tip of his sword around uneasily.

Then he joined the dance. He began performing the same movements as his opponent—they became mirror images of each other. Apparently they were adepts of the same style and had chosen to open with the same form. Laughter rippled through the crowd. And it was funny, like a mime copying a passerby. But neither of the fighters laughed.

Afterward Quentin wasn't sure exactly when this preamble ended and the fighting began. The two combatants passed too near each other, and it was like a candle flame accidentally brushing a curtain. A spark jumped the gap, the symmetry was broken, the fissile material reached criticality, and suddenly the room was full of the rapid-fire clatter of steel colliding with steel.

At this level of mastery the action went too fast for Quentin to follow. The precise details of the moves and countermoves and negotiations were lost on everybody but the combatants. Their shared style was all arcs and spins and constant motion as each side looked for openings and found only dead ends. You got the impression they were reading each other down to an atomic level, logging tiny twitches and tells and shifts of weight. The passes would start beautifully, set sequences that sometimes even included a flip or a somersault, then the flow would break and everything would be chaos until the blades tangled up and locked, and they disengaged and started all over again.

Jesus, Quentin thought. And he was going to get on a boat with one of these people. It was a little too real. But it was electrifying too: these were people who knew exactly what they were meant to do and never hesitated to do it, whether they won or lost.

Then all at once it was over: Aral overextended herself with a huge overhand chop that Bingle just managed to roll out from under, and by blind chance her blade stuck fast in the floor, in a crack between two flagstones. Coming up out of the roll Bingle kicked at it, reflexively, and it snapped neatly halfway along its length. Aral stepped back, not bothering to conceal her frustration, and indicated that she conceded the match.

But Bingle shook his head. Apparently he wasn't happy with the grounds of his victory. He wanted to keep fighting. He looked at Quentin for a ruling. So did everybody else.

Well, if he wanted to play by good-guy rules, then by all means. Quentin wouldn't mind seeing some more fighting himself. He drew his sword and offered it to Aral hilt-first. She felt the balance, nodded grudgingly, then resumed her fighting stance. The match recommenced.

Five minutes later Bingle jumped a low cut and attempted some mid-air finesse move that got tangled up in Aral's ninja wrappings. He wound up right next to her, inside her guard, and she punched him savagely in the ribs, three times. He grunted and staggered backward toward the chalk line, and Quentin was sure he was going to ring out, but at the last second he realized where he was. He spun around and leaped balletically for the wall, pushed off it, turned head over heels, and landed lightly on his feet just in bounds.

The crowd gasped and applauded. It was a circus move, stagy and over the top. Aral irritably pulled off her headscarf and shook out a surprising mass of wavy auburn hair before resuming her stance.

"Bet you anything she practiced that in a mirror," Eliot whispered.

The dynamic of the fight had changed. Now Bingle dropped the formal, balletic style they'd both been using. Quentin had assumed that that was where his training was, but it soon became apparent that he was some kind of technical freak, because he seemed to be able to shift styles at will. He went at her like a berserker, fast and furious, then cycled rapidly through a courtly dueling mode to a kind of shouting, stamping kendo style. Aral grew increasingly flummoxed trying to adjust, which was presumably what Bingle was after.

Breaking her silence, she shouted something and lunged flat out. Bingle met her attack with a parry so implausible it was vaudevillian: he stopped her blade—Quentin's blade—with the tip of his, so that the two swords met point to point.

They bent ominously, almost double, for an unendurably tense second—there was a worrying saw-blade sound of flexed metal—and then Bingle's sword snapped with a sharp, vibrant twang. He had to jerk his head to one side to avoid a flying shard.

He threw his useless hilt at Aral in disgust. The pommel clunked her on the temple, but she shrugged it off. She paused, evidently considering offering him the same largesse he'd offered her. Then, having made some inner calculation probably having to do with honor and principles and castles, she aimed an overhand cutting stroke at Bingle's shoulder, the coup de grâce.

Bingle closed his eyes and dropped rapidly to one knee. As the blade descended he didn't dodge, just brought his hands together smoothly and decisively in front of him. And then time stopped.

At first Quentin wasn't sure what had happened, but the room exploded in amazement. He stood up to get a better view. Bingle had stopped the blade between the palms of his hands, in midstrike, bare flesh against sharp steel. He must have calculated the move down to the last erg and arc and nanosecond. It took a moment for Aral to understand what he'd done, and Bingle didn't waste it. With the advantage of surprise he jerked the blade toward himself, out of her grip. He flipped it smartly, the hilt smacking solidly into his palm, and placed the blade at her throat. The match was over.

"Oh my God," Eliot said. "Did you see that? Oh my God!"

The assembled barons forgot their noble reserve. They got to their feet, huzzahing, and mobbed the winner. Quentin and Eliot cheered along with them. But Bingle didn't seem to see them. Those hooded eyes never changed their expression. He pushed his way through the crowd to Quentin's throne, where he kneeled and offered Quentin back his sword.

———

The next time Quentin visited the waterfront the *Muntjac* was crawling with workmen, like piranhas on an unlucky Amazonian explorer except in reverse. They were putting the *Muntjac* back together—bringing it back to life. There was no part of it that wasn't being aggressively sanded or varnished or tightened or reinforced or replaced. They'd got it up into drydock, propped it up on a forest of stilts, fixed the sprung boards, caulked and tarred and painted it. Out-of-sync hammer blows clattered from all quarters of the hull.

As it turned out the ship's structural elements had been basically sound, which was good, because the shipwrights didn't think they could have reproduced what they found. Deep in the hold, pieced into some of the complex joins near the prow, they'd found a complicated lump of wooden clockwork connected to taut lines leading off into various parts of the ship. They couldn't figure out what it was for, so Quentin told them to leave it alone.

The *Muntjac*'s hull was now a smart jet-black with bright white trim. Hundreds of yards of new sail were even now being sewn by an army of sailmakers, an astonishingly technical process that took place in a vast, airy sail loft the size of an airplane hangar. The sharp, honest fragrances of sawdust and wet paint bloomed in the air. Quentin breathed them in. He felt like he was coming back to life too. Not that he'd been dead, just . . . not quite alive. Something else.

With only two or three more days till the *Muntjac* could be floated, Quentin paid a visit to Castle Whitespire's map room to see what he could learn about his destination. The Outer Island was the least exciting part of this whole undertaking, but he'd better at least be able to find it. After the clamor of the docks the map room was a reservoir of cool quiet. One whole wall was windows, and the other was taken up with a glorious floor-to-ceiling map of Fillory, from Loria in the north to the Wandering Desert in the south. The map was traversed by a rolling library ladder, so you could get right up close to the part you wanted to study, and the closer you looked, the more detail resolved itself, to the point where you could pick out individual trees in the Queenswood. No dryads though.

The map was lightly animated by some subtle cartographical magic. You could follow tiny combers in as they pounded the Swept Coast, one after the other. Quentin leaned in: you could even hear them, faintly, like the roar in a shell. A line of shadow was advancing across the map, showing where it was night and where it was day in Fillory. Overhead on the vaulted ceiling, tiny stars twinkled in the velvety blue-black of a celestial map that showed the Fillorian constellations.

This was Quentin's kingdom, the land he ruled. It looked so fresh and green and magical like this. This was Fillory the way he'd thought of it as a little kid, before he'd ever been here—it looked like the maps printed on the endpapers of the *Fillory and Further* books. He could have watched it all day.

The map room wasn't exactly a hive of activity. The only visible staff was a surly teenager with thick black bangs that fell over his eyes. He was bent over a table furiously working some kind of calculation using a collection of steel cartographical instruments. It took him a minute to look up and realize that he had a patron.

The boy gave his name, grudgingly, as Benedict. He might have been sixteen. Quentin had a feeling that not a lot of people came through the map room, and still less often were those people kings; at any rate Benedict was out of practice at showing the appropriate amount of deference. Quentin sympathized. Personally he could take or leave the bowing and scraping. But he still needed a map.

"What can you show me that has the Outer Island on it?"

Benedict's eyes went blank for a second as he queried some mental database. Then he turned away and dragged himself over to a wall that was honeycombed with little square drawers. He yanked one out—they turned out to be thin but very deep—and extracted the single scroll it contained.

The centerpiece of the map room was a heavy wooden table with an elaborate brass mechanism bolted to it. Benedict nimbly fitted the scroll into it and cranked a handle. It was the only thing he did with anything remotely resembling alacrity. The crank unrolled the scroll and spread it out flat so you could get a good look at the section you wanted.

It was a lot longer than Quentin expected. Yards of almost-blank parchment scrolled by as Benedict cranked, showing curves and arcs of latitude and longitude or whatever the Fillorian equivalents were, tra-versing miles of open ocean. Finally he stopped at a tiny, irregular nug-get of land with its name underneath it in italic script: *The Outer Island.*

"That must be the place," Quentin said dryly.

Benedict would neither confirm nor deny this. He was painfully un-comfortable making eye contact. Quentin couldn't think who Benedict reminded him of until he realized that this was what he had probably looked like to other people when he was sixteen. Fear of everybody and everything, hidden behind a mask of contempt, with the greatest con-tempt of all reserved for himself.

"It looks pretty far out," Quentin said. "How many days' sail?"

"Dunno," Benedict said, which wasn't quite true, because he added, obviously in spite of himself: "Three maybe. It's four hundred and seventy-seven miles. Nautical miles."

"What's the difference?"

"Nautical's longer."

"How much?"

"Two hundred and sixty-five yards longer," Benedict said automati-cally. "And a bit."

Quentin was impressed. Somebody must have managed to beat some information into Benedict somehow. The brass map reader had many articulated arms that extended seductively outward, each one with a pos-able lens on it. Quentin swiveled one around, and a magnified version of the Outer Island swam into view. It was roughly peanut-shaped, with a star marked on it at one end. Its border was a thick dark line, with a fainter outline around it, doubling it, as if to suggest waves, or maybe the submerged edge of the landmass under the water.

It was about what he expected. A fine black thread, a single lonely stream, wandered from the interior down to the coast. Next to the star was the word *Outer,* in smaller letters. Presumably that was the name of the island's one town. The lens failed to reveal anything else. All it did was make the fine grain of the parchment look coarse.

"Who lives there?"

"Fishermen. I guess. There's an agent of the crown there. That's why it has a star."

They looked at the star together.

"It's a shit map," Benedict volunteered. He leaned down so that his nose almost touched it. "Look at the shading. Why do you want to know about it?"

"I'm going there."

"Really? Why?"

"That's actually a pretty good question."

"Are you looking for the key?"

"No, I'm not looking for the key. What key?"

"There's a fairy tale," Benedict said, as if he were explaining to a kindergartner. "That's where the key that winds up the world is. Supposed to be."

Quentin wasn't wildly interested in Fillorian folklore.

"Why don't you come along?" he said. "You could make a new map of it, if this one's so bad."

Now he was a counselor of troubled youth. Something about the boy made Quentin want to shake him up. Get him out of his comfort zone so he could stop sneering at everybody else who was out of theirs. Get him thinking about something besides his own neuroses for a change. It was harder than it looked.

"I'm not rated for fieldwork," Benedict mumbled, dropping his gaze again. "I'm a cartographer, not a surveyor." Quentin watched Benedict's eyes keep getting drawn back to the map, to that irregular peanut. Maps of places, rather than actual places, were obviously where young master Benedict preferred to live. "The linework is . . ." He made a noise through his teeth: *ch*. "Jesus Christ."

"Jesus Christ" was an expression the younger Fillorians had picked up from their new rulers. It was impossible to explain to them what it actually meant. They were convinced it was something dirty.

"In the name of the Kingdom of Fillory," Quentin intoned, "I hereby pronounce you rated for fieldwork. Good enough?"

Should've brought my sword. Benedict shrugged, embarrassed. It was exactly what Quentin would have done ten years ago. Quentin almost found himself liking the kid. He probably thought nobody could possibly understand how he felt. It made Quentin realize how far he'd come. Maybe he could help Benedict.

"Think about it. We should bring somebody to update the maps."

Though the draftsmanship looked fine to Quentin. Idly he turned the crank of the brass map-viewing contraption. It really was very neat: little half-concealed gears spun, and the Outer Island drifted away and was rolled up on the far side of the scroll. He kept cranking. Yards and yards of creamy blank paper passed by, decorated here and there with dotted lines and tiny numbers. Empty ocean.

Finally the scroll ran out, and the loose end popped out and flapped around.

"Not much out there," he said, since he felt like he should say something.

"It's the last scroll in the catalog," Benedict said. "No one's even looked at it since I've been here."

"Can I take it with me?"

Benedict hesitated.

"It's okay. I am the king, you know. It's my map anyway, if you want to be technical about it."

"I still have to sign it out."

Benedict carefully rolled up the scroll and placed it in a leather case, then gave him a slip of paper that allowed him to take it out of the map room. He had cosigned it: his full name was Benedict Fenwick.

Benedict Fenwick. Jesus Christ. No wonder he was sulky.

Quentin had an obsolete sailing ship that had been raised from the dead. He had a psychotically effective swordsman and an enigmatic witch-queen. It wasn't the Fellowship of the Ring, but then again he wasn't trying to save the world from Sauron, he was attempting to perform a tax audit on a bunch of hick islanders. It would definitely do. They left Castle Whitespire three weeks to the day after Jollyby died.

A stiff salt breeze was scouring the waterfront. The *Muntjac's* sails looked ready to lap it up and race off over the horizon in search of more. They were a glorious white with the very pale blue ram of Fillory splashed across them like a watermark, their edges snapping and vibrating with barely contained excitement. It really was a marvelous beast.

A brass band played on the waterfront. The conductor was visibly urging his charges to greater and greater volumes, but the notes were whipped away by the wind the second they left the instruments. With half an hour to spare Benedict Fenwick had turned up with the clothes on his back and an overnight bag stuffed full of clinking mapmaking equipment. The captain—once again, the unflappable Admiral Lacker—assigned him the last available quarters.

Eliot walked out onto the dock with Quentin to see him off.

"So," he said.

"So."

They stood together at the foot of the gangplank.

"You're really doing this."

"Did you think I was bluffing?"

"A little bit, yes," Eliot said. "Say good-bye to Julia for me. Don't forget what I told you about her."

Julia had already stowed herself in her cabin with the air of someone who wasn't planning to reemerge till they'd made landfall.

"I will. You'll be all right without us?"

"Better off."

"If you figure out what happened to Jollyby," Quentin said, "go ahead and kick the ass of whoever's responsible. Don't wait up for me."

"Thanks. For what it's worth I don't think it was the Fenwicks. I think they just think we're dicks."

Quentin remembered the first time they'd met, how odd Eliot's twisted jaw had looked. Now it was so familiar he didn't notice it. It looked like something natural, like a humpback whale's jaw.

"I suppose I could make a speech," Eliot said, "but nobody would hear it."

"I'll just act like you're exhorting me to further the interests of the Fillorian people and show these renegade Outer Islanders, who probably just forgot to pay their taxes, if they even have anything to pay taxes on, or with, that we stand for everything that is just and true, and they'd do well to remember it."

"You're actually looking forward to this, aren't you?"

"If you want the truth, it's taking all my self-control just to stay standing here on the dock."

"All right," Eliot said. "Go. Oh, you've got an extra crew member. I forgot to tell you. The talking animals sent someone."

"What? Who?"

"Exactly. Who or what, I never know which. It's already on board. Sorry, it was politically expedient."

"You could have asked me."

"I would have, but I thought you might say no."

"I miss you already. See you in a week."

Light on his feet, Quentin jogged up the plank, which was hastily withdrawn behind him as soon as he was on deck. Incomprehensible naval yells issued from all quarters. Quentin did his best to stay out of people's way as he picked his way back to the poop deck. The ship creaked and shifted slowly, ponderously, as it leaned and bore away from the wharf. The world around them, which had been fixed in place, became loose and mobile.

As they cleared the harbor the world changed again. The air cooled and the wind picked up and the water abruptly became gunmetal gray and ruffled. Massive swells came booming through underneath them. The *Muntjac*'s enormous sails caught hold of the wind. New wood cracked and settled comfortably into the strain.

Quentin walked to the very stern and looked out over the wake, swept clean and crushed into foam by the weight of their passage. He felt good and right here. He patted the *Muntjac*'s worn old taffrail: unlike most things and most people in Fillory, the *Muntjac* needed Quentin, and Quentin hadn't let her down. He stood up straighter. Something heavy and invisible had relaxed its taloned grip, left its familiar perch on his shoulders and winged away on the stiff breeze. Let it weigh down somebody else for a while, he thought. Probably it would be waiting for him when he got home again. But for now it could wait.

When he turned around to go below, Julia was standing right behind him. He hadn't heard her. The wind had caught her black hair and was whipping it wildly around her face. She looked outrageously beautiful. It might have been a trick of the light, but her skin had a silvery, unearthly quality, as if it would shock him if he touched it. If they were ever going to fall in love with each other, it was going to happen on this ship.

They watched together as Whitespire grew smaller behind them and was finally obscured by the point. She'd come here all the way from

Brooklyn, just like him, he thought. She was probably the only person in the world, in any world, who understood exactly what all this felt like to him.

"Not bad, right Jules?" he said. He breathed in the cold sea air. "I mean, this whole trip is ridiculous, basically, but look!" He gestured at everything—the ship, the wind, the sky, the seascape, the two of them. "We should have done this ages ago."

Julia's expression didn't change. Her eyes had never gone back to normal after the incident in the forest. They were still black, and they looked strange and ancient with her girlish freckles.

"I did not even notice we were moving," she said.

CHAPTER 4

You have to go back to the beginning, to that freezing miserable afternoon in Brooklyn when Quentin took the Brakebills exam, to understand what happened to Julia. Because Julia took the Brakebills exam that day too. And after she took it, she lost three years of her life.

Her story started the same day Quentin's did, but it was a very different kind of story. On that day, the day he and James and Julia walked along Fifth Avenue together on the way to the boys' Princeton interviews, Quentin's life had split wide open. Julia's life hadn't. But it did develop a crack.

It was a hairline crack at first. Nothing much to look at it. It was cracked, but you could still use it. It was still good. No point in throwing her life away. It was a perfectly fine life.

Or no, it wasn't fine, but it worked for a while. She'd said good-bye to James and Quentin in front of the brick house. They'd gone in. She'd walked away. It had started to rain. She'd gone to the library. This much she was pretty sure was true. This much had probably actually happened.

Then something happened that didn't happen: she'd sat in the library with her laptop and a stack of books and written her paper for Mr. Karras. It was a damn good paper. It was about an experimental utopian socialist community in New York State in the nineteenth century. The community had some praiseworthy ideals but also some creepy sexual practices, and eventually it lost its mojo and morphed into a successful silverware company instead. She had some ideas about why the whole arrangement worked better as a silverware company than it had as an attempt to realize Christ's kingdom on Earth. She was pretty sure she was right. She'd gone into the numbers, and in her experience when you went into the numbers you usually came out with pretty good answers.

James met her at the library. He told her what had happened with the interview, which was weird enough as it was, what with the interviewer turning up dead and all. Then she'd gone home, had dinner, gone up to her room, written the rest of the paper, which took until four in the morning, grabbed three hours of sleep, got up, blew off the first two classes while she fixed her endnotes, and went to school in time for social studies. Mischief managed.

When she looked back the whole thing had a queer, unreal feeling to it, but then again you often get a queer, unreal feeling when you stay up till four and get up at seven. Things didn't start to fall apart till a week later, when she got her paper back.

The problem wasn't the grade. It was a good grade. It was an A minus, and Mr. K didn't give out a lot of those. The problem was—what was the problem? She read the paper again, and though it read all right, she didn't recognize everything in it. But she'd been writing fast. The thing she snagged on was the same thing Mr. K snagged on: she'd gotten a date wrong.

See, the utopian community she was writing about had run afoul of a change in federal statutory rape laws—creepy, creepy—that took place in 1878. She knew that. Whereas the paper said 1881, which Mr. K would never have caught—though come to think of it he was a pretty creepy character himself, and she wouldn't be surprised if he knew his way around a statutory rape law or two—except Wikipedia made the same mistake, and Mr. K loved to do spot-checking to catch people relying on Wikipedia. He'd checked the date, and checked Wikipedia, and put a big red *X* in the margin of Julia's paper. And a minus after her *A*. He was surprised at her. He really was.

Julia was surprised too. She never used Wikipedia, partly because she knew Mr. K checked, but mostly because unlike a lot of her fellow students she cared about getting her facts right. She went back through the paper and checked it thoroughly. She found a second mistake, and a third. No more, but that was enough. She started checking versions of the paper, because she always saved and backed up separate drafts as she went, because Track Changes in Word was bullshit, and she wanted to know at what point exactly the errors got in. But the really weird thing was there that were no other versions. There was only the final draft.

This fact, although it was a minor fact, with multiple plausible explanations, proved to be the big red button that activated the ejector seat that blew Julia out of the cozy cockpit of her life.

She sat on her bed and stared at the file, which showed a time of creation that she remembered as having been during dinner, and she felt fear. Because the more she thought about it the more it seemed like she had two sets of memories for that afternoon, not just one. One of them was almost too plausible. It had the feel of a scene from a novel written by an earnest realist who was more concerned with presenting an amalgamation of naturalistic details that fit together plausibly than with telling a story that wouldn't bore the fuck out of the reader. It felt like a cover story. That was the one where she went to the library and met James and had dinner and wrote the paper.

But the other one was batshit insane. In the other one she'd gone to the library and done a simple search on one of the cheapo library workstations on the blond-wood tables by the circulation desk. The search had yielded a call number. The call number was odd—it put the book in the subbasement stacks. Julia was pretty sure the library didn't have any subbasement stacks, because it didn't have a subbasement.

As if in a dream she walked to the brushed-steel elevator. Sure enough, beneath the round white plastic button marked *B*, there was now also a round plastic button marked *SB*. She pressed it. It glowed. The dropping sensation in her stomach was just an ordinary dropping sensation, the kind you get when you're descending rapidly toward a subbasement full of cheap metal shelving and the buzz of fluorescent lights and exposed pipes with red-painted daisy-wheel valve handles poking out of them at odd angles.

But that's not what she saw when the elevator doors opened. Instead she saw a sun-soaked stone terrace in back of a country house, with green gardens all around it. It wasn't actually a house, the people there explained, it was a school. It was called Brakebills, and the people who lived there were magicians. They thought she might like to be one too. All she would have to do is pass one simple test.

CHAPTER 5

Waking up that first morning on board the *Muntjac,* the only thing Quentin could compare it to was his first morning waking up at Brakebills. His cabin was long and narrow, and his bed lay along it opposite a row of windows that were only a couple of yards above the waterline. The first thing he saw was those windows, speckled with droplets and bright with sunlight reflected off the water, which they were skimming over at an unbelievable clip. Bookshelves, cabinets, and drawers had been cleverly tucked in along the walls and under the bed. It was like being inside a Chinese puzzle.

He swung his bare feet down onto the wide, cold planks of his little cabin. He felt the slight pitch and the even slighter roll of the ship, and the tilt that the wind had set it at. He felt like he was in the belly of some massive but friendly marine mammal whose joy in life was to lope along the surface of the sea with him inside it. Quentin was one of those annoying people who never got seasick.

He got his clothes out of the miniature dresser that was built into the wall, or the gunwale, or bulkhead, whatever you called a wall on a ship. He admired the neat rows of books on the built-in shelves above his bed, which were held in place by a narrow board so they wouldn't fall off during a storm. He wasn't especially looking forward to finding out what they were going to have for breakfast, and the less said about the bathroom the better, but other than that he was in a state of grace. He hadn't felt this good in months. Years, maybe.

On deck he was the only person who had nothing to do. The crew of the *Muntjac* was small for a ship its size, eight hands including the captain, and all the crewmembers who were visible were very seriously engaged in steering the ship and splicing ropes and scrubbing the deck and climbing up and down things. Julia was nowhere in sight, and Admiral Lacker and Benedict were discussing some navigational nicety with a degree of animation Quentin hadn't thought either one of them was capable of.

Quentin supposed he would consult on weather magic if any was required, but Julia was better at that stuff than he was, and anyway he couldn't imagine how even Julia could improve on what they had, which was a clear sky and a cold stiff wind out of the northwest. He decided to climb up the mast.

He walked over to the last and least of the *Muntjac*'s three masts, swinging his arms forward and back, loosening up his shoulders. It was probably a stupid idea. But who hadn't at some point in his life wanted to climb to the top of a sailing ship in full flight? It always looked easy in movies. The mast wasn't exactly built for climbing—there weren't any rungs or steps or spikes. He put his foot on a brass cleat. The man at the helm looked at him. *Your king is climbing a mast, citizen. And no, he doesn't know how. Deal with it.*

It wasn't easy, but it wasn't that hard, either. Where there weren't cleats or spars there were at least ropes, though you had to be careful not to pull anything that wasn't supposed to be pulled. He skinned a knuckle, then another one, and a fat splinter stabbed straight into the soft ball of his thumb and broke off there. The mast hummed with tension—he could sense it rooted deep in the hold, taking the force of the wind and balancing it with the force of water on the keel. The thing he hadn't counted on was how cold it got, right away, like he'd climbed into another climatic zone, or maybe the lower limits of outer space.

The other thing he hadn't counted on was the angle of the ship. He barely noticed it most of the time, but the farther he got from the safety of the deck the more perilously the ship seemed to be heeling over. He had to keep reminding himself that it wasn't actually in imminent danger of rolling right over and drowning them all. Probably.

By the time he got to the top he was no longer over the deck at all.

He could have dropped a plumb line straight down into the water, which rushed along below him, a torrent of rough green glass. A blunt-nosed, milky-gray shape was keeping pace with them below the surface about fifty feet off their starboard side. It was huge. Not a whale—its tail was vertical, not horizontal. A gigantic fish, then, or a shark. Even as he watched it, it swam deeper, growing fainter and more diffuse, until he could no longer see it at all. The higher you get the more you realize how much bigger than you everything is.

Going down was easier. Once he was safely on deck Quentin decided to keep going the other way, down to the hold. The noise of the bright, busy outside world vanished as soon as he stepped through the dark hatch in the deck. There wasn't far to go: three short flights took him to the bottom of the *Muntjac*'s hollow little world.

It was warm there. He could feel the ocean pressing in on him from the other side of the damp, sweating wood. The hold was so full of supplies there was hardly room to move. It wasn't very scenic. He was making his way back to the ladder, back up to reality, or what passed for it in Fillory, when a weird, furry, upside-down face loomed out of the darkness at him.

He gave a high and not very kingly bark of alarm and hit his head on something. The face hung in midair—as his eyes adjusted he saw that the creature was hanging upside down from a crossbeam, so comfortably that it looked like it had been there its whole life. It had an alien, half-melted look.

"Hello," it said.

That was one mystery solved. Their talking animal was a sloth. It was just about the ugliest mammal Quentin had ever seen.

"Hi," Quentin said. "I didn't realize you were down here."

"Nobody seems to," the sloth said, with equanimity. "I hope you'll come visit. Often."

It took them three days to sail to the Outer Island, and every day it got hotter. They left the autumn beaches and steel waters of Whitespire for a more tropical zone. They did this while traveling east, instead of north or south, which was weird to the people from Earth, but none of the Fillorians seemed surprised. It made him wonder whether this world was even spherical—Benedict had never even heard of an equator. The crew changed into tropical whites.

Benedict stood by Admiral Lacker's side at the helm with a book of charts that laid out the approach to the Outer Island, page after page crowded with technical-looking dots and blobby concentric isobars. Working together they threaded their way through a maze of shoals and reefs that no one but they could see until the island was actually in sight: a little bump of white sand and green jungle on the horizon, with a mod-est peak in the middle, not so different from what he'd imagined. They rounded a point and entered a shallow bay.

The moment they did the wind dropped to nothing. The *Muntjac* coasted into the center of the harbor on the last of its momentum, rippling the placid green surface as it went. The sails flapped limply in the silence. It could have been a sleepy hamlet on the Côte d'Azur. The shore was a narrow sandy strand littered with dry seaweed and the fibrous bits that palm trees constantly shed, baking in the afternoon heat. A wharf and a few low structures stood toward one end, and one rather magnificent-looking building that might have been a hotel or a country club. Not a single person was visible.

Probably they were taking a siesta. In spite of himself Quentin felt a rising sense of anticipation. Don't be an idiot. This was an errand. They were here to collect the taxes.

They lowered the launch in silence. Quentin climbed in, followed by Bingle and Benedict, who lost his sullen self-consciousness for a moment in his excitement at starting his survey. At the last minute Julia appeared from below and slipped aboard. The sloth, slung comfortably from its beam in the hold, declined to go, though it enjoined them, before closing its drooping, shadowed eyes, to remember that if they came across any particularly succulent shoots, or even a small lizard, it was an omnivore.

A long, skinny, rickety pier projected from the wharves out into the water, with an absurd little cupola at the end. They rowed for it. The bay was as smooth as a pond. Throughout this entire operation they hadn't seen or heard a soul.

"Spooky," Quentin said out loud. "God, I hope it's not one of those Roanoke deals where the whole place is deserted."

Nobody said anything. He missed having Eliot to talk to, or even Janet. If Julia was amused, or even got the reference, she didn't let on. She'd been keeping to herself since they left Whitespire. She didn't want to talk to anyone, or touch anyone—she kept her hands in her lap and her elbows drawn in.

He scanned the shoreline through a folding telescope that he'd charmed so that it would show beings both visible and invisible, or most of them anyway. The waterfront was genuinely, authentically deserted. If you adjusted the telescope—it had an extra dial—it ran the view a little ways backward in time too. Nobody had visited the beach for at least an hour.

The pier creaked in the stillness. The heat was murderous. Quentin thought he should go first, as king, but Bingle insisted. He was taking his duties as royal bodyguard very seriously. He wasn't anywhere near as jolly as his name made him sound, though that would have been almost impossible since his name made him sound like a clown who entertained at children's parties.

The big building they'd seen earlier was made of wood and painted white, with Ionic columns out front and grand glass doors. Everything was peeling. It looked like an old Southern plantation house. Bingle pushed open the door and stepped inside. Quentin pushed in right behind him. If he got nothing else out of this he was going to get a little thrill of the unknown, however short-lived. It was pitch-black inside after the glare of the afternoon, and pleasantly cool.

"Have a care, Your Highness," Bingle said.

As his eyes adjusted Quentin saw a shabby but grandly appointed room with a desk in the center. At it sat a little girl with straight blond hair coloring fiercely on a piece of paper. When she saw them she turned around and shouted up the stairs:

"Mom-*my!* There's people here!"

She turned back to them.

"Try not to get sand in the house."

She went back to coloring.

"Welcome to Fillory," she added, without looking up.

———

The little girl's name was Eleanor. She was five and very adept at draw-ing bunny-pegasi, which were like regular pegasi except instead of horses with wings they were rabbits with wings. Quentin wasn't clear on whether they were real or made up; you could never be totally sure about stuff like that in Fillory. Mommy was in her late thirties or thereabouts, pretty with thin lips and a pale untropical complexion. She descended the stairs smartly, in high heels and a vaguely official-looking jacket and skirt, and shifted Eleanor roughly out of her chair, which Eleanor accepted. She took her pictures and coloring things and ran up the stairs.

"Welcome to the Kingdom of Fillory," the woman said, in a throaty alto. "I am the Customs Agent. Please state your names and countries of origin."

She opened a very official-looking ledger and held a large purple-inked stamp at the ready.

"I'm Quentin," Quentin said. "Coldwater. I'm king of Fillory."

She paused, eyebrows arched, with her hand poised to stamp. She was making a good thing out of this routine: businesslike but sexy, with some nicely judged irony in there. There was something of the vamp about the Customs Agent.

"You're the king of Fillory?"

"I'm a king of Fillory. There are two."

She put down the stamp. In the column marked OCCUPATION she wrote: *king.*

"In that case—from Fillory?"

"Well, yes."

She made another note.

"Ah, well." She sighed and closed the ledger. She didn't get to use her stamp. "There isn't much paperwork if you're from Fillory. I thought you might have come from overseas."

"Address His Highness with respect," Bingle snapped. "You're talk-ing to the king, not some wandering fisherman."

"I know he's the king," she said. "He said that."

"Then address him as 'Your Highness'!"

"Sorry." She turned to Quentin, trying, but not very hard, to suppress her amusement. "Your Highness. We don't get a lot of kings here. It takes getting used to."

"Well, all right." Quentin let it go. "Look, Bingle, I'll take care of guarding my dignity, thanks." Then to the Customs Agent: "You can still stamp my form if you want to."

Bingle shot Quentin a glance to the effect of, you have no idea how to be a king, literally none.

The Customs Agent's name turned out to be Elaine, and once she'd satisfied herself as to their immigration status she was a gracious host. It was usual on the Outer Island to have cocktails in about an hour, she explained, but before then would they like to see something of the island? They certainly would. By all means, as long as they were here. Only they should be warned that someone would wind up carrying Eleanor on his shoulders. She was a sweet child but easily distracted and very lazy.

"She's a terrible flirt. She goes straight for the men of the party, and if she figures out you're an easy mark, you'll be carrying her around for the rest of the day."

They followed Elaine through the embassy, which was what the grand building turned out to be. It was dim and surprisingly elegant, with lots of club chairs and dark wood, something like an English gentlemen's club. It was hard to picture the opulent age in which all this stuff had been shipped out here and assembled. The Outer Island must have had a heyday. They walked out the back gate and along a cart track hacked out of the tropical greenery. Elaine picked a tangy sweet-sour fruit from a low-hanging branch and offered it to Quentin.

"Try this," she purred. It had dense nests of seeds inside that one spat out into the weeds.

The spicy scent of the seaside gave way to the dense green chlorophyl fug of the jungle. Here and there they passed a wrought-iron gate, painted white but rusting, with a path curving away back into the underbrush. Elaine discoursed about the various histories and scandals of the families that lived in the houses at the ends of the paths. She was handsome and had a bright, appealing manner. Though Quentin wondered why she wasn't more affectionate to her daughter, the helpful little

Eleanor. It didn't jibe with her otherwise hospitable manner. Bingle stalked ahead of them, sword out, ready to slash or grapple any malefactors who might spring out of the jungle with designs on the king's person. Quentin thought he was being rude, but Elaine didn't seem to notice.

They stopped to admire a tropical clock-tree, which took the form of a palm tree instead of an oak. Quentin asked Eleanor if she could tell time, and she said that she couldn't and what's more she didn't want to.

"Aren't we being a little princess for the king," said Elaine. Benedict sketched effortlessly as they walked, trying not to blot his notebook with sweat. Julia stopped to study a weed, or maybe talk to it, and they left her behind. How much trouble could she get into? Quentin had had some half-formed idea of flirting with Elaine as a way of arousing Julia's competitive spirit, but if such a spirit dwelled within her it remained unaroused.

After a half mile they came to the center of town. The cart track performed a wobbly loop and rejoined itself. There was a market here, or at least some market stalls, with a fishy reek and a few discarded, trampled fruit of the kind they'd picked on the way there. At the head of the loop stood a grand official building of the town hall variety with a stopped clock on its pediment like a blind Cyclops eye and a faded but still recognizable Fillorian flag hanging limp and exhausted in the damp heat.

In the center of the loop stood a stone monument, a granite obelisk with a statue of a man on top. Monsoons had weathered it badly, and tropical weeds had managed to crack off a corner of the base, but you could still make out the man's heroic attitude, stoic in the face of what looked like impending misfortune.

"That is Captain Banks," Elaine said. "He founded the Fillorian settlement on the Outer Island, by which I mean he ran his ship into it."

Quentin wondered if there was a joke to be made about "founder" and "founder." If there was it had probably already made the rounds of the Outer Island.

"Where is everybody?"

"Oh, they're around," she said. "We keep to ourselves here, mostly."

Eleanor tried Elaine and was cuffed away. She held up her arms to

Quentin, and he hoisted her up onto his shoulders. Elaine rolled her eyes as if to say, don't say I didn't warn you. The sun was setting in an absolute bloodbath of a sunset behind the trees, and the evening insects were growing bolder.

Eleanor squealed with delight at how tall Quentin was compared with her usual mount. She pulled the edge of her skirt down over his eyes. He gently lifted it up and she squealed again and pushed it back down. It was a game. She was surprisingly strong. Quentin supposed that there were worse things to be than an easy mark.

He stood there for a long moment, in the tropical darkness that lay beneath the hem of Eleanor's skirt. Here I am, noble leader of the bold expedition to the Outer Island. King of all I survey. This was it, there really would be no surprise twist, no big reveal. The feeling of resignation was almost pleasurable, a mellow, numbing pleasure, like the first good, stiff drink of the evening.

He sighed. It wasn't an unhappy sigh, but it included the thought: as soon as I have those taxes I am so out of here.

"You said something before about cocktails," he said.

Dinner at the embassy was surprisingly good: a frighteningly toothy local fish served whole in a sweet preparation with some kind of mango-like local fruit. Eleanor waited on the guests with towering dignity, conveying salt shakers and glasses and other incidental items from kitchen to table with a straight back and slow, deliberate steps, toe-heel, as if she were walking a balance beam. Around eight thirty she dropped a crystal wineglass.

"For God's sake, Eleanor," Elaine said. "Go to bed. No dessert, just go to bed." The accused wept and demanded cake, but Elaine was unmoved.

Afterward they all sat on wicker couches and chairs on an upper porch and took cautious sips of some appallingly sugary local liquor. The bay was spread out in the darkness below them, with the *Muntjac* afloat in it, illuminated by lanterns at bow and stern and at the tops of the masts. Julia contrived a spell to keep the bugs away.

Quentin asked where the bathroom was and excused himself. It was a cover story: he stopped by the kitchen, where he found what was left of the cake sitting underneath a glass dome. He cut a slice and took it up to Eleanor's bedroom.

"Shhhhhh," he said, closing the door behind him. She nodded seriously, as if he were a spy delivering a wartime communiqué. He waited while she ate the cake, then returned the evidence—the empty plate and the fork—to the kitchen.

When he got back to the veranda Elaine was alone. Julia had gone to bed. If she felt anything about him, she wasn't about to fight over him for the sake of it. His grand outing with Julia was slipping away from him. Fine if nothing happened between them—at this point he'd be happy if he could just get her to talk to him. He was worried about her.

"I apologize about earlier," Elaine said. "Your Highness. About your being king."

"Forget about it." He refocused his attention on her with an effort and smiled. "I'm still getting used to it myself."

"It would have been easier if you were wearing a crown."

"I did for a while, but it was incredibly uncomfortable. And it always fell off at the most inappropriate moments."

"I can imagine."

"Christenings. Cavalry charges."

Under the influence of the local moonshine he was beginning to find himself insouciantly charming. *Le roi s'amuse.*

"It sounds like a public nuisance."

"It was practically an enemy of the state. Now I just maintain a kingly bearing. I'm sure you noticed *that.*"

It was difficult to make out her expression in the twilight. Mobs of exotic eastern stars were filling in the black sky overhead.

"Oh, it was unmistakable."

She began rolling a cigarette. Were they flirting? She had to be at least fifteen years older than Quentin. Here he was afloat in the wild magical tropics of Fillory and he'd stumbled on the only cougar within 477 nautical miles. He wondered who Eleanor's daddy was.

"Did you grow up here?" he asked.

"Oh, no. My parents were from the mainland—down around the Southern Orchard. I never knew my father. I've been in the diplomatic service forever. This is just another posting for me, I've been all over the empire."

Quentin nodded sagely. He wasn't aware that Fillory had a diplomatic service. He'd have to look into that when he got back.

"So do you get a lot of people coming through here? I mean from outside Fillory? Over the sea?"

"Sadly no. Actually I'll tell you a terrible secret: no one has ever come through here, not as long as I've been at the embassy. In fact in the whole history of this office, three centuries of it, nobody has ever once passed through customs from across the Eastern Ocean. The records are completely blank. In that respect I suppose you'd have to call it a bit of a sinecure."

"Well, what with there being no work and all."

"It's a shame, you should see the customs forms, they're really magnificent. The letterhead alone. You should take some. And the stamp—I'll stamp something for you in the morning. The stamp is an absolute masterpiece."

The tip of her cigarette glowed in the dimness. Quentin was reminded of the last time he'd smoked, during the brief but vigorously hedonistic period when he'd lived in New York, three years ago. Her cigarette was sweet and fragrant. He asked for one. She had to roll it for him, he'd forgotten how. Or had he ever known? No, Eliot had a clever silver device that rolled them for you.

"I hate to bring this up," Quentin said. "But there's a reason why I'm here."

"I thought as much. Is it that magic key business?"

"What? Oh. No, it's not the magic key."

She leaned back and put her feet up on a chest she used for a table.

"What then?"

"It's about the money. The taxes. You didn't send any last year. I mean the island didn't."

She burst out laughing—a big, openmouthed laugh. She leaned back and clapped her hands together once.

"And they sent you? They sent the king?"

"They didn't send me. I'm the king. I sent myself."

"Right." She dabbed at her eyes with the heels of her hands. "You're a bit of a micromanager, aren't you? Well, I suppose you're wondering where the money is. We should have sent it. We could have, no one's in any danger of starving on the Outer Island. Tomorrow I'll take you out to see the gold beetles. They're amazing: they eat dirt and poop out gold ore. Their nests are made of gold!" She kicked the chest their feet were resting on. "Take this. It's full of gold. I'll throw in the chest for free."

"Great," Quentin said. "Thanks. It's a deal."

Mission accomplished. He took a drag on the cigarette and stifled a cough. It had been a very brief phase, his smoking period. Maybe he'd had too much of whatever this was. Rum? It was sweet, and they were on a tropical island, so let's call it rum.

"We hadn't heard from you for years. There didn't seem to be any point. I mean, what do you actually do with the stuff?"

Quentin could have answered that, but even he had to admit that the answer wouldn't have been a very good one. Probably they used it to regild Eliot's scepter. Taxation without representation. She could start a revolution. She was right. It was all so unreal.

"Anyway look what happened. They sent us a king. I think we might be forgiven for feeling a little pleased with ourselves. But why are you really here? Don't tell me that's the whole reason, it's too, too disappointing. Are you on a quest?"

"I'm afraid I am going to disappoint you. I'm not on a quest."

"I was sure you were looking for the magic key," she said. "The one that winds up the world."

It was hard to tell when she was joking.

"To be honest, Elaine, I don't really know much about the key. I guess there's a story about it? Do you get a lot of people looking for it?"

"No. But it's just about our only claim to fame, aside from the beetles."

A vast orange moon was rising, as orange as their cigarette tips. It was a crescent moon, hanging so low it looked like it could snag a horn in the *Muntjac*'s rigging. Fillory's moon was actually crescent-shaped, not round. Once a day, exactly at noon, it passed between Fillory and the sun, making an eclipse. The birds all went quiet when it happened. It still seemed to take them by surprise. Quentin was so used to it he hardly noticed it anymore.

"It's not here anyway," she said.

"I figured that." Quentin poured himself more rum from a decanter. Not that he needed it, but who cared. He wondered if they'd solved the mystery of Jollyby's death yet.

"It's on After. The next island farther out."

"Sorry," he said. "I'm not following. What's where?"

"There's an island farther out from here, called After. Two days' sail, maybe three. I've never been there. But that's where the key is."

"The key. You must be joking."

"Am I laughing?" Was she? She gave him a funny half smile.

"I'm thinking this is a metaphorical key. The key to life. It's a piece of paper that says 'haste makes waste' or 'early to bed early to rise.'"

"No, Quentin, it's a real key. Made of gold. Teeth and everything. Very magical, or that's what people say."

Quentin stared at the bottom of his glass. He needed to be thinking now, but he'd taken steps to disable his thinking apparatus. Too late. Haste makes waste.

"Who makes a key out of gold?" he said. "It makes no sense. It would be too soft. It would get bent all the time."

"You'd certainly have to be careful where you stuck it."

Quentin's face felt hot. Thank God the night was cooling off, finally, and a night wind was rising in the trees around the embassy.

"So there's a magic golden key a couple of days' sail away from here. Why haven't you gone and gotten it yourself?"

"I don't know, Quentin. Maybe I haven't got any magic locks."

"It never occurred to me that the key might be real."

It was tempting. It was more than that: it was a big buzzing neon sign in the darkness that read ADVENTURELAND. He could feel the pull of it, from out over the horizon. The Outer Island was a bust, a red herring, but that just meant he hadn't gone far enough.

Elaine sat forward on the couch, looking more sober and cogent than he felt. Probably she was used to this rum stuff. He wondered what it might be like to kiss her. He wondered what it might be like to get into bed with her. They were all alone on a sweaty tropical night. The moon was up. Though if he'd been serious about that he probably should have stopped drinking a little sooner. And now that he did think about it, he wasn't entirely sure that he wanted to kiss those thin, smiling lips.

"Will you let me tell you something, Quentin?" she said. "I would think very hard about whether you want to look for the key. This island is a pretty safe place as islands go, but it's the jumping-off point. This is the end of Fillory, Quentin.

"Out there"—she pointed out to sea, past the *Muntjac*'s cozy hurricane lamps, past the faint black-on-blue outlines of the palm trees on the rim of the bay, where the hushing of distant breakers came from—"that's not Fillory. Your kingdom ends here. Here you're a king, you're all-powerful. You're not king of any of that. Out there you're just Quentin. Are you sure that's going to be enough?"

When she said it, he saw what she meant. They were on the very rim of something, the lip. The edge of that meadow in the forest, where Jollyby died. The sill of his office window, when Eliot and the others had come to fetch him on Earth. Here he was powerful. There, he didn't know what he was.

"Of course I'm not sure," he said. "That's why you go. To find out if it's enough. You just have to be sure you want to find out."

"Yes, you do, Your Highness," Elaine said. "Yes, you do."

Quentin was the last one to bed that night and the last one up in the morning. His sense of time had gotten pleasantly elastic in Fillory, since he wasn't constantly being assaulted with blinking digital clocks here the way he was in the real world, but it was late enough that the sun was already scorching. Late enough for him to feel the shame that comes with hearing other people going about their business while he was still weakly tangled up in his sweaty sheets. His room was airy and equatorial, with cool white linen and flung-open windows, and it was still suffocatingly hot.

The rum, which had seemed so delightful the night before, so absolutely good and necessary, had now revealed its true nature as a hideous toxin, a drier of mouths and a ravager of brains. He cursed the earlier incarnation of himself that drank so much of it. Then he got up and went in search of water.

There was plenty of it around. Probably there was a beautiful songbird somewhere around here that puked gallons of sparkling spring-water every morning, to go with the gold beetles. He ran himself a cool bath and sat in it and sipped more water till his head felt better. You can't feel fresher and cleaner than when you're soaking in fresh water within sight of the ocean.

Most of the night before was blotted out, or available to his memory only in the form of mental security-camera footage, grainy figures with blurred voices, but one thing remained bright and clear and high-definition: the golden key. She'd said it was real. He wondered what the magic was. He wondered what it opened. Had she told him, and he'd forgotten? No, that didn't sound right. But she'd told him where it was: After Island. He needed to know more. They had a choice to make: go on, or go home.

But by the time he came down for breakfast Elaine was already gone. She'd left a note reminding him to take the chest with him, the one with the taxes in it, and wishing him well. She also left him a slender gray book called *The Seven Golden Keys*. She didn't say where she'd gone.

I guess she won't be showing me those gold beetles after all, he thought. Or her fancy stamp. Thank God he hadn't made a pass at her.

Elaine had left behind her daughter too. Eleanor was back at her mother's desk, just as they'd found her when they arrived, industriously documenting the habits of the bunny-pegasus in bright primary-colored pencils on official Outer Island Embassy stationery. There seemed to be an unlimited supply of it.

Quentin looked over her shoulder. The letterhead really was nice.

"Good morning, Eleanor. Do you know where your mom went?"

Quentin hadn't spent a lot of time with little kids in his life. He mostly fell back on treating them like adults. Eleanor didn't seem to mind.

"No," she said lightly. She didn't look up or stop coloring.

"Do you know when she's coming back?"

She shook her head. What kind of mother would leave a five-year-old to take care of herself? Quentin felt sorry for Eleanor. She was a sweet, earnest little girl. She made him feel paternal, which wasn't a feeling he had much experience with, but he was finding that he liked it. She obviously didn't get much attention, and what she got wasn't exactly dripping with maternal affection.

"All right. We have to go soon, but we'll wait till she gets back."

"You don't have to."

"Well, we sort of do. Are you still drawing bunny-pegasi?"

"Yes."

"You know, I think they might be hare-pegasi, not bunnies. Hares are bigger, and much fiercer."

"They're bunnies."

The eternal question. Eleanor changed the subject.

"I made these for you."

With some effort she pulled open a desk drawer—the humidity made it stick, and when it came unstuck it pulled out all the way and fell on the floor. She rummaged in it and took out some papers, four or five of them, and handed them to Quentin. They were heavily scribbled over in colored pencil.

"They're passports," she said, anticipating his question. "You need them if you want to leave Fillory."

"Who said I'm leaving Fillory?"

"You need them *if* you're leaving Fillory," she said. "If you're not you don't need them. They're just in *case*."

And then more quietly: "You have to fold them in half yourself."

She must have been copying from something official, because they were in their own way impressive documents. They had the Fillorian arms on the front, or a crude facsimile thereof. Inside Quentin's—once you folded it in half—there was a picture of Quentin, more or less, with a big red smile and a golden crown on his head, and some squiggly lines representing writing. On the back were the arms of the Outer Island: a palm tree and a butterfly. She'd made one for each of them, even the sloth, whom she had never seen but had been extremely interested in. She must be bored stiff without any other kids around, Quentin thought. She must be practically raising herself.

He could relate. He was an only child too, and his parents had never paid much attention to him either. They considered their attitude toward parenting to be rather enlightened: they weren't going to be the kind of couple whose lives revolved around their child. They gave him a lot of freedom and never asked him for much. Though the funny thing about never being asked for anything is that after a while you start to feel like maybe you don't have anything worth giving.

"Thank you, Eleanor. That was very, very sweet of you." He bent down and kissed her on her blond crown.

"It's because you brought me cake," she said shyly.

"I know."

Poor moppet. Maybe when he got back to Whitespire he could start up some Fillorian equivalent of Child Social Services.

"We'll wait till your mom comes back before we go."

"You don't have to."

But he did, or he waited as long as possible. They spent the day lounging around the embassy and fishing off the dock. He made another attempt to teach Eleanor to read the palm clock-tree and was again rebuffed. Around four o'clock Quentin called it. He had Benedict take Eleanor into town—over her strident objections—to find somebody responsible to leave her with and ordered everybody else back on the freshly watered and provisioned *Muntjac.*

Benedict returned an hour later, haggard but victorious. They weighed anchor as the first stars appeared. Playtime was over. They set sail for Castle Whitespire.

CHAPTER 6

A funny thing happened to Julia after that business with her fake social studies paper. A magic trick, you might even call it: where once there had been only one Julia, there were now two Julias, one for each set of memories. The Julia that went with the first set, the normal set, the one where she wrote the paper and went home and had dinner, did normal Julia things. She went to school. She did her homework. She played the oboe. She finally slept with James, which she'd kind of been meaning to do anyway, but for some reason had been putting off.

But there was a second, stranger Julia growing inside the first Julia, like a parasite, or a horrible tumor. At first it was tiny, the size of a bacterium, a single cell of doubt, but it divided and divided and grew and grew. This second Julia wasn't interested in school, or the oboe, or even James particularly. James backed up the first Julia's story, he remembered meeting her in the library, but what did that prove? Nothing. It just proved that in addition to writing her paper on intentional communities for her, they'd gotten to James.

And James bought the story, heart and soul. There was only one James.

The problem was that Julia was smart, and Julia was interested in the truth. She didn't like inconsistencies, and she didn't let go until they were resolved, ever. When she was five she'd wanted to know why Goofy could talk and Pluto couldn't. How could one dog have another dog for a pet, and one be sentient and the other not? Likewise she wanted to know who the lazy fucker was who wrote her paper on intentional communities for her and used Wikipedia as a source. Granted that the answer, "the nefarious agents of a secret school for wizards in upstate New York," was not a league-leadingly plausible answer to her question. But it was the answer that fit her memories, and those memories were getting sharper all the time.

And as they got sharper the second Julia grew stronger and stronger, and every bit of strength she gained she took away from the first Julia, who got weaker and weaker and thinner and thinner, to the point where she was practically transparent, and the parasite behind the mask of her face became almost visible.

The funny thing, or rather one of the many funny things in this ha-ha-hilarious story, was that nobody noticed. Nobody noticed that she had less and less to say to James, or that with three weeks to go before the holiday concert she lost first chair in the oboe section of the wolfishly competitive Manhattan Conservatory Extension School Youth Orchestra, thereby forfeiting the juicy solo in *Peter and the Wolf* (the duck's theme) to the demonstrably inferior Evelyn Oh, whose rendition of it did, appropriately enough, sound like a quacking fucking duck, as did everything that came out of Evelyn Oh's quacking fucking Oh-boe.

The second Julia just wasn't that interested in James, or in playing the oboe, or in school. So uninterested in school was she that she did something really stupid, which was to pretend she'd applied to college when really she hadn't. She blew off every single one of her applications. Nobody noticed that either. But they'd notice in April, when brilliant overachieving Julia got into zero colleges. Second Julia had planted a ticking time bomb that was going to blow up first Julia's life.

That was December. By March she and James were hanging by a thread. She'd dyed her hair black and painted her nails black, in order to more accurately resemble the second Julia. James initially found this sexy and goth, and he stepped up his efforts in the sex department, which wasn't exactly a welcome side effect, but it made a break from talking to him, which was getting harder and harder. They'd never been as good a couple as they looked—he wasn't a real bona fide nerd, just nerd-friendly, nerd-compatible, and you could only explain your *Gödel, Escher, Bach* references so many times before it starts to be a problem.

Pretty soon he was going to figure out that she wasn't role-playing a sexy depressed goth chick, she had actually become a sexy depressed goth chick.

And she was enjoying it. She was dipping a toe in the pool of bad behavior and finding the temperature was just right. It was fun being a problem. Julia had been very very good for a very long time, and the funny thing about that was, if you're too good too much of the time, people start to forget about you. You're not a problem, so people can strike you off their list of things to worry about. Nobody makes a fuss over you. They make a fuss over the bad girls. In her quiet way Second Julia was causing a bit of a fuss, for once in her life, and it felt good.

Then Quentin came to visit. The question of where Quentin had gone to after first semester was one she had an inordinate amount of trouble focusing her mind on, but the mist surrounding it was a familiar mist. She'd seen it before: it was the same mist that surrounded her lost afternoon. His cover story, that he'd left high school early to matriculate at some super-exclusive experimental college, smelled like First Julia stuff to her. Made-up stuff.

She'd always liked Quentin, basically. He was sarcastic and spookily smart and, on some level, basically a kind person who just needed a ton of therapy and maybe some mood-altering drugs. Something to selectively inhibit the voracious reuptake of serotonin that was obviously going on inside his skull 24-7. She felt bad about the fact that he was in love with her and that she found him deeply unsexy, but not that bad. Honestly, he was decent-looking, better-looking than he thought he was, but that moody boy-man Fillory shit cut like zero ice with her, and she was smart enough to know whose problem that was, and it wasn't hers.

But when he came back in March there was something different about him, something otherworldly and glittery-eyed. He didn't say anything, but he didn't have to. He'd *seen* things. There was a smell coming off his fingers, the smell you got after they ran the really big Van de Graaff generator at the science museum. This was a man who had handled lightning.

They all went down to the boat launch on the Gowanus Canal, and she smoked cigarette after cigarette and just looked at him. And she knew: He'd gone through to the other side, and she'd been left behind.

She thought she'd seen him there, at the exam at Brakebills, in the hall with the chalk clock, with the glasses of water and the disappearing kids. Now she knew she was right. But it had been very different for him, she realized. When he walked into that room he'd buckled right down and killed that exam, because magic school? That was just the kind of thing he'd been waiting to happen to him his whole life. He practically *expected* that shit. He'd been wondering when it was going to show up, and when it did he was good and ready for it.

Whereas Julia had been blindsided. She had never expected anything special to just happen to her. Her plan for life was to get out there and *make* special things happen, which was a much more sensible plan from a probability point of view, given how unlikely it was that anything as exciting as Brakebills would ever just fall into your lap. So when she got there she had had the presence of mind to step back and make a full appraisal of exactly how weird it all was. She could have handled the math, God knew. She'd been in math classes with Quentin since they were ten years old, and anything he could do she could do just as well, backward and in high heels if necessary.

But she spent too much time looking around, trying to work it through, the implications of it. She didn't take it at face value the way Quentin did. The uppermost thought in her mind was, why are you all sitting here doing differential geometry and generally jumping through hoops when fundamental laws of thermodynamics and Newtonian physics are being broken left and right all around you? This shit was major. The test was the last of her priorities. It was the least interesting thing in the room. Which she still stood by as the reasonable, intelligent person's reaction to the situation.

But now Quentin was on the inside, and she was out here chain-smoking on the Gowanus boat dock with her half-orc boyfriend. Quentin had passed the test, and she'd failed. It seemed that reason and intelligence weren't getting it done anymore. They were cutting, like, zero ice.

It was when Quentin left that day that Julia really fell off a cliff.

———

It was fair to call it depression. She felt like shit, all the time. If that was depression, she had it. It must have been contagious. She'd caught it from the world.

The shrink they sent her to diagnosed her more specifically with dysthymia, which he defined as an inability to enjoy things that she should be enjoying. Which she recognized the justice of, since she enjoyed nothing, though there was a world of space inside that "should" that a dysthymic semiotician could have argued with, if she had had the energy. Because there was something she did enjoy, or would enjoy, whether or not she should. She just had no access to it. That thing was magic.

The world around her, the straight world, the mundane world, had become to her a blowing wasteland. It was empty, a postapocalyptic world: empty stores, empty houses, stalled cars with the upholstery burned out of them, dead traffic lights swaying above empty streets. That missing afternoon in November had become a black hole that had sucked the entire rest of her life into it. And once you'd fallen past that Schwarzschild radius, it was pretty damn hard to claw your way back out again.

She printed out the first verse of a Donne poem and stuck it on her door:

> The sun is spent, and now his flasks
> Send forth light squibs, no constant rays;
> The world's whole sap is sunk;
> The general balm th' hydroptic earth hath drunk,
> Whither, as to the bed's-feet, life is shrunk,
> Dead and interr'd; yet all these seem to laugh,
> Compared with me, who am their epitaph.

Apparently semicolons were the hot new thing in the seventeenth century.

But otherwise it was a pretty good summary of her state of mind. Hydroptic: it meant thirsty. The thirsty earth. The sap had sunk out of the thirsty world, leaving behind a dried husk that weighed nothing, a dead thing that crumbled if you touched it.

Once a week her mother asked her if she'd been raped. Maybe it would have been simpler if she said yes. Her family had never really understood her. They'd always lived in fear of her rapacious intellect. Her sister, a timorous, defiantly unmathematical brunette four years younger, tiptoed around her as if she were a wild animal who would snap rabidly if provoked. No sudden movements. Keep your fingers outside the cage.

As a matter of fact she did consider insanity as a possible diagnosis. She had to. What sane person (ha!) wouldn't? She definitely looked crazier than she used to. She'd picked up some bad habits, like picking at her cuticles, and not showering, and for that matter not eating or leaving her room for days at a time. Clearly—Doctor Julia explained to herself—she was suffering from some kind of Harry Potter–induced hallucination, with paranoid overtones, most likely schizophrenic in origin.

Except the thing was, doctor, it was all much too orderly. It didn't have the quality of a hallucination, it was too dry and firm to the touch. For one thing it was her only hallucination. It didn't spill over into other things. Its borders were stable. And for another thing it wasn't a hallucination. It fucking happened.

If this was madness it was an entirely new kind of madness, as yet undocumented in the *Diagnostic and Statistical Manual of Mental Disorders*. She had nerdophrenia. She was dorkotic.

Julia broke up with James. Or maybe she just stopped answering his calls and greeting him when they passed each other in the hall. One or the other, she forgot which. She did some careful calculations with her GPA, which until that point had been highly robust, and figured she could go to school two days out of five, eke out straight D's, and still graduate. It was just a matter of careful brinksmanship, and the brink was where Julia lived now.

Meanwhile she continued to see the shrink regularly. He was a perfectly decent sort, nothing if not well-meaning, with a funny stubbly face and reasonable expectations of what he could hope to achieve in life. She didn't tell him about the secret school for magic that she hadn't gotten into, though. Maybe she was crazy, but she wasn't stupid. She'd seen *Terminator 2*. She wasn't going out like Sarah Connor.

Every once in a while Julia did feel her conviction slackening. She knew what she knew, but there just wasn't a lot to go on, day to day, to keep her belief in what happened strong. The best she could hope for was that every couple of weeks Google might pop up a hit on Brakebills, maybe two, but a few minutes later it would be gone again. As if by magic! Apparently she wasn't the only person out there who had a Google alert on it, and that person was clever enough to scrub the Google cache when the alert went off. But it gave Julia something to chew on.

Then, in April, they made their first wrong move. They really blew it. Blew it wide open. Because seven envelopes arrived in her mailbox: Harvard, Yale, Princeton, Columbia, Stanford, MIT, and Caltech. Congratulations, we are pleased to accept you as a member of the class of *ha ha ha ha you must be fucking kidding me!* She laughed her fucking head off when she saw them. Her parents laughed too. They were laughing with relief. Julia was laughing because it was so goddamned funny. She kept on laughing as she ripped the letters in half, one after the other, and fed them to the recycling bin.

You goddamned idiots, she thought. Too clever for your own good. No wonder you let Quentin in, you're just like him: you can't stop outsmarting yourselves. You think you can buy off my life with this? With a bunch of fat envelopes? You are perhaps under the impression that I will accept these in lieu of the magic kingdom that is my rightful inheritance?

Oh my no. Not on your life, mister. This is a standoff, a waiting game, and I've got all day. You're looking for a quick fix to the Julia problem, but no such fix exists. You'd best settle in, my friend, because Julia is playing the long game.

CHAPTER 7

On the way home, Quentin made it his royal business to orbit the *Muntjac* and check in on everybody once or twice a day. The morning after they left the Outer Island, Quentin's first stop was Benedict. The ship was racing along under the tropical sun, its every line and sail twangingly taut and perfect, and Quentin was feeling a little silly that he'd had the *Muntjac* so thoroughly fitted out for what had amounted to a trip around the block. He found Benedict sitting on a stool in his cabin, hunched over his tiny fold-down writing desk. Spread out on it was a hand-drawn naval chart showing a few jagged little islands and peppered with tiny numbers that might have denoted the depths of the ocean. Somebody had gone over the shallow water with a pale blue wash to make it look more watery.

Benedict hadn't warmed to Quentin any since they'd left the mainland, but Quentin found himself liking him anyway. There was something bracing about the sheer consistency of his contempt for Quentin, who was, after all, Benedict's king. It took some backbone to stick to that position. And if nothing else Benedict was about the nerdiest person he'd met in Fillory, of a type that didn't really exist in the real world: he was a map nerd.

"So what have you been up to?" he said.

Benedict shrugged.

"Seasick mostly."

He hadn't seen much of Benedict, though he'd tried a couple of times to tutor him on his math. Benedict was conspicuously skillful at doing arithmetic in his head, but Fillorian mathematics weren't particularly advanced. It was amazing how far he'd gotten on his own.

"What are you working on?"

"Old map," Benedict said, without looking up. "Like really old. Like two hundred years ago."

Quentin peered over his shoulder, hands clasped behind his back. "Is that from the embassy?"

"Like I would do that. It was on the wall. In a frame."

"It's just that it has the Outer Island Embassy seal on it."

"I copied it."

"You copied the seal too?"

"I copied the map. The seal was on the map."

It was a gorgeous map. If he was telling the truth, Benedict had genuine talent. It was detailed, precise, without any hesitations or erasures.

"That's amazing. You have a real gift."

Benedict flushed at this and worked even more industriously. He found Quentin's approval and his disapproval equally unbearable.

"How've you found the fieldwork? Must be different from what you're used to."

"I hate it," Benedict said. "It's a fucking mess. Nothing looks like it's supposed to. There's no math for it." His frustration brought him out of his shell a little. "Nothing's ever correct, ever. There's no straight lines! I always got that maps are approximations, I just never understood how much they leave out. It's chaos. I'm never doing this again."

"That's it? You're giving up?"

"Why shouldn't I? Look at that—" Benedict waved at the wall, in the general direction of the heaving sea. "And now look at this." He pointed to the map. "This you can make perfect. That—" He shuddered. "It's just a mess."

"But the map isn't real. So sure, maybe it's perfect, but what's the point?"

"Maps don't make you seasick."

The irony wasn't lost on Quentin. He's the one who'd turned the ship around, back toward Whitespire. He looked at the map Benedict was working on. Sure enough, one of the little islands toward the edge of the page, almost falling into the margin, had the word *After* written next to it in tiny calligraphic script.

"After Island." There it was, right there. Quentin touched it lightly with his finger. He half-expected to get a shock. "Is that on our way?"

"It's east of here. It's the complete opposite of on our way."

"How far?"

"Two days, three days. Like I said, the map is really old. And these are outlying islands."

Benedict explained, rolling his eyes practically up into his head at Quentin's ignorance, that the islands farther out in the Eastern Ocean didn't stay still once they caught on that they'd been mapped. They didn't like it, and through some kind of tectonic magic they wandered around to make sure the maps didn't stay too accurate. More chaos.

Benedict whispered some calculations to himself, speed and time, then nimbly, precisely—you wouldn't think it was possible with those black bangs hanging over his eyes—he drew a perfect freehand circle around After Island in light pencil.

"It has to be somewhere inside this circle."

Quentin gazed at the little island-dot, lost in the web of curving lines of meridians and parallels. A net that wouldn't catch him if he fell. It wasn't Fillory out there. But somewhere in that abyss shone a key, a magic key. He could come back with that in his hand.

An image swam into his mind, an album cover from the 1970s, a painting of an old-fashioned sailing ship on the very edge of a cataract over which the green sea was roaring and pouring. The ship was just beginning to tilt, and the current was strong, but still: a bold tack in a strong wind might just save it. A sharp, barked order from the captain and it would slew around and beat back up against the current to safety.

But then where would the ship go? Back home? Not yet.

"Mind if I borrow this?" he said. "I want to show it to the captain."

With the course change they left the warm blue-green ocean behind and crashed their way into a heaving black one. The temperature dropped thirty degrees. Flail-blows of cold rain clattered on the deck. Quentin couldn't have pointed to the dividing line, but now the water around them seemed like a completely different element from the one they'd been sailing in before, something opaque and solid that had to be smashed and shoved aside rather than slipped silently through.

The *Muntjac* bulled its way gamely through the waves ahead of a firm, pressing salt wind. The ship had a surprise for them: below the waterline it seemed—it was hard to see clearly through the chop—to have put out a pair of sleek wooden fins, unfolding from pockets in the hull, which swam them forward. Whether they were animated by magic or a mechanical arrangement, Quentin didn't know. But he felt a warm surge of gratitude. The old ship was repaying his kindness and more.

He thought the sloth might know something about it, given how much time it spent down there in the hold, but when he visited he found it fast asleep, hanging by its boat-hook claws, rocking gently with the ship's rolling. If anything it was more serene in the heavy weather. The air in the hold was warm and humid and slothy, and a salad of rotting fruit rinds and less identifiable debris sloshed around in the bilge.

Julia, then. She might know. And he wanted to discuss the magic key with her. She was his only real peer on board the *Muntjac*, and she had access to sources he didn't. And he was worried about her.

Julia kept to her cabin even more than usual now that the weather had turned. She may have been spiritually one with Fillory, but the freezing drizzle had hounded even her belowdecks. Quentin lurched down the narrow passage that led to her room, with errant swells flinging him playfully against one bulkhead, then the other.

Her door was shut. For a moment, just as the *Muntjac* paused weightlessly on the crest of the wave, Quentin had a powerful sense of the romance of the scene, and his crush stirred inside him, unfolding its leathery wings. He knew it was at least partly a fantasy. Julia was so solitary, so wrapped up in Fillory, that it was hard to imagine her wanting him or anyone, or at any rate anyone human. She was missing something, but it probably wasn't a boyfriend.

Then again they were both here, far out at sea, tempest-tossed, together in a warm berth in the freezing wasteland of the ocean. It was liberating being out from under the snarky, gossipy gazes of Eliot and Janet. Surely Julia couldn't be so far gone that she didn't recognize the allure of a shipboard fling. The scene practically wrote itself. She was only human. And they would be home soon. He knocked on her door.

Always at the back of his mind, never spoken but always felt, was his awareness that Julia was from before: before Brakebills, before he knew magic was real, before everything. She'd never known Alice. If he could fall back in love with Julia, it would be like time winding itself back, and he could start over again. Sometimes he wasn't sure if he was in love with Julia or just that he wanted to be in love with her, because it would be so comforting, such a relief, to be in love with her. It seemed like such a good idea. Was there really that big of a difference?

Julia opened the door. She was naked.

Or no, she wasn't naked. She was wearing a dress, sort of, but only to her waist. The top half was hanging down in front of her, and her breasts were bare. They were pale and conical, neither full nor slight. They were perfect. When he was seventeen he'd devoted entire months of his life to constructing a mental image of Julia's naked upper body based on forensic evidence gathered from furtive surveys of her clothed form. As it turned out he'd been quite close. Only her nipples were different from what he'd expected. Paler, hardly darker than the pale skin around them.

He closed the door again—he didn't slam it, but he closed it firmly.

"Jesus Christ, Julia!" he said under his breath. Though he said it to himself more than to her.

A long minute passed. He spent it with his back against the bulkhead next to Julia's door. He could feel his heart beating hard against the hard wood. Sure, he wanted something to happen, but not that. Or at least not like that. What the hell did she mean, waving those things around? What, was this a joke to her? He could hear her moving around in her room. He took a deep breath and knocked again, slowly. When she answered the door again her dress was fully on.

"What the hell are you doing?" he said.

"Sorry," she said flatly.

She sat down on a little stool at the other end of the room, facing the windows. She didn't ask him in, but she hadn't closed the door either. Warily, he stepped inside.

Julia's quarters were the mirror image of Quentin's, but due to an irregularity in the ship's plan, an errant staircase on his side, they were a little bigger, with room for two people to sit if one of them sat on the bed. Quentin sat on the bed. Light came from a glowing blue ball that bobbed up against the ceiling like a balloon that had lost its string, an odd casting of Julia's that looked like a trapped will-o'-the-wisp.

"I'm sorry," she said again. "I forgot."

"What did you forget?" It came out angrier than he meant it to. "That your arms go in the sleeves? Look, it's not like I don't . . ." No good end to that sentence. "Never mind."

He looked at her, really looked, for the first time in a while. She was still beautiful but thin, much too thin. And her eyes were still black. He wondered if the change was permanent, and if so what else had changed that he couldn't see.

"I don't know." She stared out at the spray. "I forget what I forgot."

"Well, okay, so, but now you remembered."

"Look, I forget how things work sometimes. All right? Or not so much how but why. Why people say hello, why they take baths, why they wear clothes, read books, smile, talk, eat. All those human things." She tugged her mouth to one side.

"I don't understand this, Julia." The anger was gone. He kept revising how much trouble Julia was having, and every time he did he revised it upward. "Help me understand. You're human. Why would you forget that? *How* would you?"

"I don't know." She shook her head. Then she turned those black eyes on him. "I'm losing it. It's losing me. It's going away."

"What is? What happened to you, Julia? Do you need to go back to Earth?"

"No!" she said sharply. "I'm not going back there. Not ever."

The idea seemed to frighten her.

"But you remember Brooklyn, right? Where we're from? And James, and high school, and all that?"

"Remembering." Her delicate mouth quirked again, bitterly. She spoke in something like her old voice, with contractions and everything.

"That's always been my problem, hasn't it. I remembered Brakebills. Couldn't forget it."

Quentin remembered her remembering. She'd failed the entrance exam at Brakebills, which he'd passed, and she was supposed to forget about it afterward so the school would stay secret. They'd cast spells on her to make sure. But the spells hadn't held, and she hadn't forgotten.

But it had brought her here, he reminded himself. To a beautiful ship on a magical ocean. It had made her a queen of a secret world. The path was crooked, but it led to a happy ending, right? It was dawning on him that Fillory was his happy ending, but it might not be Julia's. She needed something else. She was still out there on the crooked path, and night was coming on.

"Do you wish you hadn't remembered Brakebills? Do you wish you'd stayed in Brooklyn?"

"Sometimes." She folded her arms and leaned back against the wall of her cabin in a way that couldn't have been comfortable. "Quentin, why didn't you help me? Why didn't you rescue me, when I came to you for help that day in Chesterton?"

It was a fair question. It's not like he'd never asked himself that before. He'd even come up with some good answers.

"I couldn't, Julia. It wasn't my choice. You know that. I couldn't get you into Brakebills, I barely got myself in."

"But you could have come to see me. Showed me what you knew."

"They would have expelled me."

"Then after you graduated—"

"Why are we still talking about this now, Julia?" Knowing he was on shaky ground, Quentin counterattacked. Your best defense is a good offense. "Look, you asked me to tell them about you. I did what you asked. I told them. I thought they'd found you and wiped your memory! That's what they always do."

"But they didn't. They couldn't find me. By the time they came looking for me I was long gone. Into thin air." She snapped her fingers. "Like magic."

"And anyway, Julia, how was it supposed to work? What, you were going to be the sorcerer's apprentice, like Mickey Mouse? And how do you think I felt about it? You didn't used to give a shit about me, then suddenly I'm Spelly McSpell and you're all over me. That's just not how it works."

"I gave a shit about you, I just didn't want to sleep with you. God!" She rounded on him in the narrow space. She'd been leaning the stool back on two legs, and now it clunked back down onto four. "Though by the way, I would have, if you'd just given me what I needed."

"Well, you got it anyway, didn't you?"

"Oh, I sure did. I got it and a whole lot more. You shouldn't be surprised about any of this, you of all people. You abandoned me out there in the real world, without magic! Everything that happened to me started with you! You want to know what it was? I'll tell you. But not until you've earned it."

A heavy silence hung in the room. Outside night was falling hard on the stone-colored waves, and her little window was splashed with seawater.

"I never wanted this for you, Julia. Whatever it is. I'm sorry."

He had to say it, and it was true. But it wasn't the only truth. There were other truths in there that weren't as attractive. Such as: he'd been angry at Julia. He'd been her lapdog in high school, trailing around after her while she screwed his best friend, and he'd quite enjoyed it when the tables turned. Was that why he hadn't rescued Julia? It wasn't the only reason. But it was a reason.

"I felt like myself again," she said dully. "Just then. When I got angry." The windowpane was beginning to mist over. Julia started drawing a shape on it, then scribbled it out. "It's going now."

Never mind the magic key. This was where his attention should be. Julia didn't need his love. She needed his help.

"Help me understand," he said. He gathered up her cold fingers in his. "Tell me what I can do. I want to help you. I want to help you remember."

Something else was glowing in the room, something besides the blue will-o'-the-wisp. He wasn't sure when it had started. It was Julia—or not Julia, but something inside her. Her heart was glowing: he could see it right through her skin, even through her dress.

"I am remembering, Quentin," she said. "Out here on the ocean, away from Fillory, it's coming back to me." Now she smiled, brightly, and it was worse than when she just looked blank. "I am remembering *so much* that I never even knew before!"

That night, after a heavy nautical dinner, Quentin went below and un-folded his pallet from against the wall and put himself to bed. The cold, the darkness, the weather, his interview with Julia, everything had combined to accelerate time to the point where he felt like he'd been awake for a week. It wasn't the hours, it was the mileage. He stared up at the rough red-brown beams over his head in the swaying light of the oil lamp.

He was cold and sticky with salt. He could have washed. He knew how to make fresh water from salt. But the spell was involved, and his fingers were stiff, and he decided he would rather live with the sticki-ness. He was warming up under the blankets anyway. When he'd come aboard he'd found a regulation navy blanket on the bed, a bristly beast that weighed about ten pounds and could have repelled chain shot. It was like being in bed with the corpse of a wild boar. He'd swapped it out for a foot-thick down comforter that was persistently damp and thoroughly nonregulation but infinitely more comforting.

Quentin waited to see if his mind would tip over into sleep. When it didn't, and it had made it clear that it wasn't going to without a fight, he sat up and looked at the books on the bookshelves. In his old life, at a juncture like this one, he would have reached for a Fillory novel, but events had overtaken that particular pleasure. But there was still the book Elaine had given him. *The Seven Golden Keys.*

Seven. That was more golden keys than he'd bargained for. He would settle for just one. The book wasn't a novel, it turned out, just a fairy tale set in large type with woodcut illustrations. A children's book. She must have filched it from Eleanor. What a piece of work that woman was. The back page bore the stamp of the embassy library. He squinched up his pillow enough to prop up his head.

The story was about a man, his daughter, and a witch. He was a widower, and the daughter was hardly more than a toddler when the witch came through town. Jealous of the little girl's beauty, and with no children of her own, the witch stole her away, cackling as she did that she was going to lock her away in a silver castle on a remote island. The man could free his daughter, but only if he could find the key to the castle, which he never would, because it was at the End of the World.

Undaunted, the man set out to find the key. It was hot, and he walked all day, and as the sun set he stopped by a river to refresh himself. When he bent down to drink he heard a tiny voice calling, open me up! Open me up! He looked around, and soon he saw that the voice belonged to a freshwater oyster that was clinging to a rock in the river. Next to it in the river mud was a minuscule golden key.

The man picked up both oyster and key, and sure enough, there was a tiny keyhole in the oyster shell, on the opposite side from the hinge. He fitted the key into the lock and turned it, and the shell began to open. He worked it farther open with his knife. As he did so the oyster died, as oysters will when their shells are opened. Inside the oyster, in the place where a pearl might have been, was another golden key, slightly larger than the first one.

The man ate the oyster and took the key and went on his way. Soon he arrived at a house in a forest, and he knocked on the door to see if the owners could give him shelter for the night. The door was slightly ajar, so he pushed his way inside. He found the house full of beds, every room was crammed with them, and in each bed a man or a woman was sleeping. He strolled through the house until he finally found an empty one for himself. There was a clock on the wall that had run down. There was no key to wind it with, so he used the key he found in the oyster's shell. Then he went to bed.

In the morning the clock struck seven, and he awoke. So did the other sleepers in the house. Each of them repeated the same story: they'd come to the house as strangers and taken beds for the night, but they appeared to have slept for years and years, in some cases centuries, right up until the clock struck. As the man packed up his things he found a golden key under his pillow, slightly larger than the one he had used to wind the clock.

It grew colder as the man walked. Perhaps it was colder everywhere since his daughter had been put in the castle. In time the man met a beautiful woman sitting in a pavilion, weeping because her harp was out of tune. He gave her the golden key to tune her harp, and she gave him a larger one in exchange. That one turned out to be the key to a chest buried under a tree root, with yet another, still larger key inside, which let him into a castle—but not the castle with his daughter in it—with a key resting on a table in the highest room of the tallest tower.

The man walked and walked, for weeks or months or years, he couldn't tell anymore. When he couldn't walk anymore he sailed, and when he couldn't sail anymore he was at the End of the World, where sat a dignified man in a dinner suit, dangling his long legs over the edge. He was patting his lapels and turning out his pockets and looking generally perplexed.

"Bother," said the well-dressed man. "I've lost the Key to the World. If I don't wind it up and set its clockwork going again, the sun and moon and stars won't turn, and the world will be plunged into an eternal nighttime of miserable cold and darkness. *Bother!*"

Being a hero, the man had observed, is largely a matter of knowing one's cues. Without a word he drew out the key he'd found in the castle.

"How the devil—?" the man said. "Well, bother. Give it here."

He took the key and lay full-length on the ground, mussing his fine suit, and reached his arm over the Very Edge of the World and began winding vigorously. A loud ratcheting sound could be heard.

"It's in my back pocket," he called over his shoulder as he worked. "You'll have to get it yourself."

Hesitantly, the man reached into the pocket—the well-dressed man never stopped winding—and drew out the last key. He retreated to his boat and sailed back the way he came.

A short time later, a surprisingly short time, he arrived at the magical castle where the witch had imprisoned his daughter, how long ago he could no longer tell. It really was an impressive affair, with gleaming silver walls that flashed in the sun, and it floated some ways off the ground, so that you had to ascend to it by way of a narrow winding silver staircase that flexed disquietingly when the wind blew.

The gate was black iron. The man fitted the last key into the lock and turned it.

The moment he finished the doors sprang open to reveal a beautiful woman standing right behind them, just as if she'd been waiting there for him all along. She was as tall as he was, and she must have been doing a great deal of studying with the witch while he was gone, because she absolutely glowed with magical power.

But he still recognized her. She was his daughter.

"Beautiful girl," the man said, "it's me. Your father. I've come to take you home."

"My father?" she said. "You're not my father. My daddy's not an old man!"

The beautiful woman cackled a not unfamiliar cackle.

"But I am your father," he said. "You don't understand. I've been searching all this time—"

The woman wasn't listening.

"Thank you anyway, for setting me free."

She kissed him on the cheek. Then she handed him a golden key and flew away on the wind.

"Wait!" he called after her. But she didn't wait. He couldn't explain. He watched her dwindle in the distance into nothing. Only then did he sit down and weep.

The man never saw his daughter again, and he never used the key either. Because where could he have gone, what door could he have opened, what treasure could he have unlocked that would have been worth more to him than the golden key his daughter gave him?

CHAPTER 8

Quentin was woken up early by the lookout calling out sonorously to the helmsman, like a subway conductor announcing the next stop, that land was in sight. He put a heavy black cloak on over his pajamas and went up on deck.

His dreams had been full of the man and the daughter and the witch and the keys. The story bothered him, not least because he didn't think it really would have ended that way. Could the man really not have explained? Did his daughter really not understand what had happened? It didn't add up. If they'd talked about it and figured things out it could have been a happy ending. People in fairy tales never just figured things out.

The clouds hung low and gray and solid, barely higher than the top of the *Muntjac*'s mainmast. Quentin squinted in the direction the lookout was pointing. There it was: the promised island was barely visible through the mist. Still hours away.

Up on the forecastle deck Bingle was going through his morning exercises. Quentin's limited interactions with him had made him worry that the greatest swordsman in all of Fillory might possibly be clinically depressed. He never laughed, or even smiled. Two swords lay beside him, still in their leather sheaths, while he performed a series of what looked like isometric exercises involving only his hands, not totally unlike the finger exercises Quentin had learned at Brakebills.

He wondered how you got to be as good at fighting as Bingle. If he was going to get any further in the adventuring business, Quentin thought, he should look into it. He liked the idea of it. A swordfighting sorcerer: the double threat. He didn't have to get as good as Bingle. He just had to get better than he was, which was none too good.

"Good morning," Quentin called.

"Good morning, Your Highness," Bingle said. He never made the mistake of calling Quentin "Your Majesty," a form of address that was reserved for the High King.

"I hate to interrupt."

Bingle didn't stop his routine, which Quentin supposed meant he wasn't technically interrupting after all. He climbed the short ladder up to where Bingle was standing. Bingle knotted his hands together, then turned the position inside-out in a move that made even Quentin wince.

"I was thinking maybe you could give me some lessons. In swordsmanship. I've had a few already, but I haven't gotten very far."

Bingle's expression didn't change.

"It will be easier to protect you," he said, "if you can protect yourself."

"That was my thinking."

Bingle unwove his fingers, which took some careful doing, and looked Quentin up and down. He reached forward and slid Quentin's sword out of its sheath. He did this so quickly and fluidly that although Quentin thought he probably could have stopped him—he had a few inches of reach on Bingle—he couldn't have sworn to it.

Bingle examined Quentin's sword, first one side then the other, felt its edge and its heft, pouting thoughtfully.

"I'll provide you with a weapon."

"I already have a weapon." Quentin pointed. "That sword."

"It's beautiful, but not right for a beginner." For a second Quentin thought he was going to do something drastic, like chuck it overboard, but he just placed it on the deck next to the two other swords.

Bingle went below and returned to present Quentin with the training sword he would be using, a short, heavy weapon of oiled steel, blunt and nearly black and devoid of any adornment whatsoever. The blade and the hilt were all made out of one single unbroken chunk of metal.

It was the most industrial-looking object Quentin had ever seen in Fillory. It weighed half again what his sword weighed. It didn't even come with a scabbard, so he wouldn't get to show off his buff sheathing-unsheathing skills.

"Hold it straight out," Bingle said. "Like this."

He straightened Quentin's elbow and brought his arm up parallel to the deck. Quentin was holding the thing at full extension. He could already feel his muscles starting to cramp.

"Point it straight forward. Keep it out there. Long as you can."

Quentin was expecting further instructions, but Bingle calmly went back to his isometrics. Quentin's arm stiffened, then glowed with pain, then caught fire. He lasted about two minutes. Bingle had him switch arms.

"What do you call this style?" Quentin asked.

"The mistake people make," Bingle said, "is thinking that there are different styles."

"All right."

"Force, balance, leverage, momentum—these principles never change. They are your style."

Quentin was pretty sure his knowledge of physics exceeded Bingle's by a couple of orders of magnitude, but he'd never thought of applying it that way.

Bingle explained that rather than practice a single fighting technique, his technique was to master all techniques and to deploy them as the circumstances and terrain required. A single grand meta-technique, if you will. He'd wandered Fillory and the lands beyond for years, seeking out martial monks in mountain monasteries and street fighters in crowded medinas and extracting their secrets, until he became the man Quentin saw before him: a walking encyclopedia of swordsmanship. Of the oaths he had made and broken, the beautiful women he had seduced and betrayed to obtain these secrets, it was best not to speak.

Quentin switched arms again, and then again. It reminded him of his days as a semi-pro sleight-of-hand magician. The beginning, the laying down of the fundamentals, was always the worst part, which he supposed was why so few people did it. That was the thing about the world: it wasn't that things were harder than you thought they were going to be, it was that they were hard in ways that you didn't expect. To take his mind off it he watched Bingle, who was now stalking the deck, staring accusingly ahead of him, whipping his own blade in a complicated pattern, drawing ampersands and Kells knots in the air with it.

A frigid spitting mist was blowing in from the ocean. He could see After Island clearly now; they'd be landing soon. He decided he was done. He should at least change out of his pajamas before he set off in search of the golden key.

"I'm knocking off, Bingle," he said. He placed his practice blade on the deck next to Bingle's other two. His arms felt like they were floating.

Bingle nodded, not breaking his own rhythm.

"Come back to me when you can do half an hour," he said. "With each arm."

He performed a spectacular no-handed roundoff that looked like it was going to take him right off the forecastle deck, but somehow he swallowed his inertia just in time to stick the landing. He finished with his blade jammed between the ribs of some imaginary assailant. He withdrew it and cleaned the blade on his pants leg.

That was probably a few more lessons down the track.

"Be careful what you learn from me," he said. "What is written with a sword cannot be erased."

"That's why I have you," Quentin said. "So I won't have to write anything. With my sword."

"Sometimes I think I am fate's sword. She wields me cruelly."

Quentin wondered what it was like to be so unselfconsciously melodramatic. Nice, probably.

"Right. Well, there won't be much cruelty on this trip. We'll be back at Whitespire pretty soon. Then you can go check out your castle."

Bingle turned to face the wind. He seemed to be living out some story of his own in which Quentin was just a minor character, a chorus member, without even a name in the program.

"I shall never see Fillory again."

In spite of himself Quentin felt a chill. He didn't like the feeling. He was chilly enough as it was.

———

After Island was a low strip of gray rocks and thin grass flocked with sheep. If the Outer Island was a tropical paradise, After could have passed for a stray member of the Outer Hebrides.

They circled it, hugging the shore, until they found a harbor and dropped anchor. A couple of rain-ravaged fishing boats were moored there, and a handful of empty buoys suggested that more were out to sea. It was a hell of a dreary spot. A more enterprising king might have tried to claim it for Fillory, Quentin supposed, except that it didn't really seem worth it. Not exactly the jewel in the crown.

There was no wharf, and the bay was crowded with surly breakers. They barely managed to get the launch in past the surf without swamping. Quentin jumped out, wetting himself to the waist, and wallowed up onto the rocky beach. A couple of fishermen watched them, smoking and mending a vast tangled net that was stretched out around them on the shale. They had the brick-red complexions of lifelong outdoorsmen, and they shared the same thickheaded look. They didn't seem to have enough forehead—their hairlines were pulled down too low over their eyebrows. Quentin would have put their age at anything between thirty and sixty.

"Ahoy there," he said.

They nodded at him and grunted. One of them touched his cap. Over a few minutes' parley the friendly one was persuaded to divulge the general direction of the nearest and probably only town. Quentin, Bingle, and Benedict thanked the men and slogged their way up the beach through the cold white sand scalloped with black tide marks. Julia trailed silently behind them. Quentin had tried to persuade her to stay on board, but she insisted. Whatever else was going on with her, she was still up for a party.

"You know what I'm waiting for on this trip?" Quentin said. "I'm not waiting for somebody to be happy to see us. I just want someone to look surprised to see us."

The weather deepened to a light wuthering rain. Quentin's wet pants chafed. The sand gave way to dunes capped with saw grass and then to a path: grassy sand, then sandy grass, then just grass. They tramped through humpy, unfenced meadows and low hills, past a lost, orphaned well. He tried to summon a heroic feeling, but the setting wasn't especially conducive. It reminded him of nothing so much as walking along Fifth Avenue in Brooklyn in the freezing rain with James and Julia on the day he took his Brakebills exam. *In olden times there was a boy, young and strong and brave-o . . .*

The town, once they found it, was a thoroughly medieval affair of stone cottages, thatched roofs, and mud streets. Its most marked characteristic was the thorough lack of interest the locals showed in the oddly dressed strangers in their midst. A half dozen of them were sitting at an outdoor table in front of a pub. They were eating sandwiches and drinking beer out of metal tankards in the face of weather Quentin would have made it a major priority to get out of.

"Hi," he said.

Chorus of grunts.

"I'm Quentin. I'm from Fillory. We've come to your island in search of a key." He glanced at the others and coughed once. It was pretty much impossible to do this without sounding like he was reciting a Monty Python sketch. "Do you know anything about that? A magic key? Made of gold?"

They looked at each other and nodded: agreed, we all know what he's talking about. They shared a family resemblance. They could all have been brothers.

"Aye, we know the one you mean," one of them said—a large, brutal-looking man encased in a huge woolly coat. His hand on his knee was like a piece of pink granite. "It's down t'road."

"Down the road," Quentin repeated.

Right. Of course. The golden key is down the road. Where else would it be? He wondered where this feeling was coming from, that he was improvising his part in a play that everybody else had a script for.

"Aye, we know it." He jerked his head. "Down t'road."

"All right. Down the road it is. Well, thank you very much."

He wondered if it was ever warm and sunny here, or if they lived in the permanent equivalent of a New England November. Did they know they were three days' sail from a tropical zone?

The travelers set off down the road. They would have looked nobler if they'd been riding horses instead of wallowing through the mud like a bunch of peasants, but the *Muntjac* wasn't set up for horses. Maybe they could hire local horses. Shaggy, sturdy ponies resigned to always being cold and damp, and to never being sleek and beautiful. He missed Dauntless.

The street changed to cobbles, rounded cubes that turned slick and ankle-breaking in the drizzle. It wasn't much of a setting for a quest or an adventure or even an errand. Maybe Bingle was right, maybe they were just minor characters in his drama.

Benedict wasn't even taking notes the way he usually did.

"I'll just remember it," he said.

There you had it: an island not even Benedict would bother to map.

It wasn't a large town, and it wasn't a long road. The last building on it was a stone building like a church, though it wasn't a church, just a boxy structure two stories high, built up out of flat gray local stones, unmortared. It had a blank façade that looked unfinished, or maybe whatever ornamentation had once been there had been stripped away.

Quentin felt like the little boy at the beginning of *The Lorax,* at the mysterious tower of the dismal Once-ler. They should have been facing down bellowed challenges from black knights bearing the vergescu, or solving thorny theological dilemmas posed by holy hermits. Or at the very least resisting the diabolical temptations of ravishing succubi. Not fighting off seasonal affective disorder.

If he'd had to put his finger on it he would have said that more than anything else the rhythm of it was wrong. It was too soon. They shouldn't have found it this quick, nor should they obtain it without a fight.

But fuck it. Maybe he was just lucky. Maybe it was destiny. In spite of everything, he felt a rising excitement. This was it. The doors were enormous and made of oak, but there was a smaller, man-sized door set in one of them, presumably for days when you couldn't be bothered to fling open an entire grand double-height oaken portal. The doorway was flanked by empty niches for statuary, past or future but not present.

They straggled to a stop in front of it, a brave company of knights assembled before the Chapel Perilous. Which of them would brave what lay within? Quentin's nose was running. His hair was wet from the rain; he did have a hat, but he felt an obstinate urge to face whatever suffering was available for him to face, and that was a cold drizzle. He and Julia sniffled at the same time.

In the end they all braved the chapel, if only to get in out of the wet. It was no warmer inside than outside. The atmosphere was of an old country church from which the verger had stepped away for a few minutes. The air smelled like stone dust. Diffuse gray light misted in through a few narrow, high windows. A collection of rusty gardening implements resided in one corner: a hoe, a shovel, a rake.

In the center of the room stood a stone table, and on the stone table lay a worn red velvet pillow, and on the pillow lay a golden key, with three teeth.

Next to it was a yellowed slip of paper on which was neatly printed:

GOLDEN KEY

The key wasn't bright, and it wasn't tarnished. It had the deep matte patina of an authentically old thing. Its dignity was undisturbed by its humble surroundings—the stillness in the room seemed to come from it. Probably the rubes around here just didn't know enough to take it seriously. Like some European village with a cannon as a war monument, and no one realizes it still has a live round in the chamber, until one day . . .

Bingle picked up the key.

"Jesus!" Quentin said. "Careful."

The guy must have a death wish. Bingle turned it over in his hands, examining both sides. Nothing happened.

Quentin realized what was going on. He'd been given a do-over. He was back on the edge of that meadow in the forest, but this time he was going in. There was more to life than being fat and safe and warm in a clockwork luxury resort. Or maybe there wasn't more, but he was going to find out. And how did you find out? You had an adventure. That's how. You picked up a golden key.

"Let me see it," he said.

Satisfied that it wasn't lethal, or at least not instantly, Bingle passed it to Quentin. It didn't buzz, and it didn't glow. It didn't come alive in his hand. It felt cool and heavy, but not cooler and heavier than he imagined a golden key should feel.

"Quentin," Julia said. "There is old magic on that key. A lot of it. I can feel it."

"Good."

He grinned at her. He felt elated.

"You do not have to do this."

"I know. But I want to do this."

"Quentin."

"What?"

Julia offered him her hand. God bless Julia. Whatever else she had lost she still had a hell of a lot of human kindness inside her. He took her hand, and with the other he felt around in the air with the key. Maybe if he—? Yes. He felt it click against something hard, something that wasn't there.

He lost it for a second—he waved the key around but couldn't find it. And then he had it again, the clack of metal on metal. He stopped with the key resting on it, then pushed and it slipped in, ratcheting past an invisible tumbler and fitting firmly. Experimentally he let go of it. It stayed there: a golden key suspended in midair, parallel to the ground.

"Yes," he whispered. "This."

He took a breath, tremblier than he wanted it to be. Bingle did an odd thing, which was to place the point of his sword on the ground and drop to one knee. Quentin gripped the key again and turned it clock-wise. Running on instinct, he felt for a doorknob and found it—he could picture it in his mind's eye, cold white porcelain. He turned it and pulled and an immense cracking, tearing sound filled the room—not a terrible sound, a satisfying sound, the breaking of a seal that had been intact for centuries, waiting to be breached. Julia's soft hand tightened on his. Air rushed from the room behind him out through the crack he was opening, and hot light flooded over him.

He was opening a door in the air, tall enough for him to walk through without stooping. It was bright in there, and there was warmth, and sunlight, and green. This was it. Already the gray stone of the After Island looked insubstantial. This was what he'd been missing—call it adventure or whatever you wanted to. He wondered if he was going somewhere in Fillory or somewhere else entirely.

He stepped through onto grass, leading Julia through after him. There was light all around them. He blinked. His eyes began to adjust.

"Wait," he said. "This can't be it."

He lunged back for the doorway, but it was already gone. There was nothing to lunge through, no way back, just empty air. He lost his balance and caught himself with his hands, skinning both his palms on the warm concrete sidewalk in front of his parents' house in Chesterton, Massachusetts.

BOOK II

CHAPTER 9

"Okay," he said. "Okay. It's disappointing."

He sat on the curb, elbows on his knees, staring up at the power lines, and attempted to reason with himself. His scraped hands smarted and throbbed. It felt like late summer. For some reason it was the power lines more than anything else that looked weird, after two years in Fillory.

That and the cars. They looked wrong, like animals. Angry alien animals. Julia was sitting on the grass, hugging her knees and rocking slightly. She looked worse off than he did.

Quentin's heart was sinking out of his chest and out of his body and down into the dirt of this goddamned useless planet. I was a king. I had a ship. I had a beautiful ship, my own ship!

It was like somebody was trying to send him a message. If so he got it. Message received.

"I get it," he said out loud. "I hear you. I get it already."

I am a king, he thought. Even in the real world I'm still a king. Nothing can take that away.

"It's all right," he said. "We're going to make this all right."

It was an experiment in saying what he wanted to be true, to see if that would make it any truer.

Julia was on all fours now. She heaved up something thin and bitter onto the grass. He went over and knelt beside her.

"You're going to be all right," he said.

"I don't feel well."

"We're going to fix this. You'll be all right."

"Stop saying that." She coughed, then spat on the lawn. "You do not understand. I cannot be here." She paused to rummage for words. "I should not. I have to go."

"Tell me about it."

"I have to leave!"

Did the key think he wanted to go home? This wasn't his home. Quentin looked up at the house. There were no signs of life. He was relieved; he wasn't in the mood to talk to his parents right now. It was a fancy suburb, with big houses that could even afford to have some lawn around them.

A neighbor was peering out at them from her living room window.

"Hi!" He waved. "How's it going?"

The face disappeared. Its owner drew the curtain.

"Come on," he said to Julia. He breathed out decisively. Let's be brave. "Let's go inside, get a shower. Maybe change clothes."

They were in full Fillorian drag. Not inconspicuous. She didn't answer.

He was fighting off panic. Jesus, it had taken him twenty-two years to get to Fillory the first time. How was he going to do it again now? He turned back to Julia, but she wasn't there. She was up and walking unsteadily down the wide, empty suburban road away from him. She looked tiny in the middle of all that asphalt.

That was another weird thing. Asphalt really wasn't like anything in nature.

"Hey. Come on." He stood up and trotted after her. "There's probably mini-Dove bars in the freezer."

"I cannot stay here."

"I can't either. I just don't know what to do about it."

"I am going back."

"How?"

She didn't answer. He caught up, and they walked together in the fading light. It was quiet. Multicolored light from giant televisions flickered in the windows. When had TVs gotten that big?

"I only knew one way to get to Fillory, and that was the magic button. And Josh had that, last we saw. Maybe we can find him. Or maybe Ember could summon us back. Other than that I think we're kind of screwed."

Julia was sweating. Her walk had a slight stagger to it. Whatever was wrong with her, this wasn't making it any better. He made a decision.

"We'll go to Brakebills," he said. "Somebody there will help us."

She didn't react.

"I know it's a long shot—"

"I do not want to go to Brakebills."

"I know," Quentin said. "I don't especially want to go there either. But it's safe, they'll feed us, and somebody there will have a line on some way to get us back."

Privately he doubted any of the faculty had a clue about getting around the multiverse, but they might know how to find Josh. Or Lovelady, the junk dealer who'd found the button in the first place.

Julia stared fixedly ahead. For a minute Quentin didn't think she was going to answer.

"I do not want to go," she said.

But she stopped walking. A sparkly blue muscle car sat parked by itself at the curb, a snouty, low-slung vehicle with a turbo hood in front and a rear spoiler. Some rich douche bag's sixteenth birthday present. Julia looked around for a minute, then stepped onto the lawn, where a landscaper had laid down a row of head-sized boulders. She picked one up like a medicine ball, hefting it surprisingly easily in her stick-thin arms, and half threw, half dropped it through the muscle car's driver-side window.

Quentin didn't even have time to offer advice or an opinion—something along the lines of, don't throw the rock through the car window. It had already happened.

It took two tries to get it all the way through—the safety glass starred and stretched before it gave way. The alarm was deafening in the suburban stillness, but incredibly no lights came on in the house. Julia reached through the hole and deftly popped the door open, then heaved the rock back out onto the asphalt and slid herself into the black vinyl bucket seat.

"You've got to be kidding me," he said.

She picked up a shard of glass and nicked the pad of her thumb with it. Whispering something under her breath, she jammed her bloody thumb-tip up against the ignition.

The alarm stopped. The car rumbled into life, and the radio came on: Van Halen, "Poundcake." She lifted up her ass and brushed the rest of the glass off the seat underneath her.

"Get in," she said.

Sometimes you just have to do things. Quentin walked around to the other side—for form's sake he really should have slid across the hood—and she peeled out before he even had the door closed. They drove away from his parents' block at speed. He couldn't believe nobody had called the police, but he didn't hear any sirens; it was either really good magic or very dumb luck. She didn't turn the Van Halen off, or even down. The gray street poured along underneath them. It beat a carriage, anyway.

Julia rolled down what was left of the broken window so that it didn't look so broken.

"How the hell did you do that?" he said.

"You know about hot-wiring?" she said. "That is 'not-wiring.' That is what we used to call it, in the old days."

"In what old days did you go around stealing cars? And who is 'we'?"

She didn't answer, just took a corner too fast, so that the car heeled over on its ridiculously too-bouncy suspension.

"That was a stop sign," Quentin said. "I still think we should go to Brakebills."

"We are going to Brakebills."

"You changed your mind."

"It happens." Her thumb was still bleeding. She sucked it and wiped it on her pants. "Can you drive?"

"No. I never learned."

Julia swore. She turned up the radio.

It was four hours from Chesterton to Brakebills, or as close as you could get to Brakebills by car. Julia did it in three. They shot west across Massachusetts the long way, whipping along old New England interstates that had been cut through pine forests and blasted through low green hills, the sides of which showed bare red rock. The rock faces were slick with water from underground springs exposed by the blasting.

The sun set. The car smelled of its owner's cigarette smoke. Everything was toxic and chemical and unnatural: the plastic walnut trim, the electric lights, the burning gasoline that was shoving them forward. This whole world was a processed petroleum product. Julia kept the radio on classic rock the whole way. It would be an exaggeration to say that she knew every single lyric of every single song that came on, but not by much.

They crossed the Hudson River at Beacon, New York, and turned off the interstate onto a two-lane local highway, winding and humped up with old frost heaves. Apart from Julia's singing they didn't speak. Quentin was still trying to make sense of what had just happened to them. It was too dark to make the trek to Brakebills tonight, so Julia showed him how to extract cash without a card from an ATM at a bug-swarmed gas station. They bought sunglasses for her, to hide her weird eyes, and they spent the night—separate rooms—at a motel. Quentin mentally dared the clerk to say something about their clothes, but no dice.

In the morning Quentin took a genuine hot shower in an actual Western-style bathroom. Score one for reality. He stayed there till all the sea salt was finally out of his hair, even though the tub was made of plastic and there were spiders in the corners and it reeked of detergents and "fresheners." By the time he cleaned up, checked out, and harvested a bona fide actual sixteen-ounce bottle of Coca-Cola from the vending machine, Julia was waiting for him, sitting on the hood of their car.

She'd skipped the shower, but she'd doubled up on the Coke. The car spit gravel on its way out of the parking lot.

"I thought you did not know where it was," Julia said. "That was what you told me when I asked you."

"I told you that," Quentin said, "because it's true. I don't know where it is. But I think there's a way to find it. At least I know someone who did it once."

He meant Alice. She'd done it as a high school senior, so they ought to be able to manage it. Strange to think of it now. He was going to follow in her footsteps.

"We'll have to walk a couple of miles through the woods," he said.

"That does not bother me."

"A vision spell should reveal it. It's veiled, but just to keep civilians out. There's an Anasazi spell. Or Mann. Maybe just a Mann reveal."

"I know the Anasazi."

"Okay. Great. Then I'll let you know when."

Quentin kept his tone carefully neutral. Nothing made Julia angrier than the feeling that she was being condescended to by a Brakebills graduate. At least she wasn't blaming him for getting them shunted back to Earth. Or probably she was, but she wasn't doing it out loud.

It was a hot late August morning. The air was saturated with bronze sunlight. A mile off, at the bottom of the valley, they caught glimpses of the huge blue Hudson River. They parked at a bend in the road.

He got that it hurt her pride, and maybe something even more vital, to be dragged back to Brakebills begging for help. It didn't change the fact that it was their first and best and possibly only option. He was not fucking staying on Earth. He wanted a quest? Now he had one. The quest was to get back to where he was when he started his goddamned quest. That ought to learn him, but good.

Before they set off Julia spent fifteen minutes on a spell that she curtly informed him would cause the car to wait an hour and then drive itself back home to Chesterton. Quentin didn't see how that was even remotely possible, on any number of levels, but he kept his doubts to himself. If he'd thought to keep more of the glass he could have at least fixed the window, but he hadn't, so hard cheese on whoever's muscle car it was. He tucked two hundred dollars in twenties into the glove compartment, then they drank the rest of the Coke and climbed over the sheet-metal guardrail.

These weren't recreational woods, meant to be hiked through and picnicked in. They hadn't been curated and made user-friendly by helpful park rangers. They were dense, and the light was dim, and walking through them wasn't fun. Quentin was constantly ducking his head too late to avoid being slashed across the face by a branch. Every five minutes he was convinced that he'd walked through a spiderweb, but he could never find the spider.

And he wasn't sure what would happen if they walked into the Brakebills perimeter without knowing it. Nothing in theory, of course, but Quentin had watched Professor Sunderland lay down the barrier after the Beast attacked. He'd seen some of the things she'd ground into those powders. Any second they could be running smack into it. The idea made his face tingle. After half an hour he called a halt.

The woods were still. There was no sign of the school, but he felt it somewhere around here, as if it were hiding behind a tree waiting to jump out at him. And he imagined he could feel older tracks running through the woods too. Like Alice's—poor cursed teenage Alice, wandering all night looking for the way in. It would have been better for her if she'd never found it. Careful what you hunt, lest you catch it.

"Let's try it here," he said.

Julia launched into the Anasazi spell in her rough, fierce casting style, clearing invisible layers away from the air in a square in front of her, like wiping fog off a windshield. He winced, inwardly, to watch some of her upper hand positions, but it didn't make her castings any less forceful. Sometimes it seemed to make them more so.

He began work on the Mann instead. It was a lot easier, but it wasn't a contest. Best to diversify.

He never finished. He heard the usually imperturbable Julia squeak and skip a step backward. Suspended in the air in front of her, in the square she'd cleared, was a face. It belonged to an older man with a goatee wearing a royal-blue tie and an appalling yellow blazer.

It was Dean Fogg, the head of Brakebills. His face was in the square because he was standing right in front of Julia.

"Soooooo," the dean said, drawing out the vowel until he practically burst into song. "The prodigal has returned."

Not five minutes later they were walking across the Sea, which was as lush and green and immense as ever. It rolled out around them, the size of half a dozen football fields. The summer sun beat down on them from directly overhead. It was June here, inside the magic walls.

It was incredible. Quentin hadn't been back here for three years, not since he'd gone to Fogg and asked to be stricken from the rolls of the magical world, but nothing had changed at all. The smells, the lawns, the trees, the kids—this place was like Shangri-la, forgotten by time, abiding in an eternal present.

"We were watching you from when you left the road. The defenses go far beyond what we had in your day. Far beyond. Double-braided lines of force—we have a remarkable young man in our theoretical department, even I don't understand half of what he does. You can see a map of the entire forest now, in real time, showing anybody in it. It's even color-coded by their intentions and state of mind. Remarkable."

"Remarkable." Quentin felt shell-shocked. On his other side Julia said nothing. God knew what she was feeling, he couldn't have guessed within a thousand miles. She hadn't been here since her failed exam in high school. She hadn't spoken since Fogg had appeared, though she had managed to shake his hand when being introduced.

Fogg rattled on about the school and the grounds and Quentin's classmates and all the impressive and respectable things they were up to. None of them seemed to have gotten themselves accidentally exiled to the wrong dimension. There was plenty of hot local news too. Brakebills had become a force to be reckoned with on the international welters circuit, thanks to the efforts of one especially sporty young professor. One of the topiary animals, an elephant calf, had broken free of its hedge and was running amok around the grounds, albeit very slowly, at the rate of about a yard a day. The Natural group was laboring mightily to corral it and bring it to justice, but no luck so far.

The library was still plagued by outbreaks of flying books—three weeks ago a whole flock of Far Eastern atlases had taken wing, terrifyingly broad, muscular volumes like albatrosses, and wrecked the circulation area, sending students crawling under tables. The books actually found their way out through the front door and roosted in a tree by the welters board, from which they raucously heckled passersby in a babel of languages until they got rained on and dragged themselves sulkily back to the stacks, where they were being aggressively rebound.

All Quentin could think was how weird it was that all this was still going on. It shouldn't be possible, it must violate a law of physics. A few students dotted the grass, girls mostly, sunning their light-starved bodies to the extent that the school uniform would permit. Classes were out for the semester, but the seniors hadn't graduated yet. If Quentin were to turn left here and walk five minutes, past that stand of live oaks, he'd get to the Cottage. And it would be full of strangers, lolling in the window seats, drinking the wine, reading the books, screwing each other in the beds. He'd wondered if he would want to see it, but now that he was here he really didn't.

The students watched the three of them pass, propped up on their elbows, full of lofty pity for those who had been stupid enough to graduate and get older. He knew how they felt. They felt like kings and queens. Enjoy it while it lasts.

"I wasn't sure we would ever see you again." Fogg was still talking. "After your—what shall we call it—your retirement? Not many people who make that choice ever come back, you know. When we lose them we lose them forever. But you, I take it you saw the—how shall I put it—the error of your ways?"

Fogg had evidently decided to take the high road, and it certainly sounded like he was enjoying the view from up there. They left the burning expanse of the Sea for the cool paths of the Maze, which opened up at unexpected intervals into little squares and circles inside of which were nestled pale stone fountains. The same fountains he'd lounged around with Alice, though the paths were different. The Maze would have been redrawn since his day—once a year every year. He followed Fogg's lead.

"I had a change of heart." The high road was wide enough for two. "But it was very generous of you to accommodate me, in my—what shall I call it—my hour of need?"

"Just as you say."

Fogg removed a handkerchief from inside his lapel and patted his forehead with it. He did look older. The goatee was new, and it was mostly white. He's been here all this time, every day, doing what he'd always done, to other kids who then moved on and left. Quentin felt claustrophobic after only five minutes. Fogg still saw him as the boy he used to be, but that boy was gone.

They walked into the House and up to Fogg's office. Before Quentin followed him inside he turned to Julia.

"Do you want to just wait out here?"

"Fine."

"Might be better tactically for me to do this man-to-man."

Julia formed a mirthless "OK" sign with her thumb and forefinger. Great. She seated herself on the bench beside Fogg's door, the one usually reserved for naughty and/or failing undergraduates. She'd be fine. He hoped.

The dean sat down and clasped his hands in front of him on the desktop. The rich, leathery, familiar smells clawed at Quentin, trying to drag him back into the past. He wondered what he would say if he could talk to the boy he had been, sitting in what looked like this exact same chair, all those years ago, wearing the rumpled clothes that he'd slept in, joggling his knee with nerves, and trying to figure out if this was all a joke. Proceed with caution? Take the blue pill? Maybe something more practical. Don't sleep with Janet. Don't go touching strange keys.

And what would his younger self say? He would look back at him the way Benedict looked at Quentin and say: like I would do that.

"So," Fogg said. "What can I do for you? What brings you back to your humble alma mater?"

The problem was how to ask for help without giving away more than he should about Fillory. Its existence—its reality—was still a secret, and Fogg was the last person he wanted to know about it. If he found out, then everybody would hear about it, and next thing you know it's the hot spot for Brakebills kiddies on spring break, the Fort Lauderdale of the magical multiverse.

But he had to start somewhere. Just pretend to be as ignorant as he is.

"Dean Fogg, how much do you know about travel between worlds?"

"A little. More theory than practice, of course." Fogg chuckled. "Some years back we had a student with an interest along those lines. Penny, I think his name was. Can't have been his real name."

"He was in my year. William was his real name."

"Yes, he and Melanie—Professor Van der Weghe—spent quite a bit of time working on that very subject. She's retired now, of course. What would be the nature of your interest, exactly—?"

"Well, I always liked him," Quentin said, improvising haplessly. "Penny. William. And I've been asking around, but nobody's seen him in a while." Since he got his hands bitten off by an insane godling. "And I thought you might have some idea about where he is."

"You thought he might have—crossed over?"

"Sure." Why not. "Yeah."

"Well," Fogg said. He stroked his goatee, mulling, or appearing to mull. "No, no, I can't go around handing out information about students left and right without their consent. It wouldn't be proper."

"I'm not asking for his cell number. I just thought you might have heard something."

The springs of Fogg's chair squawked as he leaned forward.

"My dear boy," he said, "I hear all sorts of things, but I can't repeat them. When I arranged for you to recuse yourself with that firm in Manhattan, you don't suppose I went around telling people where you'd ended up?"

"I suppose not."

"But if you're really interested in Penny's whereabouts, I'd advise you to start your search in this reality"—dry chuckle!—"rather than some other. Will you be staying for lunch?"

Julia was right. They shouldn't have come. Obviously Fogg didn't know anything, and being around him wasn't good for Quentin. He could feel himself regressing in the direction of an adolescent tantrum— it was like trying to talk to his parents. He lost all perspective on who he was and how far he'd come. He really couldn't believe the awe in which he used to hold this man. The towering, Gandalfian wizard he once cowered before had been swapped out and replaced with a smug hidebound bureaucrat.

"I can't. But thanks, Dean Fogg." Quentin clapped his hands on his knees. "Actually I think we'd better be moving on."

"Before you do, Quentin." Fogg hadn't moved. "I'd like to prolong this conversation a little further. I've heard some pretty exotic rumors about what you and your friends have been up to these past few years. The undergraduates talk about it. You're quite the campus legend, you know."

Now Quentin did stand up.

"Well," he said. "Kids. Don't believe everything you hear."

"I assure you I don't." Fogg's eyes had regained their old flinty spark from somewhere. "But a word of advice from your old dean, if I may. Notwithstanding my regrettable ignorance of interdimensional travel, I don't know what your interest in Penny might be, but I do know perfectly well that you never liked him. And no one's heard from him in years. No one's heard from Eliot Waugh or Alice Quinn in years, either. Or Janet Pluchinsky."

Quentin noticed that Josh didn't figure in Fogg's memory. He should have asked about Josh first. Though he probably would have gotten the same answer.

"And now you've turned up dressed *very* oddly, and you've brought a civilian onto the grounds, one of our rejections if I'm not mistaken, which is—well, it's just not something we ordinarily tolerate. I don't know what you're mixed up in, but I've put myself out for you over the years, quite a bit, and I have the reputation and the security of the school to think of."

Aha. There's the Fogg he used to know and fear. Not gone, he'd just been playing possum. But Quentin wasn't the naughty schoolboy he used to be.

"Oh, I do know that, Dean Fogg. Believe me."

"Well, good. Don't go digging too deep, Quentin. Don't stir. Shit. Up." Fogg enunciated the obscenity crisply. "Right now you have the air of somebody who thinks he knows better. Humility is a useful quality in a magician, Quentin. Magic knows better, not you. Do you remember what I told you the night before you graduated? Magic isn't ours. I don't know whose it is, but we've got it on loan, on loan at best. It's like what poor Professor March used to say about the turtles. Don't bait them, Quentin. One world ought to be enough for anyone."

Easy for you to say. You've only ever seen one.

"Thank you. I'll try to remember that."

Fogg sighed tragically, like Cassandra warning the Trojans, destined never to be heeded.

"Well, all right. Professor Geiger should be in the junior common room, if you need a portal. Unless you'd rather walk out the way you came."

"A portal would be great. Thank you." Quentin stood up. "By the way, that 'rejection' sitting in the hall? She's a better magician than most of your students. Most of your faculty too."

Quentin walked with Julia down to the junior common room. He had to get out of here. Everything was smaller than he remembered it—it was like *Alice's Adventures in Wonderland,* and he'd drunk the magic tonic. He felt like his head was sticking out the chimney, and his arm was out the window.

"Not going here?" he said. "You didn't miss much."

"Really?" Julia said. "You did."

CHAPTER 10

Julia was playing the long game. But the problem with the long game, it turned out, was that it was long. They knew she was out here, and sooner or later they would have to deal with her. All she had to do was wait them out. But meanwhile weeks passed. People graduated. Julia included, probably, although she didn't go to the ceremony.

The summer turned her darkened room into a convection oven, baking its contents to a hard hydroptic crisp, and then fall came and the weather relented. The ivy that ran up the house in back of them changed color and ruffled in the wind, and rain spattered the window. She could feel the neighborhood empty out as her classmates all went off to college. She didn't. She was eighteen now, a responsible adult. Her coming-of-age story was over. Nobody could make her do anything anymore.

She could breathe easier with all her old friends, First Julia's friends, out of town, but at the same time it made her nervous. She was all alone on this one. Very alone. She had made her way out to the edge of the world, hung by her fingers from the lip, and let go into free fall. Would she fall forever?

Julia would do anything to make the time pass. She killed time, murdered it, massacred it and hid the bodies. She threw her days in bunches onto the bonfire with both hands and watched them go up in fragrant smoke. It wasn't easy. Sometimes it felt like the hours had ground to a halt. They fought her as they passed, one after the other, like stubborn stools. Online Scrabble helped ease them on their way, and movies. But you could only watch *The Craft* a finite number of times, and that number turned out to be about three.

And yes, all right, she did spend six weeks in an insane asylum. There, she said it. It was awful, but she knew it was probably coming, and you couldn't blame her parents, not really. They gave her a choice, junior college or the laughing academy, and she picked door number two. What could she say, she thought they were bluffing, and she called them on it. Read 'em and weep.

So that happened. Bad as she thought it was going to be, it was worse. Six weeks of bad smells, bad food, and listening to her roommate, whose arms were crocheted with razor scars from cuff line to armpit, toss and turn and talk in her sleep about transformers, transformers, everything is a transformer, why won't they just transform?

Who's crazy now? Those movies were even worse than *The Craft*.

So she talked her shrinks in circles and took her meds, which helped to nudge the calendar along. Time sure flies when you're having fun, and by fun she meant Nardil. Sometimes she really did think death would be preferable, except she wasn't going to give those bastards the satisfaction. They couldn't wear her down. No they couldn't. No they couldn't.

Eventually she was simply returned to sender. The doctors couldn't keep her. She was no danger to herself or to others. She just wasn't that crazy.

So that was another exclusive institution she'd been kicked out of. *Badum*-ching. Thanks very much, you've been a great audience. I'll be here all week, all month, all year, indefinitely, until further notice.

Eventually, given that she had a little spare time on her hands, she opened up another front in the war. If magic was real, it stood to reason that some genuine information about how to work it must be in circulation. The Brakebills couldn't have it all to themselves. It was inevitable; anybody who knew anything about information theory would know that. You just couldn't contain a body of data that large completely hermetically. There would be too much of it, and too many pores it could leak out through. She would start tunneling from her side of the wall.

She began a systematic survey. It was good to give her always-hungry brain something to chew on—it kept it, if not happy, then at least busy. She drew up a list of the major magical traditions, and the minor ones. She compiled bibliographies of the major texts for same. She then read every one in turn, centrifuging out the practical information and ditching all the rest—the matrix of useless mystical crap in which it was suspended. This required some leaving of the house, some furtive forays into the Big Blue Room. But that had the extra effect of placating her parents a bit, so whatever, it's all good.

She ground and boiled. She sniffed and daubed. It was fun, like a scavenger hunt. She haunted head shops and organic herb sections and familiarized herself with the restaurant supply stores on Bowery—a great source for cheap hardware—and online mail-order laboratory supply houses. It was amazing what they would send you through the mail if you had a fake ID, a PayPal account, and a P.O. box. If this magic thing didn't pan out she could definitely go into domestic terrorism.

Once she spent a solid week tying like a thousand knots in a piece of string before she read ahead and realized that the string was supposed to have a strand of her hair woven into it, and she had to do it all over. She had always been a workaholic—she just couldn't get enough of that workahol, was James's joke—but even she had her limits. Twice she even killed something small, a mouse and a frog, quietly, in the backyard, under the cover of darkness. Hey, it was the circle of life. *Hakuna matata.* Which by the way is a Swahili phrase of modern origin and does absolutely fuck-all no matter how many times you chant it.

In fact, everything did fuck-all. It continued to do fuck-all as she moved out of her parents' house to a studio apartment above a bagel store, which she had to temp to pay for, but it meant she had more space to lay out pentagrams, and her sister wouldn't steal her charms and bang on her door and run away while she was chanting. (The fear effect having somewhat abated, unfortunately.) It did fuck-all even after she jacked off a simian twentysomething who couldn't believe his luck in the bathroom at a party just because he said he could get her into the Prospect Park Zoo after hours, the zoo being like one-stop shopping for some of those African preparations, let me tell you. And besides she needed some semen for a couple of things, though fortunately for the zookeeper neither of them worked.

One time, only once, did she ever get a whiff of something real. It didn't come out of a musty old codex, it came off the Internet, though it was ancient by online standards—the Internet equivalent of a musty old codex bound in finest fetal calfskin.

She'd been trolling through the archives of an old BBS run out of Kansas City in the mid-1980s. She was trying the usual search keywords, as one does, and getting the usual mountain of junk, as one does. It was like combing through stellar radiation for signs of extraterrestrial life. But one hit looked suspiciously like signal and not noise.

It was an image file. In the bad old days of 2400 baud modems, image files had to be posted in hexadecimal code in tranches of ten or twenty parts, since the amount of data in an image was many times the allowable length for a single post. You saved all the files together in a folder and then used a little utility to zip them together into a single document and decode them. Half the time a character or two got cut off along the way, and the entire frame got thrown off, and you ended up with nothing. Noise, static, snow crash. The other half of the time you wound up with a photograph of a thirtysomething stripper with baby fat and a cesarean scar, wearing only the bottom part of a high school cheerleader's uniform.

But if she was going to crack the magic racket, it wasn't going to be by half measures.

What this image was, once she had zipped and decoded it, was a scan of a handwritten document. A couplet—two lines of words in a language she didn't recognize, transcribed phonetically. Above each syllable was a musical staff indicating rhythm and (in a couple of cases) intonation. Below it was a drawing of a human hand performing a gesture. There was no indication of what the document was, no title or explanation. But it was interesting. It had a purposeful quality, draftsmanlike and precise. It didn't look like an art project, or a joke. Too much work, and not enough funny.

She practiced them separately first. Thank God for ten years of oboe lessons, on the strength of which she could sight-sing. The words were simple, but the hand positions were murder. Halfway through she went back to thinking it was a joke, but she was too stubborn to quit. She would have even then, but as an experiment she tried the first few syllables, and she discovered that something was different about this one. It made her fingertips feel hot. They buzzed like she'd touched a battery. The air resisted her, as if it had become slightly viscous. Something stirred in her chest that had never stirred there before. It had been sleeping her whole life, and now somehow, by doing this, she had poked it, and it stirred.

The effect went away as soon as she stopped. It was two in the morning, and she had a word processing shift at a law firm in Manhattan at eight. (Word processing was all she got anymore. She could type like a demon, but her appearance and phone manner had degenerated to the point where at her last receptionist assignment they'd shitcanned her on sight.) She hadn't showered or slept in two days or washed her sheets in two months. Her eyes were full of sand. She stood at her desk and tried it again.

It was two more hours before she got all the way through it for the first time. The words were right, and the pitch, and the rhythm. The hand positions were still a joke, but she was onto something. This was not fuck-all. When she stopped, her fingers left trails in the air. It was like a hallucination, the kind of optical effect you'd get from botched laser surgery, or maybe from staying up all night two nights in a row. She waved her hand and it left streaks of color across her vision: red from her thumb, yellow, green, blue, and then purple from her pinky.

She smelled that electric smell. It was Quentin's smell.

Julia went up to the roof. She didn't want to touch anything with the spell going—it was like having fresh fingernail polish on—but she had to go somewhere, so she climbed the steel ladder and cracked the trap door and emerged out into the jungle of tar paper and air conditioners. She stood on the roof and made rainbow patterns with her hands against the rapidly bluing predawn sky until it stopped working.

It was magic. Real magic! And she was doing it! *Hakuna* fucking *matata*. Either she wasn't crazy, or she'd finally gone well and truly around the bend, and she wasn't coming back. Either way she could have died for joy.

Then she went downstairs and slept for an hour. When she woke up she saw that her fingers had left multicolored stains on the sheets. Her chest felt painfully hollowed out, as if somebody had gone in and scraped out all the organs with a table knife, like scraping the pith out of a jack-o'-lantern. It wasn't until then that she thought to try to trace the poster from the BBS, but when she checked the archive the post was already gone.

But the spell still worked. She set it going again, and it worked again. Then, careful not to touch her face with her candy-colored fingers, she put her head down on her desk and sobbed like a child who'd been beaten.

CHAPTER 11

Quentin had Professor Geiger send them back to Chesterton. They materialized smoothly in the center of town. Geiger—a middle-aged woman, cheerfully overstuffed—had offered to send them directly to Quentin's house, but he'd forgotten his parents' address.

It was the middle of the afternoon. Quentin didn't even know what day it was. They sat on a bench on a historic green where a minor battle had been fought in the Revolutionary War. Sun-dazed tourists drifted past them. It was not a time for able-bodied twentysomethings like him to be out and about with nothing to do. He should have been at the office, or acquiring a graduate degree, or at the very least playing touch football stoned. Quentin felt the daylight bleaching the energy out of him. God, he thought, looking down at his leggings. I really have to get out of these clothes.

Though Chesterton was one of the East Coast's premier venues for colonial reenactments. That ought to make them a little less conspicuous.

"So that went well," he said. "Starbucks?"

Julia didn't laugh.

They were becalmed. They sat in silence under the old oaks: the king and queen of Fillory, with nothing to do. The air was full of weird modern hums and drones he never used to notice before he lived in Fillory: cars, power lines, sirens, distant construction, planes in the jet stream laying double-ruled lines across the clear blue sky. It never stopped.

He'd met Julia here once, he reminded himself, or not that far from here, in the graveyard behind the church. That was when she told him that she still remembered Brakebills.

"You do not have a plan, do you?" Julia stared straight ahead.

"No."

"I do not know why I thought you would." That haughty anger was back. She was waking up again. "You have never really been here. Out here in the real world."

"Well, I've visited."

"You think magic is what you learned at Brakebills. You have no idea what magic is."

"Okay," he said. "Let's say I don't. What is it?"

"I am going to show you."

Julia stood up. She looked around, as if she were sniffing the wind, then set off abruptly across the street at a scary angle. A silver Passat honked and scritched to a stop to avoid hitting her. She kept walking. Quentin followed more cautiously.

She led them away from Chesterton's main drag, such as it was. The neighborhood turned residential fast. The din of traffic and commerce died away, and big trees and houses bloomed on either side of the street. The sidewalk became bumpy and irregular. Julia was paying a lot of attention to the telephone poles for some reason. Every time they passed one she stopped and studied it.

"Been a while since I did this," she said, mostly to herself. "Has to be one around here somewhere."

"One what? What are we looking for?"

"I could tell you. But you would not believe me."

She was full of surprises, was Julia. Well, he happened to have some free time just now. Five more minutes went by before she stopped at one particular telephone pole. It had a couple of blobs of fluorescent pink spray paint on it, which might have been left there by a sloppy lineman.

She stared at it, her lips moving silently. She was reading the world in a way that he, Quentin, could not.

"Not ideal," she said finally. "But it will do. Come on."

They kept walking.

"We are going to a safe house," she added.

They walked for literally two miles through the suburban afternoon light, in the process crossing the town line from Chesterton into the less posh but still desirable town of Winston. Children trailing home from school eyed them curiously. Sometimes Julia would stop and study a chalk mark on a curb, or a stray spray of roadside wildflowers, then she would press on. Quentin didn't know whether to feel hopeful or not, but he would wait for Julia's plan to unfurl itself, especially since he didn't have any suggestions of his own. Though his feet hurt, and he was on the point of suggesting they steal another car. Except that that would have been wrong.

Like Chesterton, Winston was an old Massachusetts suburb, and some of the houses they passed were not just colonial-style but genuinely colonial. You could recognize them because they were more compact than the other kind, denser and set back from the road in damp, rotting pine hollows, where raggedy grass lawnlets were locked in an endless running battle with encroaching rings of pines armed with their acid needles. The newer houses, by contrast, the colonial-inspired McMansions, were bright and enormous, and their lawns had gone completely shock-and-awe on the pine trees, of which one or at most two examples still stood, shivering and traumatized, to provide compositional balance.

The house they stopped at was the first kind, authentically colonial. It was starting to get dark out. Julia had logged another couple of telephone-pole paint blobs, one of which she'd stopped and studied quite closely using some kind of visual cantrip that he hadn't caught because she hadn't wanted him to catch it—she actually hid it with one hand as she cast it with the other.

The driveway dived down sharply into the hollow. Generations of kids must have murdered themselves on skateboards and scooters trying to go down it and stop before they slammed into the garage. Student drivers must have martyred themselves on it practicing hill starts in standard-transmission cars.

They clomped down it on foot. Quentin felt like a Seventh-Day Adventist, or an overaged trick-or-treater. At first he thought the lights were off, but when he got close enough he saw that they were in fact all on. The windows were papered over with butcher paper to keep them dark.

"I give up," Quentin said. "Who lives here?"

"I don't know," Julia said brightly. "Let's find out!"

She rang the doorbell. The man who opened the door was in his mid-twenties, tall and fat, with a hair helmet and a red caveman face. He wore a T-shirt tucked into sweatpants.

He played it cool.

"What up?" he said.

By way of answering Julia did an odd thing: she turned around and pushed up her long, wavy black hair with one hand, giving the man a quick look at something on the nape of her neck. A tattoo? Quentin didn't catch it.

"All right?" she said.

It must have been because the bouncer grunted and stepped aside. When Quentin followed the man narrowed his already piggy eyes further and put a hand on Quentin's chest.

"Hang on."

He took up a pair of ridiculously tiny opera glasses, toylike, that hung on a thong around his neck, and studied Quentin through them.

"Jesus." He turned to Julia, genuinely aggrieved. "Who the hell is this?"

"Quentin," Quentin said. "Coldwater."

Quentin stuck out his hand. The man—whose T-shirt said POTIONS MASTER on it—left him hanging.

"He is your brand-new boyfriend," Julia said. She took Quentin's hand and dragged him inside.

Bass was bumping somewhere in the house, which had been a nice house before somebody did a profoundly shitty renovation job on its interior and then somebody else beat the crap out of the shitty renovation. Said renovation must have happened in the 1980s, as that was the era of chic on offer: white walls, black-and-chrome furniture, track lighting. The air was heavy with stale cigarette smoke. There were chips and divots in the plaster everywhere. This didn't look like a place where he wanted to spend a lot of time. He was doing his best to remain hopeful, but it was hard to see how this was getting them any closer to Fillory.

Warily, Quentin followed Julia up a half flight of stairs and into the living room, which contained a weird assortment of people. The place could have passed for a halfway house for teenage runaways if it weren't also a halfway house for twentysomething, middle-aged, and elderly runaways. There were your standard goth casualties, pale and skinny and worryingly scabby, but there was also a guy with five-o'clock shadow in a wrecked business suit of not negligible quality talking on a cell phone, saying "yah, yah, uh-huh" in a tone of voice that suggested that there was actually somebody on the other end who cared whether he said uh-huh or nuh-uh. There was a sixtysomething woman with an arctic-white Gertrude Stein haircut. An old Asian guy was sitting on the floor with no shirt on, all by himself. In front of him on the white pile carpet stood a burned-out brazier surrounded by a ring of ashes. Guess the cleaning lady hadn't come today.

Quentin stopped on the threshold.

"Julia," Quentin said. "Tell me where we are."

"Have you not guessed yet?" She practically glittered with pleasure. She was relishing his discomfort. "This is where I got my education. This is my Brakebills. It is the anti-Brakebills."

"These people do magic?"

"They try."

"Please tell me you're joking, Julia." He took her arm, but she shook it off. He took it again and pulled her back down the stairs. "I'm begging you."

"But I am not joking."

Julia's smile was wide and predatory. The trap had sprung and the prey was writhing in it.

"These people can't do magic," he said. "They're not—there's no safeguards. They aren't qualified. Who's even supervising them?"

"No one. They supervise each other."

He had to take a deep breath. This was wrong—not morally wrong, just out of order. The idea that just anybody could mess around with magic—well, for one thing it was dangerous. That's not how it worked. And who were these people? Magic was his, he and his friends were the magicians. These people were strangers, they were nobody. Who told them they could do magic? As soon as Brakebills found out about this place they'd shut it down with a goddamned vengeance. They'd send a SWAT team, a flying wedge with Fogg at the head of it.

"Do you actually know these people?" he said.

She rolled her eyes.

"These guys?" She snorted. "These guys are just losers."

Julia led the way back into the living room.

The only thing the denizens of the safe house had in common, besides their general seediness, was that a lot of them had the same tattoo: a little blue star, seven-pointed, the size of a dime. A heptagram, but solid, colored in. It winked at Quentin from the backs of their hands, or their forearms, or the meaty part between their thumb and forefinger. One of them had two, one on each side of his neck, like Frankenstein's neck bolts. The shirtless Asian guy had four. As Quentin watched he started in on some involved casting Quentin didn't recognize, staring glazedly through the web of his working hands. Quentin couldn't even look.

A redheaded man with freckles, a pint-sized Dennis the Menace type, was sitting up on the gray slate mantelpiece by himself, monitoring the scene, but when he saw them he boosted himself down and strutted over. He wore an oversized army jacket and carried a beat-up clipboard.

"Hi folks!" he said. "I'm Alex, welcome to my dojo. You are—?"

"I am Julia. This is Quentin."

"Okay. Sorry about the housekeeping. Tragedy of the commons." In contrast to everybody else in the room, Alex was chipper and business-like. "Check your stars, please?"

Julia did the thing again where she showed him the nape of her neck.

"Right." Alex's ginger eyebrows went up. Whatever he saw impressed him. He turned to Quentin. "And you—?"

"He does not have any," Julia said.

"I don't have any." He could speak for himself.

"So did he want to take the test? Because otherwise he can't stay here."

"I understand," Julia said.

The really incredible thing was that she wasn't even mouthing off to this guy. She was being civil! She, a queen of Fillory, respected the fucked-up protocol of this place.

"Quentin, he wants you to take a test," she said. "To show you do magic."

"I want lots of things too. Do I have to do it?"

"Yes, you have to fucking do it," she said evenly. "So do it. It is just the first level, everybody who comes here does it their first time. You just make a flash. You probably have a fancy name for it."

"Show me."

Julia ran through three well-rehearsed hand positions, lickety-split, snapped her fingers, and said:

"*ışık!*"

The snap produced a little pop of light, like a flashbulb.

"Okay?"

"Hang on," Quentin said. "Those hand positions weren't quite generic. Can you—?"

"Come on, people," Alex said, not so chipper now. "Are we doing this?"

Quentin saw now that Alex had eight stars, four on the back of each hand. That must make him king of the flophouse.

"Come on, Quentin."

"Okay, okay. Show me again."

She did the spell again. Quentin came at it, trying to crook his fingers the way she did. Brakebills taught you all straight lines, your hands approximating platonic geometry, but these positions were loose and organic. Nothing lined up. And it had been two years since he'd worked with real-world Circumstances. He tried it once, snap, and got nothing. Then nothing again.

This earned him a round of ironic applause. The locals were taking an interest in this transaction.

"I'm sorry, one more try and then you're out," Alex said. "You can come back in a month." Julia began to show him again, but Alex put a hand over hers. "Just let him try."

The bouncer, Potions Master, had come in from the front door and was watching with his arms folded. Quentin could hear other people saying "*ışık!*" Every time they did, a flashbulb would go off.

Screw this. He wasn't going to pick up some corrupt hedge-witch spell in thirty seconds that would probably screw up his technique. He was classically trained, and a master sorcerer, and a king to boot. Let there be light.

"יְהִי אוֹר וַיְהִי־אוֹר," he said. "וַיֹּאמֶר אֱלֹהִים"

Let's see who here's got good Aramaic. He closed his eyes and clapped his hands loudly.

The light was white and blinding—a flashbulb at close range, right up in your face. For a second the whole room—shitty carpet, listing torchiere lamps, staring faces—was frozen, all the color driven out of it. Quentin had to blink his vision back to normal, and he'd had his eyes closed.

There was a beat of silence.

"Holeeee . . ." someone said. Then everybody started talking at once. Alex didn't look happy, but he didn't throw them out either.

"Sign in," he said. He blinked and blotted his eyes on his sleeve. "I don't know where you learned that, but just get your flash working next time."

"Cheers," Quentin said.

Alex peeled a blue star sticker off a sheet and stuck it on the back of Quentin's hand. Then he handed Quentin the clipboard. Where it said "Name" he wrote *King Quentin* and handed it to Julia.

When she was done Quentin dragged her out through the kitchen, with its bumpy linoleum floor and its fifteen-year-old Easy-Bake-looking range and its countertops crowded with a multicolored metropolis of unwashed glassware. Enough was enough.

"What the hell are we doing here?" he hissed.

"Come on."

She led him deeper into the house, down a hall that in another, saner universe would have accessed Daddy's study and a TV room and a laundry room, until she found the cheap hollow-core door that opened on the basement staircase.

He closed it behind them. The chilly mildewed silence of suburban basements everywhere embraced them. The stairs were unfinished pine planks, shaggy with cobwebs.

"I don't understand this, Julia," he said. "You don't belong here any more than I do. You're not like these people. You didn't learn what you know from a bunch of unlicensed losers in a frat house. You can't have."

They were alone except for a roomful of taped-up cardboard boxes, a dead TV the size of a washing machine and half a Ping-Pong table.

"Maybe I am not who you think I am. Maybe I am an unlicensed loser too."

"That's not what I'm saying." Was it? He was still trying to get his head around this place. "I can't believe they haven't burned this whole house down by now."

"I think what you are trying to say is that you do not think they are good enough. They do not meet your standards."

"This isn't about standards!" Quentin said, though he felt the ground getting marshy under him. "This is about—look, I paid my dues, that's all I'm saying. You have to earn this kind of power. You don't just pick it up at the 7-Eleven with your Big Gulp and your Pokémon trading cards."

"And what did I do? You think I did not pay dues?"

"I know you paid your dues." He took a deep breath. Slow down. This place wasn't the problem. The problem was getting back to Fillory.

"What did he call this house? A 'dojo'?"

"Dojo, safe house, same thing. They are safe houses. He is just a dork."

"Are there a lot of them?"

"A hundred maybe, in this country. There are more on the coasts."

Jesus Christ. It was an epidemic.

"What was that test back there?"

"You mean the one you flunked? That is the test to be a first-level magician. You have to be one to come in here. You pass the test, you get a star tattooed on you, you can stay. Most people get them on their hands, somewhere obvious. The more tests you pass, the more levels you go up, the more stars you get."

"But who runs all this? That Alex guy?"

"He is just a den mother. Takes care of the house. The ranking system is self-policed. Any magician can ask another magician of equal or lower level to demonstrate the test corresponding to their level or any of the levels below that," she recited. "To prove they know their shit. If you do not know your shit, you get busted down pretty fast."

"Huh." He wanted to find fault with the idea but couldn't quite do it on the spur of the moment. He filed it away for later discrediting. "So what level are you?"

By way of an answer she turned around and showed him what she'd shown the doorman, and Alex: there was a blue seven-pointed star tattooed on the nape of her neck. Its upper points disappeared into the roots of her hair; she must have had to shave to get it done. It was like the ones he'd seen upstairs except bigger, a silver dollar, and it had a circle in the middle. Inside the circle was a number 50.

"Wow." He couldn't help but be impressed. "Ginger Balls back there only had eight. So you're a fiftieth-level magician?"

"No."

She took hold of the hem of her blouse, crossing her arms in front of her.

"Wait a minute—"

"Relax, playa." She yanked the back of her shirt up, but only halfway. It was covered in blue stars, dozens of them in neat straight rows. He counted ten across—there must have been at least a hundred. She dropped her blouse and turned back to him.

"What level am I? I am the best there is, that is what level I am, and fuck you for asking. Come on. I am getting us back to Fillory."

She knocked on a heavy fireproofed door, the kind that in most basements leads to a furnace room. It slid sideways on rollers. The man sliding it sideways looked like a by-the-numbers prepster, with short blond hair and a salmon-colored polo shirt, except that he was only about four feet tall. Dry prickly heat billowed from the room.

"What can I do for you this fine evening?" he said. His teeth were bright and even.

"We need to go to Richmond."

The small man wasn't completely solid either. He was translucent around the edges. Quentin didn't notice at first, until he realized that his eyes were tracking things behind the man's fingers that he shouldn't have been able to see. They were well and truly through the looking glass now.

"Full fare tonight, I'm afraid. It's the weather. Stresses the lines." He had the twinkly mannerisms of an old-timey train conductor. He gestured for her to come inside.

"Only the lady, please," said the translucent prepster. "Not the gentleman."

Deference to Julia's secret extra-Brakebills magic scene notwithstanding, enough was enough. Quentin's grasp of real-world Circumstances was rusty but not that rusty. He whispered a quick, clipped series of Chinese syllables, and an invisible hand gripped the man by the back of the neck and yanked him back against the cinder-block wall behind him so that his head bonked against it.

If Julia was surprised she didn't show it. The man just shrugged and rubbed the back of his head with one hand.

"I'll get the book," he managed. "You have credit?"

It was a furnace room, hot and made of unplastered cinder blocks. There was an actual furnace in it, with a fire bucket full of sand next to it, but there were also two old-looking full-length mirrors leaning against one wall. They looked like pier glasses that had been salvaged from an old house: fogged in places, with wooden frames.

Julia had credit. The book was a leather-bound volume in which she wrote something, stopping in the middle to do mental arithmetic. When she was finished the man looked it over and handed them each a string of paper tickets, the kind you'd get if you won at skee-ball at a carnival. Quentin counted his: nine.

Julia took hers and stepped into the mirror. She disappeared like she'd been swallowed by a bathtub full of mercury.

He thought she would. Mirrors were easy to enchant, being somewhat unearthly by nature anyway. Now that he looked at them more closely he saw the telltale sign: they were true mirrors that didn't invert right and left. Even though he'd just seen Julia walk right through it, he couldn't help closing his eyes and bracing himself to bang his forehead against it. Instead he passed through with an icy sensation.

Crude, he thought. A cleanly cast portal shouldn't make you feel anything.

What followed had the feeling of a movie montage: a series of shabby, nondescript back rooms and basements, with an attendant in each one to take one of their tickets, and another portal to step through. They were traveling on a makeshift magical public transit system, basement to basement. These amateurs must have ginned it up piecemeal. Quentin prayed that somebody out there was doing quality assurance on something other than a strictly voluntary basis, so they wouldn't end up materializing two miles in the air, or directly into the mesosphere two miles underground. That would be a real tragedy of the fucking commons.

In some cases whoever set the portal up had had a sense of humor. One was in a TARDIS-style English phone booth. One portal had a mural on the wall around it: a giant circus fat lady bending over and lifting up her dress, so that you had to step right into her ass.

One stop was completely unlike the others: a hushed executive suite somewhere high up in a skyscraper in some unidentifiable nighttime metropolis. From this height, at this hour, it could have been anywhere, Chicago or Tokyo or Dubai. Through a smoky pane of glass, possibly one-way, Quentin and Julia could see a roomful of men in suits deliberating around a table. There was no attendant here. You were on the honor system: you dropped your ticket into a little bronze idol with an open mouth, and you hit the mirror.

"There are rooms like this all over the world," Julia said as they walked. "People set them up, keep them running. Mostly they are fine. Sometimes you get a bad one."

"Jesus." They'd done all this, and nobody at Brakebills had a clue about it. Julia was right, they wouldn't have believed it was possible. "Who was that see-through prepster guy?"

"Some kind of fairy. Lower fairy. They are not allowed upstairs."

"Where are we going?"

"We are going my way."

"Sorry, that's not good enough." He stopped walking. "Where, specifically, are we going, and what are we doing there?"

"We are going to Richmond. Virginia. To talk to somebody. Good enough?"

It was. But only because the bar for good enough had gotten very, very low.

One portal was unexpectedly dead, the room empty and dark, the mirror smashed. They backtracked and haggled with an attendant who rerouted them around the dead node. They gave the last of their tickets to a meek, pretty young flower child with dishwater hair, center-parted. Julia marked the woman's ledger.

"Welcome to Virginia," she said.

They'd slipped in time as well as space somehow. When they came upstairs the first thing they saw was morning sunlight in the windows. They were in a big house, nicely appointed and immaculately kept, with a Victorian feel: lots of dark wood and oriental carpets and comfortable silence. They'd definitely traded up from the Winston house.

Julia seemed to know the layout. He followed her as she prowled through empty rooms as far as the doorway of a generous living room, which revealed another face of what Quentin had mentally tagged as the underground magic scene. An older man in jeans and a tie was holding court from an overstuffed couch to three teenagers, undergraduate-type girls in yoga pants who watched him with expressions of awe and adoration.

My God, he thought. These people were absolutely everywhere. Magic had gotten out. The antimatter containment field had collapsed. Maybe there had never been one.

The man was demonstrating a spell for his audience: simple cold magic. He had a glass of water in front of him, and he was working on freezing it. Quentin recognized the spell from his first year at Brakebills. Having completed it, in what Quentin thought was a basically correct but overly showy style, the man cupped his hands around the glass. When he took them away it had a skim of ice on it. He'd managed not to break the glass, which the expanding ice often did.

"Now you try it," he said.

The girls had their own glasses of water. They repeated the words in unison and tried to imitate his hand positions. Predictably, nothing happened. They had no idea what they were doing—their soft pink fingers were nowhere near where they needed to be. They hadn't even cut their nails.

When the man noticed Julia standing in the doorway, his face went to shock and horror for about a half second before he was able to bring up a facsimile of delighted surprise. He might have been forty, with carefully mussed brown hair and a fringe of beard. He looked like a large, handsome bug.

"Julia!" he called. "What an amazing surprise! I can't believe you're here!"

"I need to talk to you, Warren."

"Of course!" Warren was working hard to seem like the master of the situation, for the benefit of the room, but it was clear that Julia was very low on his list of people he wanted surprise visits from.

"Hang tight for a minute?" he told his acolytes. "I'll be right back."

When his back was to the undergrads Warren dropped the smile. They crossed the hall into a den. He had an odd, rolling gait, as if he were managing a clubfoot.

"What's this all about, Julia? I've got a class," he said. "Warren," he added to Quentin, with a wary smile. They shook hands.

"I need to talk to you." Julia's tone was stretched thin.

"All right." And before she could answer, he said under his breath: "Not here. In my office, for God's sake."

He ushered Julia toward a door across the hall.

"I'll just wait in the hall," Quentin said. "Call me if—"

Julia closed the door behind them.

He supposed it was fair play, considering that he'd parked Julia in the hall outside Fogg's office. This must be as weird for her as going back to Brakebills had been for him. He couldn't make out what they were saying, not without putting his ear to the door, which would have attracted even more attention from the girls in the living room, who were peering at him curiously, probably because he was still dressed in the raiment of a Fillorian king.

"Hi," he said. They all found something else to peer at.

Raised voices, but still indistinct. Warren was placating her, playing the reasonable one, but eventually Julia got under his skin and he got loud too.

". . . everything I *taught* you, everything I *gave* you . . ."

"Everything *you* gave *me?*" Julia shouted back. "What I gave you . . ."

Quentin cleared his throat. Mommy and Daddy are fighting. The whole scene was starting to seem funny to him, a clear sign that he was becoming dangerously detached from reality. The door opened and Warren appeared. His face was flushed; Julia's was pale.

"I'd like you to leave," he said. "I gave you what you wanted. Now I want you out of here."

"You gave me what you had," she spat back. "Not what I wanted."

He opened his eyes wide and spread out his arms: what do you want me to do.

"Just set the gate," she said.

"I can't afford it," he said, through his teeth.

"God, you are path-*et*-ic!"

Julia walked stiff-legged back through the house, back the way they came, with Warren trailing after. Quentin caught up with them in the mirror room. Julia was scribbling furiously in the ledger. Warren was busy with his own issues. Something odd was happening to him. A long twig was poking through his shirt at the elbow. It seemed to be attached to him.

It was like a dream that just went on and on. Quentin ignored it. They seemed to be leaving anyway.

"You see what you do to me?" Warren said. He was trying to twist and snap off the twig, but it was green and bendy, and there seemed to be another branch sticking out from his ribs, under his shirt. "Just by being here, you see what you do?"

He finally wrenched it off and waved it at her, accusingly, in his fist.

"Hey," Quentin said. He stepped in front of Julia. "Take it easy." They were the first words Quentin had addressed to him.

Julia finished writing and stared at the mirror.

"I cannot *wait* to get out of here," she said, not looking at Warren.

The meek dishwater woman looked horrified by all this. Another of Warren's acolytes, without a doubt. She had faded even farther into her corner.

"Come on, Quentin."

He got the freezing shock again, and this time when they stepped through the transition wasn't instantaneous. They were somewhere else, somewhere dim and in-between. Beneath their feet was masonry, old stone blocks. It was a narrow bridge with no guardrails. Behind them was the bright oblong of the mirror they'd come through; ahead of them, twenty feet away, was another one. Beneath them and on either side was only darkness.

"Sometimes they pull apart like this," Julia said. "Whatever you do do not lose your balance."

"What's down there? Under the bridge?"

"Trolls."

It was hard to tell if she was joking.

The room they emerged into was dark, a storeroom full of boxes. There was barely room for them to push their way out of the mirror. The air smelled good, like coffee beans. No one was there to meet them.

The coffee smell explained itself when he found a door and opened it onto a cramped restaurant kitchen. A cook barked at them in Italian to move along. They squeezed past him, trying not to burn themselves on anything, and out into the dining room of a café.

Threading their way out through the tables, they emerged onto a wide stone square. A beautiful square, defined by sleepy stone buildings of indeterminate age.

"If I didn't know better I'd think we were in Fillory," Quentin said. "Or the Neitherlands."

"We are in Italy. Venice."

"I want some of that coffee. Why are we in Venice?"

"Coffee first."

Bright sunlight on paving stones. Clumps of tourists standing around, taking pictures and studying guidebooks, looking both overwhelmed and bored by it all at the same time. Two churches fronted the square; the other buildings were a weird Venetian jumble of old stone and old wood and irregular windows. Quentin and Julia walked over to the other café on the square, the one out of whose kitchen they had not just magically burst.

It was an oasis of bright yellow umbrellas. Quentin felt like he was floating. He'd never been through so many portals in one day, and it was disorienting. They'd already ordered before they realized they had no euros.

"Fuck it," Quentin said. "I woke up in Fillory this morning, or maybe it was yesterday morning, either way I need a macchiato. Why are we in Venice?"

"Warren gave me an address. Someone who might be able to help us—a fixer, kind of. He can get things. Maybe he can get us a button."

"So that's the plan. Good. I like it." He was up for whatever as long as coffee was involved.

"Great. After that we can try your amazing plan which you do not have."

They sipped their coffee in silence. Dreamily Quentin studied the chaotic surface of his macchiato. They hadn't drawn a milky leaf on it the way they would have in America. Pigeons strutted in between the café tables, picking up unspeakably soiled crumbs, their clawed toes looking livid and pink this close up. Sunlight washed over it all. The light in Venice was like the light in Fillory: stone-light.

The world had changed again. It wasn't as neatly divided as he remembered it, between the magical and the non-magical. There was this grubby, anarchical in-between now. He didn't much care for it; it was chaotic and unglamorous and he didn't know the rules. Probably Julia didn't like it either, he reflected, but she hadn't gotten to choose, not the way he did.

Well, his world hadn't done them any good. They would go rooting around in hers for a while.

"So who was that Warren guy?" Quentin said. "Seems like you guys have some history."

"Warren is nobody. He knows a little magic, so he hangs around the college and tries to impress undergraduates and teach them some things so he can bang them."

"Really."

"Really."

"What happened to him at the end there? With his arm—what was that?"

"Warren is not human. He is something else, wood spirit of some kind. He just has a thing for humans. When he gets upset he cannot keep up the disguise."

"So did Warren 'bang' you?" he said.

Who knew where it came from. It just bubbled up out of nowhere: a flash of jealousy, sour and hot like acid reflux. He didn't see it coming. He'd had a lot to absorb in one day, or night, whatever it had just been, and it was just a little too much too fast. It spilled over.

Julia leaned across the table and slapped Quentin. She only did it once, but she did it hard.

"You have no idea what I had to do to get what was handed to you on a plate," she hissed. "And yeah, I banged Warren. I did a lot worse things too."

You could almost see the waves of anger coming off her, like fumes off gasoline. Quentin touched his cheek where she'd hit him.

"I'm sorry," he said.

"Not sorry enough."

A few people looked over, but just a few. It was Italy after all. People probably hit each other all the time.

CHAPTER 12

I t was another year and a half before Julia saw Quentin again.
He'd become a hard boy to find. He didn't seem to have a cell phone, or even a phone, or even an e-mail address. His parents talked in vaguenesses. She wasn't convinced that even they knew how to find him. But she knew how to find them, and he had to come back home once in a while, like a dog to its vomit. Quentin wasn't close to his parents, but he wasn't the type to cut them off all the way. Frankly he wouldn't have the stones for it.

Julia, though. Julia had the stones for it. She was a flight risk, no strong ties to the community. When she heard that the Coldwaters had sold up and moved to Massachusetts, she pulled up stakes and followed them. Even a suburban cultural sump like Chesterton had Internet connections and temp agencies—no, especially a suburban cultural sump like Chesterton—and that was all she needed to get by. She rented a room over a garage from a retired guy with a janitor mustache who probably had a Web cam hidden in the bathroom. She bought a beat-up Honda Civic with a wired-shut trunk.

She didn't hate Quentin. That wasn't it. Quentin was fine, he was just in the way. He had gotten it so easy, and she had it so hard, and why? There was no good reason. He passed a test, and she failed it. That was a judgment on the test, not on her, but now her life was a waking nightmare, and he had everything he ever wanted. He was living a fantasy. Her fantasy. She wanted it back.

Or not even that. She wasn't going to take anything away from him.

She just needed him to confirm that Brakebills was real, and to open a chink in the wall of the secret garden just wide enough for her to squeeze through. He was her man on the inside. Though he didn't know it yet.

So here's how it worked: every morning before work she drove past the Coldwaters' house. Every night around nine o'clock she drove by again, and got out and quietly walked the perimeter of the lawn, looking for traces of her quarry. A McMansion like that, all double-glazed picture windows, broadcast the goings-on inside it out into the night like a drive-in movie. It was summer again, and the summer nights smelled like murdered grass and sounded like crickets fucking. At first all she learned was that Mrs. Coldwater was a predictable but technically sound amateur painter in a sadly dated Pop art mode, and that Mr. Coldwater had a weakness for porn and crying jags.

It wasn't till September that the beast showed himself.

Quentin had changed: he'd always been lanky, but now he looked like a skeleton. His cheeks were sunken, his cheekbones jagged. His clothes hung on him. His hair—cut your fucking hair already, you're not Alan Rickman—was lank.

He looked like shit. Poor baby. Actually what he looked like was Julia.

She didn't approach him right away. She had to psych herself up for it. Now that she had him where she wanted him, she was suddenly afraid to touch him. She quit taking temp assignments and went full-time on Quentin. But she stayed under the radar.

Around eleven every morning she watched him slam out of the house in a brown study and whiz into town on a hilariously antique white ten-speed. She followed him at a distance. Good thing he was completely oblivious and self-obsessed or he would have noticed a red Honda with a death rattle shadowing his every move. There he was, the living, breathing forensic trace of everything she'd ever wanted. If he couldn't help her, or wouldn't, it would be over. She'd have given two years of her life for nothing. The fear of finding out paralyzed her, but every day she waited the risk that he would vanish again grew and grew. She would be back to square zero.

All Julia could think was that if it came right down to it she would sleep with him. She knew how he felt about her. He would do anything to sleep with her. It was the nuclear option, but it would work. No risk. It was her ace in the hole. So to speak.

Who knows, it might not even be so bad. Different, doubtless, from James's smartly paced gymnastic exhibitions. She didn't even know anymore why she was so determined not to like Quentin. Maybe he'd been right, maybe he was the one for her after all. It was hard to know anymore, it was tangled up with everything else, and she was out of practice at having feelings for other people. At this point it had been a long time since anybody had even touched her. Not since the zookeeper in the bathroom at the party, and that was mostly just spastic over-clothes pawing, entirely clinical in its intent. The patient struggling under the knife, while she performed the operation. She felt out of touch with her body, with pleasure of any kind. Doctor Julia noted, purely for the record, that it was scary how unloving she'd become, and how unlovable. She'd locked all that stuff away and melted down the key for scrap.

It was in a cemetery behind a church, whither Quentin had retired for more sulking, that she sprang the trap. Looking back on it she was proud of herself. She could have lost it but she didn't. She got it out. She said her piece, and hung on to her pride, and showed him that she was every bit as good as he was. She made the case. She even showed him the spell, the one with the rainbow trails, which she'd gotten down pat over the previous six months. Even those murderous hand positions, even the one with the thumbs, she had hit with icy precision. She'd never shown it to anybody before, and it felt great to finally unveil it for an audience. She took that beach like a goddamned Marine.

And when it came down to the nuclear option, when the red phone rang in the war room, Julia hadn't flinched. Oh, no. She took that call. If that's what it took, she would go there, sister.

But here was the thing: he wouldn't. She hadn't counted on that. She'd offered, as plainly as she knew how. She'd run herself through with the hook and dangled herself before him, pink and wriggling, but he hadn't taken the bait. Julia knew she'd let herself go a bit lookswise, but still. Come on. It didn't add up.

The problem wasn't her, it was him. Something or someone had gotten to him. He wasn't the Quentin she remembered. Funny: she'd al-most forgotten people could change. Time had stopped for her the day she'd gotten her social studies paper back from Mr. Karras, but outside the dark, musty interior of her room, time had gone on hurtling for-ward. And in that time Quentin Makepeace Coldwater had managed to get a boner for somebody else besides Julia.

Well, good for him.

When he left she lay down on the cold, soft, wet grass of the grave-yard. It rained on her and she let it. It wasn't that she was wrong. She'd been right. He'd confirmed everything that she'd ever suspected, about Brakebills and magic and everything else. It was all real, and it was ex-traordinary. It was everything she wanted it to be. Her theoretical work had been admirably rigorous, and she had been rewarded with full ex-perimental validation.

It was just that there was nothing he could do for her. It was all real—it wasn't a dream or a psychotic hallucination—but they weren't going to let her have it. There was a place out there that was so perfect and magical that it had made even Quentin happy. There wasn't just magic there, there was love too. Quentin was in love. But Julia wasn't. She was out in the cold. Hogwarts was fully subscribed, and her eligibility had lapsed. Hagrid's motorcycle would never rumble outside her front door. No creamy-enveloped letters would ever come flooding down her chimney.

She lay there thinking, on the rich, wet graveyard grass, before the tomb of some random parishioner—Beloved Son, Husband, Father—and what she thought was this: she'd been right about almost every-thing. She'd gotten nearly full marks. A minus again. Blew only one question.

Here's the one thing I got wrong, she thought. I thought that they could never wear me down.

CHAPTER 13

Shoplifting a city map from a tourist trap wasn't a particularly spiritually enlarging activity—where was Benedict when you needed
him?—and the magic involved was trivial. But it gave Quentin enough
time to pull himself together. He wished he hadn't said that about Warren. He wished he weren't so tired. And so stupid. He wished he could
either fall back in love with Julia or get over her all the way. Maybe he
was stuck in between forever, like the space between the portals. Food
for the trolls.

Quentin took a deep breath. He was surprised at himself. He knew
that he was being weird and kind of a dick. So what if she'd slept with
Warren and whoever and whatever else? She didn't owe him anything.
God knows he was in no position to judge her. It was partly his fault that
she had to do what she did.

He could have used someone stable to hang on to right now, but as
it happened, through no particular fault of her own, Julia was not a
person one could hang on to. She needed one of those warning decals
that they put on airplane parts: NO STEP. He would have to be that person, the stable, reliable person, the one who had his shit together, for
both of them. They could either do this together or separately, except
they had to do this together, because he was out of leads and she was
very nearly out of her mind. It wasn't a particularly glamorous role—it
wasn't the Bingle role—but it was his role. It was time he accepted it.

Though so far she'd been a lot more help than he had. When he got back to the table at the café she had undergone yet another unexpected transformation. She was smiling.

"You look happy." He sat down. "Maybe you should slap me more often."

"Maybe I should," she said. She sipped her coffee. "This is good."

"The coffee."

"I had forgotten how good it can be." She turned her pale face into the light and closed her eyes, like a cat sunning herself. "Did you ever miss it? Being here?"

"I honestly never did."

"Me neither. Not until now. I had forgotten."

Warren had written the address on a blue Post-it, which Julia had kept clutched in her fist all the way from Richmond. Now they pored over the city map together, like all the other tourists in the square were doing, until they'd figured out where they were and where they were going. Their destination was in a neighborhood called Dorsoduro, on a street a block off the Grand Canal. Not far. A bridge crossing away.

Quentin guessed it was probably only around nine or ten at night by their internal clocks, but it was midafternoon in Venice, and he felt like they'd been up for days. It was hot in the square but cool up on the bridge, in the seaborne jet stream that blew down the Grand Canal, so they stopped there to orient themselves. There were no cars in Venice, or not in this part anyway. The bridge was a wooden footbridge, disappointingly modern. It would be a hundred years at least until it started looking like it belonged in Venice.

Beneath them oily black gondolas poled along, spinning off miniature spiral whirlpools after them, and sturdy vaporetti chugged, and long thin barges glided, roiling the green water behind them into milky smoothness. Debauched, listing palazzi lined the canal, all tiles and terraces and colonnades. Venice was the only city he'd ever seen that looked the same in real life as it did in pictures. It was consoling that something in this world met expectations. The one factoid Quentin remembered about the Grand Canal was that after Byron was done screwing his mistresses he used to like to swim home along it, carrying a lighted torch in one hand so that boats wouldn't run him over.

He wondered what was happening in Fillory. Would they wait around on After Island for them? Hold an investigation? Put the locals to the sword? Or would they go back to Whitespire? The truth was, whatever was going to happen had probably already happened. Weeks could have gone by already, or years, you never knew how the time difference would work. He could feel Fillory floating away from him, into its future, leaving him behind. Hell must have broken loose when they vanished, but life would go on, they'd get back to normal. Right now Janet and Eliot could be growing old without him. They'd miss him but they'd live. Quentin, king of Fillory, needed Fillory more than Fillory needed him.

In Dorsoduro the streets were narrow and quiet. It was less like a stage set and more like a real city than the part they'd come from—people actually seemed to live and work here, they weren't just putting on a show for the tourists. As much as Quentin wanted to hurry through it, to get on with getting back to Fillory, even he couldn't ignore how conspicuously beautiful Venice was. People had been living here for what, a thousand years? More? God only knew whose crazy idea it was to build a city in the middle of a lagoon, but you couldn't argue with the results. Everything was made of old brick and stone, with carved blocks of even older stone stuck into the walls at random intervals as ornaments. Old windows had been bricked up, and then new windows had been bashed through the brick, affording glimpses of silent, secret courtyards. Every time they thought they'd left the sea behind they'd stumble on it again—a dark angular vein of water branching in between the buildings, lined on both sides with bright-colored skiffs.

Just being here made Quentin feel better. It was more suitable for a king and a queen than suburban Boston. He didn't know yet whether they were getting any closer to Fillory, but he felt closer.

Julia kept her pace brisk and her eyes fixed straight ahead. It should have been a short walk, ten minutes at most, but the street plan was so chaotic they had to stop at literally every corner to reorient themselves. They took turns snatching the map from each other and getting lost and having it snatched back. Only about one building in five had a number on it, and the numbers didn't even seem to be in sequential order. It was a city built for wandering, which was all well and good unless you had urgent business at one very particular location.

Finally they stopped at a wooden door, painted brown, that was barely as tall as they were. It was an open question whether they were on the right street, but if nothing else the door had the right number on a little stone plaque above it. It had a tiny window set in it, which had been painted over. There was no knob.

Quentin put his hand on the warm stone wall next to it. He counted a rhythmic sequence under his breath, and a thick fabric of lines the deep orange of a heating filament flashed for a minute over the old stone.

"The wards on this place are ironclad," he said. "If your fixer doesn't live here, whoever does knows what they're doing."

Either they were about to improve their situation or significantly worsen it. There being no buzzer, Quentin knocked. The door didn't resonate under his knuckles—there could have been a solid mile of rock behind it. But the window swung open promptly.

"Sì," Darkness inside.

"We'd like to talk to your boss," Quentin said.

The window shut immediately. He looked at Julia and shrugged. What else was he supposed to say? She looked back at him impassively from behind her black glasses. Quentin wanted to walk away. He wanted to go back, but there was no back to go to. The only way out was through. Onward and downward.

The street was silent. It was narrow, practically an alley, with buildings going up four stories on either side. Nothing happened. After five minutes Quentin muttered some words in Icelandic and held his palm an inch away from the door. He felt the wall around it, which was in the shade but still warm.

"Stand back," he said.

Whoever made the wards knew what they were doing. But they didn't know everything Quentin knew. He moved the heat from the wall, all of it, into the little glass window, which expanded, as glass will when it's heated. The wards were good enough that the heat didn't want to go, but Quentin had ways of encouraging it. When the glass couldn't

expand anymore it popped with a ping like a lightbulb. Warren's students would have been impressed.

"*Stronzo!*" he called through the empty frame. "*Facci parlare contuo
direttore del cazzo!*"

A minute passed. Quentin's thermal transfer spell had made a
sheen of frost appear on the old stone wall. The door opened. It was dark
inside.

"See?" he said. "I did learn something in college."

A short, heavyset man met them in the foyer, a tiny room lined with
brown ceramic tiles. He was surprisingly gracious. They must have to
replace that little window a lot.

"*Prego.*"

He ushered them up a short flight of stairs into one of the most beautiful rooms Quentin had ever seen.

He'd been snowed by Venice's bizarre topography. He'd assumed
they'd be shown into some crap Euro-trash crash pad, with white walls
and uncomfortable couches and tiny geometrical lamps, but the building's exterior was pure camouflage. They were in one of the big palaces
on the Grand Canal. They'd come in the back way.

The entire front wall was a row of tall windows with Moorish peaks,
all looking out onto the water. The obvious intention was to awe guests
into a state of trembling submissiveness, and Quentin surrendered immediately. It was like a full-scale mural, a Tintoretto maybe, with vivid
green water and boats of all shapes and sizes, imaginable and unimagi-
nable, crossing back and forth. Three hideous, glittering Murano chandeliers lit the room, translucent octopuses dripping with crystals. The
walls were stacked with ranks of paintings, classical landscapes and
scenes of Venice. The floor was old marble tiles, their lumps and scars
smothered under overlapping oriental carpets.

Everything in the room was very much just so. It was the kind of
room you wanted to spend years in. It wasn't Fillory, but things were
definitely looking up. It felt like Castle Whitespire.

Their escort departed, and for the moment they were left to their own
devices. Quentin and Julia sat on a sofa together; its legs were so deeply
carved it looked like it was going to walk away. There were four or five

other people in the room, but it was so huge that it seemed private and empty. Three men in shirtsleeves were talking in low tones over a tiny table, sipping something clear out of tiny glasses. A broad-shouldered old woman stared out at the water with her back to them. A butler, or whatever they were called in Italy, stood at the foot of the stairs.

Everyone ignored them. Julia squished herself into one corner of the couch. She pulled her feet up, putting her shoes on the nice antique upholstery.

"I guess we take a number," Quentin said.

"We have to wait," Julia said. "He will call us."

She took off her glasses and closed her eyes. She was starting to withdraw again. He could see it. It seemed to come in waves. Maybe it was because she felt safe here, she could let herself go for a while. He hoped so. He would take it from here.

"I'm going to get you some water."

"Mineral water," she said. "Fizzy. And ask him for rye."

If there was one thing being a king prepared you for, it was talking to domestic staff. The butler had both mineral water—*frizzante*—and rye. He brought the rye neat, which seemed to be how Julia wanted it. She ignored the water. He worried about her drinking. Quentin liked a drop here and there, God knew, but the volume of alcohol Julia could consume was heroic. He thought of what Eliot told him, about what he'd seen at the spa. It was like Julia was trying to anesthetize herself, or cauterize a wound, or fill in some part of her that was missing.

"Warren's fixer must be pretty good at fixing things," Quentin said. "This place is nice even by magician standards."

"I cannot stay here" was all Julia said.

She sat there sipping the rye and shivering, cupping it between her hands as if it were a magic healing cordial. She drank without opening her eyes, like a baby. Quentin had the butler bring her a wrap. She had the butler bring her another rye.

"I can't even get drunk anymore," she said bitterly.

After that she didn't speak. Quentin hoped she could rest. He occupied the other end of the couch, sipping a Venetian spritz (Prosecco, Aperol, soda water, twist of lemon, olive) and looking out at the canal and not thinking about what they'd do if this didn't work out. The palace directly opposite them was pink; the setting sun was turning it salmon. Its windows were all shuttered. Over the years it had settled unevenly—one half had sunk slightly while the other half stayed where it was, creating a fault line up the middle. It must have run through the whole building, all the rooms, Quentin thought. People were probably always tripping on it. Stripy poles stuck up at odd angles from the water in front of the pink palace.

It was strange to be in a place and not be king of it. He'd gotten out of the habit. It was like Elaine had said: nothing made him special here. Nobody noticed him. He had to admit it was strangely relaxing. It was an hour, and Quentin had cut himself off after his third spritz, before a small, intense young Italian in a pale suit, no tie, came and invited them upstairs. It was the kind of outfit an American couldn't have gotten away with in a million years.

He showed them into a small all-white salon with three delicate wooden chairs set around a table. There was a plain silver bowl on the table.

No one sat in the third chair. Instead a voice spoke to them out of the air—a man's voice, but high and whispery, almost androgynous. It was hard to tell where it was coming from.

"Hello, Quentin. Hello, Julia."

That was creepy. He hadn't told anybody their names.

"Hi." He didn't know where to look. "Thanks for seeing us."

"You're welcome," the voice said. *"Why have you come here?"*

I guess he doesn't know everything.

"We'd like to ask for your help with something."

"What would you like me to help you with?"

Showtime. He wondered if the fixer was even human, or some kind of spirit like Warren, or worse. Julia was doing her thousand-yard stare, a million miles away.

"Well, we've just come from another world. From Fillory. Which as it turns out is a real place. You probably knew that." Ahem. Start again. "We didn't mean to leave—it was kind of an accident—and we want to go back there."

"I see." Pause. *"And why would I want to help you with that?"*

"Maybe I can help you too. Maybe we can help each other."

"Oh, I doubt that, Quentin." The voice dropped an octave. *"I doubt that very much."*

"Okay." Quentin looked behind him. "Right, look, where are you?"

He was starting to feel painfully aware of how vulnerable they were. He didn't have much of an exit strategy. And the fixer shouldn't have known their names. Maybe Warren had called ahead. That wasn't a comforting thought.

"I know who you are, Quentin. There are circles in which you are not a very popular man. Some people think you abandoned this world. Your own world."

"All right. I wouldn't say abandoned, but okay."

"And then Fillory abandoned you. Poor little rich king. It doesn't seem like anyone wants you, Quentin."

"You can look at it like that if you want. If we can just get back to Fillory everything will be fine. Or at any rate it's not your problem, is it?"

"I will be the judge of what is and is not my problem."

The back of Quentin's neck prickled. He and the fixer weren't getting off to a roaring start. He weighed the advantages of laying on some basic defensive magic. Prudent, but it might spook the fixer into trying a preemptive strike. He shot Julia a glance, but she was barely following.

"All right. I'm just here to do business."

"Look in the bowl."

Looking in the silver bowl at this juncture seemed like a bad idea. Quentin stood up.

"Listen. If you can't help us, fine. We'll go. But if you can help us, give us a price. We'll pay it."

"Oh, but I don't have to give you anything at all. I did not invite you here, and I will decide when you can go. Look in the bowl."

Now there was steel in that high, whispery voice.

"Look in the bowl."

This was going south fast. It felt all wrong. He took Julia's arm and pulled her to her feet.

"We're leaving," he said. "Now."

He backhanded the silver bowl off the table and it clanged against the wall. A slip of paper fluttered out of it. Against his better judgment Quentin glanced at it. There were spells you could set off just by reading them. The paper had the words I.O.U. ONE MAGIC BUTTON written on it in crude magic marker.

The door opened behind them, and Quentin scrambled to get them both behind the table.

"Oh, shit! He looked in the bowl!"

The voice was a lot lower than the one that had been speaking before. It was a voice Quentin knew well. It belonged to Josh.

Quentin hugged him.

"Jesus!" he said into Josh's broad, comforting shoulder. "What the hell, man?"

He didn't understand how it was even possible that Josh was here, but it didn't matter. Probably it would, but not yet. He didn't even care that Josh had messed with their heads. What mattered now was that they weren't going to have a new disaster. They weren't going to have a fight. Quentin's knees were shaking. It was like he'd sailed so far from the safe, orderly world he knew that he was coming back around the other way, from the other side, and there was Josh: an island of warmth and familiarity.

Josh disengaged himself tactfully.

"So," he said, "welcome to the suck, man!"

"What the hell are you doing here?"

"Me? This is my house! What are you doing here? Why aren't you in Fillory?"

He was the same Josh: round-faced, overweight, grinning. He looked like a beer-brewing abbot, not visibly older than the last time Quentin had seen him, which was more than three years now. Josh carefully closed the door behind him.

"Can't be too careful," he said. "Got an image to protect. Kind of a Wizard of Oz thing going on, if you see what I mean."

"What's with the bowl?"

"Eh, I didn't have a lot of time. I just thought it was creepy. You know. *'Look in the bowl . . . look in the bowl . . .'*" He did the voice.

"Josh, Julia. You guys know each other."

They'd met once before, in the chaotic run-up before the great return to Fillory, before Josh had set off into the Neitherlands on his own.

"Hi, Julia." Josh kissed her on both cheeks. He must really have gone Euro over here.

"Hi."

Josh waggled both eyebrows at Quentin lewdly in a way that didn't seem like it should be physically possible. It was starting to sink in for Quentin just what a colossal stroke of luck this was. Josh would have the magic button. He was their ticket back to Fillory. Their wandering days were over.

"So listen," he said. "We've got some problems."

"Yeah, you must if you came here."

"We don't even really know where here is."

"You're in my house, that's where here is." Josh waved his arms grandly. "Here is a huge fuck-off pa-*lots*-o on the Grand Canal."

He gave them the tour. The palazzo was four floors, the lower two for business, the upper two for Josh's private apartments, to which they retreated. The floor was massive pink-swirled marble slabs, the walls crumbling plaster. All the rooms were odd sizes and seemed to have been built as they were needed, on a series of whimsical impulses that it was now impossible to reconstruct.

All glory to the great quest for Fillory, but they needed a break. Julia requested a hot bath, which frankly she badly needed. Quentin and Josh retired to the tremendous dining room, which was lit by a single modest chandelier. Over plates of black spaghetti, Quentin explained as best he could what had happened and why they were here. When he was done Josh explained what had happened to him.

With Quentin, Eliot, Janet, and Julia safely installed on the thrones of Fillory, Josh had taken the button and embarked on an exploration of the Neitherlands. He'd seen as much as he ever wanted to see of Fillory, and it hadn't been pretty, and anyway he was sick of scraping along in the others' shadows. He didn't want to be co-king of Fillory, he wanted to do his own thing his own way. He wanted to find his own Fillory. He wanted to get laid.

Josh could be careless about a lot of things—what he ate, wore, smoked, said, did—but you don't get into Brakebills without being a genius of some kind or another, and given the right stakes he was fully capable of being highly methodical, even meticulous. In this case the stakes were just right. He began a careful survey of the Neitherlands.

This was not a thing to be undertaken lightly. As far as anyone knew the squares and fountains of the Neitherlands extended an infinite distance in all directions, never repeating themselves, and each one led to a different world, and maybe a whole different universe. It would take no effort at all to get so lost that you could never find your way home.

Josh had it in mind to go to Middle Earth, as in the setting of Tolkien's *The Lord of the Rings*. Because if Fillory was real, why not Middle Earth? And if Middle Earth was real, that meant a lot of other things were probably real: lady elves and lembas wafers and pipe-weed and Eru Ilúvatar knew what else. But practically speaking anywhere would have done as long as it was reasonably warm and life-supporting and inhabited by people endowed with the appropriate organs and a willingness to make them available to Josh. The multiverse was his TGI Friday's.

He had it in mind to spiral outward from Earth's fountain, square by square, mapping carefully as he went. He wouldn't need much. You didn't really get hungry in the Neitherlands. He brought a loaf of bread, a good bottle of wine, warm clothes, six ounces of gold, and a stun gun.

"The first world was a complete bust," he said. "Desert everywhere. Incredible dunes, but no people at all that I could find, so I buttoned right back out of there. Next one was ice. Next one was pine forest. That one was inhabited—sort of a Native American thing. I stayed there two weeks. No love, but I lost about ten pounds. Also scored a fuck-ton of wampum."

"Wait, hang on. These worlds were the same all over? Like each one had a single climate and that's it?"

"Well, I don't know. I don't even know if these other worlds are spheres, you know? Or discworlds or ringworlds whatever else. Maybe they don't work the same way. Maybe they don't have latitude. But I wasn't about to hike to another climatic zone just to find out. Much easier just to hit the next fountain.

"God, the things I saw. Really, you should do it sometime. Some days I would hit a dozen worlds. I was just like free-falling through the multiverse. A giant tree that didn't have any beginning or end. A sort of magnetic world, where everything stuck to you. One was all stretchy. One was just stairs, stairs and stairs and stairs. What else? There was an upside-down one. A weightless one, where you drifted around in outer space, except that space was warm and humid and smelled sort of like rosemary.

"And you know what's real? Teletubbies! I know, right? Crazy, crazy stuff."

"You didn't . . ."

"No, I did not hit that shit. Totally could have. Anyway. Not everything was that exotic. Sometimes I'd find a world that was just like ours only one tiny thing would be different—like the economy was all based on strontium, or sharks were mammals, or there was more helium in the air so everybody had little high voices.

"I did meet a girl, after all that. Man, it was so beautiful. This world was mostly mountains, like one of those Chinese paintings, just rising out of the mist, and actually everybody looked kind of Asian. They lived in these ornate hanging pagoda cities. But there were hardly any of them left—they were always fighting these endless wars with other people on other mountains, for no special reason. Plus they fell off cliffs a lot.

"I was probably the fattest person they'd ever seen, but they didn't care about that. I think they thought it was hot. Like it meant I was a good hunter, something like that. They'd also never seen magic before, so that went a long way. I was kind of a celebrity for a while.

"I started hanging out with this one girl, big-time warrior for one of the cities. She was very into the magic thing. And also I guess their menfolk weren't especially well-endowed in the hardware aisle, if you take my meaning."

"I believe I grasp the essence of it, yes," Quentin said.

"Anyway she died. Got killed. It was awful. Really, really sad. At first I wanted to stay and fight and try to get the people who killed her, but then I couldn't do it. It was all so stupid. I just couldn't get into the war thing the way they did, and that was shameful to them, I guess, so they kicked me out."

"God. I'm sorry."

Poor Josh. The way he talked all the time, you sometimes forgot he had feelings. But they were all there, if you dug deep enough.

"No, it doesn't matter. I mean it did, but what can you do. It was never going to work out. I think she wanted to die that way. Those people weren't that into life, or maybe they were and that's what life is, *I don't fucking know.*

"That's when it all went to shit. All the fun was gone. I went to this kind of Greek world, all white cliffs and hot sun and dark seas. I slept with a harpy there."

"You had rebound sex with a harpy?"

"I don't know if that's what she was. Wings for arms, basically. Her feet were kind of talon-y too."

"Right."

"She practically took off in the middle of it. Feathers going every-where. Way more trouble than it was worth. I still have a scar from where she clawed me. I can—"

"I don't want to see it."

Josh sighed. All the humor had drained out of his face, leaving it gray under the stubble. Now Quentin saw those years that he'd missed before.

"I mean, all I was looking for basically was some kind of *Y: The Last Man* setup, right? Where I was the only dude in a world of chicks. I know it's out there. They could even all have been lesbians, and I would just watch. I'd be good with whatever.

"Anyway after that I started just sliding through worlds. Worlds worlds worlds. I stopped caring. It was like when you've surfed too much porn on the Web and none of it seems real but you keep going anyway. I'd get to a world and immediately start looking for any excuse to quit and go on to the next one. As soon as I'd see one wrong thing—oh, this one has flies, or the sky is a weird color, or no beer, anything that wasn't perfect—I'd bail.

"Then one of those times I came back and the whole Neitherlands was busted."

"What? How do you mean, busted?"

"Broken. Fucked up. Do you know about this? If I hadn't seen it, I wouldn't have believed it."

He drained his wineglass. A man came to refill it, and Josh waved him off. "Whiskey," he said.

He went on.

"At first I thought it was me, I must have broken it. I used it too much, something like that. When my head broke the water that last time it was like the cold punched me in the face. The air was freezing, and the wind was just *whipping* this dry powdery snow through the squares."

"How is that even possible?" Quentin said. "I didn't think the Neitherlands even had weather."

It made him think of that silent storm, the one that had thrashed the clock-tree back in Fillory. Maybe it was the same wind?

"Something's deeply messed up there, Quentin. Something's wrong, something basic. Like systemic. Half the buildings were in ruins. It looked like the place had been bombed. All those beautiful stone buildings just laid open to the sky. Do you remember how Penny said once that they were all full of books? I think he was right, because the air was full of pages, blowing along through the city."

Josh shook his head.

"I guess I should have grabbed a few, to see what was on them. You would have. I never even thought of it till after.

"You know what I was thinking about? Not dying. I was pretty far from the Earth fountain at that point, a mile maybe. I'd brought warm clothes, but I ditched them when I met the harpy. It was hot as hell there. And she kinda tore at my clothes a lot of the time anyway.

"So I was practically naked, and a lot of my landmarks were gone. A lot of the fountains were gone too. Some of them were leveled, some of them were frozen. You know how you can't really do magic there? A couple of times I just squatted down in a corner. I thought maybe I'd wait out the storm, but really I just wanted to go to sleep. I didn't think I could go on. I could have died, easily. I was out there for about half an hour. It's a miracle I found the Earth fountain at all. I really thought I wouldn't make it."

"It's incredible that you did." Good old Josh. Just when you were ready to write him off he kicked into gear, and when he did he really was indomitable. Like that time in Fillory, when he'd beaten the red-hot giant with his black hole spell. He'd probably outlive them all.

"I keep trying to figure it out," Josh said. "It was like somebody'd attacked the Neitherlands, or cursed it, except who could do that? I didn't see anybody there. It was just as empty as it always was. I thought maybe—I know it's silly—I thought maybe I'd see Penny."

"Yeah."

"I mean, not that I wanted to. I couldn't stand that guy. But it'd be nice to know he's not dead."

"Yeah. It would."

Quentin was already trying to calculate whether this meant he and Julia couldn't get back to Fillory through the Neitherlands. It was still possible, in theory. They'd just suit up for cold weather. Bring an ice ax.

"I always thought the Neitherlands were invulnerable," Quentin said. "They felt like they were outside time, I didn't think they ever changed. But it sounds like an earthquake hit them, an earthquake and a blizzard at the same time."

"I know, right? What are the odds?"

"I don't suppose you noticed whether the Fillory fountain was still there?" Quentin said. "I thought maybe we'd go back that way. Back to Fillory."

"No. So you are going back? I didn't exactly pop in while I was passing through. But listen, I don't know if you can go back that way anyway."

"Why not? I realize the Neitherlands is a disaster area, but it's worth a try. You got back to Earth. You seem pretty settled here. We'll just borrow the button and be on our way."

"Yeah, see, that's the thing."

Josh didn't meet Quentin's eyes. He studied a painting hanging on the flaking wall behind Quentin as if he'd never seen it before.

"What?"

"I don't have the button anymore."

"You don't—?"

"Yeah. I sold it. I didn't realize you still wanted it."

Quentin could not be hearing this.

"You didn't. Tell me you did not do that."

"I totally did!" Josh said, indignant. "How the hell do you think I could afford a fucking Venetian palazzo?"

CHAPTER 14

The old wood of Josh's dining room table felt cool against Quentin's forehead. In a few more seconds he'd sit up again. That's how long it would take to roll his brain back to the state it was in before it thought that their troubles were over. Until that happened Quentin would just enjoy the cool solidity of the table for a second more. He let the despair wash over him. The button was gone. He thought about banging his head a few times, just lightly, but that would have been overdoing it.

He was aware for the first time of how quiet the city had gotten. After dark the streets and canals seemed to empty out. As if Venice felt less of an obligation to pretend to be part of this millennium at night, and had reverted to its medieval self again.

All right. He sat up. The blood drained back out of his face. Back to work.

"Okay. You sold the button."

"Look, you must have had some other plan," Josh said. "I mean, don't tell me you were actually planning on randomly running into me in Venice and bumming the button off me. That's not a plan."

"Well, no," Quentin said, "it's not a plan. The plan was not to get booted out of Fillory, but that ship has sailed, so I'm working on a new plan. Who the hell did you sell the button to?"

"Well, that's a story too!" Josh launched straight into the tale, untroubled by any further self-reproach. If Quentin had moved on then so could he, and this was obviously a much happier story than the one about his sojourn in the Neitherlands. "See, I realized I was through with that button. I was done with the Neitherlands and Fillory and all that stuff. If I was going to get laid—and I was—I was going to get laid right here in the real world. So I looked around for something to do on Earth, and I started picking up on this underground scene. The safe houses, all that stuff. Have you heard about that?"

"Julia's been catching me up."

"I mean, I always knew there were hedge witches out there, a few of them, but this thing goes deep, man. I had no idea. There are a lot of those guys. And a lot of them come through Venice—they figure it's really old, so, hey, magic. They think maybe they'll pick something up. It's kinda sad, really. Some of them are the business, they've figured out a lot of what we know, and some stuff we don't, but most of them have no idea what they're doing, and they're desperate. They'll try anything.

"You gotta watch yourself around the desperate ones. They don't know enough to be dangerous, most of them, but they attract scavengers. Fairies and demons and whatever. Fucking jackals. That's where you get problems. The predators don't mess around with us because we're too much trouble, but those poor bastards, the hedge magicians, they want power and they'll do anything to get it. I've heard of them striking some pretty bad bargains.

"But you know what? I like them. You know I never fit in that well at Brakebills. That whole fake Oxford thing, with the wine tasting and the fancy dress and all that—that was always more your scene, you and Eliot. And, and Janet." He almost mentioned Alice but swerved away at the last second. "And it was great, don't get me wrong. But it's just not my style.

"I get along better with the underground people. People thought I was a joke at Brakebills, but here I'm a big wheel. I guess I just got tired of being the bottom of the food chain. Nobody really appreciated me there—no, not even you, Quentin. Not really. But here I'm like the king."

Quentin could have denied it—but no, he couldn't really. It was true. Everybody loved Josh, but nobody took him seriously. He'd allowed himself to think that it was because Josh didn't want to be taken seriously, but that wasn't true at all, of Josh or probably of anybody. Everybody wanted to be the hero of their own story. Nobody wanted to be comic relief. Josh had probably been carrying that around as long as Quentin had known him. No wonder he gave them a hard time in that room with the bowl.

"So is that why you sold the button? Because you felt like we didn't take you seriously?"

Josh looked wounded. "I sold the button because I got offered a fuckload of money for it. But would that have been a bad reason? Look, I had a little anger to deal with. They treat me with respect here. I never knew what that was like before. I'm the bridge between the two worlds. There's things you can't get in the underground that I know how to find and vice versa. So people come to me with problems from both sides.

"It's actually pretty wild. The underground scene has shit we never could have gotten our hands on, and they don't even know it. They have these sad little swap meets, and then something really legendary turns up, totally at random, and they don't even recognize it. One time I found a Cherenkov sphere. Nobody knew what it was, I had to show them how to hold it."

"So what about the button? Did you sell that at a swap meet?"

"Aha, yeah, you might well ask that," Josh said, unfazed. "That was more of a special transaction. A one-off. High-status client."

"Yeah, I bet. Maybe you could put me in touch with your high-status client. Maybe he'll want to have a special transaction with me too."

"No harm in trying, but I can't say I love your chances." Josh was grinning like a lunatic. There was obviously a secret there that he was dying to blow.

"Tell me."

"Okay!" Josh held up his hands, setting the scene. "So. After I get back from the Neitherlands I'm knocking around New York, just enjoying that I still have all my extremities, when I get a call on my cell from this guy, he says meet me tomorrow in Venice. Business to discuss, confidential matter, whatever. I'm like fine, I guess, but I'm kinda short on cash, so how's that going to work. I'm just walking along the sidewalk having this conversation. And even as I'm saying it this Bentley slides up next to me, and the door opens. Like an idiot I get in, and we're off to LaGuardia where there's a private jet waiting. I mean, how does he even know where I am? How does he know I don't have something important going on that day?"

"Yeah, how would he have ever guessed that." Old habits die hard. Josh didn't catch the irony anyway.

"I know, right?" Clean miss. "Plus there's an overnight bag for me with all these clothes and things in it. Really nice clothes that fit me. And that toothpaste that costs like seven dollars.

"Anyway, I'm supposed to meet the guy on such and such a dock at such and such a time, so I basically do, though the day when good old-fashioned green-and-white American street signs come to this continent will be a merry fuckin' occasion, let me just say. A guy pulls up to the dock in this fancy-pants launch. Not one of your usual Venice craporetto fart-buckets. This thing is sleek. It's like a giant knife made out of wood. Totally soundless. It glides up to the dock, this guy jumps out. He doesn't even tie up, the boat just waits for him.

"And he's a midget. Little person—sorry, little person. But way high-end little person. He's so well dressed you don't even notice he's a little person. He's from this old Venetian family, a marchese of whatever whatever. It takes him about an hour just to say his name.

"But after that things go pretty quick. He says he represents some-body who wants to buy the button. I don't even know how they know about it, but I say who is it. He's all, I can't say. I say, how much, and he's all: one hundred million dollars. And I'm all: two hundred million. Fifty. Two hundred fifty million.

"Right? Check that out! And I want to know who the buyer is. Right? Now who wasted his childhood watching like a million hours of TV? That shit is practically second nature to me.

"So the midget takes out an envelope and inside the envelope is a cashier's check for two hundred and fifty million. It's like he knew what I was going to say. And I'm all, and? And he waves me over with his little stubby fingers. I figured he was going to whisper something in my ear, so I stop and bend down, and he's all, no, and he keeps waving me right up to the edge of the dock, and then he points down into the wa-ter. And this *face* looms up at me.

"It just comes floating up toward the surface of the water. It's enormous—it looks like the front of a truck coming up at me. I practi-cally shit my pants."

"What was it?"

"It was a dragon. There's a dragon that lives in the Grand Canal! That's who bought the button."

Quentin knew about dragons, at least in theory. There weren't many of them, and they mostly lived in rivers, one to a river—they were highly territorial. They hardly ever came out or spoke to anyone. They hardly ever did anything at all, just dreamed away the lifetime of the planet in secret fluvial oblivion. Except one of them had woken up long enough to talk to an aristocratic little person, apparently. And it had bestirred itself to show its face to Josh, and to buy his—their—magic button for two hundred fifty million dollars.

"So we go to the bank, we verify that the check is valid, then we walk back to the dock. I take out the button and hand it to the little guy, who's put on one white glove, Michael Jackson–style. He looks at the button through a jeweler's loupe, then he walks to the edge and chucks it in the water. Just like that. Then he gets in his launch and drives away."

"That is pretty astonishing," Quentin said. It was hard to even be mad about it. Though not impossible.

"Can you believe a dragon bought *our* button?" Josh said. "He knows who we are! Or who I am anyway. I don't even think people knew there was a dragon in the Grand Canal. I mean, it's salt water. You know that, right? It's not actually a river, it's a tidal estuary or whatever. I don't think people know about saltwater dragons!"

"Josh, how would I go about getting in touch with that dragon?"

That brought him up short.

"Well, I don't know. I don't think you can."

"You did."

"He got in touch with me."

"Well, how would you try?"

Josh heaved an exasperated sigh.

"All right, there is this one girl I know who knows a lot about drag-ons. I guess I'd ask her."

"Okay, good. Listen. This is what's going to happen." Quentin focused his will on Josh. Now hear this. He met Josh's gaze and held it. "All due respect to your being king here, but Julia and I are king and queen of Fillory, and we have to get back there. For all intents and purposes we are on a fucking quest here. You are now on the quest team too. I am deputizing you. We have to get back to Fillory, and we don't know how we're going to do it. That's the problem."

Josh considered.

"That's a big problem."

"Yeah, and you're the big fixer. Right? So let's fix it."

He'd give Josh this: maybe he blew their only chance to get back to the secret magical land where Quentin was a king, but he bought a very nice palazzo with the money. It was a glorious, grotesque heap of fifteenth-century marble. The façade on the canal side was white, with its own tidy little dock out front. The interior teemed with curly plasterwork ornaments. Old oil paintings clung to the walls like lichen. Josh had accidentally acquired a minor Canaletto when he bought the place.

It was a serious palace, and it must have taken serious work to get it back on its feet. Josh had replumbed it and rewired it and put in a restaurant-caliber kitchen and done some work below the waterline, shoring up the foundations to keep the whole thing from slumping forward into the canal. He'd done it carefully, too, so that you wouldn't know the place had been touched until you turned on the shower.

And all it had cost was $25 million, plus $10 million more for the renovation. Not that Quentin was a math genius or anything, but he figured that that left Josh with a pretty tidy nest egg. No doubt it would be a great comfort to him during his golden years.

It was all a reminder that Josh had a capable and determined side that really did deserve respect, even though for his own private reasons he worked hard to keep that side hidden most of the time. Now that Quentin looked, really looked, something had changed about Josh. He was more confident. He stood differently. He'd lost weight in the Neitherlands, and he'd kept it off. People changed. Time didn't stand still for you, while you lounged around on cushions in Fillory.

And he could learn something from Josh. Here was somebody who was having a good time. He was doing what he wanted and enjoying himself. He'd been through everything Quentin had been through: he lost the girl he loved, and he nearly died. He didn't sit around moaning and philosophizing about it. He bounced back and set himself up in a palazzo.

Quentin slept like the dead till noon the next day, when he enjoyed a formal breakfast in the dining room. (Josh was exceptionally proud of the table he set. "Over here they use spoons for their jam. Amazing, right? Tiny spoons! It's 'fit for a king'!" Wink, wink.) They were joined by Julia, who kept her sunglasses on and ate only marmite, straight from the jar, which if anything seemed like further proof of her declining humanity.

They were also joined by Poppy, Josh's friend, the one who was supposed to know something about dragons. She was a beanpole, tall and skinny, with wide blue eyes and curly blond hair. Poppy had been to Brakebills as it happened, but only in a postgraduate capacity as a research fellow. She'd learned her magic at a college in Australia, which was where she was from.

Quentin had some idea that Australians were fun-loving and easygoing, and if that was true he could why see Poppy had gotten the hell out of Australia. She had a bright, sharp manner and a quick little voice and a lot of confidence. She was especially confident when it came to pointing out other people's mistakes. Not that she was a know-it-all—it didn't seem to be an ego thing with her. She just assumed that everybody shared her desire for everybody to be clear on everything, and she'd expect you to do the same for her. Apparently at Esquith, which was the Australian magic school in Tasmania, she'd been the academic superstar of her year. This according to Josh, but Poppy didn't contradict him, which if it weren't true would have gone against her error-hating nature.

Poppy was an academic at heart, but she wasn't the ivory tower type. She was into the real world. She was into fieldwork. Specifically she was into dragons.

Quentin supposed it was an extension of the general Australian preoccupation with fatally dangerous animals. Start with saltwater crocodiles and box jellyfish and it was just a hop, skip, and a jump up the food chain before you got to dragons. Poppy knew about as much about them as it was possible to know with actually ever having seen one. She'd followed leads all over the world, and now she'd followed one here. Josh had put out feelers for an expert on the topic, and he'd been very pleased indeed when his expert had turned out to be as good-looking as Poppy was. She'd been there for three weeks, and Josh didn't feel she'd worn out her welcome.

He introduced her as his friend, but given who Josh was, and given Poppy's undeniable prettiness, Quentin didn't think it was uncharitable to assume that Josh was trying to sleep with her or had already slept with her. He was new and improved, but he was still Josh.

Frankly Poppy got on Quentin's nerves a bit, but she was about to come in extremely handy. Josh had yet to give her the full download about the dragon of the Grand Canal. He told Quentin he'd been slow-playing it in an attempt to prolong her visit. But now the moment had arrived. They needed her. Needless to say Poppy was beyond excited. Her wide blue eyes got even wider.

"Well, okay," she said, talking at a runaway clip. "So most of the dragons have a place where you're supposed to be able to jump into their river and they'll notice. They monitor it just in case somebody worth their while wants to talk to them. If they want to talk to you, they'll take you down to where they live. But it's not a well-understood process at all. There are a lot of urban legends around it. Lots of people *say* they've talked to dragons, but it's very hard to verify. Supposedly the Thames dragon wrote most of Pink Floyd's stuff. At least after Syd Barrett left. But there's no way to prove it.

"Traditionally you approach them via the first bridge upstream from the sea, in this case I guess the Accademia. Haven't you guys heard all this stuff? I can't believe you haven't heard about this. Go at midnight. Go to the middle of the bridge. Take a copy of today's newspaper and a nice steak. Wear something nice. And that's it."

"That's it?"

"That's it. And then you jump in. It's all just tradition. I mean, God knows if any of it helps. There's so little data, and so little of it is reliable."

And then you jump in. That was all.

"But it does sometimes work?" Quentin said.

"Sure!" Poppy nodded brightly. "Uh-huh. Some dragons like to talk more than others. The valedictorian of the magic school in Calcutta makes a run at the Ganges dragon every year, and it works about half the time.

"A dragon in the Grand Canal, though. That's new. I mean, really new. I was starting to think you were full of shit." She gave Josh a sharp, reappraising look.

"Starting?" Quentin said.

"So when are you going?"

"Tonight. But listen, do me one favor. Don't tell anybody about this yet."

Poppy frowned prettily, which seemed to the only way she knew how. "Why not?"

"Just give us a week," Quentin said. "That's all I ask. The dragon isn't going anywhere, and I need to get a decent chance with it. If word gets out there's going to be a mob scene."

She thought for a second.

"All right," she said.

Something about the way she said it suggested to Quentin that she might actually keep her promise.

Recovering her high spirits immediately, Poppy addressed herself to her jam and toast. Thin as she was, she ate more than Josh, presumably burning it all in whatever inner furnace kept her at such a pitch of eager excitement all the time.

That left the rest of the day to dispense with. Life at the Palazzo Josh (formerly the Palazzo Barberino, after the sixteenth-century clan that built it and eventually sold it to a dot-com jillionaire, who never set foot in it, and who blew his jillions on Ponzi schemes and a trip to the International Space Station, after which he sold it to Josh) wasn't exactly taxing. He felt disloyal for thinking it, disloyal to Fillory, but he could almost get used to this. The palazzo's comforts were many. You could spend the morning in bed, reading and watching the Venetian light track slowly over an oriental carpet that was so fractally ornate it practically scintillated right there on the floor in front of you. Then there was all of Venice to wander around—the structural spells alone, the titanic bonds that kept the whole place from drowning itself in the lagoon, were a must-see for any tourist of the world's magical wonders.

Then there was the daily late-afternoon spritz. Taken altogether it was enough to make Quentin forget for minutes at a time that once upon a time he used to be the king of a magical otherworld.

Not Julia, though. Not quite. She found him nursing his drink on the *piano nobile* and admiring the cityscape over its heavy stone railing. Together they looked down at the traffic on the canal, much of which consisted of tourists on boats looking up at them and wondering who they were and whether they were famous.

"You like it here," Julia said.

"It's amazing. I'd never even been to Italy before. I had no idea it was like this."

"I lived in France for a while," she said.

"You did? When did you live in France?"

"It was a long time ago."

"Was that where you learned to steal cars?"

"No."

Having brought it up, she didn't seem to want to talk about it.

"It is nice here," she conceded.

"Do you want to stay here?" Quentin asked. "Do you still want to go back to Fillory?"

She set her glass down on the wide marble parapet. More whiskey, still neat. A muscle twinged in her jaw.

"I have to go back. I cannot stay here." Before when she said this she sounded angry and desperate. Now she sounded regretful. "I must keep going. Are you coming with me?"

It made Quentin's heart ache, to hear Julia ask him for something. Anything. She needed his help. People needing him: it was a new feeling. He was starting to like it.

"Of course I am." It was what she'd said when he asked her to come along to the Outer Island.

She nodded, never taking her eyes off the view.

"Thank you."

That night at five minutes to midnight Quentin was remembering that conversation and trying to hold on to that feeling as he loitered on the Ponte dell'Accademia, holding copies of *Il Gazzettino* and the *International Herald Tribune,* just to cover all the bases, and a really great, amazingly expensive raw steak, doing his very best impression of somebody who wasn't about to jump into the Grand Canal.

After the crushing, malodorous heat of the day, the night air was surprisingly frigid. From the point of view of someone who was planning to immerse himself in it, the creamy green water of the Grand Canal looked about as enticing as glacial runoff. It also looked a lot farther away than it had looked from the banks. It also looked clean, which Quentin knew it wasn't.

But somewhere under all that water there was a button. And a dragon. It didn't seem real. He half-suspected Josh of having lost the button in a sofa and making up the story about the dragon because it was less embarrassing.

"This is going to be really wretched, dude," Josh said. "You are not going to be a happy puppy in there."

"No kidding." He'd hoped Josh would offer to do it himself, or go in with him, but no such luck.

"You'll get used to it," Poppy said, hugging herself.

"Why are you here, again?" Quentin said.

"Interests of science. Plus I want to see if you'll actually go through with it."

It was a personal tic of Poppy's that she never seemed to lie when other people would. It was either tactless or admirable, depending on how you looked at it.

Quentin took some deep breaths and leaned against the splintery wooden railing, which still retained some of the fading heat of the sun. Remember what's at stake. Julia wouldn't hesitate. She'd be over the railing like a damn Olympic hurdler. At his request they hadn't told her they were going tonight, but slipped out after she went to bed. She would have insisted on going in.

"They hardly ever eat people," Poppy said. "I mean like twice a century. That we know of."

Quentin didn't respond to this.

"How deep do you think it is?" Josh said. He dragged on a cigarette. Of the three of them he looked the most nervous.

"Twenty feet maybe," Quentin said. "I read it on the Internet."

"Jesus. Well, whatever you do don't dive."

"If I break my neck and end up paralyzed just let me drown."

"Two minutes," Poppy said. An empty vaporetto churned by underneath them, off duty, lights off except for one in the cozy pilot's cabin. That water must be ninety percent *E. coli,* and the rest was probably diesel fuel. This was not a body of water intended for swimming in.

Somebody had carved what might have been a stylized dragon, or just a fancy *s,* into the wood right at the apex of the bridge.

"Are you going to take off your clothes?" Josh asked.

"You don't know how long I've been waiting for you to ask me that."

"Seriously, are you?"

"No."

Poppy said it at the same time he did.

"Seriously," she added.

Their little group fell silent. Somewhere far away glass broke. Beer bottle versus wall. Quentin wondered if he was actually going to do this. Maybe he could just drop a note in. Message in a bottle. Call me.

"Hey, remember when that little person called your cell?" he said. "Did you get his number? Maybe we could just—"

"It was blocked."

"Time!" Poppy said.

"Damn it!"

Just don't think about it. He backed up to the middle of the bridge, scrunched the papers and the bag with the steak in it up in one hand, ran at the railing, and vaulted over it sidewise. He surprised himself by how spryly he did it. Must be the adrenaline. Even so he almost clipped a sticking-out support beam going down.

Some primal instinct caused him to flap his arms and let go of the steak and the papers in midair. They separated from him and disappeared into the night. So much for that. To his left he caught a glimpse of something falling in parallel with him. Somebody—it was Poppy! She was jumping in too.

He hit hard, feetfirst more or less, and went under. His only thought as he went down was to clench or snort out air from all possible orifices to try to avoid taking in any water or other fluids. The canal was freezing and powerfully salty. For an instant he felt relief—it wasn't *that* cold—then his clothes soaked through and turned to frozen lead, and the cold pressed in on him from all sides. He panicked and thrashed—his clothes were too heavy. They were going to drag him under! Then his head broke the surface.

He'd lost a shoe. Poppy surfaced at the same moment a couple of yards away, spitting and blowing, her round face shining pale in the sodium light of the streetlights. He should have been mad at her, but the gonzo jolliness of swimming in the Grand Canal in the middle of the night made him laugh crazily instead.

"What the hell are you doing?" he stage-whispered.

If nothing else the freezing shock had taken away his irritation at her. He had to give her credit for a degree of physical courage he wouldn't have thought she possessed. They were in it together.

"Twice the chances, right? If there's two of us?" She was grinning a loony grin too. She lived for this shit. "I was wrong, we should have taken our clothes off."

He treaded water. It took about thirty seconds before he was exhausted and shivering uncontrollably. The current was sweeping them under the bridge—not the current, the tide, it must be, he reminded himself, since the canal wasn't really a river. Jesus, there could be sharks in this bitch. Somebody yelled at them from the bank, in Italian. He hoped it wasn't a cop.

Quentin peed in his pants and felt warmer for ten seconds, then even colder afterward. He tried not to think of what PCBs and other industrial toxins must be leaching their way into him upstream. From down here the canal looked enormous, the banks miles away. How did he get here, so far from where he started? How had he gone so far off track? He felt like he would never claw his way back to where he should be, back onto his cozy throne. A wavelet popped up out of nowhere and slapped him in the face. He was ready to call it a night. At least he could say he tried.

"How long are we supposed to wait?" he asked Poppy.

Just then an iron handcuff locked around his ankle and jerked him under.

He should have died right then. Surprise made him blurt out all his air in one heave, and he went down with his lungs completely empty.

But there was a spell in effect to keep him alive. It was obviously something the dragon had developed over many years for the comfort of its human visitors. It was comprehensive. It was user-friendly. It had the feel of magic finely milled by long centuries of use and cast by a past-master with wings and a tail. Quentin wasn't going to die. Or at least not by accident.

In fact he felt warm, for the first time in what seemed like hours, and he could see clearly, if dimly, which he shouldn't have been able to do. He was breathing the water. It wasn't quite like breathing air—it had more heft to it, more push and shove was required to get it in and out of his chest—but it got the job done. Oxygen continued to reach his brain. He heaved it in and out gratefully, in big gulps. He felt relaxed. Somebody was taking care of him. He was flying first-class.

Quentin had always had reservations about dragons, the real ones anyway, the ones that actually existed. He'd been raised on the tradition of high-flying, gold-hoarding, fire-breathing dragons. Beowulf dragons, Tolkien dragons, Dungeons & Dragons dragons. The news that real dragons lived in rivers, and didn't go thundering around the countryside setting trees on fire, had come as a disappointment to him. River dragons sounded colder and slimier and more newtlike than what he'd been hoping for.

So he was happy to see that the dragon that had hold of his ankle with its short but powerful right forelimb, drawing him down and placing him gently on the canal floor, like a puppy to whom it was saying "stay," was thoroughly, almost quintessentially draconian. It looked sinister and coldly calculating and like it could eat him without noticing, but it was canonical. Its massive saurian head was the size of a compact car. Its eyes flashed silver when you caught them at the right angle. Its scales were a delicate watery green. Having settled him on the soft sand, the dragon of the Grand Canal released him and crouched down in a catlike pose, resting its head on the tip of its tail. Its vast body humped up in the dimness behind it.

Quentin sneezed. His sinuses had flooded with filthy water when the dragon yanked him down, but the water around him now was clean. He was enclosed, with the dragon, in a quiet green-black dome of water. The canal bed, which should have been a swamp of trash and scrap metal and sewage, was smooth. The dragon kept its patch of sand well tended.

Quentin sat cross-legged. It was just the two of them; the dragon hadn't taken Poppy, apparently. Quentin was having a little trouble not floating away, but he found something round and heavy next to him—an old cannonball, maybe—and settled it in his lap to hold him down.

He let a minute go by, but the dragon didn't talk. All right. Game on.

"Hello," Quentin said. His voice sounded basically normal. Just distant, as if he were eavesdropping on himself from another room. "Thank you for seeing me."

The huge face didn't move. It was as unreadable as a skull. Though there went the eyes, flashing again.

"Probably you know why I came here. I want to talk to you about the button, the one you bought from my friend Josh." He felt like a kid asking the school bully for his lunch money back. He straightened his spine. "The thing is, it wasn't entirely his to sell. It also belonged to me, and some other people, and we need it. I need it to get back to my home, and my friend Julia does too."

"I know."

The dragon's voice was like some vast string instrument two levels below double bass. An octuple bass maybe, playing a perfect fifth. He felt the vibrations in his ribs and in his balls.

"Will you help us? Will you give us back the button? Or sell it back to us?"

The rest of the canal was a solid wall of darkness around them. There was a distant rumble, and Quentin risked a glance up: a late-night barge was thundering by overhead. It felt like the water was getting chillier, or maybe he was cooling off. He scooched a little closer to the dragon, who was giving off heat. If it was going to eat him it was going to eat him, and at least he'd die warm.

"No," came the reply.

The dragon's eyes closed and opened.

The door back to Fillory was shutting. He had to stick his foot in it. That world, the world of his real life, the life he was supposed to be living, was drifting away, or he was drifting away from it. The moorings had been cut, and the tide was flowing out. They never should have gone to After Island. They never should have left Castle Whitespire.

"Maybe you could loan it to us?" He willed the desperation out of his voice. "A one-time trip. If there's anything I have that you want, I'm offering it. I'm a king, in Fillory at least. I have a lot of resources there."

"I did not bring you here to listen to you boast."

"I'm not—"

"I have lived in this canal for ten centuries. Everything that enters it is mine. I have swords and crowns. I have popes and saints and kings and queens. I have brides on their wedding day and children on Christmas. I have the Holy Lance and the noose that hung Judas. I have every lost thing."

Fair enough. Quentin wondered if Byron had ever been down here. If he had, he probably thought of something clever to say.

"Okay. All right. But I don't understand, why did you bring me here if you don't want to sell me back the button?"

The dragon's pupils widened until they were almost a foot across, and it seemed to come awake and really notice him for the first time. Its head lifted off its tail. He was close enough that it had to go slightly cross-eyed to focus on him. Now that Quentin's eyes had adjusted to the dark he could make out the big scales on the dragon's back. They looked as thick as encyclopedias, and a few of them had things carved into them, sigils and pictograms that Quentin didn't recognize.

"You will not speak again, human, except to thank me," the dragon said. **"You wish to be a hero, but you do not know what a hero is. You think a hero is one who wins. But a hero must be prepared to lose, Quentin. Are you? Are you prepared to lose everything?"**

"I've already lost everything," he said.

"Oh, no. You have so much more left to lose."

The dragon was a lot scoldier than he expected. And disappointingly cryptic. Somehow in the back of his mind he'd vaguely thought that the dragon might want to be his friend, and they would fly around the world solving mysteries together. The chances of that happening now looked vanishingly small. He waited. Maybe the dragon would give him something they could use.

"The old gods are returning to take back what is theirs. I will play my part. Best you prepare to play yours."

"That sounds like a good idea, but how exactly—"

"You will not speak. The button is useless to you. The Neitherlands are closed. But the first door is still open. It always has been."

Quentin's knees suddenly felt stiff from sitting cross-legged. He wanted to spit the salt water out of his mouth, but there was nothing but more salt water to spit into. The dragon whipped its tail out from under its chin, back into the darkness, slashing up a cloud of silt.

"You may thank me now."

Wait, what? Quentin opened his mouth to speak—to thank the Dragon of the Grand Canal like a good boy, or to ask him what he meant, or tell him to fuck off for talking in riddles, he would never know, because he choked instead. He couldn't breathe. The spell was gone, and he was gagging on filthy, freezing canal water. He was drowning.

He left his one remaining shoe stuck in the mud and kicked his way crazily up toward the surface.

CHAPTER 15

O h, the return of the prodigal! The rapture with which Julia was received back into the domestic fold! The blurry, beaming faces of her parents, a pair of rain-soaked headlights trained upon her, as she presented herself to them in the form of a reprobate reformed. She had disappointed them so many times, in so many ways, they hardly dared to hope anymore. They'd been through so many stages of grief they'd lost count.

Now here she was, returned from Chesterton, her spirit crushed, ready to be part of the family again, and they let her. They actually let her. With a kindness utterly unlike anything she recognized in herself, they took her back, even though she could not have deserved it less. The wreck of the good ship Julia, out of Brooklyn, carrying the precious cargo of Their Love, was ready to be hauled off the Reef of Life and salvaged and refloated, and they did it. They took her back without a word of reproach.

Now it was Julia's turn to grieve, and they let her, which was another gift. She mourned her lost life, and she mourned the death of the magician she would never be. She buried that mighty sorceress with full honors. And with the grief, unbidden, came its ghostly golden cousin, relief. She had been trying so hard, for so long, to be something the world did not want her to be. Now she could finally stop. The world had won. She yielded to her family's embraces, and she was grateful for them. What was so great about magic anyway, compared to love? Seriously, what?

Oh, the timorous overtures of her sister, the humanist! By now she was a senior in high school herself. As she labored over her college applications, Julia reactivated her own. They worked on them together, side by side at the kitchen table, swapping tips, her sister coaching her on her essay, Julia dragging her sister through basic calculus by main force. They were a team again, the two of them. Julia had forgotten what it felt like to be part of a family. She'd forgotten how good it could feel, and how much she needed it.

Of Julia's legendary seven acceptances, only Stanford's could be salvaged, but that was enough. There was a gap or three in her résumé, sure, but if you cocked your head and blurred your eyes you could take her magical research for some sort of worthy independent ethnographic project. So it was sunny California for her. Just what she needed. Fun in the sun. Put some color in her cheeks. She'd spend a year saving up cash and matriculate in the fall. It was all arranged.

Because Julia had given up. She was packing it in. She washed her hands of the realms invisible that had so thoroughly washed their hands of her. She would take a page from the holy book of those child-raping utopian socialists she'd written about for Mr. Karras: when your sacred intentional community collapses, it's time to suck it up and sell silverware instead.

Julia would take a page from Jack Donne. At the end of the poem, hadn't he run to the Goat (by which he meant the constellation Capricorn, a footnote gallantly informed her) to find New Love? Or was it lust? Or maybe it turned out it was too late for him. Maybe that was somebody else. That poem was pretty fucking unintelligible. Anyway it had a happy ending. Ish.

She still had her bad days, no question, when the black dog of depression sniffed her out and settled its crushing weight on her chest and breathed its pungent dog breath in her face. On those days she called in sick to the IT shop where, most days, she untangled tangled networks for a song. On those days she pulled down the shades and ran dark for twelve or twenty-four or seventy-two hours, however long it took for the black dog to go on home to its dark master.

She couldn't go back, she knew that now. The magic kingdom was closed to her. But some days she couldn't see a way forward either.

She always righted herself in the end, with the help of a dandy cat-eyed new shrink, a woman this time, and her dandy 450 milligrams of Wellbutrin and 30 milligrams of Lexapro daily, and her dandy new online support group for the depressed.

Actually the support group really was pretty dandy. It was something special. It was founded by a woman who'd worked successively at Apple, and then Microsoft, and then Google. She blazed a glittering arc in the firmament at each firm for about four or five years, piling up tranches of stock options, before she rolled neurochemical snake eyes and a bout of clinical depression knocked her out of the sky. By the time Google was done with her she was forty-four and had her fuck-you money in the bank. So she retired early and started Free Trader Beowulf instead.

Free Trader Beowulf—you had to be at least forty and a recovering pen-and-paper role-playing-gamer to get the reference, but it was apt. Google it. FTB was an online support group for depressed people. But not your common run of depressed person. Oh, no.

To get in the door you first had to show them your prescriptions. They wanted credentials, solid ones. A bunch of nerds like this, they didn't want to hear your whining, and they didn't want to read your poems—sorry, Jack—or look at your doomy watercolors. This crowd wasn't soft-core. If you were depressed, they wanted to see the hard stuff, a diagnosis from an actual psychiatrist and hard-core chemical-on-neuron action. And if you were rocking double-neurochemical-penetration, like Julia was, all the better.

If that all worked out, then they sent you a video invitation. It was meaningless in itself, a red herring, just a bunch of new-agey platitudes delivered by a sympathetic hippie-type actor. But buried in it, for those who thought to look, was a clue: a single frame of what looked like white noise but which turned out to be hard data. The black-and-white pixels stood for ones and zeros that, when laid end to end, formed a sound file. The audio was of somebody speaking the phone number of an old-school dial-up BBS, which when you called it up, frog-marched you through a pretty chunky series of pure math problems, which if you solved them in six hours or less yielded a sequence of numbers that turned out to be Ulam numbers, Ulam being the password to the Web site at the IP address they gave you if you beat the test, where there was a Flash game that made absolutely no sense unless you could think in four spatial dimensions, but if you could you got a pair of GPS coordinates in South Dakota that turned out to be a geo-caching site from which you could recover a grotesquely complicated three-dimensional wooden puzzle, inside of which was etc. etc. etc.

All good clean all-American fun. A childless, clinically depressed, forty-four-year-old retiree with a genius IQ and an eight-figure bank account had nothing if not time on her hands. It was obnoxious, but nobody was twisting Julia's arm, and she had time on her hands too, as it happened. It took Julia three weeks to work her way through the intellectual obstacle course—she would've liked to see Quentin try it—but at the end of it all she recovered, on the strength of many quarters, a plastic bubble from the claw machine in a neglected video arcade on the Jersey Shore. The bubble contained a flash drive. The flash drive contained the real invitation. No tricks this time. She was in.

Free Trader Beowulf had fourteen members, and Julia made it fifteen. It was only a message board, but it felt more like home than anything had since the two hours Julia had spent at Brakebills four years earlier. The people in FTB got her. She didn't have to explain herself. They understood her gallows humor and her *Gödel, Escher, Bach* references, her sudden rages and her long silences. She picked up their arcane in-jokes and running gags pretty quickly. Her whole life she'd felt like the last living member of a lost Amazonian tribe, speaking her own extinct dialect, but here, finally, was her ethnic group. They were a bunch of depressed, overeducated shut-ins, but they seemed human to her. Or maybe not human, but whatever Julia was, they were too.

References to real life were tacitly discouraged on FTB. You didn't use real names. In most cases she had only the vaguest sense of where the other members lived or what they did for a living, whether they were married or in a few cases even what gender they were. As far as Julia knew they never met in person. FTB just wasn't a meatspace thing. Outing another member's real-world identity was an offense punishable by expulsion, or it would have been if it ever happened, but it never did. Welcome to Facelessbook: an antisocial network.

That spring was the happiest time Julia had lived through since her old life ended. She chattered away to the Free Traders all day every day. They hung around her in an invisible crowd, bantering and kibitzing on her work projects. She typed while she ate her breakfast. She typed walking down the street. The last thing she saw before she fell asleep was the Free Trader app on her smartphone on the pillow next to her, and it was the first thing she saw when she opened her eyes in the morning. She opened herself up to them in a way she never had to anyone: no irony, no caveats, no regrets. She poured out her broken heart to the Free Traders, and they took it and cleaned it up and fixed it up and gave it back to her fresh and bloody and pumping again.

She never said a thing about Brakebills—that would have been beyond the pale even for FTB—but she found to her relief that she didn't really have to. Whatever was wrong, the details didn't matter. It was enough for them to know that there was an enormous piece missing from her world, and they understood what that felt like because they were missing pieces too. Didn't matter what shape it was. Julia wouldn't have been surprised to learn that there were a few Brakebills also-rans among the Free Traders. But she never asked.

She had warm feelings for all the Free Traders, but inevitably there were a few with whom she formed tighter bonds: a little clique, a circle within the circle, comprising herself and three others. Failstaff, a gentle poster whose cultural references put him three or four decades older than Julia; Pouncy Silverkitten, whose acid sarcasm was extreme even for FTB, but who chose his targets humanely, mostly; and Asmodeus, who understood Julia's feelings with telepathic completeness, and whose facility with theoretical physics was so extraordinary, she seemed to be posting from somewhere off-planet.

Julia posted as ViciousCirce. They'd been a trio before she came along, but they were happy to accept her as one of them, and to make their never-ending conversations four-handed.

It was acceptable on FTB to take a thread private, if all parties agreed, and once in a while she and Asmo and Pouncy and Failstaff would recede into their own highly abstract world together. In those private threads they would get a little more concrete about their personal lives, though it was still considered gauche to drop any geo-specific details. That became part of the game, keeping their identities obscure, and another part of the game was constructing elaborate fictional biographies and résumés for each other. Julia did an FBI serial killer profile for each of the other three, complete with police sketches.

Another game they were fond of was called Series. It was simple: somebody would provide three words, or three numbers, or names, or molecules, or shapes, or whatever. Those were the first three terms in the series. Then you had to figure out what the next term in the series was, and what principle generated it. You wanted to make your series maximally difficult but still theoretically solvable, while also making sure there was only one possible solution, i.e., only one guiding principle that could be extrapolated from the three examples. Once the solution was cracked, second prize went to the first person who could iterate the series ten times.

FTB took over her life, and she let it. Sometimes even when she was offline it was as if FTB was running by itself in her head—her brain had spent so much time with these invisible personalities that they'd calved off little clones of themselves in her brain, pirate software versions of Asmo and Pouncy and Failstaff and all the others, that ran on Julia's hardware. She wasn't demented—she wasn't!—it was just a game she played with herself. It was a little insane, but hey, whatever got you through, right? And everything else was going fine. She'd gained weight, stopped scratching herself, barely even bit her cuticles anymore. She hadn't done the rainbow spell in ages. She knew she was obsessed, but it was turning out that she was the kind of person who needed to be obsessed with something, and she could have done a lot worse. God knows she had before.

She figured, let the fever run its course. It would break, and the patient would wake up clammy but clearheaded, and the fever dreams would fade. She'd head off to Stanford in the fall, get a new life, get some real-world, visible, analog friends. Wipe the slate clean.

But first she'd give it its head, let it run a little. Which is how Julia found herself late on a weekend afternoon in March wandering through Prospect Heights toward Bed-Stuy. She'd become a prodigious walker of late, because she needed some kind of exercise, and exposure to sunlight improved her mood. And she could take the Free Traders with her, not only in their capacity as spectral presences in her brain but as actual presences on her smartphone, for which Failstaff had ginned up a clever little app. (No iPhones, natch, Android only. The Free Traders were huge open-source snobs.) She strode the earth clad in the invisible armor of their virtual companionship.

Julia typed as she walked; she had developed a great facility in doing this, using her peripheral vision to weave around fire hydrants and dog-shit land mines and other pedestrians. A key part of successfully being Julia, it seemed, was not giving a shit if you looked weird. Today she half-listened via the app's text-to-speech feature while Pouncy and Asmodeus went back and forth on the validity of Hofstadter's strange-loop theory of consciousness as derived from Gödel numbers, or something like that.

The other half of her consciousness, Hofstadterian or no, was deployed in looking at the front doors of the houses she passed. Specifically she was looking at the way they were divided up into square and rectangular panels of different sizes. Most of them were anyway. This was not on the face of it an overwhelmingly interesting activity; in fact she would have been hard-pressed to explain to anybody exactly why she was doing it. It was just that the doors had begun to remind her of a game of Series they'd played the other day.

Pouncy had offered up a geometrical puzzle, painstakingly executed in ASCII characters, consisting of simple patterns of squares on a small grid. It had turned out—Failstaff nailed it—that the patterns could be understood as successive states of a very simple cellular automaton, so simple that they could nut out the rules in their heads once they had the general idea. Or Failstaff could anyway.

The funny thing was, Julia fancied that as she walked she could spot sequences from the series in the different configurations of the doors she was passing. It seemed like if she kept going long enough she could always find the next term.

It was just a goofy mental exercise. Sometimes the pattern was in wood, sometimes in glass, or a wrought-iron gate. Once it was in cinder blocks in a blocked-up window, which was cheating, but it was weird how often she found it. She started setting rules for herself—she would stop walking if it took her more than a block to find the next term in the series, then it had to be within a block and on the same side of the street, and so on—but the right pattern always turned up just in time. She wasn't sure if this was a significant discovery or not, but she felt a compulsion to see how long she could keep it going. She could imagine the acidity of the sarcasm Pouncy would slather all over her if she told the others what she was doing. It would be seriously corrosive, pH 0 sarcasm.

It was all working out very neatly though. The only difference between her and Pouncy's cellular automata was that hers was running backward—the rules were being applied in reverse, so it was winding back down to its initial state. That was another reason she kept walking: the series was finite. It would be over soon, whatever happened. Once she got lost for a block, but then she realized she'd munged the transformation, and once she fixed it then sure enough, there it was, an old wooden door with inset panels, three of them slightly lighter in color to pick out the right configuration. It was a will-o'-the-wisp leading her onward, farther into the perilous marsh of Bed-Stuy, deeper into a dreamlike, hypnagogic state.

A small but vigilant sector of Julia's brain wasn't that stoked about how far into Bed-Stuy she was getting. Row houses were giving way to vacant lots and chop shops and half-built apartment houses that the recession had killed off before they were finished. She had about an hour before dark, and it was no longer possible to tell herself that some of the houses were boarded up because they were undergoing very ambitious gut renovations, because those houses weren't being renovated, they were crack houses. But it wouldn't be long before she found the door that corresponded to Pouncy's starting configuration, and then the series would be at an end—which is to say, at its beginning—and she could turn around and head back to Park Slope.

And sure enough, just past Throop (pronounced "troop") Avenue, there it was. It was not a pretty house, but it wasn't a crack house, either. It was a two-story lime-green clapboard house with an antique rabbit-ears antenna on top and a surly gang of aluminum garbage cans in the cracked cement yard out front. The front door was an eight-paned glass affair. One pane, the top left corner, had been punched out and plastic-wrapped, thereby completing the series.

And that was that. It was finished. The sight of that final pattern, the initial state, released Julia from the spell. The dream logic had iterated itself out. She looked around like a sleepwalker awakened, wondering where the hell she was, exactly. Somebody was still babbling in her ear in a computer-generated voice about Hofstadter. Exhaustion broke over her in a wave. She must have walked for miles, and the sun was setting. She sat down on the stoop.

She needed a ride home. A car service would be expensive, but being mugged and/or assaulted would be even more expensive. Plus she felt like she would literally drop in her tracks if she had to take another step. She killed the FTB app and took out her earbuds, and the voices died away. Silence. Reality.

Behind her she heard the door open. She got up again and held up a hand—okay, okay, she was going. She didn't suppose that a lecture on cellular automata would really pass for an excuse for trespassing with the residents of some random lime-green shitbox house on Throop Avenue.

But the guy in the door wasn't shooing her away. He was a white guy, owlish-looking, maybe thirty, in a vintage blazer and jeans and an insta-annoying porkpie hat.

He just looked at her, assessing. Behind him she could see other people in the house, sitting and standing, chatting and moping, and doing things with their hands. Only they didn't have anything in their hands. A weird acid-green light flared for a second in the doorway, from somewhere she couldn't see, like there was welding going on in there. Somebody gave an ironic cheer. The air absolutely reeked of magic. You could barely breathe, it was so thick.

Julia squatted down on her haunches on the sidewalk, like a toddler, and put her head in her hands and laughed and cried at the same time. She felt like she was going to pass out or throw up or go insane. She had tried to walk away from the disaster, to run away from it, she really, truly had. She'd broken her staff and drowned her book and sworn off magic forever. She'd moved on and left no forwarding address. But it hadn't been enough. Magic had come looking for her. She hadn't run far enough or fast enough, or hid herself well enough, and the disaster had tracked her down and it had found her. It wasn't going to let her go.

It was about to start all over again.

CHAPTER 16

During everything that followed, all the time while he nearly got creamed by a vaporetto as he swam to shore, while he dragged himself up some ancient stone steps out of the water (the Grand Canal was well-appointed with means of egress for those who fell or flung themselves into it) and trudged back to Josh's palazzo alone—Josh having had his hands full keeping Poppy out of the clutches of the carabinieri, who showed up shortly after Quentin went under—Quentin's mind was on fire with the only piece of useful information the dragon had given him: that there was still a way back to Fillory. They weren't going to get the button, but he could let go of that now, because there was a way back. If they could just figure out what the dragon meant.

He thought about it while he rinsed off salt and oil and heavy-metal particles and worse in a half-hour shower at high temperature and high pressure and washed his hair three times and dried off and finally tossed his ruined clothes, his beloved Fillorian clothes, his royal clothes, into the trash and crawled into bed. The first door, the dragon had said. The first door. The first door. What did it mean?

Of course there were other words in there to think about. There was a lot to take away from that brief conversation. The old gods were returning. Something about being a hero. All definitely important. Of paramount importance. But the first door: that was the action item. He had the scent. He was going to do it, he was going to follow the clues, and get them out of here and back where they belonged. He was going to be a hero, damn it all, whatever the dragon said. He would lose whatever he had to lose, if that's what it took to win.

Poppy woke him up the next morning at seven. It was like Christmas morning for her. She was just so excited, and she'd waited as long as she could. She wasn't even jealous. She'd already had three cappuccinos, and she'd brought him one. Australians. He thought she was going to start bouncing on his bed.

They all worked through the possibilities together over breakfast.

"The first door," Josh said. "So it's some primal, like, door. Like Stonehenge."

"Stonehenge is a calendar," Poppy said. "It's not a door."

In the course of general orientation Poppy had almost incidentally been brought up to speed on the existence of Fillory. Irritatingly, she took it in stride, the way she did everything else. She was interested in it from an intellectual point of view. She assimilated the information. But it didn't set her imagination burning the way it had Quentin's.

"Maybe it's like a time-lock. Like on a vault."

"Dude!" Quentin said. "Forget Stonehenge! It must be something in Venice, like a sea-gate or something."

"Venice is a port. That's a kind of door. A portal. The whole city is a door."

"Yeah, but the first?"

"Or it's a metaphorical door," Poppy said. "The Bible or something. Like in Dan Brown."

"You know, I bet it's something about the pyramids," Josh said.

"It means the Chatwins' house," Julia said.

The conversation stopped.

"What do you mean?" Poppy said.

"Their aunt's house. In Cornwall. Where they discovered Fillory. That was the first door."

It was nice to see Poppy beaten to the punch for once.

"But how do you know?" Poppy asked.

"I know," Julia said. Quentin hoped that she wouldn't say what she was about to say next, but she said it anyway. "I can feel it."

"What do you mean, feel it?" Poppy said.

"Why do you care?" Julia said.

"Because I'm curious."

Quentin intervened. Julia seemed to have taken an instinctive, prickly dislike to Poppy.

"It makes sense. What's the first way people got into Fillory? Through the Chatwins' house. The clock in the back hall."

"I don't know," Josh said. He rubbed his round stubbly chin. "I thought you could never get in the same way twice. And anyway, Martin Chatwin was a little kid. That's fine for him, but no way I could fit through the door of a grandfather clock. Not even you could."

"All right," Quentin said. "Sure, but—"

"Plus it was supposed to be a personal invitation, specific to the Chatwins," Josh went on. "Like, those particular kids were particularly awesome in some way, so Ember summoned them so they could use their awesome personal qualities to fix shit in Fillory."

"We have awesome personal qualities," Quentin said. "I think we should go. It's our best lead."

"I am going," Julia said.

"Road trip!" Josh said, turning on a dime.

"All right." It felt good to be making decisions anyway, whatever they were based on. It felt good to get moving again. "We'll go tomorrow morning. Unless anybody has a better idea before then."

It was getting increasingly hard to not notice that Poppy was helpless with laughter.

"I'm sorry!" she said. "I really am. It's just that—I mean, I know it's real, or I mean I guess it's real, but you do realize that this is a kids' thing? Fillory? It's like you're worried about how to get to Candy Land! Or I don't know, Smurftown."

Julia got up and left. She didn't even bother to get annoyed. She took Fillory seriously, and she had no patience for, and no interest in, anyone who didn't. He hadn't noticed till now, but Julia could be pretty unpleasant when she wanted to be.

"You think Candy Land is real?" Josh said. "'Cause I would ditch Fillory in a red-hot minute for that shit. Chocolate Swamp and all. And have you *seen* Princess Frostine?"

"Maybe it's not real to you," Quentin said, a little stiffly. "It's just that it's very real to us. Or to me anyway. It's where I live. It's my home."

"I know, I know! I'm sorry. I really am." Poppy wiped her eyes. "I'm sorry. Maybe you just have to see it."

"Maybe you do."

But, Quentin thought, you probably never will.

The next day they all went to Cornwall.

That's where the Chatwins' house was: the house where in 1917 the Chatwin children went to stay with their aunt Maude, and met Christopher Plover, and found their way into Fillory, and the whole magnificent, wretched story began. It was incredible that the house still existed, and had been sitting there all this time, and that you could just *go* there.

But in a way it was incredible that he hadn't been there already. The Chatwin house wasn't open to the public, but its general whereabouts weren't a secret. It was a matter of historical-slash-Wikipedian record. Nobody had torn it down. It's not like somebody was going to stop them, other than possibly the current owners and the local constabulary. It was about time he went there, if only to pay his respects at what was basically the Trinity test site of the Fillorian mythos.

As far as getting there went, Josh swore up and down that he'd been doing serious work with opening portals lately, and he was pretty sure he could get one through to Cornwall. Quentin asked Josh where he thought Cornwall was, then immediately rephrased and said he would give Josh a hundred dollars if he could tell him whether Cornwall was in England, Ireland, or Scotland. Smelling a trick question, Josh went nonlinear and guessed Canada.

But when Quentin actually showed Josh where it was on a map, way down at the southwestern tip of England, Josh redoubled his swearing—that shit's practically next door! it's in *Europe*—and went into a very technically sophisticated disquisition on lines of magnetic force and astral folding. It really was time Quentin got out of the habit of underestimating him.

Poppy said she wanted to come too.

"I've never been to Cornwall," she said. "I've always wanted to meet a native speaker."

"Of English?" Josh said. "Because you know, I can probably introduce you."

"Of Cornish, jackass. It's a Brythonic language. Meaning it's indigenous to Britain, like Welsh and Breton. And Pictish. Before everything was polluted by the Anglo-Saxons and the Normans. There's tons of power in those old languages. Cornish died out a couple hundred years ago, but there's a big revival happening now. Where are we going exactly?"

They were still sitting around the breakfast table, which over the course of the morning had become the lunch table. Espresso cups and wobbly towers of plates and silverware had been transferred to the floor to make room for a massive atlas Josh retrieved from the library, along with the Fillory books and a biography of Christopher Plover.

"It's called Fowey," Quentin said. "It's on the south coast."

"Hm," Poppy said. She put a fingertip on the map. "We could come in through Penzance. It's a couple of hours' drive from there, tops."

"Penzance?" Josh said. "Like as in the pirates of? Since when is that a real place?"

"See, okay, I want to say something about this," Poppy said. She pushed the atlas away and sat back in her chair. "If I could have the floor for just a moment. Yes, Penzance is a real place. It's a town. It's in Cornwall. And it's real, as in it exists on Earth. You're all so obsessed with other worlds, you're so convinced that this one is crap and everywhere else is great, but you've never bothered to figure out what's going on here! I mean, forget Penzance, Tintagel is real!"

"Is that—didn't King Arthur live there?" Quentin said weakly.

"King Arthur *lived* in Camelot. But he was conceived at Tintagel, supposedly. It's a castle in Cornwall."

"Fuck it," Josh said. "Poppy's right, let's go there."

It was amazing. Quentin had never met a magician like Poppy. How could someone so utterly literal-minded, so resolutely uninterested in anything beyond mundane reality, work magic?

"Yes, but you see," he said, "the fact is, King Arthur probably wasn't conceived at Tintagel. Because he probably didn't exist. Or if he did exist he was probably some depressing Pictish warlord who was always killing people and breaking them on the wheel and raping their widows. He probably died of the plague at thirty-two. See, that's my problem with this world, if you really want to know. I'm pretty sure that when you say that King Arthur was 'real,' you don't mean King Arthur like in the books. You don't actually mean the good King Arthur.

"Whereas, in Fillory—and feel free to find this hilarious, Poppy, but it's true—there are actual real kings who aren't bullshit. And I'm one of them. Plus there are unicorns and pegasi and elves and dwarves and all that."

He could have added that some very bad things were real in Fillory that weren't real here. But that wouldn't have strengthened his argument.

"There are not elves," Julia said.

"Whatever! That's not the point! The point is, I could pretend I don't have a choice, and just live here my whole life. I could even go live in Tintagel. But I do have a choice, and I only have one life, and if it's all right with you I'm going to spend it in Fillory, in my castle, chilling with dwarves and sleeping on pegasus feathers."

"Because it's easier," Poppy said. "And why not do the easiest possible thing? Because isn't that always the best thing?"

"Yes, why not? Why not?"

Quentin had absolutely no idea why Poppy aggravated him so much, and so efficiently, with such great precision. And he didn't know why he sounded so much like Benedict right now either.

"All right already," Josh said. "Stop. You live here. You live in Fillory. Everybody's happy."

"Sure," Poppy chirped.

God, Quentin thought. It's like Janet all over again.

They assembled two hours later in the narrow street behind the palazzo. The building was too heavily warded to cast a portal inside it.

"I thought maybe we could do it down there." Josh peered doubtfully down the street. "There's one of those tiny Venetian micro-alleys down there. Nobody ever uses it."

Nobody else had a better suggestion. Quentin felt shifty—it was like they were looking for a place to shoot up, or have sex outside. Josh led them twenty yards down the street, which itself wasn't much more than an alley, then cut left into a gap between buildings. There was barely room for two people to walk next to each other. At the end of the alley was a bright ribbon of water and sunlight: the Grand Canal. It was deserted, but Josh hadn't been completely right about nobody ever using the alley, because somebody had definitely used it as a urinal not too long ago.

It reminded Quentin of when he used to catch a portal back to Brakebills at the end of summer. Usually they'd send him down some random local alley and put the portal at the end. The thought of it ignited a hot coal of nostalgia in his chest, for a time when he didn't know better.

"Let me just see how much of this I remember . . ."

Josh pulled a crumpled piece of paper out of his pocket, on which he'd scribbled neat columns of coordinates and vectors. Poppy, who was taller than him, kibitzed over his shoulder.

"See, it's not direct," he said, "but there's a junction you can use, it's out in the English Channel somewhere."

"Why don't you go through Belfast?" Poppy said. "Everybody does. Then you double back south. It's actually shorter in astral geometry."

"Nah, nah." Josh squinted at his writing. "This is way more elegant. You'll see."

"I'm just saying, if you miss the junction and we go in the water, it's a long swim to Guernsey . . ."

Josh stuffed the paper in his back pocket and squared off into his spellcasting stance. He spoke the words quietly and clearly, without hurrying. With a lot more confidence than Quentin ever remembered him having, he made a series of symmetrical movements with his arms, shifting his fingers rapidly through different positions. Then he squared his shoulders, bent his knees, and hooked his fingers firmly underhand into the air, like he was preparing to haul open an especially heavy garage door.

Sparks flew. Poppy yipped in surprise and stepped back in a hurry.

Josh straightened his back and heaved upward. Reality cracked, and the crack slowly widened revealing behind it something else—green grass and brighter, whiter sunlight. When the portal was halfway open Josh stopped and shook out his hands, which smoked. He outlined the top of the doorway with his fingers, then the sides—one side wasn't quite straight, and he accidentally snipped off some of the alley wall. Then he got under it again and pulled and pushed it open the rest of the way.

Quentin kept glancing at the mouth of the alley while all this was going on. He heard voices, but nobody walked by. Josh stopped to check his work. Now in the middle of the bright Venetian afternoon there stood a rectangle of cooler, somehow higher-definition English noon. Josh bunched his sleeve in his fist and rubbed off a last smudge of Venice.

"All right?" he said. "Pretty good?" His pants were scored with pin-hole burns from the sparks.

Everyone had to admit it looked pretty good.

They stepped through, one by one, gingerly—the bottom of the doorway wasn't quite flush with the pavement, and you could shear off toes on the edge if you weren't careful. But the connection was tight, with no sensation as you went through. It was a totally other level of workmanship, Quentin thought with satisfaction, from the crude portals they'd gone through between the safe houses.

They had skipped Penzance after all, as well as Belfast: Josh brought them out in a public park not far from the center of Fowey. This kind of precision over that much distance hadn't been possible even a few years ago, but Google Street View was an absolute boon to the art and craft of creating long-distance portals. Josh went through last and scrubbed it out behind them.

Quentin didn't think he'd ever seen anywhere as quintessentially English-looking as Fowey. Or maybe he meant Cornish-looking, he wasn't sure what the difference was. Poppy would know. Either way it was a small town at the mouth of a river that was also called Fowey, and Beatrix Potter could have drawn it. The air was cool and fresh after the summer fug of Venice. The streets were narrow and winding and shin-splintingly steep. The sheer volume of floral window boxes overhead almost blocked out the sun.

At the little office of tourism in the center of town they learned that the various Foweys were all pronounced "Foy," and that even aside from Christopher Plover the town was something of a hotbed of fictional settings. Manderley from *Rebecca* was supposed to be nearby, as was Toad Hall from *The Wind in the Willows*. Plover's house was a few miles out of town. The National Trust owned it now; it was enormous, and some days it was open to tourists. The Chatwins' house was privately owned, and not on any tourist maps, but it couldn't be far away. According to legend, and all the biographies, it abutted Plover's property directly.

They sat on a bench in the thin English sunlight, like clarified butter, while Poppy went off to rent a car—she was the only one of them who carried the full complement of valid IDs and credit cards. (When Julia pointed out that she could have stolen one just as easily, Poppy looked at her with wordless horror.) She returned in a peppy silver Jag—who would have thought you could even get one out here in Smurftown? she said. They knocked back a pub lunch and set out.

It was Quentin's first time in England, and he was amazed. Once they got up the coastal slope and out of town, out into the lumpy, uneven pastures dotted with sheep and stitched together with dense dark hedges, it looked more like Fillory than he'd thought anywhere on Earth could. Even more than Venice. Why hadn't anybody told him? Except of course they had, and he hadn't believed them. Poppy, in the driver's seat, grinned at him via the rearview mirror as if to say, see?

Maybe she was right, he hadn't given this world enough credit. Zipping along the narrow highways and shady lanes of rural Cornwall, the four of them could have been regular people, civilians, and would they have been any less happy? Even without magic they had the grass and that blessed country solitude and the sun flickering past between the branches and the solace of an expensive car that somebody else was paying for. What kind of an asshole wouldn't be satisfied with that? For the first time in his life Quentin seriously considered the idea that he could be happy without Fillory—not just resigned, but happy.

They were certainly as close to Fillory as you could get on Earth. They were closing in on the Chatwins' house. Even the place names sounded Fillorian: Tywardreath, Castle Dore, Lostwithiel. It was as if the green landscape of Fillory was hidden right behind this one, and this was a thin place, where the other world showed through.

Cornwall was certainly having a good effect on Julia. She was almost lively. She was the only one of them with the gift of not getting carsick while she read, so as they drove she paged through the Fillory books, applying stickies to certain passages, reading others out loud. She was compiling a list of all the different ways the children had gotten through: a practical traveler's guide to leaving this world behind.

"In *The World in the Walls* Martin gets in through the grandfather clock, and so does Fiona. In the second one Rupert gets in from his school, so that does not help us, and I believe Helen does too, but I cannot find it. In *The Flying Forest* they get in by climbing a tree. That might be our best bet."

"We wouldn't have to break into the house," Quentin said. "And we could all fit."

"Exactly. And in *The Secret Sea* they ride a magic bicycle, so let us keep an eye out for that. Maybe there is a garage or a shed with old things in it."

"You realize the fans have probably picked this place clean like years ago," Josh said. "We can't be the first people to think of this."

"Then in *The Wandering Dune* Helen and Jane are painting in a meadow somewhere nearby. Which seems like a long shot, but if we have to we can go back to Fowey for art supplies. And that is it."

"It's not quite it." Sorry, but nobody one-upped Quentin on Fillory trivia, not even Julia. "Martin gets back in in *The Flying Forest,* at the end, though Plover doesn't say how he did it. And there's a book you're missing, *The Magicians,* which is Jane's book about how she went back to Fillory to find Martin. She used the magic buttons to get in, which she found in the well, where Helen threw a whole box of them. Jane only used one to get back, so there may be more lying around."

Julia turned around in her seat.

"How do you know that?"

"I met her. Jane Chatwin. It was in Fillory. I was getting better from my injuries after we fought Martin. After Alice died."

There was silence in the car, broken by the ticking of the turn signal as Poppy took a fork in the road. Julia studied him with those empty, unreadable eyes.

"Sometimes I forget everything you have been through," she said finally, and turned around to face forward.

It only took them forty-five minutes to find Plover's house, aka Darras House, which must have once been in the deep countryside, but now you could get there on a well-maintained two-lane road. Poppy pulled over on the other side. There was no shoulder, and the Jag tilted at a perilous angle.

All four of them got out and straggled across the road. There was no traffic. It was about three-thirty in the afternoon. The grounds were surrounded by a formidable stone wall, and the gate framed, with an almost fussy architectural perfection, a view of a palatial Georgian country house set back deep in carefully tended grounds. Darras House was one of those rectangular English houses made of gray stone that probably conformed to some nutjob eighteenth-century theory about symmetry and ideal proportions and perfect ratios.

Quentin knew Plover had been rich—he'd made one fortune in America already, selling dry goods, whatever they were, before he came to Cornwall and wrote the Fillory novels—but the scale of it was still stunning. It wasn't so much a house as a cliff with windows in it.

"Jeez," Josh said.

"Yeah," said Poppy.

"Hard to imagine somebody living there all by themselves," Quentin said.

"He probably had servants."

"Was he gay?"

"Dude, totally," Josh said.

There was a sign on the gate, DARRAS HOUSE/PLOVER FARM, with a schedule of hours and tours and entrance fees. A blue plaque gave them a capsule biography of Plover. It was a Thursday, and the house was open. A large black bird retched loudly in the underbrush.

"So are we going in?" Poppy asked.

He'd thought they would, on the off chance that they might stumble on something, and so they could say they had. But now that they'd arrived the place felt empty. Nothing here called to Quentin. Plover had never gone to Fillory. All he'd done was write books. The magic was somewhere else.

"Nah," he said. "I don't think so."

Nobody disagreed. They could come back tomorrow. If they were still on Earth.

They trooped back across the road and spread out the map on the hood of the car. The exact location of the house the Chatwins had stayed at near Fowey was a matter for speculation, but not wild speculation. There was a limited number of places it could be. Plover's books were full of enchanting descriptions of how the Chatwin kids, singly and en masse, ran and skipped and cycled over from their aunt Maude's house to visit their beloved "uncle" Christopher. Plover had even famously had a little child-size gate built in the wall that separated their properties to let them through.

They had two Plover biographies with them, one a soft-focus hagiography from the 1950s, authorized by the family, the other a hardnosed psychoanalytic exposé from the early 1990s that anatomized Plover's complex and "problematic" sexuality, as symbolically dramatized in the various Fillory novels. They stuck to that one. It had better geography.

They knew that the Chatwin house was on one Darrowby Lane, which helped, although the Cornish were even less interested in signage than the Venetians. Fortunately Poppy turned out to be excellent at this kind of cross-country dead-reckoning navigation. At first they thought she must be using some kind of advanced geographical magic until Josh noticed that she had an iPhone in her lap.

"Yeah, but I used magic to jailbreak it," she said.

It was late afternoon, and they'd traversed what seemed like several hundred verdant and *Watership Down*–esque but stubbornly unmarked and unidentifiable rural byways, and the light was turning bluish, before they settled on a target property, which sat on a narrow lane that wasn't definitely not called Darrowby and as near as they could tell pretty much had to back onto Plover's enormous estate.

There was no wall or gate, just a gravel track curving back through the late-summer trees. A square stone post next to it supported a NO TRESPASSING sign. They couldn't see the house from here.

Quietly Julia read out the relevant passage from *The World in the Walls:*

The house was very grand—three stories tall, with a façade made of brick and stone, and enormous windows, and endless numbers of fireplaces and window seats and curving back stairs and other advantages, which their London house distinctly lacked. Among those advantages were the sprawling grounds around the house, which included long straight alleys and white gravel paths and dark-green pools of grass.

There was a time when Quentin could probably have said it along with her from memory.

Quentin sat in the car and stared across the road. He couldn't see much evidence of anything as nice as that. The place didn't exactly scream "portal to another world" either. He tried to imagine the Chatwins arriving here for the first time, the five of them crammed into the backseat of some sputtering black proto-automobile, more carriage than car, and with a fair amount of locomotive DNA in it as well, their luggage tied to the boot with twine and Victorian leather strappage. They would have been funereally silent, resigned to exile from London. The youngest, five-year-old Jane, the future Watcherwoman, reclining on her older sister's lap as on a chaise longue, lost in a fog of longing for her parents, who were respectively fighting World War I and raving in a posh rest home. Martin (who would grow up to become a monster who would kill Alice) keeping his composure for the sake of the youngsters, his soft boy's jaw set in grim preadolescent determination.

They'd been so young and innocent and hopeful, and they'd found something more wonderful than they could ever have hoped for, and it had destroyed them.

"What do you think?" he said. "Julia?"

"This is the place."

"All right. I'm going to go in. Look around."

"I'll come," Poppy said.

"No," Quentin said. "I want to go alone."

To his surprise it worked. She stayed put.

Becoming invisible was a simple idea in theory, but in practice it was a lot harder than you'd think. It had been done, but it took years of meticulous self-erasure, and once accomplished it was practically impossible to undo; apart from anything else you could never be sure you'd reinstated your visible self completely accurately. You came out looking like a portrait of yourself. The best work-around Quentin knew was more like an animal's protective coloring. If you were standing in front of some leaves, you looked drab and leafy. If you weren't moving or jumping around, an observer's eye tended to skate over you. Usually. If the light wasn't too good. The car door chunked shut in the stillness. He felt the others' eyes on his back as he crossed the road.

There was something on top of the stone post: buttons. They were scattered in the grass around it too. Big ones, small ones, pearly ones, tortoiseshells. It must be a fan ritual. You come by, you leave a button, the way people left joints on Jim Morrison's grave.

Still, he stopped and touched each of them, one by one, just to make sure none of them were genuine.

The camouflage spell was unbelievably crude. He picked up a big leathery oak leaf, snapped off a shingle of bark from a tree, plucked a blade of the scanty grass, and collected a granite pebble from the edge of the road. He whispered a rhyming chant in French over them, spat on them, and—the glamorous life of the modern sorcerer—stuffed them in his pocket.

Further up and further in. He stayed off the gravel driveway and picked his way through the trees for five minutes, until there were no more, and then he was looking at Aunt Maude Chatwin's house.

It was like he was looking back through time. The unpromising driveway had been a feint, a hustle. It really was a grand house; it probably would have qualified as magnificent if they hadn't just come from Plover's house. As Quentin got closer the gravel track pulled itself together and became a proper driveway, which clove in two and formed a circle with a modest but still entirely effective fountain at the center. Three rows of tall windows adorned the front, and the gray slate roof was a beautiful profusion of chimneys and gables.

Quentin hadn't known what to expect. A ruin, maybe, or some appalling new Modernist façade. But the Chatwin house was perfectly appointed and restored, and the lawns looked like they'd been trimmed that morning. It was everything Quentin had hoped for, except for one thing. It wasn't empty.

That well-maintained lawn was littered with cars. They were nice cars that made the rental Jag look poky by comparison. Yellow light spilled out of the lower floors and out into the mellowing dusk, chased by some nicely judged, not-overamplified early Rolling Stones. Whoever's private hands the house was in, they were having a party.

Quentin stood there, on the outside looking in, as a little convocation of evening gnats began to gather over his head. It seemed sacrilegious—he wanted to barge in and order everybody out, like Jesus ridding the temple of moneylenders. This was ground zero for the primal fantasy of the twentieth century, the place where Earth and Fillory had first kissed like two cosmic billiard balls. Over the chatter a roar went up, and a woman shrieked and then laughed uncontrollably.

But looking on the bright side, it was a tactical windfall. It was a big enough party that they could mingle in, the girls especially. They wouldn't sneak in at all, they would walk in the front door. Brazen it out. Then when any suspicions had been allayed they would slip upstairs and see what they could see. He walked back to the car to get the others.

They found a spot for the car on the lawn. They weren't the least plausible bunch of partygoers imaginable. Quentin had invested in some nice clothes in Venice, charged to Josh's bottomless credit card.

"If anybody asks just say John brought you."

"Good one. Dude, are you gonna . . . ?" Josh gestured at Quentin's appearance.

Oh, right. Probably better not to show up looking like a pile of mulch. He killed the camouflage spell. Crossing the threshold, Quentin closed his eyes for just a moment. He thought of little Jane Chatwin, still alive and at large somewhere. Maybe she would be at the party too.

Josh made straight for the bar.

"Dude!" Quentin hissed. "Stay on mission!"

"We're in deep cover. I'm getting into character."

For all that it was a party at Maude Chatwin's house, it was also just a party like any other party. There were pretty people and unpretty people, drunk people and undrunk people, people who didn't care what anybody thought about them and people standing in corners afraid to open their mouths lest somebody look directly at them.

Deep cover notwithstanding, Josh revealed himself to be conspicuously American by asking the bartender for beer. He wound up settling
for a Pimm's Cup, which he consumed with an air of disappointed baffle-
ment. But he and Poppy made themselves agreeable to the other guests
with an ease and skill that Quentin found awe-inspiring. Genuinely social people never ceased to amaze him. Their brains seemed to generate
an inexhaustible fund of things to say, naturally, with no effort, out of
nothing at all. It was a trick Quentin had never figured out.As an unat-
tached American male among English strangers, he felt inherently suspi-
cious. He did his best to affiliate himself with small groups and nod along
politely in response to people who weren't especially talking to him.

Julia found a wall to put her slender back against and looked deco-
rously mysterious. Only one man dared to approach her, a tall Canta-
bridgian type with a half-grown beard, and she sent him packing in
terms so uncertain he had to salve his wounds with cucumber sandwich.
After a half hour of this Quentin felt he could begin a slow drift toward
the stairs—not the grand Tara-style ones in front but a more unassum-
ing, utilitarian staircase toward the back of the house. One by one he
caught the others' eyes in turn and inclined his head. We were just looking for a bathroom? All four of us? Too bad they didn't have drugs; that
would have made a better cover story.

The staircase performed a tight switchback up to the second floor, a
hushed and darkened maze of white walls and parquet. The rumble and
tinkle of the party was still clearly audible, but hushed now, like distant
surf. There were a few kids up here, helling along the hallways and rack-
eting in and out of rooms, laughing a little too hysterically, playing some
game nobody knew the rules of, flopping down on the coats when they
got tired, the kind of forced pack of one-shot friends that exists on the
margins of all grown-up parties.

The World in the Walls wasn't a how-to manual, and it was irritatingly
vague as to the precise location of the famous clock. "One of the back
corridors of one of the upper floors" was all the detail Plover gave them.
Maybe it would have been better to split up, except that would have
violated the basic teaching of every movie ever made. Quentin would
have worried that everybody else would slip through into Fillory with-

out him, leaving him behind in reality like the last man standing in a game of Sardines.

Whoever lived here now didn't use the top floor at all, and it had gone unrestored. Another piece of luck. They hadn't even refinished the floors—the varnish had worn off them, and the walls were old wallpaper, with even older wallpaper showing through in places. The ceilings were low. The rooms were full of mismatched and broken furniture under sheets. The quieter it got the realer Fillory began to feel. It loomed in the shadows, under beds, behind the wallpaper, in the corner of his eye, just out of view. Ten minutes from now they could be back on the *Muntjac*.

This was the place. This was where the children played, where Martin vanished, where Jane watched, where the whole terrible fantasy began. And there in the hallway, the back hallway—as it had been written, as the prophecy foretold—stood a grandfather clock.

It was a beast of a clock, with a big fat brass face orbited by four smaller dials tracking the months and the phases of the moon and the signs of the zodiac and God knew what else, all framed in plain, uncarved dark wood. The works must have been hellishly complex, the eighteenth-century equivalent of a supercomputer. The wood was the wood of a Fillorian sunset tree, it said in the book, which shed its flaming orange leaves every day at sundown, endured a leafless winter overnight, and then sprouted fresh green new ones at dawn.

Quentin, Julia, Josh, and Poppy gathered around it. It was like they were re-enacting a Fillory book—no, they were in one, a new one, and they were writing it together. The pendulum wasn't moving. Quentin wondered if the connection could still be live, or whether it had broken after the children went through. He couldn't feel anything. But it had to work, he would make it work. He was going back to Fillory if he had to cram himself into every fucking piece of cabinetry in this house.

Even so it was going to be a tight fit. Maybe if he breathed out all his air and wriggled through sideways. Not how he planned to make his triumphant return to Fillory, but at this point he'd take whatever worked.

"Quentin," Josh said.

"Yeah."

"Quentin, look at me."

He had to tear his eyes away from the clock. When he did he found Josh watching him with a gravity that didn't suit him. It was a new-Josh gravity.

"You know I'm not going, right?"

He did know. He'd just let himself forget in all the excitement. Things were different now. They weren't kids. Josh was part of a different story.

"Yeah," Quentin said. "I guess I do know. Thanks for coming this far. What about you, Poppy? Chance of a lifetime."

"Thank you for asking me." She seemed to mean it, to take it in the spirit in which it was offered. She put a hand on her chest. "But I've got my whole life here. I can't go to Fillory."

Quentin looked at Julia, who'd taken off her shades in deference to the gloom of the top floor. Just you and me, kid. Together they stepped forward. Quentin got down on one knee. The roar of their imminent escape thundered in his ears.

As soon as he got up close he could see that it wasn't going to work. The thing wasn't ticking, but more than that it just looked too solid. The clock was what it was and nothing more—it was brute, mundane matter, wood and metal. He turned the little knob and opened the glass case and looked in at the hanging pendulum and chimes and whatnot other brass hardware, dangling there impotently. His heart had already gone out of it.

It was dark in here. He reached in and rapped the back of the case with his knuckles. Nothing. He closed his eyes.

"Goddamn it," he said.

Never mind. It wasn't over. They could always try climbing trees. Though at that moment he felt less like climbing a tree than he'd ever felt like doing anything in his entire life.

"You're doing it wrong, you know."

Their heads turned in unison. It was a little kid's voice, a boy. He was standing at the end of the corridor in his pajamas, watching them. He might have been eight years old.

"What am I doing wrong?" Quentin said.

"You have to set it going first," the boy said. "It says in the book. But it doesn't work anymore, I tried it."

The boy had fine tousled brown hair and blue eyes. A more quintessential English moppet it would have been hard to find, right down to his having a spot of trouble pronouncing his *l*'s and *r*'s. He could have been cloned from Christopher Robin's toenail clippings.

"Mummy says she's going to send it to the shop, but she never does. I climbed the trees too. And I did a painting. Lots of them actually. D'you want to see?"

They stared at him. Not finding himself rebuffed, he walked over on bare feet. He had that dismal air of sprightly self-possession that some English children have. Just looking at him, you knew you were going to have to play a game with him.

"I even had Mummy pull me round in an old wagon we found in the garage." He said it *ga*rage. "It's not the same as a bicycle, but I had to try it."

"I can see that," Quentin said. "I can see where you would have to do that."

"But we can keep looking though," he said. "I like it. My name's Thomas."

He actually held out his little paw for Quentin to shake, like a tiny alien ambassador. Poor kid. It wasn't his fault. He must be so chronically neglected by his parents that he had taken to press-ganging random party guests into paying attention to him. He made Quentin think of faraway Eleanor, the little girl on the Outer Island.

The really awful thing was that Quentin was going to go along with it, and not for the right reasons. He took the proffered paw. It wasn't that he felt bad for Thomas, though he did. It was that Thomas was a valuable ally. Adults never got into Fillory by themselves, at least not without a magic button. It was always the kids. What Quentin needed, he realized, was a native guide to act as bait. Maybe if he let young Thomas here course along ahead of him, like a hound across the moors, he just might flush out a portal or two. He was going to use Thomas to chum the waters.

"Just get me a drink," Quentin said to Josh as Thomas pulled him away. As they passed Poppy, Quentin firmly grabbed her hand. The misery train was leaving the station, and Quentin wasn't going to travel alone.

It emerged, with remarkably little prompting from Quentin or Poppy, that Thomas's parents had bought the Chatwin house a couple of years ago from the children of Fiona Chatwin; Thomas and his parents were themselves, through some connection that Quentin couldn't follow, distantly related to Plover. Maybe that was where the money came from. Thomas had been simply mad with excitement when he heard the news. Weren't all his friends at school jealous! Of course now he had all new friends, because before he'd been in London, and now they were in Cornwall. But his friends here were much nicer, and he only missed London when he thought about the Rainforest Life exhibit at the zoo. Had Quentin ever been to the zoo in London? If he could choose, would he be an Asian lion or a Sumatran tiger? And did he know that there was a monkey called a red titi monkey? It wasn't rude, you could say it because it was a real kind of monkey. And didn't he agree that, under certain extreme circumstances, the murder of children was completely ethically justifiable?

Towed by Thomas the tank engine, they toured the grounds. As a threesome they conducted a deep-cavity search of the top floor, including closets and attics. They made seven or eight circuits of the enormous green behind the house, with special attention paid to rodent burrows and spooky trees and copses large enough for a human being to infiltrate. Meanwhile Josh kept up an underground railroad of gin-and-tonics, handing them off to Quentin whenever he happened to pass by, like a spectator handing Gatorade to a marathoner.

It could have been worse. The view from the back terrace was even grander than the front. An orderly English estate had been hacked out of the rough Cornish countryside by main force, including a flat, still swimming pool that by some landscaper's artifice had mostly escaped looking anachronistic. Beyond it a perfect Constable vista rolled down and away, green hills and fallow hay fields and pocket villages, all slowly dissolving in the viscous light of a golden English sunset.

Thomas enjoyed the attention. And Poppy—he'd give her this—was a heroically good sport. She had no real stake in how all this turned out, but she pitched right in. She was nothing if not game. Moreover she was better at it than he was, hardened as she was by many tours in the babysitting trenches.

It all finished up, predictably, in Thomas's bedroom. By ten thirty even Thomas, with his titanically fresh-faced lust for life, couldn't be coaxed into one more round of Find Fillory. They all sat or sprawled on the rainbow-colored woolly yarn rug in Thomas's room. It was a huge room, a little kingdom all Thomas's own. It even had an extra bed in it, in the shape of a space rocket, as if to cruelly emphasize Thomas's only-childhood, the hilarious sleepovers he wasn't having. Josh and Julia joined them there. The party raged on beneath them, into the night, having degenerated from a cocktail party into a regular party party.

They should leave, obviously. At this point Thomas had gone from harasser to harassed. Maybe Josh was right, maybe they'd try Stonehenge next. But not before they'd burned this bridge right down to its charred pilings.

So they played other games. They ground out rounds of Animal Snap and rummy and Connect 4. They played board games, Cluedo and Monopoly and Mouse Trap, until Thomas was too tired and they were too drunk to follow the rules. They dug deeper into Thomas's toy closet, and thus further back into Thomas's childhood, for games so mathematically simple they were barely games at all, lacking as they did almost any strategic element: War and Snakes and Ladders and Hi Ho! Cherry-O and finally High C's, a primally simple alphabet game in which the main goal seemed to be to win the pregame argument with your fellow players over who got to be the dolphin. After that everything else was blind chance and cartoon fish.

Quentin took a slug of flat, warm gin-and-tonic. It tasted like defeat. This was how the dream died, in a welter of plastic primary-colored board game pieces, upstairs at a bad party. They would keep looking, they would knock on all the first doors they could think of, but for the first time, lying there sprawled on the spare bed, his long legs flat out, with his back against Thomas's rocketship headboard, Quentin took seriously the possibility that he wasn't going back after all. Probably hundreds of years had gone by in Fillory anyway. The ruins of Whitespire were dissolving in the rain, white stones softening like sugar cubes under green moss, by a now nameless bay. The tombs of King Eliot and Queen Janet were probably long since overgrown with ivy, twin clock-trees rising from their twin plots. Perhaps he was remembered as a legend, King Quentin the Missing. The Once and Future King, like King Arthur. Except unlike Arthur he wasn't coming back from Avalon. Just the Once King.

Well, it was a fitting place to end it, in the Chatwins' house, where everything started. The first door. The really funny thing was that even though he'd hit bottom, he couldn't honestly say that it was all that bad there. He had his friends, or some of them. They had Josh's money. They still had magic, and alcohol, and sex, and food. They had everything. He thought of Venice, and the pure green Cornish landscape they'd just driven through. There was so much more to this world than he thought. What the hell did he have to complain about?

Fuck-all was the answer. One day he'd have a house like this too, and a kid like Thomas, who lay fast asleep with the lights on and his arms thrown up over his head, a marathon runner breaking the tape in his dreams. He and some lovely and talented Mrs. Quentin (Who? Poppy? Surely not) would get married, and Fillory would fade away like the dream it so fundamentally was. So what if he wasn't a king. It had been lovely for a while, but here was real life, and he would make the most of it like everybody else. What kind of a hero was he, if he couldn't do that?

Julia kicked his foot. By unspoken agreement they were all grimly determined to finish the game of High C's, and it was his turn. He flicked the spinner and moved forward two waves. Josh, who was playing as the whale, had a commanding lead, but Julia (the squid) was making a late charge, leaving Poppy (fish) and Quentin (jellyfish) to battle it out for a distant third place.

Josh spun. He was on a charade square.

"Caw!" Josh said. "Caw! Caw!"

"Seagull," they all said in unison. It was like when they were geese. Josh spun again. Julia belched.

Quentin slumped over behind Poppy's warm back, onto the infinitely soft and sweet-smelling pillows. From this point of view it was apparent that Poppy was wearing a thong. The bed was not entirely stable. The drinks were catching up with him. It wasn't clear whether the spins were going to spin themselves out or gather speed and power and wreak a terrible vengeance upon him for his many transgressions. Well, time would undoubtedly tell.

"Caw!" Josh said.

"Enough already," Quentin said.

"Caw! Caw!"

"Seagull! I said seagull!"

The light hurt his eyes. It was uncomfortably bright in Thomas's room. That was enough drinking for tonight. Quentin sat up.

"I know, man," Josh said. "I heard you."

"Caw!"

The cawing didn't stop, nor did the spinning. The bed was definitely in motion, not so much spinning as rocking gently. They all froze.

Poppy reacted first.

"No way." She lunged off the bed and landed in water. "Goddamn it! No fucking way!"

The sun was hot overhead. A curious albatross was circling over them, making respectful inquiries.

Quentin jumped up on the bed.

"Oh my God! We did it. We did it!"

They had broken through. It wasn't the end, it was all about to start all over again. He spread his arms wide to the daylight and let the hot sun slam straight down into his face. He was a man reborn. Julia was looking around her and sobbing as though her heart would break. They were back. The dream was real again. They were adrift on the high seas of Fillory.

BOOK III

CHAPTER 17

"Thomas will be so disappointed," Poppy said. "He missed every-thing."

She sat glumly on a sail locker on the deck of the *Muntjac,* wrapped in a rough ship's blanket. Her curly hair was flat from the salt water. She'd tried to swim away, back to Earth, back to Thomas's little-boy bed-room, but when she saw that she had no shot she stroked back to the bed instead, and they'd hauled her dripping back up onto it to await rescue. She was a strong, easy swimmer, which was somehow not surprising.

The bed, while a top-quality bed that contained a fair amount of actual bona fide wood—Thomas's parents had spared no expense—was only so-so as a raft and had trended downward rapidly as the bedclothes and then the mattress soaked through and lost their buoyancy. Josh sat heavily on it, crisscross applesauce, resigned, Buddha going down with the ship, while the bed gradually swamped, and the cold seawater lapped up over his knees.

But the *Muntjac* was already in view by then, sheering keenly through the waves toward them, the force of a fresh wind setting it at a rakish angle. Its sails—his sails, Quentin's sails, with the pale blue ram of Fillory—stood out in taut, proud curves. The power of it, the color, the solidity, the reality of it, were almost too thrilling. A tiny action-figure sailor was already at the railing, pointing in their direction.

Quentin hadn't for a second doubted that the *Muntjac* would be there. It seemed like years since he'd seen it. They had come to take him home.

As it bore down on them he'd had a moment of worry: what if centuries had passed, what if Eliot and Janet really were dead, and the *Muntjac* was the last survivor of the Brakebills era, and he was going home to a court of strangers? But no, there was Bingle at the railing, looking just as he always had, ready to haul his royal body back on board and get back to guarding it.

Though even as they were toweling off, and hugging each other, and making introductions, and securing fresh clothes and hot tea, he could see that not everything aboard the *Muntjac* was exactly as he'd left it. The ship was older. Not that it was shabby, but it had aged, settled into itself some. What had been glossy—the paint on the railings, the varnish on the deck—was now rubbed to matte. Ropes that had once been bright and prickly were now smooth and soft and dun-colored from having been run through blocks over and over again.

Also Quentin was no longer in charge of the *Muntjac*. Eliot was.

"Where have you been!" he said, when he was done embracing Quentin. "You ridiculous, ridiculous man. I was starting to think you were dead."

"I was on Earth. How long have we been gone?"

"A year and a day."

"God. It was only three days for us."

"That makes me two years older than you now. How do you think that makes me feel? How was Earth?"

"The same. It ain't Fillory."

"Did you bring me back anything?"

"A bed. Josh. An Australian girl named Poppy. I didn't have a lot of time. And you know how hard you are to shop for."

Quentin was still in a euphoric state, but the adrenaline was wearing off, and his eyes felt sandy and jet-lagged. Twenty minutes ago it had been midnight, the tail end of a long and arduously alcoholic party, and now it was early afternoon again. They went below to Quentin's cabin, which was now Eliot's cabin, and he dried off and changed clothes and cursed Ember that He hadn't thought to bless Fillory with the miracle of coffee beans.

Then he lay down on Eliot's bed and looked up at the low woodwork ceiling and told Eliot about everything that had happened. He told him about going back to Brakebills, and about Julia's safe houses, and how Josh had sold the button. He told him about the Neitherlands being in ruins, and about the dragon, and about the Chatwins' house.

Eliot sat at the foot of the bed. When Quentin was done Eliot watched him for a minute, slowly tapping the hollow of his upper lip with the tip of his index finger.

"Well," he said finally. "This is interesting."

Yes, it was. Although Quentin's immediate personal interest in it was faltering. He wanted to fall asleep and moreover felt confident of his ability to do so very quickly. Being back in Fillory was a massive dose of comfort, a huge inflatable cushion of relief of the kind stuntmen fall into from great heights without injury, and he sank into it.

Though if Quentin could have had absolutely everything exactly the way he wanted it, he would have asked for one more thing: he didn't want to be on a boat anymore. He wanted to go home, meaning not just to Fillory but specifically to his room in Castle Whitespire, with its high ceiling and its big bed and its special calm hush. Quentin did not consider himself a great interpreter of signs and wonders, but the lesson of the golden key seemed pretty clear to him. It was this: you've already won the game, so quit playing. Remain where you are, in your castle, and you will be safe. No further action on your part is required.

"Eliot," he said. "Where are we?"

"We're east. Very far east. Even farther than you went. We left After Island behind two weeks ago."

"Oh, no."

"We're over the horizon."

"No, no, no." Quentin closed his eyes. "We can't be." He wanted it to be dark, but surly yellow late-afternoon sun continued blasting in through his—Eliot's—cabin window unabated. "All right. We are. But we're going back now, right? You found me and Julia. Mission accomplished. End of story."

"We will go back. We just have to do one more thing first."

"Eliot, stop. I'm serious. Turn the ship around. I'm never leaving Fillory again."

"Just one thing. You'll like it."

"I don't think I'm going to like it."

Eliot smiled broadly, or as broadly as his bad teeth would allow.

"Oh, you're going to love it," he said. "It's an adventure."

It was unbelievable. Never mind Thomas: he, Quentin, had missed everything. It had started as soon as he left for the Outer Island.

This all came out at a massive feast belowdecks that evening. By then Quentin had almost come to accept that when you were surfing the great interdimensional divide certain days were just destined to stretch out to about thirty-six hours long, and there was nothing you could do except to wait them out till they ended. The new arrivals ate like wolves—their exhaustion had turned into a raging hunger. They'd never had a proper dinner the night before anyway, just the occasional passed hors d'oeuvre. Only Julia picked at her food, managing a bite every few minutes, like her body was an unloved pet that she was being forced to babysit.

"I knew something was up," Eliot said, cracking open a massive, lethal-looking crimson crab. Like Julia he never seemed to eat, but somehow he got through massive quantities of food anyway, which of course never made him any less skinny. "First off, two days after you left Whitespire, someone tried to kill me in my bath."

"Really?" Josh said with his mouth full. "And that tipped you off?"

It hadn't taken long for Josh to get acclimated aboard the *Muntjac*. Discomfort just wasn't in his nature. He'd picked up with Eliot exactly where they'd left off two years ago.

"That's awful," Quentin said. "Jesus."

"It was! I was lolling in my bath of an evening, as one does, blameless as a newborn child—more so, if you've ever met such a creature, they're absolutely horrible—and one of my own towel boys came creeping up behind me with a big curvy knife in his hand. He tried to cut my throat.

"I'll spare you the details"—which is what Eliot said when he was going to march you through everything blow by blow—"but I grabbed his arm, and he went in the water. He'd never been a particularly good towel boy. Perhaps he felt he was meant for better things. But he was no great success as an assassin either, I can tell you. He got his knife against my neck, but nowhere near the artery, and he hadn't braced himself properly at all. So in he went, and I scrambled out of the water, and I froze it."

"Dixon's charm?"

He nodded. "It was no great loss. I was about to get out anyway. I'd put in so many bath salts I didn't know if it would take, but it froze solid right away. He looked like Han Solo frozen in carbonite. The resemblance was actually quite striking."

"You and your towel boys," Josh said. "But I ask for a harem and it's all, morality this, human rights that."

"Well, and I spared you a good stabbing, didn't I?"

Eliot didn't tan, he was too pale for that, but the sun and the wind had put some texture in his otherwise immaculate pallor, and he'd grown some nicely naval stubble. He'd dropped some of the god-king preciousness that had dominated his persona back at Whitespire, shed some of the gold leaf. He spoke to the crew with an air of easy familiarity and command—even the ones like Bingle whom he'd never met before the ship sailed, and in Quentin's mind wasn't supposed to know. Now he knew them better than Quentin did. They'd been at sea together for a year.

"I let him out, of course. I didn't have the heart to let him suffocate. But would you believe it, he wouldn't tell us a thing! He was a fanatic of some kind. Or a lunatic, maybe. Same thing. Do you know, some of the generals wanted to torture him? I think Janet would have done it too, but I couldn't. But I couldn't just let him go either. He's in prison now.

"I was shaken, but I suppose you're not really High King until somebody tries to kill you in your bath. If they ever succeed, by the way, make sure you leave me in there and have a painting done. Like Marat.

"I wanted to let the whole thing drop, but I couldn't. It wouldn't let me drop. I don't know what *it* was. Fillory, I suppose. At any rate, that's when the wonders started.

"That's what everyone called them, and I couldn't think of another name for them. It started out just as feelings. You would look at something, a carpet, or a bowl of fruit, and the colors would seem different. Brighter, more vivid, more saturated. Sudden rushes of grief or excitement or love would come over you for no reason. Some very unmanly crying jags were observed among the barons.

"It was like drugs more than anything else, but I hadn't taken any drugs. I remember one night in my bedroom lying there smelling spices in the darkness, one after the other. Cinnamon, jasmine, cardamom, something else—something wonderful I couldn't place. Paintings started to change as I walked by them. Just the backgrounds. The clouds would move, or the sky would go from day to night.

"Then I saw a hunting horn hovering before me at dinner. Some of the others saw it too. And one night in the middle of the night I opened the bathroom door, and it opened onto deep forest instead. It's all the same when it comes to taking a piss, I suppose, but still. It put me right off my game.

"For a while I thought I was going mad, literally mad, until the tree came. A clock-tree grew up right in the middle of the throne room, right through the carpet, in broad daylight. It did it all at once, all in one go, with the whole court watching. And then it just stood there, silently, like a hallucination, ticking and sort of swaying with the energy of its just having grown. It was as if it were saying, 'Well, here I am. This is me. What are you going to do about it?'

"After that I knew it wasn't me that had gone mad. It was Fillory.

"I don't mind telling you I found the whole business more than a little provoking. I was being called, you understand, and I most definitely did not want to come. I understand the appeal this sort of thing has for you, quests and King Arthur and all that. But that's you. No offense, but it always seemed a bit like boy stuff to me. Sweaty and strenuous and just not very *elegant,* if you see what I mean. I didn't need to be called to feel special, I felt special enough already. I'm clever, rich, and good-looking. I was perfectly happy where I was, deliquescing, atom by atom, amid a riot of luxury."

"Nicely put," Quentin said. Eliot must have mounted this set piece before.

"Well, and then that damned Seeing Hare came bolting through the room during our afternoon meeting. Scattered the whiskey service and frightened one of my more sensitive protégés half to death. Everyone has a limit. Next morning I called for my hunting leathers, saddled a horse, and went riding out alone into the Queenswood. And you know, I *never* go anywhere alone, not anymore, but these things have certain protocols and not even the High King—or I suppose especially not the High King—is exempt."

"The Queenswood," Quentin said. "Don't tell me."

"But I am telling you." Eliot finished his wine, and a rangy, shaven-headed young man refilled his glass without his having to ask. "I went back to that ridiculous meadow of yours, the round one. You see, you'd been right to want to go in. It was our adventure after all."

"I was right." Quentin felt crestfallen. He stared down at his hands. "I can't believe it, I was right!"

If he hadn't been so tired, and a bit drunk, it probably wouldn't have struck him the way it did. But as it was he felt himself filling up with a sense of—how could he put it? He thought he'd learned a lesson about the world, and now he was realizing that the lesson he learned might have been the wrong one. The right adventure had been offered to him, and he'd walked away. If being a hero is a matter of knowing your cues, like the fairy tale said, he'd missed his. Instead he'd spent three days faffing around on Earth for nothing, and nearly got stuck there forever, while Eliot was off on a real quest.

"It's true," Eliot said. "Statistically, historically, and however else you want to look at it, you are almost never right. A monkey making life decisions based on its horoscope in *USA Today* would be right more often than you. But in this case, yes, you were right. Don't spoil it."

"It was supposed to be me, not you!"

"You should have gone on it when you had the chance."

"You told me not to!"

"Janet told you not to. I don't know why you listened to her. But look, I know." Eliot put a hand on his arm. "I know. I had no choice. Whoever is in charge of handing out quests has a damned peculiar sense of humor.

"At any rate, off I went. And I did feel something, you know, as I set off that morning. Nip in the air, sun on my armor, a knight pricking across the plain. I wished you could have been there.

"Though I looked much better than you would have. I had special questing armor made, just for that day, embossed and damascened within an inch of its life. I won't lie to you, Quentin. I looked magnificent."

Quentin wondered what he'd been doing at that moment. At least he'd gotten to drink a Coke. That was something. He wished he had one now. He was exhausted.

"It took me three days to find that fucking meadow, but finally I did. The Seeing Hare was there, of course, waiting for me under the branches of that hideous great tree, which was still thrashing away in its invisible wind."

"Intangible," Poppy said in a small voice. "All wind is invisible."

Good to see she was finding her feet.

"The hare wasn't alone. The bird was there as well, and the monitor, the Utter Newt, the Kind Wolf, the Parallel Beetle—it does a geometrical thing, it's so boring I can't even explain it. All of them, all the Unique Beasts, the full conclave. Well, except the two aquatic ones. The Questing Beast sends you his regards by the way. I think he's fond of you for some reason, even though you shot him.

"Well, when I saw them all there together, standing in two neat rows, the little ones in front, like they were posing for a class picture, I knew the jig was up. It was the newt that did the talking. He let it be known that the realm was in peril, and nothing else would do but my recovering the Seven Golden Keys of Fillory. I asked him why, what good were they, what were they for, what did they unlock. He wouldn't say, or he couldn't. He said I would know when it was time.

"I haggled a bit of course. I wanted to know, for example, how rapidly these keys would have to be recovered. I could imagine doing one every few years. Organize my holidays around it. At that rate I might even look forward to it—it's always nicer traveling when you have some business to do. But apparently it's a time-sensitive issue. They were very insistant about that.

"They gave me a Golden Ring that the keys were supposed to go on, and I left. What else could I do? When I got back Whitespire was up in arms. There were all kinds of terrible portents, all over the kingdom. That storm had spread—all the clock-trees had started thrashing the way that first one did. And you know the waterfall at the Red Ruin? The one that flows up? It started flowing down. You know, the regular way. So that was about the last straw.

"And then the *Muntjac* came screaming into port, and they told me you and Julia had vanished."

In full hero mode, Eliot took command of the *Muntjac*. He spent a day repairing and provisioning it while the whole kingdom buzzed with anxiety and excitement. High King Eliot was going on a quest! Apart from everything else it was a public relations triumph. The docks were mobbed by volunteers offering to join the search for the Seven Keys. The dwarves sent over a trunkload of magical keys they happened to have been kicking around in their vaults, in case there was a match in there, but most of them turned out to be useless.

One, though, fit on the key ring. So six to go. Funny how every once in a while the dwarves came up trumps.

Eliot left Janet in sole possession of the castle. He felt bad about making her shoulder everything even more than she already did, but she was practically licking her chops as he left. She would probably be running a fascist dictatorship by the time they got back. So he set off.

Eliot had no idea where he was going, but he'd read enough to know that a state of relative ignorance wasn't necessarily a handicap on a quest. It was something your dauntless questing knight accepted and embraced. You lit out into the wilderness at random, and if your state of mind, or maybe it was your soul, was correct, then adventure would find you through the natural course of events. It was like free association—there were no wrong answers. It worked as long as you weren't trying too hard.

And Eliot was in no danger of trying too hard. The *Muntjac* ran fast before a warm wet wind, out past the Outer Island, and After, out of Fillory and out of the known world.

A hush settled over the table. For a moment the creaking of the ship's ropes and timbers could be heard, and Quentin felt for the first time how far off the map they were. He thought how they would look to someone far above them: a tiny lighted ship, lost in the immensity of an empty uncharted nighttime ocean.

Eliot studied the ceiling. He was actually groping for words. That was a new one on Quentin.

"You wouldn't have believed it, Q," he said finally. Something like an expression of actual awe had come over Eliot's face. "You really wouldn't. We've been all over the Eastern Ocean. The lands we saw. Some of the islands . . . I don't know where to begin."

"Tell him about the train," said the shaven-headed young man. All at once Quentin recognized him. It was Benedict. But a new Benedict, reborn with ropy muscles and flashing white teeth. The floppy bangs and the sullen attitude were long gone. He looked at Eliot with a respect Quentin had never seen him show anybody before.

"Yes, the train. We thought it was a sea serpent at first. We barely brought the ship around in time. But it was a train, one of those slow freight trains that are always about a million cars long, all tankers and boxcars, except that this one never ended. It broke the surface, seawater streaming off the sides of the cars, rumbled along beside us for a couple of miles, then it sank back under the sea again."

"Just like that?"

"Just like that. Bingle hopped onto it for a while, but we could never get any of the cars open.

"And we found a castle floating on the ocean. At first we just heard it, bells ringing in the middle of the night. The next morning we came up on it: a stone castle, riding on a fleet of groaning wooden barges. No one inside, just bells tolling in one of the towers with the rocking of the waves.

"What else? There was an island where no one could tell a lie. Goodness that was awkward for a while. We aired a lot of dirty laundry there, I can tell you."

Rueful smiles went around the room among the crew.

"There was one where the people were really waves, ocean waves, which I know, but I just can't explain it anymore than that. There was a place where the ocean poured into a huge chasm, and there was only a narrow bridge across it. A water-bridge that we had to sail across."

"Like an aqueduct," Benedict put in.

"Like an aqueduct. It was all so strange. I think magic gets magnified out here, gets wilder, and it creates all sorts of impossible places, all by itself. We spent a week trapped in the Doldrums. There was no wind, and the water was as smooth as glass, and there was a Sargasso Sea there, a big swirl of flotsam in the ocean. People lived there, picking through it. Everything people forget about ends up there one day, they said. Toys, tables, whole houses. And people end up there too. They get forgotten as well.

"We were almost trapped there, but the *Muntjac* sprouted a bank of oars to help us get away. Didn't you, old thing?" Eliot knocked familiarly on the bulkhead with his fist. "You could take things away with you, from the Sargasso Sea, but you had to leave something behind. That was the deal. Bingle took a magic sword. Show them your sword, Bing."

Bingle, sitting at the far end of the table, stood up and drew his sword halfway out of its sheath, almost shyly. It was a narrow length of bright steel chased with swirly silver patterns that glowed white.

"He won't say what he left behind for it. What did you leave, Bing?"

Bingle smiled and touched the side of his nose and said nothing.

Quentin was weary. He'd woken up in Venice that morning, and spent the day in England, and another half day in Fillory. He'd already been drunk once and sobered up, and now he was getting drunk again, sitting there on a hard splintery bench in the *Muntjac*'s galley. Probably Eliot would have enjoyed a little jaunt back to Earth, he thought, where the wine and coffee were better. Though who knows, maybe it wouldn't have worked if it had been the other way around. Maybe he couldn't have done it—maybe he would have gotten trapped in the Sargasso Sea. And maybe Eliot wouldn't have found his way to Josh, wouldn't have gone to see the dragon, wouldn't have played with Thomas. Maybe he would have failed where Quentin succeeded, and vice versa. Maybe this was the only way it could have gone. You didn't get the quest you wanted, you got the one you could do.

That was the hard part, accepting that you didn't get to choose which way you went. Except of course he had chosen.

"Don't keep us in suspense," he said. "Did you find the keys?"

Eliot nodded.

"We found some of them. It was always either a fight or a riddle, one or the other. One was a huge beast like a giant spiny lobster. It had the key inside its heart. Then there was a beach that was all made of keys, millions of them, and we had to go through them till we found the right one. There was probably a trick to that one, but no one could think what it was, so we brute-forced it instead—took shifts, trying keys on the key ring, round the clock. After a couple of weeks we got a fit.

"Now I'm sorry if I'm a bit direct about this, but you have to remember, we've been at this for a full year, week in and week out, and frankly all this questing is wearing pretty thin. So here it is: we have five of the seven keys. One the dwarves gave us, and four we found. Do you have one? The one from After Island?"

"No," Quentin said. "Julia and I left it behind when we went through the door. Didn't somebody take it?"

Quentin looked at Bingle, then at Benedict. Neither one of them met his eye.

"No? But we don't have it either."

"Damn," Eliot said. "That's what I was afraid of."

"But what happened? It can't just have disappeared. It must still be on After Island."

"It's not," Benedict said. "We looked everywhere."

"Well, we'll just have to keep looking." Eliot sighed and raised his glass to be refilled. "So it looks like you're going to see some adventuring after all."

CHAPTER 18

The house in Bed-Stuy was Julia's first safe house, and it was the end of Stanford. She was never going to college now. It was her parents' hearts broken for the second and final time. It was too terrible to think about, so she dealt with it by not thinking about it.

She could have said no, of course. She could have finished dialing the number of the car service, and turned her back on the man with the porkpie hat, and waited till the black town car came, and gotten in and repeated her home address to the Guatemalan highlander behind the wheel until he finally understood and whisked her away from it all. Or she couldn't have, but she wished she could. She wished it then, and she would rewish it many times in the years to come.

But she couldn't walk away, because the dream, the dream of magic, wasn't dead. She'd tried to kill it, to beat the life out of it with work and drugs and therapy and family and the Free Traders, but she couldn't. It was stronger than she was.

The owlish young man who was working the door of the Bed-Stuy safe house that night was named Jared. He was about thirty, not tall, with a bright smile and heavy black stubble and heavy black glasses. He'd been working on a doctorate in linguistics at NYU for the past nine years. Nights and weekends, he worked magic.

They weren't all like that—nerdy, academic, what you'd think. It was a surprisingly heterogeneous crowd. There was a twelve-year-old prodigy from the neighborhood, and a sixty-five-year-old widow who drove

down from Westchester County in a BMW SUV on weekends. In all
there was a rotating cast of about twenty-five: physicists and reception-
ists and pipe fitters and musicians and undergrads and hedge-fund guys
and barely functional, socially marginal nutjobs. And now there was
Julia.

Some of them came in once a month to work on spells, and some of
them showed up at six in the morning every morning and stayed till ten
at night, or slept there, though house rules kept that to a minimum.
Some of them were high-functioning in their daily lives, had careers and
families and no obvious signs of eccentricity or physical debilitation. But
doing magic alongside all that other stuff was a tricky balancing act, and
when you lost it and fell you hit the floor hard. Even if you got up again,
you got up limping. And everybody fell sooner or later.

See, when you had magic in your life, it turned out, when you lived
the double life of a secret underground magician, you paid a certain
price, which was that your secret other life pulled at you always. Your
magician self, that loopy doppelgänger, was always with you, tugging
at your sleeve, whispering silently that your real life was a fake life, a
crude and undignified and inauthentic charade that nobody was really
buying anyway. Your real self, the one that mattered, was the other one,
the one waving her hands around and chanting in a dead Slavic dialect
on the busted-ass couch in the lime-green clapboard house on Throop
Avenue.

Julia kept her job, but she was at the house most nights and all day
on weekends. The lust was back, and this time it looked like she could
slake it. She had the scent, and she was going to make the kill. She went
quiet on FTB. The Free Traders could wait. They were used to members
dropping off the grid unexpectedly for months or years at a time. In the
chronic mood disorder community, that was well within normal operating parameters.

As for her parents . . . Julia cut herself off. She knew what she was
doing, and she knew how hard it would be for them, watching her fall
back into the obsession and get skinny again and stop bathing and all
the rest of it, and she did it anyway. She felt like she had no choice. It
was an addiction. Thinking about the consequences for her family, re-

ally thinking about them, would have annihilated her with remorse. So she didn't. The first morning she caught herself absentmindedly, almost sensuously, running a thumbnail along her arm at the breakfast table, leaving a red line behind, or rather when she caught her mother catching her doing it, no words were spoken. But she saw part of her mother die that morning. And Julia did not take heroic measures to resuscitate her.

Julia could have died that morning too, she knew. She almost did. But you let a drowning woman cling to you, she'll drag you down with her, and what's the point of that? That's what she told herself, anyway. You have to look her in the eye and pry her fingers off your arm and watch her sink down into the airless green depths and perish there. It's either that or you'll both die. What's the point?

Her sister knew that. You could see the disappointment in her quick brown foxy eyes, then you could see it change and harden into something clear and smooth and protective. She was young enough, she could still swerve around the wreck and keep moving. She let Julia go, her sister with her black secrets. Smart kid. She had made a sensible deal. Julia made one too.

And what did Julia get, for her deal? When you put your family and your heart and your life and your future up on the block, how much does that net you? What do you walk away with in return? Show her what she's won, Bob!

A lot, it turns out. A motherfuckingload of arcane lore is what it gets you, for starters.

That first day they tested her. From the second you got in the door—Jared actually started up the stopwatch widget on his iPhone as she crossed the threshold—you had fifteen minutes to learn and execute the flash spell that Quentin punted at the Winston safe house, or you had to leave, and you couldn't come back for a month. They called it, boringly, the First Flash. You could try again at another safe house, of course—they didn't share information—but there were only two in New York City, so if you wanted to get your magic on in the five boroughs you had to go big or go home.

Tired as she was Julia did it in eight minutes flat. If she'd had any muscle tone left over from her rainbow-witch phase she wouldn't even have needed that long.

As it turned out, they didn't know the rainbow spell, so she printed out the scan she'd downloaded from the Internet that one time, it was already two years ago now, and brought it in. Jared the linguist, with great pomp and ceremony, encased it in a transparent plastic sleeve, punched the sleeve with a three-hole punch, and added it to a tatty duct-taped three-ring binder in which they kept the club's spell list. A three-ring binder: that's what they had by way of a spellbook.

And they called it the Spellbinder. That should have tipped Julia off.

Still, it increased twentyfold the sum of Julia's information about magic, and that was a joy beyond measuring. Under Jared's tutelage, or whoever the senior magician in the house on any given day happened to be, she worked her way through the book. She learned how to stick things together with magic. She learned how to light a fire at a distance. She learned a spell to guess a coin flip, and to keep a nail from rusting, and to take a magnetic charge off a magnet. They competed with each other to see how many everyday tasks they could do with magic: opening jars, tying their shoes, buttoning buttons.

It was a bit random, and it was a bit small potatoes, but it was a start. Nail by nail, magnet by magnet, she began to force the world to conform to her specifications. Magic: it was what happened when the mind met the world, and the mind won for a change.

There was another binder, of hand exercises, much battered from having been thrown across the room in frustration, and she started work on them too. Soon she had the book memorized, and she did the exercises all the time: in the shower, under the table at mealtimes, under her desk at work, at night as she lay in bed. And she got serious about her languages. Magic wasn't just a math thing, it turned out.

As she learned spells, she gained levels. Yes, levels: that's what they called them. The lameness of the level system, borrowed wholesale from Dungeons & Dragons (which must have borrowed it from Freemasonry, she supposed), was not deniable, but it did keep things orderly, and it kept the hierarchies clearly defined, which Julia liked more and more the higher she rose in them. She began the tattoos on her back. She took care to leave a lot of room, because she was learning fast.

It took her a month to realize that she was learning faster than the other regulars at the safe house, and another three months to realize just how much faster. By that point she had seven stars, which was as many as Jared had, and he'd been at it for three years. Probably at Brakebills she would have been just another apprentice, but she wasn't at Brakebills, was she, she was here, and here she stood out. The others just didn't seem to have any flare for the theoretical side of magic. They learned their spells by rote, but they weren't interested in the basic patterns that underlay them. Only a few of them went into the deeper linguistic work, the grammars and the root systems. They preferred to just memorize the syllables and gestures and forget the rest.

They were wrong. It sapped the power of their casting, and it meant that every time they started a new spell they were starting over from scratch. They didn't see the connections between them. And you could forget about doing any original work, which Julia was already looking forward to. Along with Jared she started an ancient languages working group. They only got four other members, and most of those were there because Julia was hot. She kicked them out one by one when they didn't keep up with the homework.

As for the hand exercises, she worked doubly hard at those, because she knew she wasn't naturally gifted at them. Nobody kept up with her on the hand exercises, not even Jared. They didn't have her taste for pain.

Much as she hated Brakebills, with a red glowing hatred that she kept carefully burning in some inner brazier, blowing on it if it ever sank too low, she could see why they kept things exclusive there. A lot of riffraff came through the Throop Avenue safe house.

Julia had always had a nasty competitive streak. In the past she'd done her best to keep it under wraps. Now she reversed that policy. With no one to check her, she nurtured it and let it flower. As Brakebills had humiliated her, so she would humiliate anybody who couldn't keep up with her. Hey, magic's not a popularity contest. Throop Avenue would be her own private Brakebills. Any visitor who came to the Throop Avenue safe house rocking a level equal to or less than Julia's had better come to play. Any bullshit you were walking around with, you would be called on.

It didn't matter if you were black or white or tired or sick or twelve. It was amazing, truly in*cred*ible, how many magicians were faking their way through this shit. It made Julia furious. Who issued these people their stars? You gave some of these other safe houses a little push and they fell over like houses of cards. It was dispiriting, is what it was. She'd finally found a magic school, of sorts, to call her very own, and it was barfing out a bunch of fakers and cheats.

On the strength of Julia's bedside manner, the Throop Avenue safe house began to get a bit of a reputation. They didn't get quite so many drop-ins anymore, and some of the drop-ins they did get got ugly. As in physical. Bullshitters don't like being called on their bullshit, and there was a considerable Venn diagram overlap between people who were into magic and people who were into martial arts.

But I'm sorry, where did you think you were, motherfucker? Connecticut? You're in a magic safe house in Bed-Stuy, borough of Brooklyn. There was a considerable Venn diagram overlap between people who lived in Bed-Stuy and people who had motherfucking *guns.* Fool. Welcome to New Dork City.

Still, even with Julia's crusade for magical rigor bringing up the general tone of things, there was a problem at the Bed-Stuy safe house, and that was its three-ring binder. The Spellbinder. Every once in a while a visitor would drop by who meant business, and they'd know a spell that wasn't in the book, and if that was the case, and if the book contained a spell that they didn't know, a swap might be arranged, and the book would grow.

But such transactions were frustratingly infrequent. Julia needed to grow faster than that. It didn't make sense: where did these spells come from in the first place? What was the source? Nobody knew. Turnover was high at safe houses, and institutional memory was short. But more and more Julia suspected that somebody out there was operating on a much higher level than she was, and she wanted to know who, and where, and how, and now.

So Julia turned it around. She became a visitor. She'd hung on to the Civic from her Chesterton days, and she quit her job troubleshooting networks and started putting miles on it, sometimes by herself, sometimes with Jared riding shotgun. Safe houses weren't easy to find—they hid their locations from the wider world, but also from one another, because safe houses had been known to go to war, and that usually resulted in mutual annihilation. But sometimes you could coax an address out of a friendly visitor. She'd gotten good at coaxing. If all else failed she had the power of the bathroom handjob, and she wielded it with an iron fist.

And some safe houses were bigger than others, and some were big enough and safe enough that they'd allowed themselves to get a little famous, at least within the scene, on the strength of their belief that they were big enough that nobody could fuck with them. The binder she was handed in an old repurposed bank building in Buffalo was so thick it made her fall on her knees and weep. She stayed there for a week, uploading magical knowledge into her starving brain by the terabyte.

All that summer she roamed north into Canada, west as far as Chicago, south to Tennessee and Louisiana and all the way down to Key West, a back-breaking, clutch-grinding, vinyl-sticky trip that yielded a face-palmingly disappointing twelve-page spellbook in a cat-infested bungalow next door to the Hemingway Home. It was Julia's wandering period. She crashed on spare beds and in motels and in the Civic. When the Civic quit on her, she got into not-wiring cars off the street. She met a lot of people, and some people who weren't people. The more rural houses occasionally played host to minor demons and lesser fairies and local geo-specific nature spirits and elementals who lent street cred to the establishment in return for God knows what in the way of goods and services, she didn't ask. There was a certain romance to these beings; they seemed to embody the very promise of magic, which was to deliver unto her a world greater than the one into which she had been born. The moment when you walk into a room, and the guy playing pool has a pair of red leather wings sticking out of his back, and the chick smoking on the balcony has eyes of liquid golden fire—at that moment you think you'll never be sad or bored or lonely again.

But Julia got to the bottom of those beings pretty fast, and once she got there she often found someone who was just as desperate and confused as she was. That was how Julia got mixed up with Warren, and that was the lesson she learned.

At any rate her back was filling up with seven-pointed stars. She had to put the big 50-spot on her neck to save space. It was unconventional, but conventions were there to make it easy on the fakers and cheats. You had to bend conventions to make room for somebody like Julia.

But Julia was running out of steam. She was a freight train of magical pedagogy, but that train ran on information, new data, and fuel was growing scarce, and what there was wasn't of the best quality. The potatoes were too small. Every time she walked into a new safe house she did so with her hopes high, but her hopes were dashed more and more often. It went like this: she pushed open the door, accepted the ogling gazes of the local males, showed off her stars, intimidated the ranking officer into showing her the binder, which she leafed through listlessly, expecting to find and finding nothing she didn't already know, whereupon she dropped the binder on the floor and walked out, letting Jared make her apologies for her.

This was bad behavior, and she knew it. She did it because she was angry and because she disliked herself. The more she disliked herself, the more she took it out on other people, and the more she took it out on other people the more she disliked herself. There's your proof, Mr. Hofstadter: I am a strange loop.

Sure, she could have lit out for the West Coast, or made a run for the Mexican border, but she had a feeling she already knew what she would find there. In the looking-glass world of the great magical underground, perspective appeared to be reversed: the closer you got to things, the smaller they looked. Objects in mirror were farther away than they appeared. Put another way: how many coin flips could one girl predict? How many nails could she protect from rust? The world was not in urgent need of more demagnetized magnets. This was magic, but it was chickenshit magic. She had tuned in to the choir invisible, and it was singing game-show jingles. She'd put her entire life down as a deposit on this stuff, and it was starting to look like she'd been taken.

After all she'd been through, all she'd sacrificed, that was more than she could stand. She wondered for a while if Jared could be holding out on her, if he knew something she didn't, but she was pretty sure that wasn't the case. Just to make sure she deployed the nuclear option. Nope. Zero. Oh, well.

To be absolutely honest, she'd deployed the nuclear option a few times on her travels, and she was starting to feel a bit like a nuclear wasteland herself: irradiated and toxic. She didn't like to think about it. She didn't even name it to herself: *nuclear* was the code word, and she kept those memories encoded, never to be decrypted. She'd done what she had to do, that was the end of it. She no longer even fantasized about real love. She couldn't imagine it anymore, her and it being in the same world. She'd given it up for magic.

But nuclear winter was coming, and magic wasn't keeping her warm. It was getting cold, tainted snow was falling, and the earth was getting thirsty again, thirsty for balm. The black dog was hunting. Julia was feeling it again, the blackness.

Or really blackness would have been a relief, blackness would have been a field trip compared with where she was headed, which was despair. That stuff had no color. She wished it were made of blackness, velvety soft blackness, that she could curl up and fall asleep in, but it was so much worse than that. Think of it as the difference between zero and the empty set, the set that contains nothing, *not even zero.* These but the trappings and the suits of woe. *All these seem to laugh,/Compared with me, who am their epitaph.*

December came, and the days shortened. Snow quietened the traffic on Throop Avenue. And then one day, St. Lucy's Day as it should happen, the day of the Donne poem, it all went down. And when it did, it went down Western-style: a stranger came to town.

She had a nice look about her, the stranger, an Ivy League look. Twenty-nine maybe, dark suit, dark hair pulled back and secured with crossed chopsticks. A round face, baby fat, nerd glasses, but hard: there might once have been a time when she was pushed around, but that time was long past. As per Throop Avenue protocol, as soon as she was in the door the big gun stepped to her, the big gun being Julia.

Well. Ivy League took off her jacket and unbuttoned her cuffs. Both arms were sleeved in stars up to the shoulders. She spread them wide, in the manner of our savior, to show a 100-spot on the inside of each wrist. The room got very quiet. Julia showed Ivy League her stars. Then Ivy League made her prove it.

This had never happened to Julia before, but she knew the drill. She would have to walk through every spell she knew, every test she'd ever passed, to satisfy Ivy that she had earned her stars. Step-by-step, level by level, coins, nails, fires, magnets, the whole utility belt, from level one to level seventy-seven, which was as far as Julia had gotten. It took four hours, while the sun set and the short-timers and day students went home.

Of course Julia lived for this shit. She only flubbed a couple, in the midfifties, but the bylaws allowed her a few retakes, and she got through it, shaking but still fierce. Whereupon Ivy League nodded coldly, rolled down her sleeves, put her jacket back on, and left.

It took all of Julia's pride not to run after her, shouting, "Take me with you, mysterious stranger!" She knew who that must have been. That was one of the Others, the people who had a line on real magic, the pure shit. Ivy League had been to the source, where the spells came from. Julia had known they were out there just by the way they perturbed the universe, like a black planet, and she'd been right. Finally they'd shown themselves to her. They'd tested her.

And just as Brakebills had, they'd found her wanting. There must be a flaw in her, one that she couldn't see, but obvious to those who looked for it.

It wasn't till she got home that she found the card in her pocket. It was blank, but a complex unlocking enchantment revealed a message printed on it in Old Church Slavonic: *Burn This.* She burned it in an ashtray, using not a simple conflagration spell but rather the forty-third-level one, which did basically the same thing but did it in fourteenth position and in Old Church Slavonic.

The flame flashed violet and orange, rhythmically. The flashes were Morse code. The Morse code spelled out a pair of GPS coordinates, which turned out to correspond to a microscopic hamlet in the south of France. The hamlet was called Murs. It was all very Free Trader Beowulf.

At last, Julia had been called. The fat envelope had arrived. This time she was really going. She had put down her bet a long time ago, and finally, finally, it was showing signs of paying off.

How to explain all this to her parents, who you would have thought would have been way past caring. She was twenty-two now, how many times were these people going to make her break their hearts? But as much as she dreaded the conversation, it went better than she expected. She hid a lot from her parents, but one thing she couldn't hide from them was that she actually felt hopeful for once. She believed that she had a shot at happiness now, and she was taking it. It seemed like—it was—years since she'd felt that way. Her parents understood that somehow, and they weren't upset. They were happy for her. They let her go.

Speaking of letting people go, she dumped owlish Jared, the not-so-cunning linguist, on his pale and bony ass. Call me when you finish that dissertation, porkpie.

One fine day in April Julia boarded a plane, bringing with her none of her worldly possessions, and flew to Marseille, on the lurid blue Mediterranean Sea. She felt so light and free, she could have flown there under her own power.

She rented a Peugeot that she would never return and drove north for an hour, negotiating a typically French *rond-point* every one hundred meters, turned right at Cavaillon, and got lost eighty times near Gordes, a spectacular *village perché* that clung vertiginously to the side of the Luberon Valley as if it had been plastered there with a trowel. She rolled into sleepy, tiny Murs at three in the afternoon, in the heart of photogenic Provence.

And lo and behold, it was a little gem, a largely untouristed clump of old houses built from strangely light-emitting bleached-brown southern French stone. It had one church and one castle and one hotel. The streets were medieval and paint-scrapingly narrow. Julia stopped the car in the town square and took in the heartbreaking World War I memorial. Half of the dead had the same last name.

The GPS coordinates were ten minutes outside of town. They corresponded to a handsome farmhouse afloat all by itself in a sea of hay and lavender fields. It had sky-blue shutters and a white gravel driveway in which she parked her scraped-up Peugeot. A clean-cut man only a little older than Julia answered the door. He was handsome—you got the impression that he hadn't always been clean-cut, that he'd lost a lot of weight at some point in his life. It had left behind some interesting lines on his face.

"Hello Circe," he said. "I'm Pouncy Silverkitten. Welcome home."

CHAPTER 19

Standing at the bow with Eliot the next morning, two kings of Fillory plowing eastward into the unknown, into the rising sun, never knowing what God or Fate or Magic was going to send rearing up at them over the horizon next, this now: this was much more like it. This was the stuff.

At first it had been hard to admit it, to change gears, again, and just go with it, but then suddenly it wasn't. Not with the morning sun on his face, and the *Muntjac* surging and galloping along under him. He'd missed a lot here, but he wasn't going to miss anything more. Earth was the dream, not Fillory, and it was going to that part of his brain where dreams went—the kind of anxiety-ridden, fiendishly detailed dreams that felt like they lasted for years, through endless meaningless plot twists, which delivered you ultimately to a fate not even of death but merely of permanent embarrassment. Fillory had taken him back. Welcome to the Quest for the Seven Keys. Your adventure is already in progress.

Bingle was atop the forecastle as usual, just like back in the day, but now he was sparring vigorously with another swordsman. It was Benedict, stripped to the waist, lean and brown, grimacing as he gave ground and then, unbelievably, beating Bingle back and pressing his advantage. The whole time he kept his wrist on his hip, swashbuckler-style. The air rang with the loud scraping of steel on steel, like the gnashing of a huge pair of scissors.

Their swords locked. Stalemate. They broke apart, clapping each other on the shoulder and laughing—laughing!—about some point of technical swordsmanship. It was like watching an alternate-timeline version of himself, a timeline in which he'd stayed in Fillory and learned to hold his sword at full extension for more than two minutes. Quentin caught Benedict's eye, and Benedict saluted him, smiling with those bright white teeth. Quentin saluted back. They squared off again.

Bingle had found his disciple.

"Those guys are amazing."

He hadn't heard Poppy come up beside him. She was watching the action too.

"Can you do that?" she asked.

"Are you kidding?" Poppy shook her head. She was not kidding. "I wish I could. The one on the right, the older guy? He's the best swordsman in Fillory. We had a contest."

"It all still looks like a movie to me. I can't believe it's all real. Wow!" Bingle did one of his signature gymnastic tumbling passes. "Oh my God. I thought he was going over the side."

"I know. I was going to take lessons with him."

"That sounds exciting. What happened?"

"I accidentally went back to the real world. Then a year went by here in three days."

"Well, I can see now why you wanted to come back. It's beautiful here. I'm sorry I thought it was funny before. I was wrong."

Quentin had expected Poppy to be miserable on board the *Muntjac*. After all, she'd effectively been abducted from everything she knew and cared about and brought here. It was an outrage to every principle she lived by.

And all that was true, and she'd spent a day being outraged about it. Well, half a day. Poppy had spent yesterday afternoon sulking, then she showed up at breakfast this morning with a brand-new can-do attitude. She just wasn't temperamentally suited to long-haul sulking. Sure, all right, she'd been accidentally transported to a magical world that until recently she had understood to be fictional. The situation wasn't ideal. But it was what she had to work with, so she would work with it. She was a tough one, Poppy.

"I talked to the other one at dinner last night," she said. "The kid. Benedict. He's a big fan of yours."

"Benedict? Really?"

"Did you see how he lit up when he saw you watching him just now? Look at him, he's killing himself to impress you. You're a father figure for him."

Quentin hadn't seen. How was Poppy here for one day and she'd seen all that?

"To be honest I always thought he hated me."

"He's gutted he didn't get to go to Earth with you."

"You must be joking. And miss out on all the adventures here?"

Now Poppy directed her guileless blue gaze at him instead of the sword fight.

"What makes you think what happened to you on Earth wasn't an adventure?"

Quentin started to answer, and stopped with his mouth open. Because it turned out he had nothing to say.

It was five more days before they sighted land.

They were having breakfast al fresco on deck: Quentin, Eliot, Josh, and Poppy. It was a practice Eliot had instituted: the crew set up a table on the poop deck, with a blinding white tablecloth clipped on to keep it from blowing away. He kept this up in a surprising range of meteorological conditions. Once Quentin saw him up there alone in a squall, munching on marmalade toast that was obviously soaked through with salt spray. It was a matter of principle with him.

But today it was nice out. The weather was almost tropical again. Sunlight flashed off the silverware, and the sky was a perfect blue dome. Though the food itself was getting pretty grim, the kind of unspoilable stuff that came out of deep storage late in an ocean voyage: hard biscuits and meat so salty it was more salt than meat. The only thing that was still good was the jam. Quentin used a lot of it.

"So is this how it works?" he said. "The questing? We just keep sailing east till we hit something?"

"Unless you have a better idea," Eliot said.

"No. Just remind me why we think it's going to work?"

"Because that's how quests always work," Eliot said. "I don't pretend to understand the mechanics of it, but the lesson seems to be that you just can't force the issue with a whole lot of detective work. It's a waste of energy. The ones who go around knocking on doors and looking for clues never find the thing, the Grail or whatever it is. It's more a matter of having the right attitude."

"What attitude is that?"

Elliot shrugged.

"I haven't got a clue. I guess we're supposed to have faith."

"I never really took you for the faith-having kind," Quentin said.

"I didn't either. But it's worked out so far. We've got five of the seven keys. You can't argue with results."

"You can't," Quentin said, "but that's actually not the same thing as having faith."

"Why do you always try to ruin everything?"

"I'm not ruining it. I just want to understand it."

"If you had faith you wouldn't have to understand."

"And why exactly are you looking for these keys?" Poppy asked brightly. "Or I guess, why are we looking for them?"

"Yeah, why are we?" Josh said. "I mean, don't get me wrong, they're cool and all. They sound cool. Can I see them?"

"We don't really know why," Eliot said. "The Unique Beasts wanted us to find them."

"But find them and do what with them?" Poppy said.

"I suppose once we have them all they'll tell us. Or perhaps we'll know when we have them. Or perhaps we'll never know. They might just take the keys and pat us on the behind and send us on our way. I don't know. I've never done a quest before."

"So . . . the journey is the arrival, kind of thing?" Josh said. "I hate that stuff. I'm an old-fashioned arrival-is-the-arrival kind of guy."

"For what it's worth, they told me the realm was in peril," Eliot said. "So there is that. But it's not like the Holy Grail was actually *useful* for anything."

"I told everybody the Neitherlands are jacked, right?" Josh said.

"You think that's part of this?" Quentin said. "You think they're connected?"

"No. Well, maybe." Josh stroked his chin with his thumb and fore-finger. "But *how?*"

"The Neitherlands are down." Quentin ticked them off. "Jollyby is dead. The realm is supposedly in peril. Seven Golden Keys. A dragon collecting buttons. If there's a thread running through all that, I'm not seeing it."

Maybe he didn't want to see it. That would be a hell of a thread. You'd want to think twice about yanking on it.

Someone up in the rigging shouted that he could see an island.

The boat's prow scrunched almost soundlessly into the damp white sand. Quentin vaulted over the bow just as it spent the very last of its momentum and landed on his feet on powdery white sand with his boots still dry. He turned back toward the launch, bowed, and received a smattering of applause from its passengers.

He grabbed the painter and hauled on it as the others—Eliot, Josh, Poppy, Julia, Bingle, Benedict—scrambled out on both sides. The air was quiet and still. It felt weird to be standing on solid ground again.

"Worst away team ever," Josh said, wading up onto land. "Not a single redshirt."

Pretty: that was the impression the island had made from a distance. Chalk cliffs that parted to reveal a small bay with a tidy beach. A row of single trees stood out against the skyline, so fine and still and green against the blue sky they looked like they'd been carved in jade. Vacation paradise.

It was late afternoon; it had taken them most of the day to make landfall. They stood together on the shore in a knot. The sand was as clean as if it had been sifted. Quentin slogged across it and up the first dune to the crest to see what was beyond it. The dune was steep, and just short of the top he flopped down on the slope and peered over the crest. It was like being a kid at the beach. Beyond the dune were more dunes topped with scrub, then a meadow, then a line of trees, then Ember knew what else. So far so good. Pretty.

"Welp," Quentin said. "Let's get questin'."

But first there were more mundane matters to attend to. Quentin and Poppy and Josh had been in Venice three days ago, but this was the first land the men had seen in something like three weeks. They piled ashore in twos and threes; some of them cannonballed off the *Muntjac's* sides into the flat green sea. After a suitable interval for goofing off Eliot mustered them on the shore and sent them out in teams to find fresh water, gather wood for fires and new spars, set up tents, harvest the local fruit, hunt for local game.

"We've fallen on our feet," Eliot said, once everybody had a job to do. "Don't you think? So far I would rate this an above-average island."

"It's so beautiful!" Poppy said. "Do you think anybody lives here?"

Eliot shook his head.

"I don't know. We're two months' sail out from Castle Whitespire. I've never heard of anyone else coming this far. We could be the first human beings ever to set foot here."

"Think of that," said Quentin. "So do you want to . . . ?"

"What?"

"You know. Claim it. For Fillory."

"Oh!" Eliot considered. "We haven't been doing that. It seems a little imperialist. I'm not sure it's in good taste."

"But haven't you always wanted to say it?"

"Well, yes," Eliot said. "All right. We can always give it back." He raised his voice, using the one he used to call meetings to order back at Castle Whitespire. "I, High King Eliot, hereby claim this island for the great and glorious Kingdom of Fillory! Henceforth it will be known as"—he paused—"as New Hawaii!"

Everybody nodded vaguely.

"New Hawaii?" Quentin said. "Really?"

"It's not really tropical," Poppy said. "The vegetation's more temperate."

"What about Farflung Island?" Quentin said. "Like as one word: Farflung."

"Relief Island." Poppy was getting into the spirit of it. "Whitesand Island. Greengrass Island!"

"Skull Island," Josh said. "No wait, Spider-Skull Island!"

"Okay, the Island to Be Named Later," Eliot said. "Come on. Let's find out what's on it before we name it."

But by then the sun was low in the sky, so instead they pitched in bringing sticks and dry grass back from the meadow. With five trained magicians on hand, starting a fire wasn't a problem. They could have made a fire with just sand. But it wouldn't have smelled as good.

The hunting party came back flushed with pride, hauling two wild goats on their shoulders, and one of the foragers had spotted a patch of something very closely analogous to carrots growing wild at the edge of the woods, that seemed self-evidently safe to eat. They all sat in circles on the cooling sand, the cold sea air at their backs, the warmth of the fire on their faces, and savored the feeling of being on firm ground again, with enough space to stretch out their arms and legs and not touch anything or anybody. The beach was covered with footprints now, and as the sun got lower the light made monkey-puzzle shadow patterns on it. They were very far from home.

The setting sun moved behind a cloud, lighting it up from the inside like a pall of smoke, sunlight leaking out around the edges. Strange stars came swarming across the blackening sky. No one wanted to get back on the *Muntjac,* not yet, so when the light was all gone the travelers wrapped themselves up in blankets right there on the sand and fell asleep.

The next day everything seemed a little less urgent than it had when they first arrived. Yes, the realm was in peril, but was it in immediate peril? It was hard to imagine a place that felt less imperiled than the Island to Be Named Later. There was a touch of lotus land about it. And anyway adventure would find them when it was ready, or so the theory ran. You couldn't rush it. You just had to keep the right state of mind. For now they would savor the anticipation, and stay well rested.

Even Julia wasn't pushing.

"I was afraid we would not get back," she said. "Now I am afraid of what will happen if we go forward."

They hiked up to the top of the cliffs on one side of the bay and from there got a good look at more green island, with rocky hills heaped up in the interior. Birds roosted along the clifftops in bunches—they had dull gray feathers on their backs and wings, but they had a way of turning in the air in unison and suddenly showing you their rose-colored chests all at once. Quentin was going to name them rose-breasted swoopers, or something along those lines, when Poppy pointed out that they already had a name. They were galahs. They had them in Australia too.

The cook was a keen fisherman, and he pulled a prodigious number of fat, tiger-striped fish out of the surf, one after the other. In the afternoon Quentin watched Benedict and Bingle fence with foils—they stuck wine corks on the tips for safety. He spent an hour just lying back on his elbows and looking at the waves. They were nothing like the brutally cold, puritan waves of his East Coast youth, which had sternly discouraged anything so frivolous as surfing or frolicking. These waves came sloping in smoothly, building up heads of boiling cream foam on top, reared up for a moment, mint green and paper-thin in the sunlight, then broke in a long line with a sound like fabric tearing.

He wiggled his toes in the hot sand and watched the weird moire optical effects that the miniature sand avalanches created. They went to bed that night hardly having explored more than the thin crescent of island they'd already seen. Tomorrow they would strike inland, into the forest and up into the hills.

Quentin woke early. The sun wasn't even up yet, though there was a gray blur of predawn to the east. He wondered what happened out there, in the extreme east. The rules were different in Fillory. For all he knew the world was flat, and the sun ran on tracks.

Everything was gray: the sand, the trees, the sea. Deep red embers smoldered under the gray ashes of the bonfires. It was warm out. The sleepers on the beach looked as though they had fallen there from a great height. Poppy had kicked off her blanket—she slept with her arms crossed over her chest, like a knight on a tomb.

He would have gone back to sleep, but he was dying for a piss. He got up and jogged to the top of the dune and down the other side. It didn't seem quite far enough for hygienic purposes, so he went one farther, and at that point he figured he might as well get as far as the field and pee there.

It was undeniably a vulnerable feeling, as he let fly into the tall grass, but the morning was as still as a painting, and they hadn't been completely stupid about it. Anybody who knew the proper reveal spells—meaning almost no one—would have seen a gossamer-thin line of magical force, pale blue in color, looped along the edge of the forest like a trip wire. They'd set it up the day before. It wouldn't hurt anybody who walked into it, not permanently, but the magicians would know they were there, and they wouldn't be walking anymore. They'd be lucky if they were conscious. They'd already caught a wild pig that way.

Even the insects were hushed. Quentin sneezed—he was mildly allergic to some local plant—and wiped his eyes. On the far side of the meadow something slipped into the forest. It went just as his eye began to track it—it must have been standing there, stock-still, watching him while he pissed. He got an impression of something large, the size of a big boar maybe.

Quentin fastened his trousers—zippers were foreign to Fillory, and so far impossible to reverse-engineer, you just couldn't explain them to the dwarves—and walked across the meadow to where the animal had been. Standing just on the near side of the blue line, he peered in among the trees. They were thick enough that it was still full night in the forest. Still, he caught the faintest shadow of a pair of heavy animal haunches receding into it.

Is this it? Is it starting? Carefully, like he was stepping over an electric fence, he put one leg over the invisible blue line, then the other, and walked into the forest. He was pretty sure he knew Who he was chasing even before He was fully in view.

"Hey, Ember," he called. "Ember! Wait up!"

The god looked at him impassively over His shoulder, then continued to trot.

"Oh, come on."

The ram-god had not been seen in Fillory since the Brakebills took the thrones, or not as far as Quentin knew. He looked fully recovered from the beating He'd taken from Martin Chatwin. Even His hind leg, which had been crippled the last time Quentin saw Him, was restored and could take His weight without a limp.

Quentin had complicated feelings about Ember. He wasn't like Ember was in the books. Quentin was still angry that He hadn't been able to save them—to save Alice—in the fight against Martin. He supposed it wasn't Ember's fault, but still. What kind of a god wasn't at the top of the food chain in His own world?

The big woolly kind with horns, apparently. Quentin didn't have any particular beef with Ember, he just didn't want to bow down to Him the way He always seemed to expect people to do. If Ember was so great He should have saved Alice, and if He wasn't that great, Quentin wasn't bowing. QED.

Still, if Ember was here, it meant they were on the right track. Things were going to get very real soon, or at least very Fillorian. He just didn't know which Fillory it was going to be—the beautiful, magical Fillory or the dark, frightening one. Either way this would be a good moment for a shipment of divine wisdom to arrive. Guidance from on high. A pillar of fire, a tree of smoke.

Ember led Quentin uphill, into the interior of the island. Quentin was starting to get winded. After five minutes Ember finally slowed down enough to let him catch up. By that time they were halfway up a hill, and the sun had at last pushed a hot-pink sliver of itself up over the horizon. They were high enough that Quentin could look out across the forest canopy.

"Thanks," Quentin said, taking big heaving breaths. "Jesus." He leaned on Ember's flank for a second before wondering if maybe that was too familiar, mortal to god. "Hi, Ember. How's it going?"

"Hello, my child."

That resonant bass voice instantly sent Quentin right back to the cavern under Ember's Tomb. He hadn't heard it since then, and his guts clenched. That was not a place he wanted to go back to.

He would keep the tone light.

"Fancy meeting You here."

"We do not meet by chance. Nothing happens by chance."

That was Ember for you. No small talk. The ram began to climb again. Quentin wondered if He knew that behind His back Quentin and the others called him Ram-bo. And, less kindly, Member.

"No, I guess not," Quentin said, though he wasn't actually sure that he agreed. "So. How did You get all the way out here?"

"Fillory is my realm, child. I am everywhere, and therefore anywhere."

"I see that. But couldn't You have just magicked us here, instead of making us sail all this way?"

"I could have. I did not."

Forget it. Quentin could look back now and see the *Muntjac* at anchor, neat and perfect. You could have put it in a bottle. He could even see the camp on the beach, the bonfires and blankets. But there was no time to admire the view, the ram was taking the rocky slopes of the hill at speed. Which was fine for Him, He was built for it. He was a ram. Quentin panted and eyed the fluffy pale gold wool on His broad back and wondered if Ember would let him ride on Him. Probably not.

"You know," Quentin went on, "while I've got You, I've been wondering. About these Seven Keys. If You're basically omnipresent, and probably omniscient too, why don't You go around and just collect the keys Yourself? If they're so important to the realm? I mean, You could probably do it in half an hour, tops."

"There is Deeper Magic at work here, my child. Even the gods must bow to it. That is the way."

"Oh, right. The Deeper Magic. I forgot about that."

The Deeper Magic always seemed to come up when Ember didn't feel like doing something, or needed to close a plot hole.

"I do not think you understand, my child. There are things that a man must do, that a god may not. He who completes a quest does not merely find something. He becomes something."

Quentin stopped, blowing, hands on hips. The horizon to the east was a solid band of orange now. The stars were going out.

"What's that? What does he become?"

"A hero, Quentin."

The ram kept going, and he followed.

"Fillory has need of gods, and kings, and queens, and those it has. But it has need of a hero too. And it has need of the Seven Keys."

"Fillory doesn't ask for much, does it?"

"Fillory asks for everything."

With a lumbering lunge, awkward but powerful, Ember surged ahead and surmounted a rocky dome that turned out to be the top of the hill. From there He turned His head and looked down at Quentin with His strange, peanut-shaped eyes. Supposedly sheep evolved that way so they could see wolves coming out of the corners of their eyes. Better peripheral vision. But the effect was disconcerting.

"That's a big ask."

"Fillory asks for what it needs. Do you, Quentin? What do you need? What do you ask for?"

The question stopped him. He was used to scolding and pseudo-Socratic interrogation from Ember, but here was a rare gem: a good question. What did he want? He'd wanted to get back to Fillory, and he'd done that. He thought he'd wanted to go back to Castle White-spire, but now he wasn't so sure. The terror of almost losing Fillory had been extreme, but he'd found his way back. Now he wanted to find the keys. He wanted to finish the quest. He wanted his life to be exciting and important and to mean something. And he wanted to make Julia better. He felt like he would do anything to help Julia, if he only knew what to do.

"I guess it's like what You said," Quentin said. "I want to be a hero."

Ember turned away again and faced the rising sun.

"Then you will have your chance," He said.

Quentin scrambled up onto the rocky summit and watched the dawn alongside Him. He was going to ask Ember about it, about the sun, and what it was, and what happened out there at the rim of the world, or whether Fillory even had a rim. But when he turned to ask Him he was alone on top of the hill. Ember was gone.

Just when things were getting interesting. He turned slowly, in a full circle, but there was no sign of Him. Vanished without a trace. Oh, well. Now that He was gone Quentin almost missed Him. There was something special about being in the divine presence, even when the divinity was Ember.

He stretched, standing at the top of the island, and then jumped carefully down from the rocks and began trotting back down the hill to the beach. He couldn't wait to tell the others what had happened, though the whole thing already felt like a dream, an early morning, half-awake dream tangled up with sheets and pillows and dawn light through closed curtains, the kind you only remembered by chance hours later, for a few seconds, when you were going to sleep again at the end of the day. He wondered if anyone else was up yet. Maybe he could still go back to bed.

He should have noticed that something had changed, but he'd been distracted on the way up. He'd been practically running, and plus he'd been talking to a god. And he'd never been an especially assiduous observer of flora and fauna. He wouldn't have noticed a spectacular beech tree or an unusual elm because he didn't know what the difference between them was, if any.

Still, after a few minutes he began to wonder if he was coming down a different way than he'd come up, because it all seemed a little rockier than he remembered—the ratio of rocks to plants and dirt to grass wasn't quite what it had been. He didn't let it worry him too much, because if it worried him too much he would have to climb back up the hill and find a new way down, and that was the kind of thing he wanted to avoid. And besides, he was keeping the rising sun on his right hand, and that's how navigation works, right? If things really went wrong he could go all the way down to the beach and cut along the coast. No way he could miss the camp that way. He still had hopes of getting back to the beach in time for breakfast.

One thing he couldn't ignore, though, although he tried to for as long as he could, was that the shadows of things weren't getting shorter anymore, in the usual manner of shadows cast by a rising sun. They were getting longer. Which would have meant that the orange-red stew boiling at the edge of the sky was somehow no longer a sunrise, but a sunset instead.

And it would mean he was on the wrong side of the island. But that was impossible. The strangest thing was that he didn't even realize that somebody had hit him with a sword till after it had happened.

All he knew at first was that suddenly he'd lost his balance, and his left arm was numb.

"Shit!" he said.

He staggered and caught himself with his good right hand on the cold turf. There was a man behind him, a large young man with a round pale face and a goatee. The two of them were stuck together somehow. They were connected by a short broad-bladed sword that was stuck in Quentin's collarbone, and the man was trying to wrench it out.

What had saved him was this: half of Quentin's collarbone was made of hardwood, put there by the centaurs to replace what Martin Chatwin had bitten out of him. The man with the sword, not knowing this, had unluckily chosen that side when he attempted to cut Quentin in half from behind.

"Son of a bitch!" Quentin said. He didn't mean the man specifically; he didn't know who, or Who, he meant.

If he'd been thinking clearly Quentin might have actually tried to win the tug-of-war over the sword, but in the moment he just wanted it out of him, badly. They both did—their interests were temporarily aligned. In a state of almost disembodied fear Quentin reached up and gripped it with the opposite-side hand. It cut his palm. The man planted a booted foot on Quentin's back and yanked the sword out with a grunt.

They faced each other, both panting. The quietness of it was weird: real fights happened without a sound track. The man was lightly armored, wearing some kind of blue livery, and not even as old as Quentin. It felt strangely personal—there, alone in a clearing on a silent island, in low-angle morning (evening) light, Quentin felt the *you*ness of the man intensely. For an endless second they stared at each other while Quentin, like everyone else who has ever faced a blade unarmed, made little feinting motions in either direction, as if he were a defender and the man with the sword was going to try to cut past him to the basket. Just in case he lost that matchup, Quentin whispered the opening words to a spell, a Persian fainting charm, he could do it with one hand, which was lucky because he still couldn't feel his left—

Rudely, the man didn't wait for him to finish. He advanced, cutting off Quentin's angles, then lunged appallingly fast, stabbing this time rather than chopping. Quentin twisted desperately to his right and away, but not quite far enough because the sword cut into him. It was incredible that he hadn't made it, in his mind he was so absolutely sure he would make it, but instead the metal went right into his right side, through his clothes and into his body.

He'd twisted so far around that it went in from behind. At first the sensation was just strange, this hard, awkward presence taking up space where usually his body was, grinding against his ribs. Then it felt warm, almost pleasantly warm, then almost immediately hot, searing hot, as if the sword wasn't just sharp but glowing white from a forge.

"Ahhhh . . ." Quentin said under his breath, and he sucked air through his clenched teeth, exactly as if he'd cut himself chopping an onion.

The man was obviously a soldier, but Quentin had never really thought about what that meant. He was a professional killer, efficient and businesslike. He had none of Bingle's elegance. He was like a baker, except instead of making bread he made corpses, and he wanted to make Quentin into one. He wasn't even breathing hard. He jerked the sword out so he could go in again, right away, this time aiming for something more vital. Time to make the donuts. Quentin couldn't think.

"*ışık!*" he shouted. He snapped his fingers.

It was just what came to him; it had been nagging at the back of his mind ever since the safe house. He'd gotten it right this time: light flared between them in the clearing. Startled, the man fell back a step. He must have thought Quentin had hurt him somehow. It didn't take him long to figure out that he was all right, but it didn't take Quentin long to blurt out the Persian fainting charm either.

The man dropped his sword and fell forward onto the thin grass. Quentin stood there panting and holding his side. Blood soaked his shirt. That was too close. Too close. He almost died. The pain was amazing, like a pulsing flare hanging there in the softening early evening, an evening star. Not looking, he couldn't have said with absolute confidence if the pain was even located inside his body. When it couldn't get any worse he threw up. Sour fish from last night's dinner. Then it got even worse than that.

Gingerly he took off his shirt, detaching it in one go from the wounded place, and ripped off one of the sleeves. He folded the sleeve into a pad and pressed it against the wound, then tried as best he could to tie the rest of the shirt around him to hold it in place. When it was done he spent a minute just gritting his teeth and trying not to pass out. His heart was fluttering in his chest like a trapped sparrow. He kept repeating the phrase *damage control* under his breath. It helped for some reason.

When he could inspect it again he saw that the wound was bleeding but not pumping blood. There seemed to be a sharp limit to how deep a breath he could take without his vision going gray with pain. He tried to think what was in there. From the pain when he moved the sword must have cut muscle, but it couldn't have reached his lung. Could it? What the hell else was over there? Probably it had just gone into the flank meat.

Adrenaline was flooding his system, dimming the pulsing flare of pain, pulling oxygen away from it. It was there, but he started to be able to bear it. As he did he realized what was happening. It dawned on him with a terrible, fiery power. He was having an adventure. A real one this time. That's what the pain was.

He looked at his hands. He could feel his left one again. He made fists with both of them. There was a chunky notch in his wooden collarbone, but no deep structural damage. The kind of thing you'd fill in with Bondo. He shook his head. It seemed clear. Or clearish.

He looked at the man snoring facedown on the stubby island grass. He picked up his sword and began walking in the direction the man had come from.

The castle was a small three-part affair: a stodgy boxy keep with two outlying watchtowers, all built out of gray stone, with enormous trees growing around them. The whole layout was visible from where he stood on the rocky hillside. It was built on a grassy knob of land at the foot of the hills that Quentin could now see dominated one coast of the island, screening the castle from other angles of view. No wonder he and the others had missed it.

Quentin crept from rock to rock, keeping out of sight of whoever might be monitoring the hillside, zigzagging downhill toward the castle. He didn't meet any more soldiers. Maybe it had just been bad luck. Not wanting to push it, he picked his way down a rocky defile to the edge of the sea. He would approach by creeping along the shore.

A narrow crust of rocky beach ran along it, barely enough to keep his feet dry. The sea lapped at it excitedly with dark, rapid wavelets. Quentin wasn't even thinking about what he was doing. If he had to explain it to anybody, that he was preparing a one-man *Die Hard* magical assault on a castle, it would have been difficult to justify. He might have said that he was performing vital reconnaissance, probing its defenses, but all that meant was that if he got scared enough he was going to run away. What he was really thinking was that this was what Ember had meant, what Ember had given him. His chance. Something was in there, something to do with the keys, or Jollyby, or Julia, or all of them, and he was going to get it and bring it back.

And then he stopped. A boat was drawn up on the thin shingled beach, a gray, weathered rowboat. The oars were there, laid neatly inside it like the folded wings of a dragonfly. It was in good repair. The painter was knotted around an overhanging branch.

Just like that Quentin got stuck, mentally stuck. It felt like no force on Earth could compel him to walk past the boat without getting in it. He was going to get into it and retreat. He would row back around to the other side of the island, to where his friends were. His sword wound would compromise his rowing ability, but not fatally. The sudden sense of inertia was overwhelming. No one could reproach him for cowardice; indeed it would be foolhardy to keep going, selfish even.

He was actually untying the thin rope from the tree branch—he had to do it with his left hand, since he couldn't lift his right arm above his head—when a pale face appeared at the far end of the beach. Another soldier.

It was eerie how long it took them both to react. Quentin didn't want to believe that the man could see him, or if he did that he would recognize Quentin as an intruder, but even though the daylight was going by the minute there was no actual way that either of those things was possible. A cold wavelet broke over Quentin's foot.

If the man had run and raised the alarm, that would have been the end of it. But he didn't. Instead he advanced—he strode down the beach toward Quentin, drawing a short stubby sword as he came, the twin of the one Quentin was holding. Guess everybody wants to be a hero. Quentin supposed he didn't look especially imposing.

But appearances were deceiving. Quentin stuck the first soldier's sword point-down in the sand and squared off.

Kinetics: he was good with them. He was a Physical Kid. Whispering fast, reaching back to a Brakebills seminar he hadn't thought about in, what, five years, he held out both hands, palms up, and waved them toward the soldier as if he were shooing away a flock of pigeons. As one, the black pebbles on the shore rose up at the man in a dark stream, like a swarm of angry bees, pelting him in the chest and the face with a rattling sound like a gravel truck dumping its load. Confused, the man turned to run, but he fell after only a few steps, and the rocks buried him into unconsciousness.

There now. All at once the fear was gone again, and the pain was gone, and the inertia was gone. Quentin was free to move. He could pass the boat. He'd been free his whole life, if only he'd known it.

He walked over to where the man lay half-covered. A warm, damp wind was coming in from offshore. Quentin kicked some rocks away from his face: a narrow sunburned face, ravaged by acne scars. His story was over for now. Quentin picked up his sword and chucked it as hard as he could out to sea. It skipped once, twice, and sank.

He picked up a small flat stone and slipped it into his pocket.

A skinny, windy path led up from the end of the beach through the trees toward the near watchtower. The grade was steep, and he walked up it bent over; it made his burning side feel better. He was afraid of nothing except losing momentum. He rehearsed spells to himself under his breath without actually casting them, feeling the energy build and then letting it die away again.

The watchtower was round and built on a steep slope, so coming up on it even the ground floor was above him. He put a hand on the old exposed foundation. He wondered who'd built it. The bricks felt cool and permanent. Who had placed them in this careful, elegant way, rectangular bricks approximating a smooth circle? Who was inside it? Was it enough that fate, or Ember, or whoever, had stuck these people in his way, that he was now going to hurt or kill them? After all he couldn't keep this nonlethal shit up all night. Was it enough that one or really two of them had tried to kill him—one of them had even gone so far as to stick a sword in him?

Enough thinking. Sometimes it felt like all he did was think, and all other people did was act. He was going to do the other thing for a while. See how that felt.

He blew five minutes on a silent ritual that was supposed to enhance his senses, at least in theory, though he hadn't done it since he was an undergraduate, and even then he'd never done it sober. His best bet would be to fly up the outside of the tower and surprise whoever was inside from above. Flight was a surprisingly major arcanum, bigger than you'd think, and he worried that using it would leave him with too little juice for a fight. But on the other hand, huge points for style. Nothing made you feel more like a fucking sorcerer than aviating under your own power. Yippee ki-yay, motherfuckers.

Up he rose through the twilight air. The ancient brick rushed by his face in the dimness. There was no noise. He felt his chest empty out a little with the effort. It wasn't so much a feeling of being weightless as one of being supported, touchlessly, somewhere around your shoulders. You were a baby being lifted up by a giant parent. Who's a good boy?

Quentin's long legs hung down as he cleared the treetops. He wished the others could see him. He shot up above the rim of the tower, arms spread out, one hand holding his stolen sword, the other lit up and crackling with violet witchery in the dimness. At the last second he cocked one knee up, the way superheroes did in comic books.

The man on the rooftop had time to stop swinging his arms back and forth and crane his neck back in shock, squinting, all blond hair and buckteeth, before Quentin extended his hand toward him, two fingers pointed. Two deep indigo pulses shot out of them and caught the man in the forehead and dropped him; the pulses ricocheted off into the darkness to points unknown. Quentin had had a long time to tinker with Penny's old Magic Missile spell, and now it ran smooth and precise, with glowy special effects on top. The man's head snapped back and then forward, and he went down on his hands and knees. Another shot, to the ribs, sent him sprawling over on his side.

Three down. Quentin landed lightly on the stone roof, which had a low wall around it. Again he felt the absence of a sound track keenly. There was a gun up here, a squat black cannon with a neat pyramid of cannonballs next to it. He took the flat rock that he'd collected from the beach out of his pocket. Drawing a dagger from the belt of the unconscious lookout—it was all the man was armed with—he began scratching a rune on it. It was a complicated business, but he could see the rune in his mind—could picture the page of the book where he'd read about it, a left-hand page. It didn't have to be exact, straight lines and right angles, but the structure of it had to be right. You couldn't mung up the topology.

When it was done, when he connected the last line to the first one, Quentin felt the join in his gut. It was good enough. The power was locked in there. The stone buzzed and jumped in his hand as if it were alive.

He waited for just a moment at the top of the stairs. Once he threw that rock there would be no going back, no slipping off into the darkness. The warm ocean wind poured over him under the darkening sky. The weather was picking up, and the sea was flecked with combers. A storm was rolling in. He had a sudden worry about the man he'd left down on the beach. What if the tide came in? Quentin was pretty sure the water would wake him up before it drowned him.

A quick, soundless flicker of blue-white light caught Quentin's eye, in his peripheral vision. It came from the other watchtower, on the far side of the keep, through the trees—it was exactly as if somebody had taken a flash photo inside it. He squinted into the half darkness. Had he been spotted? Had he imagined it? A long moment passed. Ten seconds. Twenty. He relaxed again.

The other tower ripped open. Something hot and bright and white exploded inside it. The whole top floor blew out, and arcs of power flashed out in all directions, setting the treetops around it on fire. Stones went crashing away through the underbrush. The tower's roof pancaked down onto the floor below it.

Just then, out at sea, the rough, bold shape of the *Muntjac* came heeling silently around the point. It was like an enormous friendly dog he hadn't seen for weeks and weeks, bounding toward him. The others had come. It was all happening.

Grinning like a loon, Quentin threw his stone down the stairs and stepped away.

A colossal *whump* made the roof under his feet resonate like a drum, as the stone gave up the energy he'd locked inside it all at once, explosively. Dust spurted up from between the roof tiles, and air blasted out of the mouth of the stairs. Instinctively Quentin half squatted, and for a second he wondered if he'd overdone it, but the tower held together. He ran down the steps, prepping another spell, the tip of his sword scraping the wall. The room was dark—he could just make out two men, one lying prone under a broken table, the other trying to get to his feet.

Quentin kept running. His mind was clear and ringing with excitement. As he ran he blew into his hand and shook it to get another spell charged up. Not a moment too soon, because yet another man came pelting up the stairs, hurriedly tugging on gloves. Quentin stiff-armed him straight in the chest, which might or might not have worked anyway, but Quentin's hand was amped up like a Taser, and the charge blew the man back down the stairs.

Quentin hurdled the groaning body and kept on running, out into the square in front of the castle.

It had four sides: the keep on the left, watchtowers on either end, ocean on the right. There was a small obelisk in the middle. A moment later Poppy came walking into the open air from the opposite corner. He hadn't realized what he must look like, shirtless and bloody, until she saw him and he saw her expression. He waved in what he hoped was a cheerful and not moribund way. He was about to jog across to her when a stick clattered across the cobblestones next to him. He looked at it curiously, then scrambled violently backward out of the courtyard when he saw that it was an arrow.

Poppy saw it at the same time he did. She darted behind the pedestal, singing something in rapid-fire Polish, and a green tracer appeared in the air, like a green laser, connecting the arrow to the roof of the castle. She had back-traced its path through the air.

She didn't faze easily. It must be an Australian thing. Probably she grew up fighting off snakes and dingoes and whatever else. He'd never seen her cast anything before, and it was amazing. He'd never in his life seen anybody move their hands that quickly.

"Oy!" she called, her back to the stone obelisk. "Are you all right?"

"I'm all right!"

"Eliot and Benedict are finishing in the tower!" she shouted.

"I'm going in!" He pointed to the keep.

"Wait! No! Bingle's coming too!"

"I'm going in!"

He didn't hear what she said next. He was overjoyed to see them, and somehow weirdly Poppy, good old Poppy, most of all, but he felt a surge of longing at the same time. This was his chance. If he didn't stay ahead of them, if he didn't get there first, he would lose it, and he didn't want to be selfish about it, but if it was all the same to them he wanted this one to be his show. Quentin whispered a few words to his sword and struck it twice on the ground. It took on a golden sheen. Poppy was working on the end of the green trail from the arrow now. The end became a spark, and the spark raced along the trail like a lit fuse. It disappeared over the parapet, and there was a crack of thunder.

Quentin ran for the doorway of the keep. The feeling was absolutely glorious. He didn't know how he knew what to do, but he did. With the others at his back, his last doubt was gone.

The doors were made of foot-thick iron-bound beams. He took a skip-step, wound up with the sword, and smashed it into them overhand. The spell he'd put on it didn't affect the way the sword felt to him, but it acted on everything else as if it weighed about half a ton. The whole structure vibrated, and the wood cracked and split. More dust. The boom echoed out into the night. Another hit smashed the door halfway in, and another cleared the doorway.

Striding into the castle Quentin felt so full of power it was almost painful. It was bursting out of him. He didn't know where it was coming from—his chest felt huge, its contents under maximum pressure. He was a walking bomb. Five men stood in the hall behind the broken door, pointing swords and spears at him, and a shout of wind rushed out of Quentin's hands and blew them backward. He blinded them with a flash of light and then threw them bodily down the great hall. It was just so *obvious*.

He turned and put one hand on the ruins of door he'd just knocked out, and it began to burn. This seemed like a good idea, and very dramatic, but just in case it caused problems later he hardened his skin against fire.

He was discovering, in a way for the first time, what it felt like to truly be a Magician King. That fat bastard he'd been when he was sitting around Castle Whitespire, playing with swords and getting drunk every night? That was no king. This was a king. Master and commander. This was the culmination of everything that had started the day he'd walked into that frozen garden in Brooklyn, all those years ago. He had at last come into his own. Maybe all he'd needed was Ember's permission. You have to have faith.

The ritual he'd done to ramp up his senses was actually working: he was so wired, he could feel where people were through the walls—he could sense the electricity in their bodies, the way a shark does. Time, that dull mechanism that usually reliably stamped out one second after another, like parts on a conveyor belt, erupted into a glorious melody. He was getting it all back now, everything that he'd missed and more. Poppy was right, that time on Earth, it had been an adventure after all. It wasn't just blundering around, it was the buildup to this. And this was living. He would live like this from now on.

"This is me," he whispered. "This is me."

He trotted up the front stairs and through a series of grand rooms. When people approached him, objects flew at them and battered them to the floor—chairs, tables, urns, chests, whatever he could get traction on with a spell. Lightning struck and stunned them. Lazily, he stopped a thrown ax in midair with one outstretched hand, and sent it back the way it came. Breathing in, he sucked the oxygen out of rooms until the people in them choked and passed out, lips blue, eyes bulging. Pretty soon they began to run when they saw him coming.

He felt altered, like he had grown physically giant. It didn't stop the spells pouring out of him, one after another, effortlessly. The enemy troops were mixed, human and fairy and a few exotics: a stone golem of some sort, a water elemental, a red-bearded dwarf, a rather tatty talking panther. It didn't matter, he was an equal-opportunity hero. He was a gusher, a fire hose. He barely even felt the wound in his side anymore. He threw his sword away. Screw swords. A magician doesn't need a sword. A magician doesn't need anything but what's inside him. All he had to do was be who he was: the Magician King.

He had no idea where he was going, he just worked room to room, clearing the building. Twice he heard the *Muntjac*'s guns boom in the distance. Once he threw open a door and found Bingle and Julia backing down a crowd of soldiers amid the wreckage of a drawing room full of ornate furniture. Bingle's magic sword flickered in front of him, as fast and precise as an industrial machine, its glowing tracery leaving hypnotic neon tracks in the air. He seemed to be in a state of martial ecstasy, his tunic wringing with sweat but his face calm, his hooded eyes having drooped almost to slits.

But the real terror was Julia. She'd summoned a kind of transformative magic Quentin didn't know, or maybe whatever it was in her that wasn't human had come to the surface in the fight. He hardly recognized her. Her skin was shining with that phosphorescent silver, and she'd grown at least six inches. She fought bare-handed—she advanced on the soldiers till somebody was foolish enough to thrust a spear at her, at which point she simply grabbed it like he was moving in slow motion and began beating the shit out of him and his friends with it. Her strength looked enormous, and metal blades just skated off her skin.

She didn't look like she needed help. Quentin found the stairs up to the top floor. He kicked open the first door he saw and almost died when a massive fireball rolled over him.

It was a colossally powerful casting. Someone had spent a long time setting it up and pumping energy into it. It enveloped him completely, and he felt the flames licking him, icy through the fireproofing spell. But the spell held. When the fire had dissipated his limbs were smoking but undamaged.

He was standing in the doorway of a darkened library. Inside, sitting at a desk with two lanterns on it, was a skeleton in a nice brown suit. Or not quite a skeleton, a man, but an obviously dead one. He still had flesh on him, but it had shrunk and turned leathery.

It was very still in the library. Bookshelves smoldered and crackled quietly on either side of Quentin, from the fireball. The corpse watched him with eyes like hard dry nuts.

"No?" it said finally. Its voice buzzed and flapped, a blown-out speaker. It obviously didn't have much left in the way of vocal cords. Some unnatural force was keeping it alive, long after its sell-by date. "Well. That was my only spell."

Quentin waited. The thing's face was immobile, unreadable. Its dried lips didn't cover its teeth completely. It wasn't pretty to look at, but for some reason Quentin didn't feel angry at it. Why were they fighting again? For a second Quentin really couldn't remember. He wondered if he'd gotten too far ahead of the others. But no, this was on him. He'd started it. And this was the boss fight.

The corpse came to convulsive life again and whipped a throwing knife at him with one skinny, loose-jointed marionette arm. Quentin ducked, purely out of instinct, but it was a wild throw, nowhere near him. It went through the open door behind him and skittered on the flagstones.

"All right," it said. "Now I'm really done."

The corpse might have sighed.

"Where's the key?" Quentin said. "You have one, don't you?" For a terrible second he worried that it might not.

"I don't even know what I'm doing anymore," the corpse said wheezily. It pushed a small wooden box toward him with one shriveled hand. The skin had worn off some of the knuckles, like the leather off the arms of an old chair. "It used to be my daughter's."

"Your daughter's," Quentin repeated. "Who are you?"

"Don't you know the story?" It sighed again. It seemed much more resigned to its fate than Quentin expected. He didn't know if it had to breathe anymore, but apparently it could still suck air in and out of its leathery chest like a bellows when it wanted to. "I thought everybody knew it."

Now that he'd stopped moving he realized he was covered with sweat. It was cold in the nighttime island air.

"Wait. You're not going to tell me you're him. The man from the fairy tale. *The Seven Golden Keys.*"

"Is that what they're calling it? A fairy tale?" Air hissed between its teeth. Was that laughter? "I suppose it's a little late to quibble about things like that."

"I don't understand. I thought you were one of the good guys."

"We can't all be heroes. Then who would the heroes fight? It's a matter of numbers really. Just work out the sums."

"But isn't this the key your daughter gave you?" Quentin had a terrible feeling he'd grasped the wrong end of something. "That's what the story said. You set her free, from the witch, and she didn't remember you, but she gave you the key."

"That was no witch, that was her mother." More hissing laughter. Only its lower jaw moved when it talked. It was like talking to an animatronic president at a theme park. "I left them to look for the Seven Keys. I suppose I wanted to be a hero. They never forgave me for it. When I finally came back my own daughter didn't know me. Her mother told her I was dead.

"The key kept me alive. It's just as well, your taking it like this. It's terrible living in a dead body, I can't feel anything. You should see how the others look at me."

Quentin opened the wooden box. A golden key lay inside it. He was part of the fairy tale now, he supposed. He'd crashed through a shared wall into an adjoining story. Enter the Magician King.

"Just tell me," the corpse said. "What is it for? I never knew."

"I don't know either. I'm sorry."

Footsteps behind him. Quentin risked a glance back. Just Bingle, catching up at last.

"Don't be sorry. You've paid for it. You paid the price." The life had started going out of it as soon as it let go of the box. It slumped forward, and its head hit the table with a bang. It muttered the last words directly into the wooden desktop. "Like me. You just don't know it yet."

It didn't move again.

Quentin snapped the box shut. He heard Bingle walk in beside him. Together they stared at the dome of the corpse's head, which was as bald and mottled and seamed as a globe.

"Well done," Bingle said.

"I don't think I killed him," Quentin said. "I think he just died."

"It is all good." He must have picked that up from Josh.

Quentin's crazy power levels were dropping rapidly toward normal again, leaving him feeling wrung out and shaky. He was vaguely aware that he was giving off a nasty burnt-hair smell. The fireproofing hadn't been perfect.

"It was that man," Quentin said. "The one from the fairy tale. But his version was different. How did you know to come get me?"

"The cook caught a talking fish. It told us what to do. It had a bottle in its belly, with a map inside. What happened to you?"

"Ember came."

That was enough explanation for now. Together they walked back down the hall toward the stairs, Bingle eyeing every doorway and alcove for holdouts and dead-enders.

They'd done it: another key found. One to go. Quentin was on the scoreboard. They met a chattering Poppy, flush with her first Fillorian outing—"We did it!"—and a silent, still-fluorescent Julia wandering the halls. Quentin showed them the prize and hugged them both, Julia a bit awkwardly, since she didn't really hug him back, and moreover had retained the extra height from her battle form. Poppy was right, they had done it, and Quentin had led the way. He held on to that victorious feeling, weighed it in his hands, felt its warmth and its heft, making sure he would always remember it. Bingle rooted a straggler out from behind a curtain, but he'd already laid down his weapons. He didn't have a lot of fancy ideas about dying for lost causes.

Outside the *Muntjac* had drawn right up to the wharf—it loomed up abruptly over the stone square. The bay must have been deeper than it looked. Somebody—Eliot, probably—had conjured some floating lights, basketball-sized globes that hovered over the courtyard, bathing it in soft yellow-rosy illumination and giving it a country-fair atmosphere. The wind had picked up even more, and the glowing spheres trembled and bobbed as they tried to stay in position.

And there was Eliot, standing with Josh out on the pier, with the great comforting bulk of the *Muntjac* behind them. Why were they just standing there? The high was all gone now, and Quentin's knees were weak. It was tiring work, being a hero. He felt hollowed out, a limp empty skin of himself. The ache in his side was getting hot again. The thought of his cozy shipboard berth was crushingly comforting. Now that they had the key he could curl up in it and the great beast would bear him away. He raised a weary hand in greeting. There would be talking now, and explanations, and congratulations—the hero's welcome—but for now he just wanted to get past them and back aboard.

Eliot and Josh didn't greet him. Their faces were grave. They were looking down at something on the pier. Josh spoke, but the wind snatched his words away, spirited them off and out over the black ocean. They were both waiting for Quentin to notice Benedict lying there on the rough wet wood.

There was an arrow through his throat. He was dead. He'd barely made it off the boat. He lay curled around himself, and his face was dark. He hadn't died right away. It looked like he'd clawed at the arrow for a while first, before he finally choked on his own blood.

CHAPTER 20

The house at Murs was the best thing that had ever happened to Julia in her entire life. In any of her entire lives.

Pouncy was right, she had come home. Her life up until now had been one vicious, un-fun, never-ending game of tag, where everyone else was it and you could never stop running. Only now had she finally found home base. She could rest. Unlike the safe houses, this house was actually safe. This was her Brakebills, for real this time. She had made a separate peace.

There were ten people at Murs, counting Julia. Some were from Free Trader Beowulf, some weren't. Pouncy was there, and Asmodeus, and Failstaff. So were Gummidgy and Fiberpunk: timid, infrequent posters who were the last people Julia would have figured were involved with magic. Now she realized they'd probably spent most of their time trading spells in private threads.

Asmodeus and Failstaff and Pouncy weren't who she thought they were either, at all. She'd figured Pouncy for a girl, or a gay man, but she didn't get a gay vibe off him in person, and either way she didn't think he'd be so good-looking. Online he came across as somebody with something to be angry about, who was always on the edge of losing it in the face of some intolerable outrage against his person, and who kept it together through sheer force of will. Julia's pet theory had been that he was an accident victim of some kind, a paraplegic maybe, or somebody in chronic pain who was struggling to be philosophical about his condition. No way she would have pegged him as all Abercrombie & Fitch like that.

Failstaff wasn't handsome. In Julia's mind he'd been a silver-haired retiree, a gentleman of the old school. In fact he was about thirty, and he might have been a gentleman, but if he was he was one of the largest gentlemen she'd ever seen. Six foot five, maybe, and built like a butte. He wasn't fat, exactly, there was just a shitload of him. He must have weighed four hundred pounds. His voice was a subsonic rumble.

As for Asmodeus, she turned out to be even younger than Julia, seventeen at the most, a fast talker with a big smile and heavy V-shaped eyebrows that gave her a naughty-schoolgirl look. She had a bit of a Fairuza Balk thing going on. Shades of *The Craft.* They were her best friends, and Julia didn't even recognize them.

They were also magicians, and good ones, better than she was. And they lived in a big house in the south of France. It would take her a while to get used to them.

And to forgive them.

"When were you going to tell me?" she demanded, as they sat ranged around some deep glasses of local red at a stylish reclaimed-wood table on the stone patio behind the house. A blue swimming pool shimmered in the late afternoon sun. It was like a goddamned cigarette ad.

"Really! I'd like to know! You were here all this time, doing magic and scarfing humane local foie gras and I don't even know what else and you didn't even tell me? Instead you made me pass a test. Another test! As if I haven't passed enough tests in my life!"

Maddeningly, a tear coursed down her cheek. She snapped her hand to her face like she'd been stung.

"Julia." You could practically feel it when Failstaff talked, his voice was that deep. It practically rattled the silverware.

"We're sorry," Asmodeus said, all sisterly. "We all went through it."

"Believe me, it gave us no pleasure to think about you at that Bed-Stuy safe house." Pouncy set his wine glass aside. "But think about it. When you dropped off the radar on FTB we had a pretty good sense that you'd hooked up with the magic scene. So we waited. We gave you time to get your feet under you, get the basics out of the way, all that low-level crap. Get your finger positions straight, crack the major language groups. To see if this was for you or not."

"Well, thanks a fucking million. That was really thoughtful of you." All that time she'd spent wandering in the wilderness, wondering if there was anything out there, and they'd been here this whole time, watching her. She took a shaky breath. "You don't know what I went through."

"We know," Failstaff said.

She looked at them, sipping their wine, a fancy Rhône red so dark it was almost black, lolling in the golden fucking Merchant-Ivory sunlight. The house was surrounded by hay fields gone to seed. They seemed to absorb sound, leaving them alone in an ocean of hush.

"You were paying your dues," Pouncy said. "Call it a rite of passage."

"Let's call it what it is," Julia said. "You were testing me. Who do you think you are? To test me?"

"Yes, we fucking tested you!" Pouncy was exasperated, but in a decorous, good-natured way. "You would have done the same thing to us! We tested the shit out of you. Not to see if you were smart. We know you're smart. You're a goddamned genius, though Iris says your Old Church Slavonic is crap. But we had to know why you were here. It wouldn't work if you were just here to play with us. It wasn't enough for you to love us. You had to love magic."

"We all did it, Julia," Asmodeus repeated. "Everybody here did, and we were all pissed when we found out the truth, and we all got over it."

Julia snorted. "You're what, seventeen? Are you going to tell me you paid your dues?"

"I paid, Julia," she said evenly. A challenge.

"And to answer your question," Pouncy said, "who do we think we are? We are us. And you're one of us now, and we're damn glad you're here. But we don't take chances on people." He waited for that to sink in. "There's too much at stake."

Julia crossed her arms fiercely, or with all the ferocity she could muster, to avoid giving them the impression that they were entirely forgiven. But God damn them all to Hades, she was curious. She wanted to know what the hell this place was, and what they were up to. She wanted to know what the game was, so she could play too.

"So whose house is this?" she said. "Who paid for all this?"

Obviously there was a lot of money washing around here. She'd stood by while Pouncy called the rental car company and, in fluent French, simply bought the scraped-up Peugeot with a credit card.

"It's Pouncy's," Asmodeus said. "Mostly. He was a day trader for a while. He was pretty good at it."

"Pretty good?" Pouncy lifted his finely drawn eyebrows.

Asmo shook her head. "If you'd gone into the math just a little further you could have done so much better. I keep telling you, if you look at the market as a chaotic system—"

"Whatever. It wasn't an interesting problem. It was a means to an end."

"If you'd just stake me—"

"We all put in money when we came here," Failstaff said. "I put in all mine. What was I saving it for? What else is money for except to live like this, with them, somewhere like Murs?"

"No offense, but it all sounds kind of culty."

"That's exactly what it is!" Asmodeus said, clapping her hands. "The Cult of Pouncy!"

"I think of it more like CERN," Pouncy said. "It's an institute for high-energy magical studies."

Julia hadn't touched her wine. More than wine right now, she wanted control, a thing that was not fully compatible with wine.

"So I'm looking around for like a Large Hadron Collider or its magical equivalent."

"Bup-bup-bup," Pouncy said. "Baby steps. First we power-level you up to two hundred fifty. And then we shall see what we shall see."

It emerged that the house at Murs was, in its way, a natural outgrowth of the safe-house scene. The scene was a filter: it caught a very few, rather unusual people, culled them out of the everyday world and into the safe houses, and gave them magic to chew on. Murs filtered the filtered, double-distilled them. Most people in the magic scene were happy chilling in the safe houses, faffing around with three-ring binders. It was a social thing for them. They liked the double-life aspect of it. They'd gone behind the veil. They liked knowing they had a secret. It was what they needed, and it was all they needed.

But some people, a very few people, were different. Magic meant something else to them, something more primal and urgent. They didn't have a secret, the secret had them. They wanted more. They wanted to penetrate the veil behind the veil. They did not faff, they learned. And when they hit the ceiling of what they could learn in the safe-house scene, they banged on it till somebody in the attic opened up a trap door.

That's when they ended up in Murs. Pouncy and his gang skimmed off the cream of the safe houses and brought them here.

Life was easy in Murs, at least at first. There was a living wing and a working wing. Julia was assigned a beautiful bedroom with a high ceiling and wide floorboards and big stripey-curtained windows that let in floods of that champagne-y French light. Everybody cooked and everybody cleaned, but they'd worked out a lot of magic to smooth the way— it was amazing to watch the floors repel dust and herd it into neat little piles, like iron filings in a magnetic field. And the produce was second to none.

The others didn't welcome her with open arms, exactly. They weren't open-arms types. But there was respect there. She was geared up to prove herself all over again, since based on her life thus far she was used to having to prove herself to a new gang of assholes every six months or so. And she would have, she really would have. But they weren't going to make her. The proving was done with. The journey was the test, and she had arrived. She was in.

It wasn't Brakebills. It was better. She felt like she'd finally won— she'd won ugly, but she'd won.

They knew about Brakebills at Murs. Not much, but they knew. Their attitude toward it was bracingly snobbish. They considered Brakebills— to the extent that they considered it at all—rather cute: a sanitized, safety-wheeled playpen for those who didn't have the grit and the will to make it on the outside. They called it Fakebills, and Breakballs. At Brakebills you sat in classrooms and followed the rules. Perfectly fine if you like that kind of thing, but here at Murs you made your own rules, no adult supervision. Brakebills was the Beatles, Murs was the Stones. Brakebills was for Marquis of Queensberry types. Murs was more your stone-cold street-fighting man.

Most of them had even been in for the Brakebills exam, like her, though unlike her they didn't realize that till they'd gotten to Murs and Failstaff, who had a special touch with memory spells, had wafted away the magic that was fogging their brains. They took a certain pride in it, the refuseniks. Gummidgy (Julia never did figure out what the deal with her name was) even claimed to have beaten the exam and then—a historic first—declined Fogg's offer to matriculate and walked away. She'd chosen the life of a hedge witch instead.

Privately Julia thought that that was completely demented, and that the Brakebills crowd probably had slightly more on the ball than the others were giving them credit for. But she enjoyed the snobbism none-theless. She'd earned that much.

They were an odd bunch at Murs. It was a menagerie—you needed a genius IQ to get into Murs, but eccentricity was not an impediment, and you'd have to be some kind of outlier to go through the grinder of the safe-house scene and not come out a little skewy. A lot of their magic was home-brewed, and as a result the range of different styles and techniques on display was bewildering. Some of them were graceful and balletic, some were so minimalist they barely moved at all. One guy was so herky-jerky he looked like he was practically break dancing. There was some popping and locking going on there.

There were specialists too. One guy mostly made magic artifacts. Gummidgy was a dedicated psychic. Fiberpunk—a short, thickset spec-imen almost as wide as he was tall—self-identified as a metamagician: he dealt in magic that acted on other magic, or on itself. He rarely spoke and spent a lot of time drawing. The one time Julia looked over his shoul-der he explained, in a whisper, that he was drawing two-dimensional representations of three-dimensional shadows cast by four-dimensional objects.

Life was easy in Murs, but work was hard. They gave her a day to deal with her jet lag and her personal baggage, then Pouncy told her to report to the East Wing first thing the next morning. Julia didn't fancy being told to report anywhere by Pouncy Silverkitten, whom she was accustomed to thinking of as a friend and an equal. But he just unbut-toned his shirt and showed her his stars. (Also his annoyingly smooth, well-muscled chest.) He had a lot of them. Equals they might be, but only in some abstract philosophical sense. Practically speaking he could still kick her ass at magic.

Which was why, swallowing her pride, and possibly some other feelings, she obeyed Pouncy and reported to an upstairs room in the East Wing called the Long Study at eight o'clock in the morning.

The Long Study was a narrow room lined with windows along one side—more of a gallery, really. There was nothing obvious to study with there. There were no books, or desks, or furniture of any kind in the Long Study. What there was was Iris.

Baby-faced, chopstick-haired, Ivy League Iris, last seen breaking Julia down into her component parts back at the Bed-Stuy safe house. It was almost like meeting an old friend. On her home turf Iris went casual: jeans and a white T-shirt that showed off her stars.

"Hi," Julia said. It came out a tad querulous. She cleared her throat and tried again. "How are you?"

"Let's do it again," Iris said. "From the top. Start with the flash."

"The flash?"

"We're going to run your levels. Start with the flash. You miss one, you go back to the beginning. You do them all, one to seventy-seven, no mistakes, three times in a row, and then we can start work."

"You mean start leveling me?"

"Start with the flash."

For Iris, meeting Julia again was not like meeting an old friend. For Iris meeting Julia was more like when the grizzled sergeant in the Vietnam movie meets the newbie private fresh from Parris Island. Eventually the private will lose his cherry and become a man, but first the sergeant is going to have to drag him through the jungle until such time as the private can unfold his entrenching tool without shooting his balls off.

Of course Iris had every right. That's how the system worked. She was doing Julia a fucking favor. Babysitting the noob was evidently not considered a premium assignment at Murs, and she wasn't going to pretend to enjoy it. Which whatever, but this did not oblige Julia to pretend to be grateful either. Really she ought to dog it a few times, she thought, just to piss Iris off. Show her that Julia had nothing to prove. See how long it took her to lose her shit. *Fuck* her and her flash.

But in truth it was not necessary for Julia to dog it. She screwed it up the old-fashioned way, involuntarily, four times before she made it to seventy-seven even once. Twice she muffed the same spell, level fifty-six, a thumb-cracking affair rich in Welsh *ll*'s that was designed to toughen glass against breakage. Even averaging a bit more than two minutes a level, which was really machinelike efficiency, they were two and a half hours into it when she went down for the second time. Iris sat down cross-legged on the floor.

But Julia had decided that she was not going to swear or twitch or sigh in front of Iris, whether she muffed level fifty-six twice or two hundred times. She was going to be all sweetness and light. How do you *ll*ike them apples.

At two in the afternoon Julia spiked spell number sixty-eight on an otherwise perfect run-through. Iris rolled her eyes and groaned and lay down full-length on the wooden floor and stared up at the ceiling. She couldn't even look at Julia anymore. Julia didn't pause but went right back to the beginning, whereupon she stuffed level fourteen, a gimme spell that even Jared knew cold.

"God!" Iris shouted at the ceiling. "Get it right!"

By the time Julia rattled off two perfect runs, right through to seventy-seven, it was six thirty in the evening. They hadn't broken for lunch. Julia hadn't even sat down. The setting sun, angling in from the west, painted the long wall a chalky pink. Her feet were killing her.

"All right," Iris said. "That's it. Same time tomorrow."

"But we're not done."

Iris levered herself up off the floor.

"Nope, we're done. Finish tomorrow."

"We're not done."

Iris stopped and stared at Julia through her nerd glasses. Maybe Iris was annoyed at having to babysit the new fish, but Julia had so much more anger than Iris did at her disposal. She was making a withdrawal from her stockpile now, spending a little of the principal, and it hardly made a dent. She walked over to a window and punched it. It would have broken if she hadn't already cast level fifty-six on it three times that day.

"All right, Julia, I get it. I was tough on you. I'm sorry. Come on. Let's get some dinner."

"We're done when I say we're done."

Julia cast a locking spell on the door (level seventy-two). It was a symbolic gesture, as there were in fact two doors out of the Long Study, and Iris could probably have unpicked her level seventy-two in a couple of minutes anyway. That wasn't the point. The point was that Julia had been waiting four years to get to Murs. Iris could skip dinner.

Iris sat back down and put her head in her hands.

"Whatever."

She could stand to skip a few meals anyway, Julia thought. She's working on a muffin-top situation with those jeans.

Julia started again. She was going slower now, and when she was done the room was dark. It was almost nine o'clock. Iris stood up. She tried the door Julia had locked, swore, and walked the length of the Long Study to the other door without looking back or saying a word. Julia watched her go.

There was no touching moment of female bonding. The grizzled sergeant didn't chuck her on the shoulder and grudgingly admit that the rookie might make a hell of a soldier one day after all. But when she reported to the Long Study at eight o'clock the following morning it was tacitly understood that they could now skip the alpha-chick bullshit.

Let the power-leveling begin. Here come the big secrets. At least she didn't have to fuck anybody this time.

She didn't have to stand up, either: apparently she now qualified for some furniture. She and Iris sat on chairs and faced each other across an actual table, a sturdy chunk of old butcher block. On the table was, yes, a three-ring binder, but it was the most beautiful three-ring binder Julia had ever seen: leather-bound, with those sturdy steel rings—none of this bendy aluminum Trapper Keeper shit—and above all thick, thick, thick. It was stuffed with neatly transcribed spells.

Under Iris's steady gaze Julia went up two levels that day. The next day she did five. Every level she gained wiped out a little bit of what she'd been through in Brooklyn. Julia had a hungry mind, she always had, and she'd been on starvation rations for longer than she cared to think about. She'd even worried that her brain might be starving to death, losing its plasticity, that she'd been running on fumes for so long she might not have the mental muscle tone to wrangle large tranches of hard data. But she didn't think so. If anything, wandering in the information jungle had made her tough and efficient. She was used to doing a lot with a little. Now that she had a lot, she was going to work wonders with it. And she did.

It was frustrating having to pound levels while the others were off doing God knew what. She was running through new fields of power, *frisking* through them, but she was already eager to get on to whatever it was the rest of them were up to. She kept trying to run ahead, and Iris had to drag her back and make her trudge through the levels in order. I mean, it was so blindingly obvious that if you took the kinetic elements from level 112, and borrowed the reflexive bits from the self-warming spell at level 44, then you had a basic working model for how to make yourself hover a few feet off the ground. But that wasn't till 166, and level 166 was 54 more levels away.

And meanwhile she was being treated like a little kid around whom everybody had to watch their language. Whenever she looked out the window of the Long Study it seemed like Pouncy and Asmodeus were walking by, heatedly engaged in what was obviously the most interesting conversation in the history of spoken communication. Either they were sleeping together—though even in France Asmodeus was practically jail-bait, so whatever—or there was some deal going on here that Julia was not yet senior enough to be cut in on. Conversations went quiet whenever she walked into the dining room. It's not that they weren't glad to see her, it's just that she had apparently developed the ability to instantly make people forget what they'd been about to say, causing them instead to make some remark about the weather or the coffee or Asmo's eyebrows.

One night she woke up from a dead sleep at two in the morning— she was so tired from running levels with Iris that she'd gone straight up to her room and slept through dinner. At first she thought there was a phone ringing in her room on vibrate, except that she didn't have a phone. Then the vibrations got stronger than that, stronger and stronger to the point where the whole house was throbbing every five seconds or so. It sounded like when cars rolled down her street in Brooklyn with the bass cranked up and too much funk in the trunk. Things were starting to rattle. It was like giant footsteps were approaching the house, over the sleeping fields of Murs.

The whole thing took maybe two minutes. The pulses got bigger and bigger until whatever it was was right on top of her. The windows rattled till she thought the old glass would crack. On the final beat her bed vibrated a foot to the left, and she could feel three-hundred-year-old plaster dust sift down from the ceiling onto her face. Somewhere in the house something did shatter, a window or a plate. Light burst soundlessly out of the lower floors of the house, illuminating the row of cypresses across the lawn.

And then it was gone, just like that, leaving behind it only a ringing, burnt-out silence. Later, it might have been an hour later, she heard the others coming up to bed. Asmo said something in a furious whisper, something about how they were wasting their time, and somebody else shushed her.

The next morning everything was as it had been. Nobody copped to anything having happened at all. Though Fiberpunk was now sporting a ripe purple bruise on his temple. *Hmmmmmmmm.*

When Julia hit level 200 they baked her a cake. Two weeks later, six weeks after she'd driven into Murs, she went to bed having hit level 248, and she knew that tomorrow would be it. And it was: at three in the afternoon Iris walked her through a complex casting that, when properly done, rolled back entropy in a local area by five seconds. The effect was very local, a circle a yard across, but no less spectacular for that.

The theory behind it was a rat's nest of interwoven effects. She could hardly believe something that kludgy even worked, but Iris could do it, and after a few hours so could Julia. She knocked down a pile of blocks. She cast the spell. The blocks knocked themselves back up again.

And that was level 250. When she dropped her hands Iris kissed her on both cheeks—*zo Fransh*—and told her they were finished. She could hardly believe it. Just to be sure she offered to run the full set, 1 through 250, to Iris's satisfaction, but Iris declined. She'd seen enough.

Julia spent the rest of the afternoon just walking the shady lanes that ran in comforting right angles between the sun-baked fields that surrounded the farmhouse. Her brain felt bloated and replete, like after a big meal—it was the first time she could ever remember it not being hungry. She spent an hour playing computer games, then that night Fiberpunk cooked them an elaborate bouillabaisse, with monkfish and saffron, and they opened a bottle of Châteauneuf-du-Pape with dust on its shoulders and a really boring-looking label that didn't even have a little line drawing on it, which meant it must have been hair-raisingly expensive. Before they went to bed Pouncy told her to come to the Library the next morning. Not the Long Study, the Library.

She woke up early. It was midsummer, but the heat hadn't come up yet. She haunted the lumpy, un-landscaped grounds for an hour, startling weird French bugs out of her way, studying the tiny white snails that were everywhere, getting her shoes soaked with dew, waiting for everybody else to wake up. It was like morning on her birthday. Superstitiously Julia avoided the dining room while the others ate breakfast. At 7:55 she snatched a roll out of the kitchen and gnawed it nervously on her way over to the Library.

The day she'd stepped into that elevator in the library in Brooklyn, she'd dropped into the void. It might as well have been an empty shaft. She'd been falling ever since. But it was almost over. She was about to touch solid ground again. She could barely even remember what it felt like to be where she belonged, on the same side of the glass as everybody else.

She'd tried the door to the Library once before but it hadn't opened for her, and she hadn't bothered trying to hack the locking charm. She was tired of picking locks. She stood in front of the door for a minute, plucking at the fabric of her summer dress, watching the second hand of the clock in the hall.

At the appointed hour the door opened by itself. Julia lowered her chin and went inside.

They were all there, sitting around a long worktable. The Library was clearly the crowning achievement of whoever had renovated the Murs farmhouse. They'd hollowed out the space completely, cut away three floors and exposed the roof beams thirty feet up. Morning sunlight lasered in through tall thin windows. Bookshelves soared along the walls, all the way up, which would have been totally impractical except for some tasteful oak platforms that floated magically alongside them, ready to hoist the browser up to whatever level he or she wanted to be at.

They stopped talking when she came in. Nine faces turned to look up at her. Some of them had books and folders of notes in front of them. They could have been a corporate board meeting, if the corporation were Random Genius Freaks LLC. Pouncy sat at the head of the table. There was an open seat at the foot.

She pulled out the chair and sat down, almost demurely. Why weren't they talking? They just looked at her calmly, like a parole board.

So. She'd met their expectations. It was time they met hers. Cards on the table. Show me whatcha got. Read 'em and weep.

"All right," she said. "So what are we doing?"

"What would you like to do?"

It wasn't Pouncy who spoke, it was Gummidgy. You tell me, Julia wanted to say. You're the pyschic. She was built like a model, tall and skinny, though her face was too long and severe to be really beautiful. Julia couldn't place her ethnicity. Persian?

"Whatever comes next. Whatever comes after level two hundred fifty. Two hundred fifty-one. I'm ready."

"What makes you think there is a level two hundred fifty-one?"

Her eyes narrowed. "The fact that there were levels one through two hundred fifty?"

"There is no level two hundred fifty-one."

Julia looked at Pouncy, Failstaff, Asmodeus. They looked back at her patiently. Asmo nodded.

"How can there be no level two hundred fifty-one?"

"There's nothing after two hundred fifty," Pouncy said. "Oh, you can craft more spells. We do it all the time. But at this point you have all the building blocks, all the basic components, that you're going to have. The rest is just permutations. After two hundred fifty you're just rearranging base pairs on the double helix. The power levels plateau."

Julia had a weightless, floating feeling. Not a bad feeling, but like she'd been cut adrift. So this was it. As mysteries went it wasn't exactly a showstopper.

"That's it? That's all there is?"

"That's it. You're done leveling."

Well. You could do a lot with what she had. She already had some ideas about spells involving extreme temperatures, extreme states of matter. Plasmas, Bose-Einstein condensates, that sort of thing. She didn't think they'd ever been tried. Maybe Pouncy would front her some money for equipment.

"So that's what you're doing here. Running the permutations."

"No. That's not what we're doing."

"Though we have run a hell of a lot of permutations," Asmo put in.

She took over the narrating.

"Once we realized that the way forward consisted of an indefinite series of incremental advances, we began to wonder if there was an alternative to that. A way to break the cycle. To take the power curve nonlinear."

"Nonlinear," Julia said slowly. "You want to find a magical singularity, kind of thing."

"Exactly!" Asmodeus grinned her wide Cheshire grin at Pouncy, as if to say, see? I told you she'd get it. "A singularity. An advance so radical that it takes us into another league, power-wise. Exponentially bigger energies."

"We think there's more to magic than what we've seen so far," Pouncy said. "A lot more. We think we're just dicking around in the minors while there's power sources out there that could put us in the bigs. If we could just access the right power grid."

"So that's what you're doing here. Trying to get on the big power grid."

She realized she was repeating their words while her mind tried to take in what they meant. So there was more to it. Funny, she had almost been relieved for a minute there, when she thought that that was it, that was all there was.

She'd crammed a lifetime's worth of magical study into the last four years, and the rest of her, the non-magical parts, was feeling somewhat neglected. Empty. She wouldn't have minded spending some time filling in those blanks in a big French farmhouse with some close friends. The big energies could wait. Or they could have. But her close friends didn't want to wait. And Julia would go with them, because—and it was so painfully tender to say it, even to herself, that she didn't say it, even to herself—she loved them. They were what she had instead of a family. So excelsior. Onward and upward.

"That's what we're doing here." Pouncy sat back and laced his hands behind his head. It was early, but there were already dark patches of sweat under his arms. "Unless you have any better ideas."

Julia shook her head. Everybody was watching her.

"All right," she said. "Well, show me what you've got so far."

Read 'em and weep.

CHAPTER 21

They carried Benedict's body up the gangplank, all together, Quentin and Josh and Eliot, struggling awkwardly with his heavy rag-doll limbs. Death seemed to have made his lanky adolescent body strangely dense. Slipping on the wet wood, they had none of the gravitas that would have been appropriate for pallbearers. Nobody had worked up the courage to take the arrow out of his throat, and it pointed crazily in all directions.

Once Benedict was laid out on the deck Quentin went and got a blanket from his cabin and spread it over the body. His side was throbbing hotly, in sync with his pulse. Good. That's what he wanted. He wanted to feel pain.

It was Bingle who drew the arrow expertly out of Benedict's throat; he had to snap it in half to get it out, because one end was barbed and the other feathered. It began to rain steadily, the drops tapping and splashing on the deck and on Benedict's pale unflinching face. They moved the body inside, into the surgery, although there was no surgery to be done.

"We're going," Quentin said aloud, to nobody and everybody.

"Quentin," Eliot said. "It's the middle of the night."

"I don't want to stay here. We've got a good wind. We should go."

Eliot was officially in charge, but Quentin didn't care. This was his ship first and he didn't want to spend another night on this island. It's all fun and games till somebody gets an arrow through the throat.

"What about the prisoners?" somebody said.

"Who cares? Leave them here."

"But where are we going to go?" Eliot said, reasonably.

"I don't know! I just don't want to stay here! Do you?"

Eliot had to admit he didn't especially want to stay either.

There was no way Quentin was going to bed. Benedict wasn't going to get warm tonight, so how could he? He was going to get the ship ready. Looking down at Benedict's blank, unfeeling face, Quentin was almost angry at him for dying. Things had been going so well. But that was being a hero, wasn't it? For every hero, don't legions of foot soldiers have to die in the background? It was a matter of numbers, like the corpse in the castle said. Just work out the sums.

So Quentin, the Magician King, leader of men, helped corral the rest of the defeated soldiers and got the crew watering and provisioning the *Muntjac*, even if it was the middle of the night and pissing rain. Somebody else would have to plot the course, since Benedict was dead, but that wasn't a problem because they didn't know where they were going. It didn't matter. He didn't understand what they were doing anymore. It was obviously a very effective way to procure magic keys, but how was that going to help Julia? Or rebuild the Neitherlands? Or calm the clock-trees? What could the keys possibly be good for that was worth this—Benedict curled up on the dock like a little boy trying to get warm?

They all worked together through the night, whey-faced and industrious. Julia sat with the corpse, slowly reassuming her human form, her mourning dress for once entirely appropriate for the occasion. Also fully in character was Bingle, whose haunted demeanor had darkened to funereal. He spent the night by himself haunting the ship's bow, hunched in on himself in his cloak like a hurt bird.

Once Quentin went forward to see if he was all right, but he heard Bingle mumble to himself:

"Not again. I must go where I can do no further harm."

And Quentin thought, maybe I'll leave him to work that out by himself.

The sky was paling through the rain clouds when Quentin went out alone into the square in front of the castle to finish the job. He was chilled through and bone tired. He felt like the living corpse in the library. He wasn't the best person for this job, but it was his job to do. He got down on one knee in front of the little obelisk with a hammer and a chisel, which he'd borrowed from the ship's carpenter.

Probably this could be done by magic, except he couldn't remember how just now, and he didn't want to do it by magic anyway. He wanted to feel it. He set the point of the chisel against the stone and started chipping. When he was done there were two words there, ragged but legible:

BENEDICT ISLAND

Back on the ship he gave the order—eastward ho—though everybody knew what the order was before he gave it. Then he went below. Quentin heard the anchor being weighed. The world tilted and came unmoored, and he was finally gone.

The *Muntjac* ran fast ahead of a freezing gale. It drove them across vast, island-less stretches of ocean, punishing the sails, which meekly accepted the abuse and ran even faster. Enormous emerald-green swells urged them onward from below, rising up under them and then rolling on ahead of them, as if even the sea had had enough of them and couldn't wait for this to be over. Eliot had made the voyage out sound like nonstop riches and wonders, islands of mystery twenty-four-seven-three-sixty-five, but now the ocean was a complete blank, scrubbed mercifully free of anything remotely fantastical. A clean miss.

Maybe the islands were moving out of their way. They had become untouchable. They didn't see land once—it was as if they were taking a grand leap outward into nothingness.

The only miracle that happened, happened on board. It was a small miracle, but it was a real one. Two nights after Benedict died, Poppy came to Quentin's cabin to say she was sorry about what had happened and to see how he was. She didn't leave till the next morning.

It was a strange time to have something nice happen. It was the wrong time, it wasn't appropriate, but maybe it was the only time it could have happened. Their emotions were raw and close to the surface. Quentin was surprised to say the least, and one of the things that surprised him was how much he wanted her. Poppy was pretty, and Poppy was smart, at least as smart as Quentin, probably more so. And she was kind, and funny when she let her guard down a little, and her long legs were as absolutely wondrous as anything Quentin had ever seen in this or any world.

But beyond that Poppy had something Quentin wanted almost as badly as the wordless physical forgetting of sex—which would have been enough, God knows, it really would—and that was a sense of perspective. She wasn't completely caught up in the grand myths of quests and adventures and whatever else. Deep down she didn't especially give a shit about Fillory. She was a tourist here. Fillory wasn't her home, and it wasn't the repository of all her childhood hopes and dreams. It was just a place, and she was just passing through it. It was a relief to not take Fillory too seriously for a while. When he'd imagined something like this might happen, he'd always imagined it with Julia. But Julia didn't need him, not this way. And when it came right down to it, the person he needed wasn't Julia either.

Quentin hadn't been celibate since Alice died, but he hadn't exactly been cutting a swath either. The problem with sleeping with people who weren't Alice was that somehow it made Alice even more gone. It meant really, truly knowing and admitting that she was never coming back. With Poppy he let himself know it a little more, and that should have made it hurt more, but strangely it made it hurt a little less.

"Why don't you stay?" he said one day, while they were eating lunch in his cabin, cross-legged on his bed. Fish again. "Come live in a castle for a while. I realize you're not a Fillory nerd like me, but haven't you ever wanted to live in a castle? Haven't you ever wanted to be a queen?"

If or when they eventually made it back to Castle Whitespire, with or without that last key, it was going to be something less than a triumphant homecoming. It would be good to have Poppy beside him when he sailed back into that harbor, for moral support. And for immoral support too.

"Mmmm." Poppy salted her fish within an inch of its life, then drenched it in lemon juice. No amount of flavor seemed to be too much for her. "You make it sound romantic."

"It is romantic. That's not just me. Living in a castle is objectively romantic."

"See, this is spoken like somebody who didn't grow up in a monarchy. Australia still has a queen. There's a lot of history there. Remind me to tell you about the constitutional crisis of 1975 sometime. Very unromantic."

"I can promise you there will be no constitutional crises if we go to Whitespire. We don't even have a constitution. Or if we do I promise you nobody's ever read it."

"I know, Quentin." She pressed her lips together. "But I don't think so. I don't know how much longer I can stay here."

"Why not? What do you have to get back to?"

"My entire life? Everybody I know? The real world?"

"This world is real." He scooched over next to her, so that their hips touched. "Here. Feel."

"That is not what I meant."

She put her plate on the floor and lay back on the bunk. She hit her head on the wall. It wasn't made for a tall person, let alone two.

"I know." Quentin didn't know why he was fighting her on this. He knew she wasn't going to stay. Maybe that's what made this so easy, that he knew the outcome in advance. There was no chance that she would get too close. He was playing to lose. "But seriously, what's back there for you? Your dissertation? On dragon-ology, or whatever? Or tell me you don't have a boyfriend."

He took her foot in his lap to rub. She had new calluses from walking around the ship barefoot, and he picked at one. She snatched the foot back.

"No. But yes, my dissertation on dracology. I'm sorry if that seems very boring to you, but it's my thing and I happen to like it."

"There are dragons in Fillory. I think. Well, maybe there aren't. I've never see one."

"You don't know?"

"You could find out. You could apply for a royal research grant. I can promise you your application would be looked upon favorably."

"I would have to start all over again. I'm not ripping up four chapters of my dissertation."

"Anyway, what's wrong with a little unreality?" Quentin said. "Unreality is underrated. Do you know how many people would kill to be where you are?"

"What, in bed with you?"

He pushed up her shirt and kissed her stomach, which was flat and covered in very fine downy hair.

"I meant here in Fillory," he said.

"I know." She sighed, prettily and genuinely. "I just wish I were one of them."

It was all very well to decide that Poppy was going back to the real world—or not very well, but it was what it was—but it was an open question how they were going to get her there. They could be confident that at some point Ember would turn up to kick her out of Fillory, as He always did with any visitors. But that could take weeks, or months, you never knew, and she didn't want to wait. Quentin might have been in paradise, but Poppy was in exile.

In the end they decided to try the keys. They didn't have the one from After, which had gotten Quentin and Julia to Earth so efficiently, but they all looked more or less the same apart from the size. They started with the last and biggest, the one they'd found on Benedict Island. It was stowed in Quentin's cabin, still in the wooden box it came in. They brought it up on deck. Poppy had come with nothing, and she had nothing to pack. Quentin supposed Josh would want to go back too, in the fullness of time, but he didn't seem to be in any hurry. He was already talking about which room he'd get back at Whitespire. And Quentin preferred to give Poppy a private send-off.

The key had lain in its box so long, its three-toothed jaw had worn a shadow of itself into the red velvet. He offered it to her, like a fancy cigar. She picked it up.

"Careful."

"It's heavy." Poppy turned it over in her fingers, weighing it. "Wow. It's not just the gold, it's magic. The spellwork on this thing is thick. Dense."

They looked at it, then at each other.

"I sort of felt around with it in the air," Quentin said. "You should find an invisible keyhole. It's hard to explain, it's more a learn-by-doing thing."

She nodded. She got it.

"Well."

"Wait." He took both of her hands. "I didn't ask you properly before. Stay here. Please stay. I want you to."

She shook her head and kissed him softly on the lips. "I can't. Call me next time you're in reality."

He knew she would say that. But it made him feel better, knowing he'd really asked.

Poppy made a few experimental, self-conscious pokes in the air with the key. Quentin wondered idly if the key understood that they were on a moving ship. Suppose it opened a door in the air and then got stuck and they immediately left it behind—the key tugged out of Poppy's hands, the door lost behind them in midair and midocean. He halfway hoped it would happen.

But no such luck. Old magic usually had any obvious bugs or loop-holes like that worked out long ago. Quentin didn't hear the click, but he saw when her hand met resistance in the air. The key slid in. Keeping one hand on it, she gave him another kiss, this time with some extra sugar in it, then she turned the key. With her other hand she found the doorknob.

A crack opened, and there was a *poof* of air pressure equalizing. The sun didn't shine through like it had before. It was dark. It was odd to see an oblong of night standing upright like that, on the deck of a ship in broad daylight. Quentin walked around behind her and tried to peer through it. He felt a cold draft. Winter air. She looked back at him: so far so good?

He wondered what month it was on Earth, or what year even. Maybe the time-streams had gone haywire and she'd be walking into a far-future Earth, an apocalypse Earth, a cold dead world orbiting an extin-guished sun. His arms goose-bumped, and a couple of errant snowflakes spun out and melted on the warm wood of the *Muntjac*'s deck. *I had a dream, which was not all a dream.* Good old Byron. Something for every occasion.

Poppy let go of the key, ducked her head—the portal was slightly too low for her beanpole frame—and stepped through. He saw her look around and shiver in her summer dress, and he caught a glimpse of what she was looking at. A stone square. The door began to close. The key must have let her out at her last known permanent residence, namely Venice. It made sense. She could crash at Josh's for a bit. She would know people. She would be safe there.

Or no, she wouldn't. That wasn't Venice, and she was all alone. Quentin lunged forward through the closing door after her.

"Poppy!"

She'd stopped just over the threshold, and he barreled into her from behind. She squeaked, and he grabbed her around the shoulders to keep them both from falling over. Then he reached back to keep the door from closing, but it was already gone. The air was freezing. The sky was full of strange stars. It was night, and they were not on Earth. They were in the Neitherlands.

For a second Quentin was almost glad to see them. He hadn't been to the Neitherlands for two years, not since he and the others had traveled to Fillory. They made him feel nostalgic. The first time he'd seen the Neitherlands he'd felt, maybe for the last time in his life, pure joy: the kind of uncut, pharmacy-grade, white-hot joy that comes with believing, or not just believing but knowing, that everything was going to be all right, not just then or for the next two weeks, but forever.

He'd been wrong, of course. In actuality that knowledge had lasted about five seconds—just up until Alice had punched him in the face for cheating on her with Janet. It turned out that everything was not going to be all right. Everything was chance and nothing was perfect and magic didn't make you happy, and Quentin had learned to live with it, which it turned out that most people he knew were already doing anyway, and it was time he caught up with them. But you didn't forget that kind of happiness. Something that bright leaves a permanent afterimage on your brain.

But the Neitherlands he knew had always been warm and peaceful and twilit. This Neitherlands was pitch-dark, and bitter cold, and it was snowing here. More snow had drifted in the corners of the square, huge creamy swaths of it.

And the skyline was different. Of the buildings around the square, the ones on one side looked exactly the way they always had, but the ones on the other side were half-gone. Their black silhouettes stood out jagged against the deep-blue sky, and the snow in front of them was mixed with big blocks of fallen stone. You could see all the way through to the next square over, and through that into the next.

"Quentin," Poppy said. She looked back for the door too, trying to account for both his presence and her surroundings. "I don't understand. What are you—where are we?"

She hugged herself against the cold. They really weren't dressed for this. She wasn't panicking though.

"This isn't Earth," Quentin said. "This is the Neitherlands. Or these are the Neitherlands, I've never really made up my mind which it is. This is the world in between Earth and Fillory and all the other worlds."

"Right." He'd told her about the Neitherlands. "Okay. Well, it's nice and all, but it's cold as hell. Let's get out of here."

"I'm not actually sure how we're going to do that. You're supposed to come in through the fountains, but you need a button to do that."

"Okay." Their voices vanished in the frozen air as soon as they spoke. "Well, but do a spell or something. Why did it take us here?"

"I don't know. They've got a sense of humor, those keys." It was hard to think in the bitter cold. He studied the empty air they'd just appeared out of, his breath smoking. There was really nothing left of the portal back to Fillory. Poppy walked stiff-legged over to the fountain. They were in the Fillory square; the fountain had a statue of Atlas in it, coiled and braced under the crushing weight of a marble globe.

The water in the fountain was frozen. The level of the ice was actually above the stone rim. She felt it with her hand.

"What the shit," she said quietly. She didn't sound like herself.

It was dawning on Quentin how much trouble they were in. It was cold here, really cold. It couldn't have been more than 15 or 20 degrees. There was no wood, nothing to make a fire with, nothing but stone. Quentin remembered Penny's warning not to do magic here. They might have to test that.

"Let's go over to the Earth fountain," he said. "It's a couple of squares from here."

"Why? What good would it do if we don't have a button?"

"I don't know. Maybe there's somebody there. I don't know what else to do, and we have to start moving or we're going to freeze to death."

Poppy nodded and sniffed. Her nose was running. She looked more frightened now than she had back on the island, when they were fighting for the key.

They started to walk but immediately broke into a jog instead, to warm up. Apart from their footsteps the silence was absolute. The only light was starlight, but their eyes were adjusting rapidly. All Quentin could think was that this wasn't going to work, and after it didn't work things would get very bad. He tried to do mental calculations about thermodynamics. There were too many variables, but hypothermia wasn't far in their future. A few hours at most, maybe not even that.

They trotted through the broken cityscape. Nothing moved. They crossed a bridge over a frozen canal. The air smelled like snow. A stupid mistake, and now they were both dead, he thought giddily.

The Earth square was bigger than the Fillory one, but it was in no better shape. One of the buildings showed a row of empty windows through which the stars were visible. The façade had survived the catastrophe, but the building behind it was gone.

This fountain was frozen too. The ice had plugged the great bronze lotus flower and cracked it all down one side. They stopped in front of it, and Poppy slipped on black ice under the snow and just managed to catch herself. She popped back up, slapping the wet off her hands.

"Same," she said. "All right. We need a way out of here. Or we need shelter and something to burn."

She was rattled, but she was hanging on to her nerve. Good old Poppy. She set a good example, and it woke him up a little.

"The doors on some of these buildings look like wood," he said. "And there are books inside the buildings. I think. Maybe we could get some and burn them."

Together they walked the square till they found a broken door, a Gothic-arched monster that had been knocked askew. Quentin touched it. He broke off a splinter. It felt like ordinary wood. They would have to try a fire spell. He explained about how magic acted in the Neitherlands: it was supercharged, explosive. Penny had said never to use it at all. Desperate times.

"How far away can you cast a fire spell from?" he said. "Because we'd better be as far away as we can get when it goes up."

"It goes up" came out of his numb lips sounding like "id go dup." He said it again, enunciating a little more clearly, but only a little. This was going downhill faster than he'd thought. They didn't have long at all. Maybe fifteen minutes more in which they could plausibly get a spell off.

"Let's find out," she said.

She began pacing backward away from the door, back toward the center of the square. He couldn't help thinking that this was just a stop-gap, a way station on the road to the inevitable. After they'd figured out how to light a fire, they'd have to find shelter. After they found shelter they'd need food, and there wasn't any food. His mind churned uncontrollably. They could melt snow to drink, but they couldn't eat it. Maybe they could find some leather bookbindings to chew on. Maybe there were fish under the ice in the canals. And even if they could survive indefinitely—which they couldn't—how long till whatever broke the Neitherlands came along and broke them?

"All right!" Poppy called. "Quentin, move!"

He pressed his palm against the wood, if that's what it was. If this didn't work, could they make a magic button from scratch? Not in fifteen minutes. Not in fifteen years.

There was a crack between the two doors. Thin blue light shone faintly through it. Starlight. But it wasn't starlight. It flickered.

"Hang on!" he said.

"Quentin!" He caught a note of desperation in her voice. She had her hands jammed in her armpits. "We don't have much time!"

"I thought I saw something. There's something in here."

He pressed his face up against the frozen wood, but he couldn't see anything more. He went from window to window, but they were all dark. Maybe from the other side. He yelled at Poppy to come on and ran through an archway to the next square over.

The building was a huge Italianate palace with evenly spaced windows. He considered for a moment the possibility that they might be even worse off if whatever was in there making blue light came out here, but it seemed unlikely that it could offer them a more lingering, unpleasant death than the one they were about to experience anyway. He wondered if, before he died, he'd sink so low that he would pray to Ember to save him. He thought he probably would.

There was no door at all on this side of the palace, but the façade was broken: it ended in jagged stone above the second rank of windows. He could probably get over it if he had to, which he did. A frozen wind was coming up. He wondered what had happened here. It had been so still and protected before, a world under glass. Someone had cut the power and smashed the windows and let the elements come roaring in.

A running jump got him up on the first window ledge. He thanked God, or Ember, or whoever, for the architect of the Neitherlands' excessive fondness for baroque ornamentation. He could tell the rough stone was taking skin off his cold fingers, but he couldn't feel it.

"Stand there," he said, and pointed. He put a foot on Poppy's shoulder, which she accepted with good grace. From there he could get a foot on the upper molding, and a hand on the window ledge above it, which wasn't enough for a good grip but was all he was going to get. From there he jumped and grabbed the top of the broken wall. He had to will his fingers to bend.

With his cheek pressed against the cold stone, Quentin risked a look down. Poppy was watching him expectantly. Her lovely face was pale and grave in the starlight. Slowly he hauled himself up until he got a forearm over the wall, then clumsily hiked his knee up onto it. He looked down for the first time into the interior of the Neitherlands.

It looked like he remembered pictures from the London Blitz looking. There was no roof, and most of what had been the second floor had fallen in and lay in ruins on top of the first. The floor was awash with paper, stirred in slow circles by the wind. Books large and small lay sprawled in various states of intactness, some whole, some spread-eagled and eviscerated.

At the far end, where remnants of the upper floor formed a partial shelter, someone had arranged some of the more intact books into tall, neat stacks. The man who presumably had arranged them stood among them. Or no, he wasn't standing, he was floating a foot off the ground, with his arms spread out.

That's where the blue light was coming from. There were runes on the floor below him that gave off a faint cold glow. Either he was a fellow refugee from the destruction or the author of it. It seemed like a good moment to take a bad risk.

"There's someone inside!" he called down to Poppy. He raised his voice. "Hey!"

The man didn't look up.

"Hey!" Quentin yelled again. "Hi!" Maybe he was Fillorian.

"Quentin," Poppy said.

"Hang on. Hi! Hi!"

"Quentin, the doors are opening."

He looked down. So they were. The doors were opening outward, all by themselves.

"Okay. I'm coming down."

It wasn't much easier coming down; he'd lost all feeling in his fingers. He took Poppy's numb hand in his own. This really was their last chance.

"Shall we?" he said. It sounded even thinner than he meant it to.

CHAPTER 22

They picked their way through the rubble, trying out of politeness to step on as few pages as possible. Quentin almost turned an ankle on a stone that rolled under his foot.

The blue light from the runes seemed to be what was supporting the man. His bare feet hung a yard off the ground. He had sandy hair and a large round face—his round head could almost have been what was holding him up, like a balloon. Around him in a cloud hung a dozen books, and a few more single sheets of paper, all opened in his direction, presumably so he could consult them simultaneously. The pages of two of the books were turning slowly.

He didn't greet them or even look at them as they approached. He had long sleeves that fell over his hands, but there was something odd about the way the material hung. As Quentin got closer it became obvious what it was: the man had no hands. It was Penny.

Quentin hadn't recognized him without the mohawk, and his hair fully grown in. He'd never known what Penny's natural hair color was, only that it probably wasn't metallic green. Penny rotated in place to face them, gazing down from where he hung in midair. He was thinner than he once was, much. He didn't used to have cheekbones.

Quentin stood at the edge of the eerie blue letters etched in the ground. The cold had gotten into his core. He couldn't stop his shoulders from shaking.

"Penny," he said lamely. "It's you."

Penny watched him calmly.

"This is my friend Poppy," Quentin said. "It's good to see you, Penny. I'm glad you're all right."

"Hello, Quentin."

"What happened to you? What happened here?"

"I joined the Order."

He spoke softly and calmly. Penny didn't seem to feel the cold at all.

"What is that, Penny? What's the Order?"

"We care for the Neitherlands. The Neitherlands is not a natural phenomenon, it is a made thing. An artifact. It was built long ago by magicians whose understanding of magic went far, far deeper than yours does."

Not mine, mind you. Just yours. Good old Penny. His losing his hands the way he did was a catastrophe Quentin would never really get over, but if anybody was born to be a mystical floating monk with no hands, it was Penny. They were going to freeze to death before he was done with his dramatic exposition.

"Ever since then men and women like myself have watched over it. We repair it and defend it."

"Penny, I'm sorry, but we're really cold," Quentin said. "Can you help us?"

"Of course."

When Penny lost his hands Quentin thought he would never do magic again. Counting Penny out was a mistake he apparently couldn't stop making. Hanging in the air in front of them, Penny joined his empty wrists together in front of him and began rhythmically reciting something in a language Quentin didn't know. He was making some kind of physical effort under his robe, but Quentin couldn't tell what.

All at once the air around them went from frigid to warm. Quentin shook even more uncontrollably as he warmed up. The relief was immense. He couldn't help himself, he bent over, and his mouth filled with saliva. He thought he might throw up, and that seemed incredibly funny, and he started laughing. Beside him he could hear Poppy moaning as her body recovered.

He didn't throw up. But it was a minute before either of them could talk again.

"What happened here?" Poppy said finally. "Who destroyed this place?"

"It was not destroyed." Penny corrected her with a trace of his old touchiness. "But it was damaged, badly. Perhaps irreparably. And there is worse to come."

The books and papers that surrounded Penny closed and zipped off to their places in various stacks and piles. Penny began floating in the direction of the open doors of the palazzo. Apparently those blue runes weren't all that was holding him up. The Order seemed to adhere to the principle of suckers walk, players ride.

"It is better if I show you," Penny said.

Quentin took Poppy's hand, and they followed him out into the square. Quentin was coasting on an endorphin high. He wasn't going to die—probably—and after that all news was good news. Penny talked as he floated along. His head was still a couple of feet above theirs. It was like having a conversation with somebody who was riding a Segway.

"Did you ever wonder," Penny said, "where magic comes from?"

"Yes, Penny," Quentin said dutifully. "I did wonder about that."

"Henry had a theory. He told me about it when we were at Brakebills."

He meant Dean Fogg. Penny only ever referred to the Brakebills faculty by their first names, to show that he thought of himself as their equal.

"It seemed wrong to him that humans should have access to magic. Or not wrong, but strange. It didn't make sense. He thought it was too good to be true. As magicians we were taking advantage of some kind of cosmic loophole to wield power that by rights we were never meant to have. The inmates had found the keys to the asylum, and we were running amok in the pharmacy.

"Or think of the universe as a vast computer. We are end users who have gained admin-level access to the system, and are manipulating it without authorization. Henry has a whimsical mind. He isn't a rigorous theorist, by any means, but he does have moments of insight. This was one of them."

They had left the square, Poppy and Quentin walking with their arms around each other now, pooling their heat. The zone of warm air was centered around Penny and moved with him, so that the cold nudged them along if they lagged too far behind him. He had a captive audience. Even being lectured by Penny was preferable to freezing to death.

"Now push Henry's theory a little. If magicians are hackers who broke into the system, then who are the system's rightful administrators? Who built the system—the universe—into which we have broken?"

"God?" Poppy asked.

It was good to have her here when dealing with Penny. Penny didn't get on her nerves. He didn't push Poppy's buttons the way he pushed Quentin's. She just wanted to know what he knew.

"Precisely. Or more precisely, the gods. There's no need to get overly theological about it: any magician who could work magic on such a fundamental scale would be, almost by definition, a god. But where are they? And why haven't they caught us and kicked us out of their system? They must have worked spells on an energy scale that to us is no longer conceivable. Their power would have dwarfed even that of the mages who built the Neitherlands.

"You should see it, Quentin. I mean really see the Neitherlands, the way I have. It's not infinite, you know, but it goes on for thousands of miles in all directions. It's wonderful. They show you everything when you get in the Order."

It was funny about Penny. He was an arrogant prick—notice the way he all but ignored Poppy—and he'd suffered terribly, but deep down under it he was still very innocent, and every once in a while his innocence overpowered his arrogance. Quentin didn't quite have it in him to like Penny, but he felt he understood Penny. Penny was the only person he'd ever met who loved magic, really loved it, the same way he did: naively, romantically, completely.

"After a while you get to be able to read the squares, like a language. Each one is an expression of the world it leads to, if you understand the grammar of it. No two are the same. There's one square, just one, that's a mile on each side, and it has a golden fountain in the center. They say the world it leads to is like heaven. They haven't let me go through yet."

Quentin wondered what heaven would be like for Penny. Probably in heaven you were always right and you never had to stop talking. God, he could be a dick where Penny was concerned. Probably in heaven you had hands.

They were silent for a bit, as they crossed a stone bridge over a canal. Little whirling snow-devils chased each other across the ice.

"Where did the gods go?" Poppy asked.

"I don't know. Maybe they've been in heaven. But they're back. They've come back to close the loophole. They're taking magic back, Quentin. They're going to take it all away from us."

They'd come to a square that looked no different from any of the others except that the fountain in the center was closed. A tarnished bronze cover, ornately inscribed, fitted over the basin. It was held shut by a simple latch. Penny glided over to the fountain, over the snow, the tips of his bare toes brushing it. He let himself float gently to the ground.

Quentin was trying to process what Penny had said. This must have been what the dragon had meant, back in Venice. This must be the mystery at the root of it all. But it couldn't be real. It had to be a mistake. The end of magic: that would mean the end of Brakebills, of Fillory, of everything that had happened to him since Brooklyn. He wouldn't be a magician anymore, nobody would be. All of their double lives would become single ones again. The spark would go out of the world. He tried to work out how they'd gotten here. A trip to the Outer Island, that's all it was supposed to be. He'd pulled a thread, and now the whole world was coming unraveled. He wanted to unpull it, to put it back, weave it back together again.

Penny was waiting for something.

"Open this for me, please," he said. "You have to undo the catch."

Right. No hands. Numb, but not from cold now, Quentin unhooked the bronze hook that held the cover on, then worked his fingertips between the cover and the stone. It was heavy—the metal was an inch thick—but with Poppy's help he heaved it up and part of the way to one side. They peered in.

It took a second for the perspective to resolve, and when it did they both backed away instinctively. It was a long way down.

There was no water in the fountain. Instead it was just a vast, echoing darkness. It was like they were looking down through the oculus of an

enormous dome. This must be what lay beneath the Neitherlands. Far
down, Quentin would have guessed a mile, was a flat pattern of glowing
white lines, like a schematic diagram of circuitry, or a maze with no
solution. Among the lines, waist deep in them, stood a silvery figure. It
was bald and muscled, and it must have been enormous. It was dark, but
the giant made its own light. It glowed with a lovely steady silvery luminescence.

The giant was busy. It was at work. It was changing the pattern. It
grasped one line, disconnected it, bent it, connected it to another line.
Because they were the size of derricks, its arms moved slowly, traversing
enormous distances, but they never stopped moving. Its handsome face
showed no expression.

"Penny? What are we looking at?"

"Is that God?" Poppy said.

"That is *a* god," Penny corrected her. "Though that is really just a
term to describe a magician operating on a titanic power scale. We've
seen at least a dozen of them; it's hard to tell them apart. There's one at
each of these access points. But we know what they're doing. They're
fixing it. They're rewiring the world."

Quentin was staring down at the exposed circuitry of creation, and
at the master of it. It looked a little like the Silver Surfer.

"I suppose," Quentin said slowly, "you're going to say that that is a
being of sublime beauty and power, and he only looks like that because
my fallen mortal eyes are incapable of perceiving his true magnificence."

"No. We think that's actually pretty much it."

"Come on," Poppy said. She tilted her head. "He is pretty impressive.
He's big. And silvery."

"A big silvery janitor. Penny, this can't be how the universe works."

"In the Order we call it 'inverse profundity.' We've observed it in any
number of cases. The deeper you go into the cosmic mysteries, the less
interesting everything gets."

So that was him. The biggest bastard of them all, top of the food
chain. That's where magic came from. Did he even understand what
he'd made, how beautiful it was, how much people loved it? He didn't
look like he loved anything. He just was. Though how could you make
anything as beautiful as magic and not love it?

"I wonder how he found out," Poppy said. "About us using magic. I wonder who tipped him off."

"Maybe we should talk to him," Quentin said. "Maybe we can change his mind. We could, I don't know, prove ourselves worthy of magic or something. Maybe they have a test."

Penny shook his head.

"I don't think they can change their minds. When you get to that level of power and knowledge and perfection, the question of what you should do next gets increasingly obvious. Everything is very rule-governed. All you can ever do in any given situation is the most gloriously perfect thing, and there's only one of them. Finally there aren't any choices left to make at all."

"You're saying the gods don't have free will."

"The power to make mistakes," Penny said. "Only we have that. Mortals."

They watched the god work for a while without talking. It never paused or hesitated. Its hands moved and moved, bending lines, breaking one connection, making another. Quentin couldn't see why one pattern was better than another, but he supposed that was his mortal fallibility. He felt a little sorry for it. He supposed it was happy, never doubting, never hesitating, eternally certain of its absolute righteousness. But it was like a giant divine robot.

"Let's cover it up," he said. "I don't want to look at it anymore."

The bronze cover grated against the stone, then dropped with a clang back into place. Quentin latched it. Though who the latch was going to keep in or out, he couldn't imagine. They stood around it as if it were a grave they'd just finished filling.

"Why is this happening now?" he said.

Penny shook his head.

"Something caught their attention. Somebody somewhere must have tripped an alarm and summoned them back from wherever they were. They may not even have realized they were doing it. We didn't know they were here until the cold started. Then the sun went out, and the snow came, and the wind. The buildings started to collapse. It's all ending."

"Josh was here," Quentin said. "He told us about it."

"I know," Penny said. He shifted uncomfortably under his robe. He forgot himself and spoke in his old voice again. "The cold makes my stumps ache."

"What's going to happen?" Poppy asked.

"The Neitherlands will be destroyed. It was never part of the divine plan. My predecessors built it in the space between universes. The gods will clear it away, like a wasp's nest in an old wall. If we're still here we'll die with it. But it won't stop there. It's not even the Neitherlands they're after, it's what it runs on."

You could say one thing for Penny, he could look a hard truth in the face. He had a weird integrity about things like that. He was calm and collected. He didn't flinch. It wouldn't occur to him to.

"Magic is the problem. We're not supposed to have it. They're going to close whatever loophole they left open that lets us use it. When they're done it will go dead, not just here but everywhere, in every world. That power will belong to the gods only.

"Most worlds will simply lose magic. I think Fillory may fall apart and cease to exist entirely. It's a bit special that way—it's magical all the way through. I have a theory that Fillory itself might be the loophole, the leak through which magic first got out. The hole in the dike.

"The change would have started already. You may have seen signs."

The thrashing clock-trees. They must be something like Fillory's early warning system, sensitive to any signs of trouble. Jollyby's death: maybe Fillorians can't live without magic. Ember and the Unique Beasts up in arms.

They were fixing the world. But Quentin preferred it broken. He wondered how long it would take. Years, maybe—maybe he could go home and not think about it and it would all happen after he was dead. But he wasn't getting that impression. Quentin wondered what he would do if magic went away. He didn't know how he would live in that world. Most people wouldn't even notice the change, of course, but if you knew about it, knew what you'd lost, it would eat away at you. He didn't know if he could explain it to a non-magician. Everything would simply be what it was and nothing else. All there would be was what you could see. What you felt and thought, all the longing and desire in your heart and mind, would count for nothing. With magic you could make those feelings real. They could change the world. Without it they would be stuck inside you forever, figments of your own imagination.

And Venice. Venice would drown. Its weight would crush those wooden pilings, and it would disappear into the sea.

You could see the gods' point of view. They made magic. Why would they want an ignorant insect like Quentin playing around with it? But he couldn't accept it. He wasn't going to. Why should the gods be the only ones who got magic? They didn't appreciate it. They didn't even enjoy it. It didn't make them happy. It was theirs, but they didn't love it, not the way he, Quentin, loved it. The gods were great, but what good was greatness if you didn't love?

"So is it going to happen?" he asked. For now he would be stoic like Penny. "Is there any way to stop it?"

He was warm again, but the chill kept creeping back in through the soles of his boots.

"Probably not." Penny began to walk, like a regular mortal, with his actual feet. The snow didn't seem to bother him. Quentin and Poppy walked with him. "But there is a way. We always knew this might happen. We prepared for it. Tell me, what's the first thing a hacker does once he breaks into a system?"

"I don't know," Quentin said. "He steals a bunch of credit card numbers and subscribes to a lot of really premium porn sites?"

"He sets up a back door." It was good to know that even having attained enlightenment Penny was still impervious to humor. "So that if he's ever locked out, he can get back in."

"The Order did that?"

"So they say. A back door was built into the system, metaphorically speaking, that would let magic back out into the universe, if the gods ever returned to claim it. It just has to be opened."

"Oh my God." Quentin didn't know whether he should dare to hope or not. It would almost be too painful if it turned out not to be true. "So you can fix this? You're going to fix this?"

"The 'back door' exists." Penny mimed doing quotey-fingers, which he couldn't actually do. "But the keys to it were hidden a long time ago. So long ago now that not even we know where they are."

Quentin and Poppy looked at each other. It couldn't be that simple, it just couldn't. No way were they that lucky.

"Penny, there wouldn't by any chance be seven of these keys?" Quentin said.

"Seven, yes. Seven golden keys."

"Penny. Jesus Christ, Penny, I think we have them. Or six of them. We have them back in Fillory. It has to be them!"

Quentin had to sit down on a block of stone, even though it was a little outside Penny's circle of warmth. He put his head in his hands. That was the quest. It wasn't fake, and it wasn't a game, it was real. It mattered after all. They'd been fighting for magic all along. They just hadn't known it.

Of course Penny took this in stride. He would never be so uncool as to give Quentin credit for saving the universe or anything.

"That's very good. That's excellent. But you must recover the seventh key."

"Right. I got that far. We'll find the seventh key. And then what?"

"Then take them all to the End of the World. The door is there."

This was it. He knew what to do now. He'd received his cue. It was like how he felt back on the island, in the castle, but calmer this time. This must be what the gods felt like, he thought. Absolute certainty. They had arrived at Penny's building, back where they'd started.

"Penny, we have to get back to Fillory, back to our ship, to finish the quest. Can you send us back? I mean, even with the fountains frozen over?"

"Of course. The Order has made me privy to all the secrets of interdimensional travel. If you think of the Neitherlands as a computer, then the fountains are merely—"

"Awesome. Thanks, man." He turned to Poppy. "Are you in on this? Or do you still want to go back to the real world?"

"Are you kidding?" She grinned and pressed herself against him. "Fuck reality, baby. Let's go save the universe."

"I will prepare the spell to send you back," Penny said.

It was snowing harder, the flakes blowing slantwise through their little dome of warmth, but Quentin felt invulnerable now. They were going to fight this, and they were going to win. Penny began chanting in that same incomprehensible language he'd used before. It had some vowel sounds that Quentin barely recognized as human.

"It needs a minute to take effect," he said when he was done. "Of course, from this point forward the journey will be undertaken by members of the Order."

Wait.

"What do you mean?"

"My colleagues and I will return with you to your ship and carry out the remainder of the quest. You may observe, of course." Penny gave them a moment to take that in. "You didn't think we would leave a mission of this importance to a group of amateurs, did you? We appreciate the good work you've done to get us this far, we truly do, but it's out of your hands now. It's time for the professionals take over."

"Sorry, but no," Quentin said. "It isn't."

He wasn't giving this up. And he definitely wasn't inviting Penny along.

"I suppose you'll find your own way back to Fillory then," Penny said. He crossed his handless arms. "I take back the spell."

"You can't take it back!" Poppy said. "What are you, nine? Penny!"

He'd finally gotten under even Poppy's skin.

"You don't understand," Quentin said, though he wasn't totally sure he understood himself. "This is our job. Nobody else can do it for us. That's not how it works. You have to send us back."

"I have to? Are you going to make me?"

"Jesus! Penny, you are unbelievable! Literally unbelievable! You know, I actually thought you'd changed, I really did. Do you even get that this isn't about you?"

"Not about me?" Penny lost his grip on his interdimensional monk voice again and spoke in his old, higher-pitched voice, the one he used to use when he felt especially aggrieved and self-righteous. "Spare me that, Quentin. You haven't spared me much during our long acquaintance, but spare me that. I found the Neitherlands. I found the button. I took us to Fillory. You didn't do all that, Quentin, I did."

"And I got my hands bitten off by the Beast. And I came here. And now I'm going to finish this, because I started it."

Quentin imagined it: Penny and his fellow Blue Oyster Cult members showing up on the *Muntjac* and ordering everybody—ordering Eliot!—around. Probably they were better magicians than he was, technically. But still, no, he couldn't do it. It was impossible.

They glared at each other. It was a stalemate.

"Penny, can I ask you something?" Quentin said. "How do you do magic now? I mean, without your hands?"

The funny thing about Penny was that you knew questions like that weren't going to make him uncomfortable, and it didn't. In fact his mood brightened immediately.

"At first I thought I would never do magic again," Penny explained. "But when the Order took me in they taught me another technique that does not depend on hand motions. Think about it: what's special about hands? What if you were to use other muscles in your body to cast spells? The Order showed me how. Now I can see how limiting it was. To be honest I'm a little surprised you're still doing it the old way."

Penny wiped his chin with his sleeve. He always used to spit a little when he got excited. Quentin took a deep breath.

"Penny, I don't think you or the Order can finish this quest. I'm sorry. Ember assigned this one to us, and He must have had His reasons. I think that may just be the way it works. It's His will. I don't think it would work for anybody else."

Penny mulled this for a minute.

"All right," he said finally. "All right. I can see there is a certain logic to it. And there is a great deal for the Order to do in the Neitherlands. In fact in many respects the crucial effort will take place here, while you retrieve the keys."

Quentin had a feeling that was the best he was going to get.

"Great. I appreciate that. If you wanted to, you could take this opportunity to say that you're sorry about sleeping with my girlfriend."

"You were on a break."

"Okay, look, just get us the hell out of here, we have to go save magic." If they stayed here any longer Quentin was going to doom the universe all over again by killing Penny with his bare hands. Though it would almost be worth it. "What are you going to do while we do that?"

"We—the Order and I—are going to engage the gods directly. This will delay them while you recover the last key."

"But what could you possibly do?" Poppy asked. "Aren't they all-powerful? Or practically?"

"Oh, the Order can do things you wouldn't believe. We've spent millennia studying in the library of the Neitherlands. We know secrets that you never dreamed of. We know secrets that would drive you mad if I whispered them to you.

"And we're not alone. We'll have help."

A deep, muffled thump filled the square from over by the fountain that led back to Earth. It shook the air—they felt it in their knees. A stone fell somewhere. Another thump followed it, and another, as if something was knocking, trying to force its way into the world from somewhere underneath it. Was it the gods? Maybe they were too late.

There was a final thump, and all at once the ice in the fountain exploded upward. Quentin and Poppy ducked as chunks of it shot in all directions and went skittering across the paving stones. With a metallic groan the great bronze lotus flower tore open, the petals spreading out in all directions as if it were blooming, and a huge, sinuous form came surging and wriggling up out of it. The thing lunged violently up into the air, spreading its wings and shaking off water and beating its way into the night sky, whipping the falling snow into great whorls and circles around it.

Another one followed it, and then a third.

"It's the dragons!" Poppy shouted. She clapped her hands like a little girl. "Quentin, it's the dragons! Oh, look at them!"

"It's the dragons," Penny said. "The dragons are going to help us."

Poppy kissed him on the cheek, and Penny smiled for the first time. You could tell he didn't want to, but he couldn't help himself.

The dragons kept coming, one after the other. They must have emptied out every river in the world. The square lit up as one of them roared a gout of flame at the misty sky.

How did he know that was going to happen right then?

"You planned that, didn't you," Quentin said, or tried to say, but just then Penny's spell took effect, and Quentin was no longer in the same world as the person he was talking to.

BOOK IV

CHAPTER 23

That morning in Murs, sitting around the table in the library, they gave Julia the full download.

In a way she was lucky she was only getting in now. She'd missed the early days, when they spent a lot of time just ruling things out. For example: they'd blown six months on a theory that spells picked up extra power the closer you got to the center of the Earth. A minor effect, barely measurable, but if it could be verified it would open up huge, ripe fields of new theory. It would change everything.

That had kicked off a barnstorming tour of abandoned mines and salt domes and other deep subterranean topography, not excluding an expensive sequence involving a rented tramp steamer and a secondhand bathysphere. But all they'd learned from half a year's hard spelunking and deep-ocean diving was that Asmodeus's spellwork performed slightly better once you got half a mile underground, and that the most probable explanation for that was that spelunking got Asmodeus really excited.

They pushed on into astrology and ocean magic and even oneiromancy—dream magic. Turns out you can cast some truly amazing shit in your dreams. But after you wake up it all seems kind of pointless, and nobody really wants to hear about it.

They worked with the Earth's magnetic field, using apparatus cribbed from some Nikola Tesla drawings, right up until the night when Failstaff almost flipped the planet's magnetic poles, whereupon they dropped that whole line of investigation and backed away slowly. Gummidgy

spent a sleepless week developing a witheringly abstract hypothesis related to cosmic rays and quantum effects and the Higgs boson, which
in the end even she only half-understood. She swore she could prove it
mathematically, but the calculations required were so involved that they
would have required a computer the size of the universe, running for a
length of time that would have taken them past the projected heat-death
of the universe, to work them out. It was pretty much the definition of
moot.

That's when they turned to religion.

At this Julia pushed her chair back from the table. She could feel her
intellectual gag reflex about to kick in.

"I know," Pouncy said. "But it's not what you think. Hear us out."

Failstaff began unrolling a huge, closely annotated diagram that was
almost as big as the table.

Religion had never been a subject that interested Julia. She considered herself too smart to believe in things she had no evidence for, and
that behaved in ways that violated every principle she'd ever observed or
heard plausibly spoken about. And she considered herself too tough-
minded to believe in things just because they made her feel better.
Magic was one thing. With magic you were at least looking at reproducible results. But religion? That was about faith. Uneducated guesses
made by weak minds. As far as she knew, or thought she knew, her views
on this matter were shared by the other Free Traders.

"There was a piece missing," Pouncy went on. "We thought we'd gone
back to first principles. But what if we hadn't? What if there were principles before the first principles we'd gone back to?

"We were assuming, until it could be proved otherwise, that there were
bigger energies out there, far bigger, and that there was a technique by
which those energies could be manipulated. Humans have not, so far as
we know, in the modern era, gained access to those energies. But suppose
there were another class of beings who did have access to them. Maybe
not humans."

"Another class of beings," Julia said flatly. "You're talking about God."

"Gods. I wanted to find out more about them."

"That's insane. There's no such thing as gods. Or God. You know,
Pouncy, one of the things I love about the fact that I didn't go to college

is that I didn't have to sit around a freshman dorm getting high and arguing about shit like this."

But Pouncy was not withered by her scorn.

"'Once you've eliminated the possible, whatever remains, however impossible, must be the truth.' Sherlock Holmes."

"That's not actually the quote. And it doesn't mean that gods are real, Pouncy. It means you need to go back and check your work, because you screwed it up somewhere."

"We checked it."

"Then maybe you should give up," Julia said.

"But I don't give up," Pouncy said. His eyes had a wintry, sleety gray to them that was distinctly un–Abercrombie & Fitch. "And neither do they." He indicated the others sitting around the table. "And neither do you. Do you, Julia."

Julia blinked and held his gaze to indicate that she would keep listening, but that she made no promises. Pouncy went on.

"We're not talking about monotheism. Or at least not in its latter-day form. We're talking about old-time religion. Paganism, or more precisely polytheism.

"Forget everything you ordinarily associate with religious study. Strip away all the reverence and the awe and the art and the philosophy of it. Treat the subject coldly. Imagine yourself to be a theologist, but a special kind of theologist, one who studies gods the way an entomologist studies insects. Take as your dataset the entirety of world mythology and treat it as a collection of field observations and statistics pertaining to a hypothetical species: the god. Proceed from there."

Fastidiously at first, with rubber gloves and tweezers and haughty distaste, as if they were handling the intellectual equivalent of medical waste, Pouncy and the others took up the study of comparative religion. Much as Julia had done with magic back in her apartment above the bagel store, they began combing the world's religious narratives and traditions for practical information. They called it Project Ganymede.

"What the hell were you hoping to find?" Julia said.

"I wanted to learn their techniques. I wanted to be able to do what gods did. I don't see any real distinction between religion and magic, or for that matter between gods and magicians. I think divine power is just another form of magical praxis. You know what Arthur C. Clarke said about technology and magic, right? Any sufficiently advanced technology is indistinguishable from magic. Turn it around. What is advanced magic indistinguishable from? Any sufficiently advanced magic is indistinguishable from the miraculous."

"The fire of the gods," Failstaff rumbled. Jesus, he was a true believer too.

But despite herself—and she took care not to show it—Julia felt her curiosity stirring. She reminded herself that she knew these people well. They were as smart as she was, and they were at least as big intellectual snobs as she was. She probably wasn't going to come up with a lot of objections that they hadn't already thought of.

"Look, Pouncy," she said. "I know enough about religion to know that even if there are gods, they don't exactly hand out holy fire like candy. There's only one way this story ends. It's Prometheus all over again. Phaëthon. Icarus. Pick your sucker. You fly too close to the sun, the thermal energy from the sun overwhelms the weak attractive forces that allow the wax in your wings to maintain its solid form, and down you go, into the sea. No fire for you. And that's if you're lucky. If you're unlucky you end up like Prometheus. Birds eat your liver forever."

"Usually," Failstaff said. "There are exceptions."

"For example, not everybody is such a complete dink that they make their wings out of wax," Asmodeus said.

Briskly, Failstaff walked Julia through the enormous diagram on the table in front of them, sketching arcs and connections with his thick, soft fingers. The diagram showed the primary narratives of the major and minor religious traditions, collated and cross-referenced—and color-coded!—to highlight areas where they overlapped and confirmed one another. Apparently if you're enough of a power nerd, there is nothing that cannot be flowcharted.

"The hubristic scenario, the pride that challenges the gods and leads to the death of the challenger, is only one of a number of possible scenarios. And usually the bad outcome can be traced to poor preparation on the part of the principals. It does not at all imply that it is categorically impossible for a mortal to gain access to divine power."

"Hm," Julia said. "Theoretically."

"No, not theoretically," Asmodeus said sharply. "Practically. Historically. Technically the process is called ascension, or sometimes assumption, or my favorite word for it is *translation*. They all mean the same thing: the process by which a human being is brought bodily into heaven, without dying, and accorded some measure of divine status. And then there's apotheosis, which is related, whereby a human actually becomes a god. It's been done, tons of times."

"Give me examples."

"Mary." She ticked off a finger. "As in Jesus's mom. She was born mortal and ended up divine. Galahad. Arthurian legend. He was Lancelot's son. He found the Holy Grail and was taken directly up into heaven. So was Enoch—he was an early descendant of Adam's."

"There's a couple of Chinese generals," Gummidgy said. "Guan Yu. Fan Kuai. There's the Eight Immortals of Taoism."

"Dido, Buddha, Simon Magus . . ." Pouncy chimed in. "It just goes on and on."

"Or look at Ganymede," Asmo said. "Greek legend. He was a mortal, but of such great beauty that Zeus brought him up to Olympus to be a cupbearer. Hence the project name."

"We think *cupbearer* was probably a euphemism," Failstaff added.

"No kidding," Julia said. "Okay, I get the point. Not everybody ends up like Icarus. But these are just stories. There's immortals in *Highlander,* but that doesn't mean they're real."

"Those aren't gods," Failstaff said. "Sheezus, have you even seen the movie?"

"And these aren't just ordinary mortals you're talking about. They were all special in some way. Like you said, Enoch was a descendant of Adam."

"And you're not?" Asmo said.

"Galahad was inhumanly virtuous. Ganymede was inhumanly beautiful. Which I don't think anybody here exactly qualifies for either. You all seem pretty human to me."

"Very true," Pouncy said. "Very true. It's an issue. Listen, for the moment we're talking proof of concept. We're in initial trials. We're nowhere near drawing definitive conclusions yet. We just don't want to rule anything out."

Like a professor showing around a prospective graduate student, Pouncy took Julia on a tour of the parts of the East Wing she hadn't been allowed into before. She passed room after room stuffed with the paraphernalia of a hundred churches and temples. There were raiments and vestments. There were altars and torches and censers and miters. There were a thousand flavors of incense.

She picked up a bundle of sacred staffs tied together with twine—she recognized a bishop's crosier among them, and a druidical shillelagh. This was a different class of hardware from what she was used to handling, to the say least. It looked like rubbish to her. But who could tell for sure without testing? Maybe this was the industrial-strength stuff. Maybe this really was the big iron, the magical equivalent of the Large Hadron Collider. You couldn't rule it out till you'd ruled it out. Could you?

So Julia joined Project Ganymede. She pitched in with the others, doing what nerds do: she sliced and diced, organized and spreadsheeted, drew up checklists and then checked the hell out of them. The magicians of Murs chanted, drank, sacrificed, fasted, bathed, painted their faces, consulted the stars, and huffed odd gases from bubbling liquids.

It was hard to assimilate the sight of the solemn, gawky Gummidgy ululating and tripping on peyote, topless and in full face paint, but as Pouncy pointed out, in the context of their present field of study, this was what rigor looked like. (Asmodeus swore, in hushed tones, glittering with suppressed merriment, that Pouncy and Gummidgy were running Bacchic sex rituals on the sly, but if she had proof she declined to make it available to Julia.) They had to find out if there was a magical technique behind all this messy crap, and if there was, who knew, maybe it would make the stuff in the three-ring binders look like bar mitzvah magic.

At the point when Julia joined Project Ganymede, Pouncy didn't have much to show by way of results, but he'd seen enough to keep hoping that it wasn't a complete waste of time, all red herring and no white whale. Apparently Iris had been trying a new transcription of a Sumerian chant the other night when something like a swarm of insects issued—no other word really applied—from her mouth. It hovered in the middle of the room for a second, buzzing fiercely, and then broke a window and

disappeared outside. Iris couldn't speak for two days afterward. The
thing had scorched her throat coming out.

There were other hints too, scattered manifestations of something,
nobody even had a theory as to what. Objects moving by themselves.
Glasses and pots shattering. There were those phantom giant footsteps
that had woken Julia up. Fiberpunk—the fireplug metamagician—had
fasted and meditated for three days, and on the morning of the fourth
he swore he'd seen a hand in a ray of sunshine, felt it reach down and
gently touch his pudgy face with its hot fingers.

But nobody else could make it happen. That's what was frustrating.
Magic wasn't a perfect linear grid or anything, but compared with magic
religion was just chaos, a complete junk pile. Sure, it was plenty ritualized, and formalized, and codified, but the rituals didn't deliver consis-
tent, reproducible results. The thing about real magic was, once you
learned a spell, and you cast it properly, and you weren't too tired, and
the Circumstances hadn't shifted while you weren't looking, then it
worked, generally speaking. But this religious stuff didn't give good
data. Pouncy was convinced that if they could drill down far enough,
parse the underlying grammar, they'd have the basis for an entirely new
and radically more powerful magical technique, but the further down
they drilled the more chaotic and less grammatical it got. Sometimes it
felt like there was some capricious, mischievous presence on the other
side that was pressing buttons and pulling levers at random, just to piss
them off.

Pouncy had the patience for it, to sit and wait out the noisy data until
the patterns emerged, but Pouncy was a singular individual. So while he
and his acolytes pored over sacred texts, and filled hard drive after hard
drive with chaotic pseudo-data, Asmodeus took a smaller group out into
the field in search of a shortcut. She went looking for a live specimen.

Pouncy wasn't thrilled to find Asmo leading a splinter movement,
but she stood up to him with the icy firmness of a seventeen-year-old
corporate vice president. There was, she explained, although everybody
already knew, a population of magical beings on Earth. It was a modest
population, as Earth wasn't an especially hospitable environment for
them. Magically speaking, the soil was rocky and bitter, the air thin, the
winters harsh. Life on Earth for a fairy was analogous to life in the Arc-

tic for a human. They survived, but they did not thrive. And yet some few remained—the Inuits, by analogy, of the magical world.

Among those few there was a hierarchy. Some were more powerful, some less so. At the bottom were the vampires, seedy serial killers from whose population the non-sociopaths had been bred hundreds of generations ago by natural selection. Empathy was not a survival trait among the *strigoi*. They were not well liked.

But above them were any number of orders of fairies and elementals and lycanthropes and one-off oddities, leading up the power chain. And this was where Asmodeus saw her opportunity: if she worked her way up the ladder, patiently, rung by rung, who knows where she might get. She might not get all the way to gods, but she might meet somebody who knew somebody who had the gods' fax number. It beat fasting.

To begin with they kept things local: day trips to hot spots within easy striking distance. Enough of Provence was still farmland and parkland that they could still ferret out indigenous sprites, minor river sirens, even the odd wyvern without much trouble. But that was small-fry. As July turned to August, and the hills around Murs lit up with lavender fields so idyllically beautiful they looked like something you'd see on a calendar in a dentist's office, Asmodeus and her handpicked team, which now included Failstaff as well, disappeared into the field for days at a time.

Their efforts were not at first conspicuously successful. Asmo would knock on Julia's door at three in the morning, dead leaves in her hair and holding a two-thirds-full bottle of Prosecco, and they would sit on Julia's bed while Asmo described a night of fruitless bullshitting in Old Provençal with a bunch of lutins—basically the French equivalent of your common leprechaun—who kept trying to crawl up under her (admittedly invitingly short) skirt.

But there was progress. Failstaff kept a special room, neatly swept, with a white tablecloth set with fresh food, as a kind of honeypot for local spirits called fadas, who would come bearing good luck in their right hands, bad in their left. Asmo woke her up crowing about having gotten an audience with the Golden Goat, a being usually seen only by shepherds, and from a distance.

It wasn't all good luck and Golden Goats. One night Asmo came back with wet hair, shivering in the early autumn chill, after a drac, in the middle of an otherwise perfectly civil interview, had abruptly pulled her right into the Rhône. The next day she saw the thing in the supermarket in the shape of a man, stocking its shopping cart with jars of anchovies. It winked at her merrily.

Plus somebody was stealing their hubcaps. Asmo thought it must be a local trickster-deity called Reynard the Fox. He was supposed to be some kind of anti-gentry, anti-clerical hero of the peasantry, but she just considered Him a pain in the ass.

One morning Julia saw Failstaff at breakfast looking as grim as she'd ever seen him. Over espresso and muesli he swore to her that he'd seen a black horse with a back as long as a school bus, with thirty crying children mounted on it, match speeds with them last night as they drove home in the van. It paced them for two solid minutes, sometimes trotting on the ground, sometimes galloping along up on power lines or across the treetops. Then it leaped straight into a river, kids and all. They stopped and waited, but it never came back up. Real, or illusion? They searched the papers for stories about missing kids, but they never found anything.

Most days the two groups would debrief at noon, over lunch for Pouncy's team and breakfast for Asmo's, who were out all night in the field most nights and got up late. Each side presented its data, and each side would feed what the other side had learned back into the next stage of its investigations. There was a certain amount of healthy competition between the two sides. Also some unhealthy competition.

"For fuck's sake, Asmo," Pouncy said one day in September, interrupting her mid-report. The hay fields all around the house were turning a toasted brown. "How is this getting us anywhere? If I have to hear one more word about that Golden fucking Goat I'm going to go mental. Absolutely mental. The Goat knows nothing. This whole region is just chickenshit! I would kill for something Greek. Anything. God, demigod, spirit, monster, I don't even care what. A cyclops. There's got to be a few of those things left. We're practically on the Mediterranean!"

Asmodeus stared at him balefully across a table strewn with baguette crusts and smears of local jam. Her eyes looked hollow. She was wiped out from lack of sleep. A huge wasp, its legs dangling limply, airlifted from one jam smear to the next.

"No cyclops," she said. "Sirens. I could get you a siren."

"Sirens?" Pouncy brightened up. He banged the table with the flat of his hand. "Why didn't you say so! That's great!"

"They're not Greek sirens though. They're French. They're half-snake, from the waist down."

Pouncy frowned. "So like a gorgon."

"No. Gorgons have snakes for hair. Except anyway, I don't think gorgons are real."

"A half-snake woman," Julia said, "would be a lamia."

"She would be," Asmodeus snapped, "if she were in Greece. But we're in France, so she's a siren."

"All right, but maybe she *knows* a lamia," Pouncy said. "Maybe they're related. Like cousins. You gotta think all the snake-bodied women have a network—"

"She doesn't know a lamia." Asmodeus put her head down on the table. "God, you have no idea what you're asking."

"I'm not asking you, I'm telling you, you've got to widen your search. I'm so sick of this cutesy Frenchy-French shit. Ever wonder why *Clash of the Lutins* was never a movie? The power levels around here are nothing! We can fly you to Greece, the money isn't a problem. We can all go to Greece. But you've hit a wall here and you're too stubborn to admit it."

"You don't know!" Asmodeus sat up, her red eyes flaming. "You don't understand what I'm doing! You can't just go knocking on doors like you're taking a census. You have to build up trust. I'm running a network of agents here now. Some of these things haven't talked to a human for centuries. The Golden Goat—"

"God!" He stuck a finger in Asmodeus's face. "No more with the Goat!"

"Asmo's right, Pouncy."

All eyes turned to Julia. She could see that Pouncy had expected her to back him up. Well, she wasn't here to play power games. If there's one thing magic had taught her it was that power wasn't a game.

"You're thinking about this the wrong way. The answer isn't wider, it's deeper. If we start hopping around the globe cherry-picking myths and legends we're going to burn through all our time and money and end up with nothing."

"Well, so far we've got Golden fucking Goat cheese."

"Hey now," Failstaff said. "That stuff was perfectly edible."

"You're missing the point. If we go out there looking for something specific we'll never find anything. But if we focus on someplace rich and really deep-dive it, work our way down through what's there, we're bound to hit something solid eventually. If there's anything solid to hit."

"Someplace rich. Like Greece. It's like I was saying—"

"We don't need to go to Greece," Julia said. "We don't need to go anywhere. All this stuff has to be connected at the roots. Everybody came through Provence: the Celts were here, the Romans, the Basques. The Buddhists sent missionaries. The Egyptians had colonies, and so did the Greeks, Pouncy, if you absolutely need the Greeks to get you hard. They even had Jews. Sure, it all got covered over with Christianity, but the mythology goes all the way down. If we can't find a god in all that, there are no gods to be found."

"So what are you saying?" Pouncy regarded her skeptically, not pleased by her display of disloyalty. "We should drop all the world religion stuff and just do local folk and myth?"

"That's what I'm saying. That's where our sources are. Let's bear down on those and see what they get us."

Pouncy pursed his lips, considering. Everyone looked at him.

"All right." He threw up his hands. "All right! Fine. Let's do a month just on Provençal stuff and see what it gets us." He glared around the table. "But no more dicking around with leprechauns. Take us up the food chain, Asmo. I want to know who runs this area. Find out who all these small players are afraid of and then get that guy's number. That's who we want to talk to."

Asmodeus heaved a sigh. She looked years older than she had in June.

"I'll try," she said. "I really will, Pouncy. But you don't know what you're asking."

You'd never hear Pouncy cop to it, but Julia turned out to be right. When they narrowed their focus to the local mythology only, Project Ganymede began to get traction. Once they started looking at just one corner of the puzzle—and stuck all the rest of the pieces back in the box—everything started to fit together.

Poring through Gregory of Tours and other, nameless medieval chroniclers, Julia began to get a feel for the local magic. Like wine, Provençal magic had its own distinctive terroir. It was rich and chaotic and romantic. It was a night-magic, confabulated out of moons and silver, wine and blood, knights and fairies, wind and rivers and forests. It concerned itself with good and evil but also with the vast intermediate realm in between, the realm of mischief.

It was also mother-magic. Gradually Julia began to become aware of something, or someone, who was standing behind the old dead pages, just out of view. Julia couldn't see her, or name her, or not yet, but she felt her. She must have been old, very old. She must have gotten here early, long before the Romans. Nothing Julia read spoke of her directly— you couldn't look straight at her, but you knew she was there because of the small ways she perturbed the universe around her. Julia picked up on her only by triangulation, via tiny traces, little glimpses, like the curious Black Madonna figures you saw scattered around Europe, and especially around Provence. Black Madonnas were otherwise ordinary images of the Virgin Mary, but with an inexplicably dark complexion.

But she was older than the Virgin Mary, and wilder. Julia thought she must be some kind of local fertility goddess from out of the darkness of the region's deep, preliterate past, before the cosmopolitan conquerors came in and scraped everything smooth and clean and paved it over with official homogenizing Christianity. A distant cousin of Diana or Cybele or Isis, ethnographically speaking. When the Christians arrived they would have lumped her in with Mary, but Julia thought she might still be out there on her own. She sensed the goddess looking out from behind the mask of Christian dogma, the way the second Julia had looked out from behind the mask of the first Julia.

The goddess called to Julia—Julia, who had turned her back on her own mother to save herself, and now heard about her only in oblique and infrequent e-mails from her sister, sent from the safe bosom of a small, top-flight liberal arts college in western Massachusetts. Julia remembered the grace and forgiveness with which she had been received back into her home, when she came crawling back from Chesterton. It was like nothing else she had ever experienced, before or since. It was the closest to the divine she'd ever been.

The more Julia read and cross-checked and deduced and collated, the more she was convinced her goddess was real. Nothing she longed for that ardently could fail to exist—it was like the goddess was just on the other side of all these useless words, trying to find Julia as Julia was searching for her. She wasn't a great and grand world-ruling goddess, a Hera or a Frigga. She was more of a middleweight, a team player on a big pantheon. She wasn't a grain-goddess like Ceres—Provence was rocky and Mediterranean, not wheat country at all. Julia's goddess dealt in grapes and olives, the dark, intense fruit of hard, gnarled trees and vines. And she had daughters too: the dryads, ferocious defenders of the forests.

The goddess was warm, even humorous, and loving, but she had a second aspect, terrible in its bleakness: a mourning aspect that she assumed in winter, when she descended to the underworld, away from the light. There were different versions of the story. In some she grew angry at mankind and hid herself underground half the year out of rage. In some she lost one of her dryad-daughters and retired to Hades in grief. In others the goddess was fooled by some Loki-type trickster-god and bound to spend half the year hiding her warmth and fruitfulness in the underworld, against her will. But in each version her dual nature was clear. She was a goddess of darkness as well as light. A Black Madonna: the blackness of death, but also the blackness of good soil, dark with decay, which gives rise to life.

Julia wasn't the only one to hear the call of the goddess. The others talked about her too. The Free Trader Beowulf alumni in particular, who tended not to have been the beneficiaries of world-class mothering as children, felt drawn to her. In the crypt under Chartres Cathedral there was an ancient druidical well, and nearby a famous statue of the Black Madonna that was known as *Notre Dame Sous Terre*. So that's what they called the goddess, for lack of a real name: Our Lady Underground. Or sometimes, when they were being familiar, just O.L.U.

Asmo began to take Julia out on some of the nighttime raids. These were conducted in Julia's former rental Peugeot or, in the event that they were considering extracting and transporting someone or something, a long-suffering Renault Trafic van. One night they followed a tip deep into the Camargue, the vast swampy delta of the Rhône River where it flowed into the Mediterranean: three hundred square miles of salt marshes and lagoons.

It was a two-hour drive. The Camargue was, allegedly, home to a creature called the tarasque. When Julia asked Asmodeus for details she just said, "You wouldn't believe me if I told you."

She was right. Having squelched through miles of rotten, boot-sucking ground, they finally tracked the thing down and chivvied it out of its hiding place in a hollow full of stunted, broken marsh pines. It faced them in the moonlight, making a miserable whuffling sound, like it had a nagging cold.

"What," Julia said, "the fuck."

"Holy shit," said Failstaff.

"This is exceeding expectations," Asmo said.

The tarasque was a beast about the size of a hippo, but with six legs. It had a scorpion tail, a kind of lion-human head with stringy long hair, and on its back a turtle shell with spikes coming out of it. It was the turtle shell that did it. It looked like Bowser from *Super Mario Bros.*

The tarasque crouched low to the ground, wheezing, its chin resting on a wet stump, looking up at them with its unbelievably ugly face. Its posture was not so much defensive as resigned.

"Leave it to the French to come up with the most fucked-up-est dragon ever," Asmodeus sighed.

Once the tarasque realized they weren't going to attack it, it began to talk. In fact they couldn't get it to shut up. The thing didn't need a roving strike team of folklorist-wizards, it needed a therapist. They sat there all night on tree stumps listening to it complain about how lonely and insufficiently damp it was. Not till dawn did it lumber back into its hollow.

But the tarasque turned out to be worth it. It was a champion whiner, and if they were trying to figure out who people around here were afraid of, well, it was afraid of practically everyone. They were spoiled for choice.

The tarasque was too big for the small fry to pick on, but reading between the lines it was clear that it was a whipping boy for the upper ranks of mythological society. Apparently Reynard the Fox teased it a great deal, though it begged them not to mention anything about that to Reynard, for fear of reprisals. More interestingly, the tarasque was subjected to periodic beatings by a holy man of some kind who had been haunting the slopes of Mont Ventoux for the past millennium or so.

It was the tarasque's terrifying appearance, see, that caused it to be so often misunderstood. A being of such ferocious magnificence as itself was too often assumed to be evil, and scourged and vilified should it devour even so much as six or seven village folk! That was why it had taken to spending its days wallowing in the salt bogs of the Camargue, nomming the occasional wild horse to stay alive. Why not join it? It was cool and safe here. And you know, it so rarely found anyone nice to talk to. Not like that nasty holy man. They were so much nicer than he was.

Driving back along empty predawn highways, squinting out at the flatness of the swamp through gummy eyes, they all agreed that the holy hermit sounded like a very nasty customer indeed. Exactly the kind of nasty customer they should get to know better.

A new atmosphere had settled over the house at Murs. It had always been a basic tenet there that luxury and comfort were integral parts of the magical lifestyle, not just for its own sake but as a matter of principle. As magicians—Murs magicians!—they were the secret aristocracy of the world, and Goddamn it, they were going to live like it.

Now that was changing. Nobody said anything, and certainly no edicts came down from Pouncy, but the atmosphere became more spartan. The serious nature of their investigation was cooling and tempering their collective mood. Less wine came out with dinner, and sometimes none at all. The food became plainer. Conversations were conducted in hushed tones, as they would be in the halls of a monastery. An attitude of seriousness and austerity was taking root among them. Julia suspected some of the others of fasting. From a high-energy magical research center Murs was turning into something more like a religious retreat.

Julia felt it too. She began getting up at dawn. She spoke only when necessary. Her mind was clear and sharp, her thoughts like birds calling to one another in an empty sky. At night she slept heavily—deep-ocean sleep, calm and dark, adrift with strange, silent, luminous creatures.

One night she dreamed that Our Lady Underground visited her in her room. She came in the form of a statue of herself, the one from the crypt at Chartres, stiff and cold. The statue gave Julia a wooden cup. Sitting up, Julia lifted it to her lips and drank like a feverish child being given medicine in bed. The liquid was cool and sweet, and she thought of the Donne poem about the thirsty Earth. Then she lowered the cup, and the goddess leaned down and kissed her, with her hard, gilded icon's face.

Then the statue broke apart, its outside crumbling like an eggshell, and from inside it stepped the true goddess, clear at last. She was grave and unbearably lovely, and she held her attributes in either hand: a gnarled olive staff in her right, a bird's nest with three eggs in it in her left. Half of her face was in shadow, for the half of the year she spent underground. Her eyes were full of love and forgiveness.

"You are my daughter," she said. "My true daughter. I will come for you."

Julia woke to the sound of Pouncy pounding on her door.

"Come look," he whispered when she opened it. "You have to see this."

Still drowsy in her nightgown, Julia followed him through the darkened house. She felt as if she were still dreaming. The floor creaked loudly, as it always did when one tried to creep through a house by night. They padded down stone steps to a basement room reserved for high-impact experiments. Pouncy practically ran ahead of her.

The lights were off. A single coherent shaft of moonlight entered the room through a high window, which was at ground level outside. She rubbed the sleep out of her eyes.

"Okay," Pouncy said. "Before we lose the light."

There was a table in the room, with a white tablecloth and a small round mirror on it. Pouncy drew a sigil on it three times with his finger.

"Hold out your hands, like this." He cupped his hands.

When Julia cupped hers, he held the mirror so that it reflected the moonbeam into them. She gasped. Immediately she felt her hands fill with something cold and hard. Coins. They made a sound like rain.

"They're silver," Pouncy said. "I think they're real."

One of the coins jingled on the floor and rolled away. This was powerful magic. It felt like nothing else she'd ever seen.

"Let me try," she whispered.

She copied the sign he'd made on the mirror. This time instead of silver the moonbeam became something white and liquid. It pooled on the table, soaking into the cloth. She touched a finger to it and tasted it. Milk.

"How did you do this?" she said.

"I'm not sure," Pouncy said, "but I think I prayed."

"Oh God." She forced down a hysterical giggle. "Who did you pray to?"

"I found it in one of these old Provençal books. Langue d'oc stuff. The language looked like an incantation, but I was wondering why there were no gestures to go with it. So I just got on my knees and clasped my hands and said the words." Pouncy flushed. "I thought about—well, I thought about O.L.U."

"Let's have a look under the hood."

There were simple spells to make magic visible: they showed you the ways the energy was running in and around an object with an enchantment on it. But what Julia saw when she cast one on the mirror defied explanation. It was the densest weave of magic she'd ever seen: a tracery of fine lines in an ornate pattern like a tapestry, so dense that it almost obscured the mirror underneath it. It should have taken a team of magicians a year at least to put all those channels in place. Instead Pouncy had done it alone, in one night, with a simple chant. It was unlike any working she'd ever heard of.

"You did this? Just now?"

"I don't know," he said. "I don't think so. I said the words, but I think somebody else must have done the work."

Her hands and her body felt strangely light. There was a sweet smell in the air. Acting on an impulse, she dabbed a little of the milk on each of her eyelids. Instantly her vision sharpened and clarified, like when they change the settings at the ophthalmologist's.

"We're getting close, Julia," Pouncy said. "We're getting close to the divine praxis. I can feel it."

"I don't like feeling things," she said. "I like knowing them."

But she had to admit, she felt it too. The only word she could think of to describe this magic was *grave*. There was nothing light or playful about it: it was dead fucking sober magic. Serious as a heart attack. Where was the line between a spell and a miracle? Turning moonlight into silver coins wasn't exactly parting the Red Sea, but the effortlessness with which it was accomplished spoke of much larger possibilities. It was a minor effect running off an enormous power source.

The next morning Asmodeus was at breakfast. Real breakfast, not her usual lunch-breakfast. She was practically vibrating with excitement. She refused any food.

"I found him," she said, with finality.

"Who?" Julia said. It was a little early for Asmodeus in her maximum-intensity mode. "Whom did you find?"

"The hermit. The tarasque's holy man. He's a saint. Or not a saint, exactly, not in the strictly Christian sense. But he calls himself one."

"Explain," Pouncy said around a hunk of the almost penitentially coarse bread they'd been eating.

"Well," and here Asmodeus shook off her manic fatigue for a minute and entered her business mode, "as close as I can figure out, this guy is about two thousand years old. Right? He calls himself Amadour—says he used to be a saint, but they defrocked him.

"I found him living in a cave. Red hair, beard down to here. Says he serves the goddess, the old one, the one we're always hearing about. He wouldn't name her, but it has to be her. Our Lady, O.L.U. For a while he passed as a Christian saint, he told me, saying he worshipped the Virgin Mary, but eventually he got outed as a pagan and they tried to crucify him. He's been living in a cave ever since.

"And at first I was all, sure, buddy, saint or crazy homeless guy, it's a fine line. But he showed me things. Weird things, guys, things we don't know how to do. He can shape rock with his hands. He heals animals. He knew things about me, things nobody knows. He—he healed a scar I have. Had. He made it go away."

Her voice faltered. Julia had never seen Asmodeus look so serious. She

glared at them, angry that she'd let a secret slip. Julia had never seen Asmodeus's scar. She wondered if she meant a physical one or something else.

"Can you take us to him?" Pouncy's voice was gentle. He seemed to
sense how close to the edge she was.

She shook her head quickly, trying to recover herself and not
succeeding.

"You only see him once," she said. "You could go find him yourself,
maybe, but I can't tell you where the cave was. I mean, I remember, but
I can't tell you. Literally—I tried just now." She shrugged helplessly.
"Nothing comes out."

They all looked at each other over the cold crusts and dead coffee.

"I almost forgot," she said. "He gave me something." She unzipped
her backpack and rummaged in it for a sheet of parchment, closely written. "It's a palimpsest. Can you believe it? So old-school. I watched him
scrape the ink off some priceless ancient hymnal or something to make
it. Probably a Dead Sea Scroll or something. He wrote out how to call
on the goddess. Our Lady Underground."

Pouncy took the paper from her. His fingers shook slightly.

"An invocation," he said.

"So that's it then," Julia said. "The Lady's phone number."

"That's it. It's in Phoenician, I think, if you can believe it. He didn't
know if she'd come, but . . ."

Asmo picked up the heel of Pouncy's loaf and started chewing it,
without seeming to know she was doing it. She closed her eyes.

"Shit," she said. "I have to go to bed."

"Go." Pouncy didn't look up from the paper. "Go. We'll talk after
you've slept."

CHAPTER 24

The *Muntjac* was becalmed, tossing on the gentle swell in the restless, unsettled way that boats do when they're built for speed but making no headway. Its slack ropes and tackle jostled and banged against the masts. It didn't like standing still.

Rain fuzzed the surface of the sea into a cloudy gray blur. Nobody spoke. A week had gone by since Quentin and Poppy came back from the Neitherlands, bearing news of the coming magical apocalypse and the true nature of the keys. The long, low-ceilinged cabin where they ate their meals was filled with the sound of drops drumming on the deck overhead, so that they would have had to practically yell at each other to be understood anyway.

They were going to find the last key. Definitely. They just weren't sure yet precisely how they were going to do it.

"Let's go over it again," Eliot said, raising his voice to be heard over the rain. "These things always work by rules, you just have to figure out what they are. You went through with Julia." He pointed at Quentin. "But you didn't take the key with you."

"No."

"Could it have fallen through before the door closed? Could it be in the grass on your parents' lawn?"

"No. Impossible." He was almost sure. No, he was sure. The grass was like a damn putting green, they would have seen it.

"But then you"—he turned to Bingle—"you searched the room and found no key."

"No key."

"But just now when you two"—Quentin and Poppy—"went through to the Neitherlands, that key remained behind, here, on this side."

"Correct," Poppy said. "Don't tell me it's gone too."

"No, we have it."

"What happened to it when the door closed?" Quentin asked. "Did it stay hanging there in midair?"

"No, it fell on the deck when the door closed. Bingle heard it and picked it up."

The conversation stopped, and the drumming rain filled in the silence. It was neither warm nor cold. The deck overhead was watertight, but the air was so wet that Quentin felt like he was soaked through anyway. Every surface was sticky. Everything wooden was swollen. His damn collarbone was swollen. There was a glum scraping as people shifted in their wooden chairs. Above his head Quentin heard the footsteps of whatever poor bastard was standing watch on deck.

"Maybe there was some space in between," Quentin said. "One of those gaps between dimensions. Maybe it fell in there."

"I thought the Neitherlands *was* the gap between dimensions," Poppy said.

"It is, but there's a different gap too. When a portal pulls apart. But we would have seen that."

The *Muntjac* groaned softly as it swayed in place. Quentin wished Julia were here, but she was below with a fever that might or might not have been related to whatever else was going on with her. She'd been down ever since the fight for the last key. She lay on her bed with her eyes closed but not sleeping, breathing quickly and shallowly. Quentin went down there a few times a day to read to her or hold her hand or make her drink water. She didn't seem to care much, but Quentin kept it up anyway. You never knew what might make a difference.

"So you searched the whole After Island," Quentin said.

"We did," Eliot said. "Look, maybe we should call on Ember."

"Call Him!" Quentin said it more vehemently than he meant to. "I doubt if it'll do much good. If that fucking ruminant could get the key He would just do it and leave us out of it."

"But would He?" Josh asked.

"Probably. He'll die too if Fillory goes."

"What is Ember, anyway?" Poppy said. "I mean, I thought He was a god, but He's not like those silver guys."

"I think He's a god in this world, but nowhere else," Quentin said. "That's my theory. He's just a local god. The silver gods are gods of all the worlds."

Although Quentin was still in close touch with the exalted frame of mind he'd been in when he came back from the Neitherlands, his connection to it had grown more tenuous. The urgency was still there: every morning he woke up expecting to find magic shut off everywhere like an unpaid power bill and Fillory collapsing around him on all sides like the last days of Pompeii. And they were certainly making good time, or they had been till this morning. Admiral Lacker had found, tucked away in a secret wooden locker, a marvelous sail that caught light as well as wind. Quentin recognized it: the Chatwins had one aboard the *Swift*. It hung slack through most of the night, limping along on whispers of moon- and starlight, but during the day it billowed out like a spinnaker in a gale and hauled the ship forward almost singlehandedly, needing only to be trimmed according to the angle of the sun.

That was all fine. But Fillory wasn't doing its part. It wasn't giving up the key. All the wonders seemed to be in hiding. In the past week they had reached heretofore unknown islands, stepped out onto virgin beaches, infiltrated choked mangrove swamps, even scaled a rogue drifting iceberg, but no keys presented themselves. They weren't getting traction. It wasn't working. Something was missing. It was almost as if something had gone out of the air: a tautness had gone slack, an electric charge had dissipated. Quentin racked his brain to think what it was.

Also it wouldn't stop raining.

After the meeting Quentin forced himself to take a break. He lay down in his damp berth and waited for the heat from his body to propagate its way through the clammy, tepid bedclothes. It was too late to take a nap and too early to go to sleep. Outside his window the sun was dropping over the rim of the world, or it must have been, but you couldn't tell. Sky and ocean were indistinguishable from each other. The world was the uniform gray of a brand-new Etch A Sketch the knobs of which hadn't yet been twiddled.

He stared out at it, gnawing the edge of his thumb, a bad habit left over from childhood, his mind adrift in the emptiness.

Somebody spoke.

"Quentin."

He opened his eyes. He must have fallen asleep. The window was dark now.

"Quentin," the voice said again. He hadn't dreamed it. The voice was muffled, directionless. He sat up. It was a gentle voice, soft and androgynous and vaguely familiar. It didn't sound completely human. Quentin looked around the cabin, but he was alone.

"Who are you?" he said.

"I'm down here, Quentin. You're hearing me through a grating in the floor. I'm down in the hold."

Now he placed the voice. He'd forgotten it was even on board.

"Sloth? Is that you?" Did it have a name other than Sloth?

"I thought you might like to pay me a visit."

Quentin couldn't imagine what would have given the sloth that idea. The *Muntjac*'s hold was dark and smelled of damp and rot and bilge, and for that matter it smelled of sloth. All in all he would have been fine talking to the sloth just where he was. Or not talking to it at all.

And Jesus, if he could hear the sloth that clearly it must have overheard everything that happened in this cabin since they'd left Whitespire.

But he did feel bad about the sloth. He hadn't paid very much attention to it. Frankly it was a tiny bit of a bore. But he owed it some respect, as the shipboard representative of the talking animals, and it was warm down in the hold, and it wasn't like he had somewhere more pressing to be just now. He sighed and peeled the bedclothes off himself and fetched a candle and found the ladder that went down below.

The hold was emptier than he remembered it. A year at sea would have that effect. Black water sloshed around in a channel that ran along the floor. The sloth was a weird-looking beast, maybe four feet long, with a heavy coat of greenish-gray fur. It hung upside down by its ropy arms at about eye level, its thick curved claws hooked up over a wooden beam. Its appearance smacked of evolution gone too far. The usual pile of fruit rinds and sloth droppings lay below it in an untidy heap.

"Hi," Quentin said.

"Hello."

The sloth raised its small, oddly flattened head so that it was looking at Quentin right-side up. The position looked uncomfortable, but the sloth's neck seemed pretty well designed for it. It had black bands of fur over its eyes that gave it a sleepy, raccoony look.

It squinted at the light from Quentin's candle.

"I'm sorry I haven't been down to see you very often," Quentin offered.

"It's all right, I don't mind. I'm not a very social animal."

"I don't even know your name."

"It's Abigail."

She was a girl sloth. Quentin hadn't realized. A hard wooden chair had been brought down to the hold, presumably in case someone was enjoying their conversation with the sloth so much that he or she just had to sit down to enjoy it even more.

"And you've been very busy," she added charitably.

A long silence ensued. Once in a while the sloth masticated something, Quentin wasn't sure what, with its blunt yellow teeth. It must be somebody's job to come down here and feed it. Her.

"Do you mind if I ask," Quentin said finally, "why you came on this voyage? I've always wondered."

"I don't mind at all," Abigail the Sloth said calmly. "I came because nobody else wanted to, and we thought we should send someone. The Council of Animals decided that I would mind it the least. I sleep a great deal, and I don't move around very much. I enjoy my solitude. In a way I am hardly in this world at all, so it doesn't very much matter where I am in it."

"Oh. We thought the talking animals wanted a representative on the ship. We thought you'd be insulted if we didn't take one of you along."

"We thought you'd be insulted if we didn't send someone. It is humorous how rife with misunderstanding the world is, is it not?"

It sure was.

The sloth didn't find the long silences awkward. Maybe animals didn't experience awkwardness the way humans did.

"When a sloth dies, it remains hanging in its tree," the sloth said, apropos of nothing. "Often well into the process of decomposition."

Quentin nodded sagely.

"I did not know that."

It wasn't an easy ball to throw back.

"This is by way of telling you something about the way sloths live. It is different from the way humans live, and even from the way other animals live. We spend our lives in between worlds, you might say. We suspend ourselves between the earth and the sky, touching neither. Our minds hover between the sleeping world and the waking. In a sense we live on the borderline between life and death."

"That is very different from how humans live."

"It must seem strange to you, but it is where we feel most comfortable."

The sloth seemed like somebody you could be frank with.

"Why are you telling me this?" he said. "I mean, I'm sure you have a reason, but I'm not making the connection. Is this about the key? Do you have an idea about how to find it?"

He didn't know how much the sloth knew about what was going on above deck. Maybe she didn't even know they were on a quest.

"It is not about the key," Abigail said in her liquid, unhurried voice. "It is about Benedict Fenwick."

"Benedict? What about him?"

"Would you like to speak with him?"

"Well, sure. Of course. But he's dead. He died two weeks ago."

It was still as unthinkable, almost unsayable, as it had been that first night.

"There are paths that are closed to most beings that are open to a sloth."

Quentin supposed it went without saying that patience was a big deal when having a conversation with a sloth.

"I don't understand. You're going to hold a séance, and we can talk to Benedict's ghost?"

"Benedict is in the underworld. He is not a ghost. He is a shade."

The sloth returned her head to its inverted position, a maneuver she accomplished without once dropping Quentin's gaze.

"The underworld." Jesus Christ. He hadn't even realized Fillory had an underworld. "He's in hell?"

"He is in the underworld, where dead souls go."

"Is he all right there? Or I mean, I know he's dead, but is he at peace? Or whatever?"

"That I cannot tell you. My understanding of human moods is imprecise. A sloth knows only peace, nothing else."

It must be nice to be a sloth. Quentin was unsettled by the idea of Benedict in the underworld. It bothered him that Benedict could be dead but still—not alive, but what? Conscious? Awake? It was like he was buried alive. It sounded awful.

"But he's not being tortured, right? By red guys with horns and pitchforks?" It never did to assume anything was impossible in Fillory.

"No. He is not being tormented."

"But he's not in heaven either."

"I do not know what 'heaven' is. Fillory has only an underworld."

"So how can I talk to him? Can you—I don't know, put in a call? Patch me through?"

"No, Quentin. I am not a medium. I am a psychopomp. I do not speak to the dead, but I can show you the path to the underworld."

Quentin was not sure he wanted to be shown that. He studied the sloth's upside-down face. It was unreadable.

"Physically? I could physically go there?"

"Yes."

Deep breath.

"Okay. I would really love to help Benedict, but I don't want to leave the world of the living."

"I will not force you. Indeed, I could not."

It was spooky down in the hold, which was lightless except for the flame of Quentin's candle, which stayed perfectly upright as the ship pitched forward and back. The hanging sloth did too—she swayed slightly, like a pendulum. Quentin's eyes kept wandering off into the darkness. It was otherworldly down here. The ship's curved sides were like the ribs of some huge animal that had swallowed them. Where was the underworld? Was it underground? Underwater?

The sloth chose this moment to engage in some self-grooming, which she did with her customary slowness and thoroughness, first with her tongue and then with a thick, woody claw, which she slowly and laboriously unhooked from around the beam.

"In a way"—she said, as she licked and clawed—"we sloths are like . . . small worlds . . . unto ourselves."

Nobody could wait out a pause like a sloth. Or survive on less conversational encouragement. He wondered if to a sloth the human world appeared to move past at blinding, flickering speed—if humans looked twitchy and sped-up to her, the same way the sloth looked slowed-down to Quentin.

"There is a species of algae," she said, "that grows only . . . in sloth fur. It accounts for our unique . . . greenish tint. The algae helps us blend in with the leaves. But it also serves . . . to nourish an entire ecological system. There is a species of moth that lives only . . . in the thick, algae-rich fur . . . of the sloth. Once a moth arrives on its chosen sloth"—here she tussled with a particularly gristly knot of fur for a long minute before continuing—"its wings break off. It does not need them. It will never leave."

Finally finished, she rehooked her claw over the beam and returned to her quiescent, upside-down state.

"They are called sloth moths."

"Look," Quentin said. "I want to be clear. I don't have time to go to the underworld right now. At any other time grieving for Benedict would be the biggest thing in my life, but the universe is going through a crisis. We're searching for a key, and there's a lot riding on that. A lot. It could be the end of Fillory if we don't find it. This will have to wait."

"No time will pass while you are in the other realm. For the dead there is no change, and therefore no time."

He couldn't afford to get distracted. "Even if it takes no time. Anyway what good would it do? I can't bring him back."

"No."

"So I hate to be blunt, but what's the point?"

"You could offer Benedict comfort. Sometimes the living can give something to the dead. And perhaps he could offer you something too. My understanding of human emotions is . . ."

The sloth paused to ponder her choice of words.

"Imprecise?" Quentin said.

"Precisely. Imprecise. But I do not think Benedict was happy with his death."

"It was a terrible death. He must feel very unhappy."

"I think perhaps he wants to tell you that."

Quentin hadn't considered that.

"I think perhaps he could give you something too."

The sloth regarded him with her gelatinous, glittering eyes, which seemed to pick up light from somewhere other than in the room. Then she closed them.

The ship grunted patiently as the waves beat against its hull, over and over again, monotonously. Quentin watched the sloth. By now he had learned enough to know that when he was getting annoyed at somebody else, it was usually because there was something that he himself should be doing, and he wasn't doing it. He pictured Benedict, trapped and languishing in a poorly drawn cartoon netherworld. Would he want someone to come visit him? He probably would.

Quentin felt responsible for him. It was part of being a king. And Benedict had died before he found out what the keys were for. He thought that he'd died for no reason. Imagine chewing on that for eternity.

One of the things Quentin remembered from reading about King Arthur was that the knights who had sins on their consciences never did very well on the quest for the Grail. The thing was to go to confession before you set out. You had to face yourself and deal with your shit, that's how you got somewhere. At the time Quentin thought that that was obvious, and he never understood why Gawain and the rougher knights didn't just suck it up, get shriven, and get on with it. Instead they blundered around getting into fights and succumbing to temptation and eventually ended up nowhere near the Grail.

But being in the middle of it, it wasn't that obvious. Maybe Benedict's death was—if not a sin on his conscience, exactly, then something unresolved. The sloth was right. It was weighing on his soul, slowing them all down. Maybe this was one of those times when being a hero didn't involve looking particularly brave. It was just doing what you should.

Well, bottom line, no time is the perfect time to visit the dead in the underworld. And if the sloth was telling the truth, he could be back before anyone knew he was gone.

"So I can do this in no time at all?" he said. "I mean, literally no time will pass here?"

"Perhaps I exaggerated. No time will pass while you are in the underworld. But you will have to make certain preparations before you go."

"And I can come back."

"You can come back."

"Okay. All right." Unless he changed he was going to be visiting the underworld in his pajamas. "Let's get started. What do I need to do?"

"I neglected to mention, the ritual must be performed on land."

"Oh. Right." Thank God, he could go back to bed after all. Hell could wait. "I thought we were going right here and now. Well, so I'll just pop down next time we get—"

There was a distant clatter of boots overhead, and a bell rang.

"We just sighted land, didn't we," Quentin said.

The sloth gravely closed her eyes and then opened them again: indeed, yes, we just sighted land. Quentin was going to ask her how she did that but stopped himself, because asking would mean that he'd have to sit through the answer, and he'd had about enough slothly wisdom for the time being.

Not more than an hour later Quentin was standing on a flat gray beach in the middle of the night. He'd wanted to slip off to the underworld and back quietly, unbeknownst to the rest of the gang. Then maybe he would bring it up later, just drop it into conversation that by the way, he'd been to hell and back, no big thing, why do you ask? Benedict says hi. He hadn't planned on doing this in front of an audience.

But an audience had assembled: Eliot, Josh, Poppy, and even Julia, who had roused herself from her stupor to observe. Bingle and one of the sailors stood nearby with a long oar resting between them on their shoulders, and from the oar dangled the sloth. They had carried it out to the beach like that, like a side of beef. It had seemed the easiest way.

Of them all only Poppy didn't seem convinced he should go.

"I don't know, Quentin," she said. "I'm just trying to picture it. It's not like visiting somebody in the hospital. Get well soon, here's a bunch of balloons to tie to the bedpost. Imagine if you were dead. Would you want the living to visit you, when you knew you couldn't go back with them? I'm not a thousand percent sure I would. It seems a little like rubbing it in. Maybe you should let him rest in peace."

But he wasn't going to. What's the worst that could happen? Benedict could send him away if he wanted. The others hugged themselves in robes and overcoats in the chilly air. The island wasn't much more than an overgrown sandbar, flat and featureless. The tide was out, and the sea was not so much calm as limp. Every few minutes it worked up enough energy for a wave that rose up half a foot and then flopped onto the strand with a startling smack, as if to remind everyone that it was still there.

"I'm ready," Quentin said. "Tell me what to do."

The sloth had asked them to bring a ladder and a long, flat board from the ship. Now it instructed them to stand them up and lean the two together to form a triangle. The ladder and board didn't want to stay like that, the triangle kept collapsing, so Josh and Eliot had to hold them up. As a former Physical Kid Quentin was used to making magic out of unpromising raw materials, but this was crude even by his standards. The crescent moon of Fillory looked down on them, flooding the scene with silver light. It rotated eerily swiftly, once every ten minutes or so, so that its horns were always pointing in a different direction.

"Now climb the ladder."

Quentin did. Eliot grunted with the effort of keeping it upright. Quentin got to the top.

"Now slide down the slide."

It was clear what the sloth meant. He was supposed to slide down the plank like a playground slide. Though this wasn't a playground slide, and it was a bit of a circus act to get into position without any bars to hang on to. The slide wobbled and at one point almost collapsed, but Josh and Eliot managed to hold it together.

Quentin sat at the top of the triangle. He hadn't imagined that his journey to the underworld would be quite this ridiculous. He'd rather hoped it would involve drawing unholy sigils in the sand in letters of fire ten feet high, and flinging open the portal to hell. You can't win them all.

"Slide down the slide," the sloth said again.

It was a raw pine board, so he had to scooch himself along for a few feet, but eventually he managed to slide the rest of the way to the bottom. He was ready at any moment for a splinter to stab him in the ass, but none did. His bare feet planted in the firm cold sand. He stopped.

"Now what?" he called.

"Be patient," said the sloth.

Everyone waited. A wave flopped. A gust of wind ruffled the fabric of his pajamas.

"Should I—?"

"Try wiggling your toes a little."

Quentin wiggled them deeper into the cold, damp beach. He was about to get up and call it a night when he felt his toes break through something into nothing, and the sand gave way, and he slid down through it.

The moment he passed beneath the sand the slide became a real slide, made of metal, with metal guardrails. A playground slide. He slid down it in total darkness, with nothing around him as far as he could tell. It wasn't a perfect system—every time he got up a decent head of speed he would get stuck and have to scooch again, his butt squeaking loudly in the pitch-black.

A light appeared, far ahead and below him. He wasn't moving very fast, so he had plenty of time to check it out on his way down. It was an ordinary unshaded electric light set in a brick wall. The brickwork was old and uneven and could have used some repointing. Below the light was a pair of metal double doors painted a gray-brown. They were absolutely ordinary, the kind that might have opened onto a school auditorium.

In front of it stood someone who looked too small to be standing in front of the entrance to hell. He might have been eight years old. He was a sharp-looking little boy, with short black hair and a narrow face. He wore a little-boy-sized gray suit with a white shirt, but no tie. He looked like he'd gotten fidgety in church and come outside for a minute to blow off steam.

He didn't even have a stool to sit on, so he just stood in place as well as an eight-year-old boy can. He tried and failed to whistle. He kicked at nothing in particular.

Quentin thought it prudent to slow down and stop about twenty feet from the bottom of the slide. The boy watched him.

"Hi," the boy said. His voice sounded loud in the silence.

"Hi," Quentin said.

He slid down the rest of the way and then stood up, as gracefully as he could.

"You're not dead," the boy said.

"I'm alive," Quentin said. "But is this the entrance to the under-world?"

"You know how I could tell you were alive?" The boy pointed behind Quentin. "The slide. It works much better if you're dead."

"Oh. Yes, I got stuck a few times."

Quentin's skin prickled just standing there. He wondered if the boy was alive. He didn't look dead.

"Dead people are lighter," the boy said. "And when you die they give you a robe. It's better for sliding than regular pants."

The bulb made a bubble of light in the darkness. Quentin had a sense of towering emptiness all around them. There was no sky or ceiling. The brick wall seemed to go up forever—did go up forever, as far as he could see. He was in the subbasement of the world.

Quentin pointed behind him at the double doors. "Is it all right if I go inside?"

"You can only go inside if you're dead. That's the rule."

"Oh."

This was a setback. You'd think Abigail the Sloth would have briefed him on that wrinkle. He didn't relish the thought of trying to climb back up that long slide, if that was how you got back to the upper world. He seemed to remembered from being a kid that it was possible, just about, but that slide must have been half a mile long. What if he fell off? Or what if somebody died and came sliding down it while he was going up?

But it would also be a relief. He could get back to business. Back to the search for the key.

"The thing is, my friend Benedict is inside. And I need to tell him something."

The boy thought for a minute.

"Maybe you could tell me, and then I'll tell him."

"I think it should come from me."

The boy chewed his lip.

"Do you have a passport?"

"A passport? I don't think so."

"Yes, you do. Look."

The boy reached up and took something out of the shirt pocket of Quentin's pajamas. It was a piece of paper folded in half. It took Quentin a beat to recognize it: it was the passport the little girl had made for him, what was her name, Eleanor, all the way back on the Outer Island. How had it gotten into his pocket?

The little boy studied it with an eight-year-old's version of intense bureaucratic scrutiny. He looked up at Quentin's face to compare it with the picture.

"Is this how you spell your name?"

The boy pointed. Under his picture Eleanor had written in colored pencil, all capitals: KENG. The *K* was backward.

"Yes."

The boy sighed, exactly as if Quentin had just bested him at a game of Chinese checkers.

"All right. You can go in."

He rolled his eyes to make sure that Quentin knew that he didn't really care if Quentin went in or not.

Quentin opened one of the doors. It wasn't locked. He wondered what the boy would have done if he'd just barged in past him. Probably he would have transformed into some unspeakably horrible *Exorcist* thing and eaten him. The door opened onto a vast open space dimly lit by banks of buzzing fluorescent lights overhead.

It was full of people. Stale air and the muttering roar of thousands of conversations washed over him. The place was a gymnasium, or that was the closest analogy he could come up with off the cuff. A recreation center. The people in it were standing and sitting and walking around, but mostly what they were doing was playing games.

Right in front of him a foursome was listlessly swatting a shuttlecock back and forth over a badminton net. Farther off he could see a volleyball net set up that no one was using, and some Ping-Pong tables. The floor was heavily varnished wood and striped with the overlapping curving lines of various indoor sports, painted over each other at odd angles, in odd colors, the way they were in school gyms. The air had the empty, echoing quality of large stadiums, where sound travels a long way but doesn't have much to bounce off of, so it just gets gray and ragged and indistinct.

The people—the shades, he supposed—all looked solid, though the artificial light washed all the color out of them. Everybody wore loose white exercise clothing. His pajamas wouldn't look that out of place after all.

The dry air pressure pushed into his ears. Quentin resolved to take everything as it came, not think too hard, not try to figure it out, just try to find Benedict. That's why he was here. This was a situation where you really needed a Virgil to show you around. He looked behind him, but the doors had already closed. They even had those long metal bars on them that you pressed to open instead of a doorknob.

Just then one of the doors opened, and Julia slipped inside. She looked around the room, the same way Quentin had, but without his air of utter bewilderment. Her ability to take things in stride was just awesome. Her fever and her listlessness seemed to be gone. The door closed behind her with a metallic clunk.

For a second he thought she was dead, and his heart stopped.

"Relax," she said. "I thought you might want company."

"Thank you." His heart started up again. "You were right. I do. I'm so happy you're here."

The shades didn't seem especially happy to be in the underworld. They mostly looked bored. Nobody was running for shots on the badminton court. They were swinging limp-wristed, and when somebody netted a shot his partner didn't look especially pissed off about it. Mildly chagrined, maybe. At most. They didn't care. There was a scoreboard next to the court, but no one was keeping score. It showed the final score of the game before it, or maybe the game before that.

In fact a lot of them weren't playing the games at all, they were just talking or lying on their backs staring up at the buzzing fluorescent lights, saying nothing. The lights hardly even made sense. There was no electricity in Fillory.

"Did he take your passport?" Quentin said.

"No. He didn't say anything at all. He did not even look at me."

Quentin frowned at that. Weird.

"We'd better start looking," he said.

"Let us stay together."

Quentin had to force himself to start walking. The deeper they went into the throng, it felt like, the greater the risk that they would get stuck here forever, whatever the sloth said. They threaded their way between the different groups, sometimes stepping over people's legs, trying not to tread on people's hands, like it was a crowded picnic. He was worried he would attract attention by being alive, but people just glanced up at him and then looked away. It wasn't an underworld like in Homer or Dante, where everybody was dying to talk to you.

It was more depressing than spooky, really. It was like visiting a summer camp, or a senior center, or somebody else's office: it's all well and good, but the knowledge that you don't have to stay there, that you can go home at the end of the day and never come back, makes you so relieved you get dizzy. Not all the equipment was in its first youth. Some of it was actually fairly shabby—the board games had cracked leathery creases across the center where they folded up, and some of the badminton rackets were waving a loose string or two. He got his first real shock when he saw Fen.

He should have expected it. She'd been one of his guides on their trip down into Ember's Tomb. She was the good one, the one who didn't betray them. He barely knew her in life, but she was unmistakable, with her fishy lips and her short dykey haircut. The last time he'd seen her she was being simultaneously crushed and set on fire by a giant made of red-hot iron. Now she looked as healthy as she ever had, if a little wan, playing a slow-paced, low-pressure game of Ping-Pong. If she recognized him she didn't show it.

Now he allowed himself to wonder the thing he'd been trying not to wonder ever since the sloth first brought it up: whether Alice was here. Part of him was yearning to see her, would have given anything if one of the faces in the crowd could just belong to her. Another part of him hoped that she wasn't here. She was a *niffin* now. Maybe that counted as still alive.

There were big metal pillars here and there holding up the ceiling, and Benedict was sitting leaning against one of them, staring off into the pale, empty distance. Half a game of solitaire was arranged in front of him, but he'd lost interest in it, even though it was pretty obvious he wasn't stuck. He could put a red five of diamonds on a six of clubs.

He looked more like the Benedict Quentin had first met in the map room, than the suntanned bravo he'd become on board the *Muntjac*. He was pale and thin-armed, with his old black bangs falling over his eyes. His hair had grown back. He looked like a sullen Caravaggio youth. Death made him seem younger.

Quentin stopped.

"Hello, Benedict."

"Hello," Julia said.

Benedict's eyes flicked over to Quentin, then back to the distance.

"I know you can't take me with you," he said quietly.

The dead didn't mince words.

"You're right," Quentin said. "I can't. That's what the sloth said."

"So why did you come?"

Now he did look at Quentin, accusingly. Quentin had worried that he would have a gaping wound in his neck, but it was smooth and whole. He's not a zombie, he's a ghost, Quentin reminded himself. No, a shade.

"I wanted to see you again."

Quentin sat down next to him and leaned back against the pillar too. Julia sat down on his other side. Together the three of them looked out at the milling throngs of dead people.

A period of time passed, maybe five minutes, maybe an hour. It was hard to keep track in the underworld. Quentin would have to watch that.

"How are you, Benedict?" Julia said.

Benedict didn't answer.

"Did you see what happened to me?" he said. "I couldn't believe it. Bingle said to stay on the ship, but I thought—" He didn't finish, just frowned helplessly and shook his head. "I wanted to try some of the stuff we'd been practicing. For real, in a real fight. But the minute I stepped off the boat, *tschoooo!* Right in my throat. Right in the hollow of it."

He pressed his index finger into the soft part below his Adam's apple, where the arrow went in.

"It didn't even hurt that much. That's the funny thing. I thought they could pull it out. I turned around to get back on the boat. Then I realized I couldn't breathe, so I sat down. My mouth was full of blood. My sword fell in the water. Can you believe I was worried about that? I was trying to figure out whether we could dive down later and get my sword back. Did anybody get it?"

Quentin shook his head.

"I guess it doesn't matter," Benedict said. "It was just a practice sword."

"What happened next? You went down the slide?"

Benedict nodded.

Quentin was evolving a theory about that. The slide was humiliating, that's what it was. Deliberately embarrassing. That's what death did, it treated you like a child, like everything you had ever thought and done and cared about was just a child's game, to be crumpled up and thrown away when it was over. It didn't matter. Death didn't respect you. Death thought you were bullshit, and it wanted to make sure you knew it.

"So did you get the key?" Benedict said.

"I wanted to tell you about that," Quentin said. "We did get the key. There was a big fight, and we got the key, and it turned out to be really important. I wanted you to know that."

"But nobody else got killed. Just me."

"Nobody else died. I got stabbed in the side." Not much to brag about under the circumstances. "But what I wanted to tell you is that it was important, what we were doing. You didn't die for nothing. Those keys—we're going to use them to save Fillory. There was a point to it all. Without them all magic is going to go away, and the whole world will collapse. But we can use the keys to fix it."

Benedict's expression didn't change.

"But I didn't do anything," he said. "My dying didn't make a difference. I could have just stayed on the boat."

"We do not know what would have happened," Julia said.

Benedict ignored her again.

"He cannot hear me," Julia said to Quentin. "Something strange is going on. No one here can see or hear me. He does not know I am here."

"Benedict? Can you see Julia? She's sitting right next to you."

"No." Benedict frowned the way he used to, like Quentin was embarrassing him. "I don't see anybody. Just you."

"I am like a ghost here," she said. "A ghost among ghosts. A reverse ghost."

What was different about Julia, that the dead couldn't see her? It was a serious question, but not one they were going to answer right now. Instead they watched the crowd some more, and listened to the *kuh-tik kuh-tak* of the Ping-Pong games. For all the time they had to practice, the dead didn't seem to be that good at it. Nobody ever tried for a slam, or a fancy serve, and the rallies only ever went a few shots before the ball hit the net or went bouncing off into the crowd.

"This whole place," Benedict said. "It's like somebody almost tried to make it nice, with all the games and stuff, but then they didn't quite care enough to think it through. You know? I mean, who gives a shit? Who wants to play games forever? I'm just so bored of everything, and I haven't even been here that long."

Somebody. Those silvery gods, probably. Benedict kicked at his solitaire game, messing up the nice straight rows.

"You don't even get powers. You can't even fly. I'm not even see-through." He held up his hand, to demonstrate his opacity, and let it drop again. "Because you know, that would have been too cool or whatever."

"What else can you do here? Besides the games and such?"

"Not a lot." Benedict put his hands in his hair and looked up at the ceiling. "Talk to the other shades. There's nothing to eat, but you don't get hungry. A few people fight or have sex or whatever. You can totally watch them do it even. But after a while, I mean, what's the point? It's just the new people who do it.

"Once they did a human pyramid, to try to reach up to the lights.

But you can't reach them. They're too high. I never had sex," he added. "In the real world. Now I don't even want to."

Quentin talked on for a while, filling Benedict in on everything that had been happening.

"Did you have sex with that Poppy girl yet?" Benedict said, interrupting.

"Yes."

"Everybody said you were going to."

They did? Julia, a ghost's ghost, smirked.

Out of the corner of his eye Quentin couldn't help but notice that they were attracting some attention. Nothing obvious, but a couple of people were pointing at them. A kid—he might have been thirteen—stood there watching him fixedly. Quentin wondered how he died.

"I am starting to understand," Julia said. "It is really gone. The part of me that was human, the part of me that could die—it is gone, Quentin. I have lost it forever. That is why they canot see me." She was talking to him, but her black eyes were fixed on the distance. "I am never going to be human again. I did not understand it till now. I have lost my shade. I suppose I knew it. I just did not want to believe it."

He started to answer, to tell her he was sorry for what she had lost, sorry he couldn't do more, sorry for everything that had and hadn't happened, whatever it was. But there was so much he didn't understand. What did it mean, losing your shadow? How did it happen? How did it feel? Was she less than human now, or more? But she held up her hand, and then Benedict spoke.

"I hope you fail," he said suddenly, as if he'd just made a decision about it. "I hope you never find the key, and everybody dies, and the world ends. You know why? Because then maybe this place would end too."

Then Benedict was crying. He was sobbing so hard he wasn't making any noise. He caught his breath and started sobbing more.

Quentin put a hand on his back. Say something. Anything.

"I'm so sorry, Benedict. You died too soon. You didn't have your chance."

Benedict shook his head.

"It's good I died." He took a shuddering breath. "I was useless. It's good it was me and not anybody else." His voice went away to a squeak at the end.

"No," Quentin said firmly. "That's bullshit. You were a great map-maker, and you were going to be a great swordsman, and it's a fucking tragedy that you died."

Benedict nodded at this too.

"Will you—will you say hi to her for me? Tell her I liked her."

"Who do you mean?"

Even though his face was red from crying, and dripping with tears, Benedict's face had all its old adolescent contempt.

"Poppy. She was nice to me. Do you think she could come visit? Down here I mean?"

"I don't think she has a passport. I'm sorry, Benedict."

Benedict nodded. There were more shades around the two of them now. A group was definitely gathering, and it wasn't at all clear that their intentions were friendly.

"I'll come back," Quentin said.

"You can't. That's the rule. You can only come one time. Didn't they take your passport? They didn't give it back, did they?"

"No. I guess they didn't."

Benedict took a shaky breath and wiped his eyes on his white sleeve.

"I wish I could have stayed. I can't stop thinking about it. It's so stupid! If I'd just waited on the boat I'd still be up there. I looked at that arrow and thought, this little stick, this little piece of wood, is taking my whole life away. That's all my life is worth. One little stick can erase it all. That's the last thing I thought." He looked directly at Quentin. It was the one moment when he didn't seem angry or ashamed. "I miss it so much. You don't understand how much I miss it."

"I'm so sorry, Benedict. We miss you too."

"Listen, you better go. I don't think they want you here."

A whole crowd was standing around them now, silently, in a rough semicircle. Maybe it was Quentin's nonstandard pajamas. Maybe they could just see that he was alive somehow. That kid was one of them, who'd been staring at him before. Quentin wished the shades weren't so solid-looking.

Quentin and Benedict both stood up, with their backs to the pillar. So did Julia.

"I have something," Benedict said, suddenly shy again. "I was going to give it back."

He dug something out of his pocket and pressed it into Quentin's hand. His fingers were cold, and the thing was hard and cold too. It was the golden key.

"Oh. My God." It was the last one. Quentin held it up in both hands. "Benedict, how did you get this?"

"Quentin," Julia said. "Is that it?"

"I had it all along," Benedict said. "After you and Queen Julia went through the door I picked it up when no one was looking. I don't know why. I didn't know how to give it back. I thought maybe I'd pretend to find it. I'm sorry. I wanted to be a hero."

"Don't be sorry." Quentin's heart was hammering in his chest. This was it. They were going to win after all. "Don't be sorry at all. It doesn't matter."

"Then it came down here with me when I died. I didn't know what to do."

"You did the right thing, Benedict." He'd been so wrong about everything. After all that, he hadn't had to kill a monster or solve a riddle. He just had to come down here, to see how Benedict was doing. "Thank you. You are a hero. You really are. You always will be."

Quentin laughed out loud and clapped poor Benedict on the shoulder. Benedict laughed too, reluctantly, and then not so reluctantly. Quentin wondered when the last time was that anybody laughed down here.

"It is time," Julia said. "I am ready."

It was. It was time to go, if that's what she meant. But the shades didn't seem to want them to leave. They stood around them in a semi-circle, maybe a hundred of them, blocking the way back to the door. He couldn't push his way through them, there were too many. He backed up, hoping to get the pillar in between him and the mob, trying to think. His heart leaped for a second when he spotted Jollyby sitting on the floor, maybe fifty yards away, with his good legs and his big beard.

But he was just watching, too apathetic even to stand up. He wasn't going to do anything.

The key. He could open a portal. Quentin jabbed at the air with it frantically, but it didn't catch on anything. He couldn't find the lock. He jabbed more vigorously and more wildly. God knew where it would take them, but anywhere was better than here.

"That won't work down here," someone called out, in a schoolboy English accent. "Magic doesn't work." It was that kid, and Quentin recognized him now. It was Martin Chatwin himself. But young—his shade looked about thirteen. That must have been what he looked like just before he became a monster, before he died for the first time.

"I don't see your girlfriend," Martin said nastily. "She'll not save you."

Maybe it was that Quentin could still die—that's what attracted them. By killing him they could change something, do something, however terrible, that made a difference in the world above.

A couple of shades in the front row started forward, the first wave of the inevitable rush, but Benedict stepped forward to meet them and they hesitated. He grabbed a badminton racket out of somebody's hand and brandished it at them like a sword.

"Come on, you bastards!" There he was: the warrior Benedict should have been. He assumed the perfect dueling stance he'd learned from Bingle and pointed the racket at Martin Chatwin. "Come on, who's first?" he shouted. "You? Come on then!"

Quentin stepped up next to him, though with nothing in his hands and no magic in play, he was painfully aware that he didn't look very dangerous. Too bad he didn't bring a sword. He squared off and put up his fists and did his best to look like he had the faintest idea what to do with them.

"I am changing," Julia said matter-of-factly behind him. And then she repeated, "It is time."

Not now. Please not now. Let nothing new happen now. Quentin stole a glance back at Julia, then stopped and stared. Everyone else was staring too. Julia was taller, and her eyes had become a brilliant green. Something was happening. She was staring down at her arms with a small, deliberate frown on her face as she watched them become longer, and stronger, watched her skin take on a lustrous, pearly luminescence. It was like she'd looked in the fight at the castle, but more so. She was becoming something else.

Then she was smiling, really smiling. She looked past him at the assembled shades, and they fell back like they were facing a strong wind. Benedict gaped.

"Can you see me now?" she said.

He nodded, goggling.

She was something else now, something no longer human. A spirit? She had been beautiful before, but now she was magnificent. Something about being here must have caused her, or allowed her, to finish becoming what she'd been becoming all this time. She was as tall as Quentin now, though she seemed to be stopping there. With an air of curiosity she picked up a stick from the floor, a hockey stick it looked like. When she touched it, it grew. It came to life and became a long staff with a knobby crown. She hefted it, and the shades scrambled back even farther, even Martin Chatwin.

"Come," she said to him. Her voice was Julia's voice, but amplified, and with reverb. "Come fight."

Martin didn't come any closer. He didn't have to, Julia came to him. In a flash, quicker than a human could move, like a poison fish striking, she had him by his shirt front. She picked him up and threw him overhand into the crowd, his arms and legs splayed out like a starfish. Her strength was surreal. Quentin wasn't sure if she could hurt Martin—it's not like he could die a third time—but he sure as hell must have found it daunting.

The crowd was like a soccer crowd: the front ranks scrambled back, but behind them the shades were flooding in from all directions, pushing them forward again. Their voices and the sound of their feet were loud in the enormous room. Word had gone out. Something was happening. There was no end to them. Julia could probably fight her way to the door through them, but he didn't think she could save them all.

Julia saw it too.

"Do not worry," she said. "It's going to be all right."

Quentin had said that to her on his parents' lawn in Chesterton. He wondered if she remembered too. It certainly sounded better coming from her now.

Julia thumped the end of her staff on the floor, and then Quentin had to look away. The light was that bright. He couldn't see, but he heard the massed shades of the underworld of Fillory gasp in unison. The light was different—it wasn't the thin fluorescent gruel that passed for light down here, it was real rich white-gold sunlight, with all its wavelengths intact. It was like a gap had opened in the clouds.

A voice spoke.

"Enough," it said. Or she said: it was a woman's voice. It was a thrilling thing that harmonized with itself.

When Quentin could look again, he saw a woman standing in front of Julia, where her staff had struck the floor. She was a vision of power. Her face was lovely, warm and humorous and proud and fierce all at once. It was the face of a goddess. And there was something else there too—half Her face was in shadow. There was gravity there, and an understanding of grief. Everything will be all right, She seemed to say, and whatever is not, we will mourn.

In one hand She held a gnarled staff like Julia's. In the other She carried, oddly, a bird's nest with three blue eggs in it.

"Enough," She said again.

The shades did what She said and kept still. Julia knelt in front of the goddess, her face buried in her hands.

"My daughter," the goddess said. "You are safe now. It is over."

Julia nodded and looked up at Her. Her face was streaming with tears.

"You're Her," she said. "Our Lady."

"I have come to take you home."

The goddess motioned to Quentin. She wasn't glowing exactly, but it was hard to look at Her, the same way it's hard to look at the sun—She was that intense. Only now did Quentin really register the scale of Her. She must have been ten feet tall.

The dead watched them mutely. No more Ping-Pong. For a moment the entire underworld was silent.

Julia rose to her feet, drying her tears.

"What happened to you?" Quentin said. "You've changed."

"It is over," Julia said. "I am a daughter of the goddess now. A dryad." I am partially divine," she added, almost shyly.

He looked at her. She looked magnificent. She was going to be all right.

"It suits you," he said.

"Thank you. We must go now."

"I'm not going to argue with you."

The goddess gathered them both in with one tremendous arm. She held them, and together they all began to rise into the air. Someone cried out, and Quentin felt Benedict's hand grab his ankle and hang on.

"Don't leave me here! Please!"

It was like the last chopper out of Saigon. Quentin reached down to grab Benedict's wrist and for a moment he had it.

"I've got you!" he yelled.

He didn't know what he was doing, but he knew he was going to hold on to Benedict with all the strength he had. They were ten feet up, twenty. They could do this. They were going to steal one soul back. They were going to reverse entropy. Death would win the war, but it wasn't going to do it with a perfect record.

"Hang on!"

But Benedict couldn't hang on. His hand slipped from Quentin's and he fell back down among the shades without a word.

Then they were flying up past the fluorescent lights, and then up through where the ceiling would have been. There was nothing more he could do. Without Benedict to hang onto, Quentin gripped the key so hard it bit into his palm. He had lost Benedict, but he wasn't going to lose that. They rose up into the darkness, through fire, through earth, through water, and then out into the light again.

CHAPTER 25

Before they did it they took a vacation. It would take a week to order some of the necessary materials: mistletoe, more mirrors, some iron tools, chemically pure water, a few exotic powders. The ritual was pretty involved, more so than Julia would have thought, given the source. She'd expected something crude and pagan, a brute force play, but the reality was more complex and technical than that. They would have to clear a lot of space.

So while they waited for the FedEx guy to arrive, and for a few slow-rolling preparatory spells to mature, the magicians of Murs, the secret genius-aspirants to the sacred mysteries of the godhead, played tourist. It was the final furlough before their unit shipped out overseas—some last-minute R&R. They went to Sénanque Abbey, which despite being familiar from a million advertisements and in-flight magazines and five-hundred-piece jigsaw puzzles, was stunningly beautiful, the oldest, stillest place Julia had ever been. They went to Châteauneuf-du-Pape, which really had been the pope's new castle at some point, though all that was left of it now was a single scrap of wall with a few empty windows in it that stood out above the flat vineyards around it like an old, rotten tooth. They drove down to Cassis.

It was October, the ass-end of the season, and Cassis was the ass-end of the Côte d'Azur, barely part of it at all, low-rent and chock-full of teenage day-trippers out of Marseille. But the sun was hot, and the water, while it was colder than Julia thought water could be and still remain in liquid form, was a legitimate and spectacular azure. There was a small hotel there, not far from the beach, in a grove of stone pines full of invisible cicadas that trilled incessantly and amazingly loudly. When they sat on the porch they could barely hear each other talk.

They drank the local rosé, which supposedly lost its flavor if you drank it anywhere besides Cassis, and took a boat tour of the calanques, the hull-shredding limestone fingers that stuck out into the sea all along the coast. Nobody noticed the magicians. Nobody looked at them twice. Julia felt wonderfully normal. The beaches were all pebbles, no sand, but they spread out their towels over them and did their best to get comfortable, alternating long stretches of sunbathing with terrified, hilarious dashes into the water. It was so freezing it felt like it would stop your heart.

They all looked pale in their swimsuits. Following the local custom, Asmodeus took off her top, and Julia thought Failstaff's heart would stop just from that. And it wasn't just Asmodeus's breasts, which were indeed small and high and remarkably jiggly. Failstaff was obviously in love with Asmodeus. Six months in a house with them, and how the hell had Julia missed that? These were her friends, the closest thing she had to a family now. All this business about being gods was impairing Julia's ability to think like a human. Which was never her strong suit to begin with. She'd have to watch that. Something was getting lost in translation.

Julia watched the seafoam draw webs and Hebrew letters on the surface of the water and then erase them again. She shook her head and closed her eyes against the hot white Mediterranean sunlight. She felt happy and contented, like a seal on a rock, with her seal family around her. She was coming out of a dream, and all her friends were here with her—it was like the end of *The Wizard of Oz*. But the frightening thing was that she knew she was about to sink down into the dream again. It wasn't over. This was just a brief lucid interval. The anesthetic was going to kick back in in a second, the dream would take her, and she didn't know if she would ever wake up again.

That was why, that night in the hotel, when everybody else was asleep, she found herself walking the halls. She wanted something—she wanted Pouncy. She knocked on his door. When he answered she kissed him. And after she kissed him, they slept together. She wanted to feel like a human being, a creature of stormy, messy emotions, one more time. Even if it was a slightly slutty human being.

She'd slept with people in the past because she thought she should—like James—or to get something out of them that she needed—Jared, Warren, fill in your own examples. She didn't think she'd ever done it just because she wanted to before. It felt good. No, it felt fantastic. This was the way it was supposed to work.

She seemed more into it than Pouncy did. When she'd first gotten a look at him, that first day, she'd thought, aha, yes, let's not jump to any conclusions, but by all means, this could happen. She'd always gone for the clean-cut type, viz James, and Pouncy fell well within the acceptable parameters. But whenever she looked into Pouncy's flat slate eyes, and steeled herself for the drop as she fell for him, it never quite came. There wasn't quite enough of him there.

There was someone in there, she knew there was. She could see him perfectly clearly when they were online. But when they were together in person, face-to-face, Pouncy retreated somewhere far below the surface, deep under the ice. His security was too tight to crack, even for a hacker of her credentials.

She told Pouncy all this afterward, lying in bed, with those cicadas still shrilling away outside, though thankfully muted by the shutters. For a long time he didn't answer.

"I know," he said carefully. "I'm sorry."

It was the easy answer. Though at least he'd given it a shot.

"Don't be sorry. It doesn't matter." It really didn't. They looked at the ceiling and listened to the cicadas some more. She felt pleasantly fleshly. She was mind and body both, for once.

"But just so I know, is that why you want this so much?" she asked, sitting up. "The power? Like, if one day you're that strong, then maybe you'll be safe enough that the rest of you can come out?"

"Maybe." He grimaced, incidentally showing off those interesting lines around his mouth. She traced one with her finger. "I don't know."

"You don't know, or you won't say?"

Nothing. Blue screen of death: she'd crashed his system. Oh, well. Boys were so unstable that way, full of buggy, self-contradictory code, pathetically unoptimized. She flopped back down on the thin hotel pillow.

"So where would you put Project Ganymede's chances of success?" she said, just making conversation now. "Percentage-wise?"

"Oh, I like our chances," Pouncy said, his personality, such as it was, coming back online now that he was back on safe ground. "I'm gonna go seventy-thirty us. You?"

"More like even steven. Fifty-fifty. What are you going to do if it doesn't work out?"

"Try again somewhere else. I still think Greece is ground zero for this stuff. Would you come if I did?"

"Maybe." She wasn't going to reassure him just for the sake of it. "The wine's better here though. I'm not an ouzo girl."

"That's what I like about you."

He played with her fingers on top of the scratchy hotel blanket, studying them.

"Listen, I lied before," he said. "I think I do know why I'm doing this— what's in it for me. Or part of it. It's not about power for me, not really."

"Okay. What then?"

This oughta be good. Julia propped herself up on an elbow, and the sheet slid down off her shoulders. It was strange to be naked in front of Pouncy after all the time they'd spent together clothed. It was strange to be naked in front of anybody. It was like that cold water out there in the bay: scary, you didn't think you could stand it, but then you plunged in and pretty soon you got used to it. There was enough hiding in life. Sometimes you just wanted to show somebody your tits.

"I was in Free Trader before you. You weren't there when I came in."

"So?"

"So to be crude about it, you haven't seen my prescriptions." Pouncy grinned, ruefully, a different smile from his regular smile. "In terms of raw dosage, I am the official all-time record-holder for Free Trader Beowulf. At first they didn't even think they were real."

"And they're for . . . depression?"

He nodded. "Ever notice how I never drink coffee? Or eat chocolate? Can't. Not with this much Nardil in my system. I've had a half dozen courses of ECT. I tried to kill myself when I was twelve. My brain chemistry, it's just hosed. Not viable, in the long term."

Now it was Julia who felt panicky. She wasn't good in these moments, and she knew it. Hesitantly she put her hand on his smooth chest. It was all she could think of. It seemed to work well enough. God, did he actually manscape?

"So you think Our Lady Underground can heal you? Like with Asmo, that scar, whatever that was?"

It was sinking in, what he was saying. This wasn't an intellectual exercise for him, or a power grab.

"I don't know." He said it lightly, like he didn't care. "I really don't. It would be a miracle, and I guess miracles are O.L.U.'s business. But to be honest I wasn't thinking of it that way."

"How then?"

"If you laugh I swear to God that I will kill you."

"Careful, She might be listening."

"I'll plead insanity. I can back it up."

Pouncy's face wasn't a naturally expressive one. His cut cheekbones might have worked for a model, if he'd been a little taller, but never for an actor. But for a second she could really see what he was feeling, as he felt it.

"I want Her to take me home with Her," he said. "I want Her to take me back with Her, into heaven."

Julia didn't laugh. She understood that she was looking at another person like herself, a broken person, but Pouncy was even more broken than she was. She was used to feeling sorry for herself, and angry at other people. She was less used to feeling sorry for someone else, but she felt it now. She would never be in love with Pouncy, but she felt love for him.

"I hope she does, Pouncy," she said. "If that's what you want, I truly hope she does. But we'll miss you if you go."

Back at Murs Julia did something she hadn't done since she'd gotten there in June. She went online.

None of them had been on Free Trader Beowulf in ages. It took them a while to crack the new log-in routine, which changed every couple of months. They raced each other, alone in their bedrooms but yelling trash talk back and forth. (Except for Failstaff, who was too much the gentle giant to talk trash, which may have contributed to his eventual victory. Asmo quit early and futzed around hacking the router instead, so she could kick Pouncy offline at will.) Once she was in Julia didn't announce her presence—you didn't have to, you could slip in without the system pinging everybody—because she didn't want a blizzard of IMs from Free Traders wanting to catch up after her long absence. For a couple of hours she just lurked, cruising through old threads, and new ones that had sprung up while she was offline. There had been some turnover in the membership—there were a couple of new fish, and a couple of old fish were gone, or in hiding.

It seemed like years since she'd been there. She felt so much older now. You could customize the Free Trader interface any number of ways, but Julia had always gone for a bare-bones look, ASCII characters only, approximating the look and feel of an olde-timey Unix shell. Her eyes filled with tears just looking at everybody's user names, picked out in green-on-black text. So much had changed since then, since she'd been living a life of quiet desperation in a mundane universe, racking up hours at the IT shop and killing time till she could take off for Stanford. So much that couldn't be changed back. But not much had changed here.

Pouncy, Asmo, and Failstaff were running a private thread just like back in the day. She checked in.

```
[ViciousCirce has joined this thread!]
PouncySilverkitten: hey VC!
Asmodeus: hey
Failstaff: hey
ViciousCirce: hey
```

Electric silence for a minute. And then:

```
Asmodeus: so. big damn show tomorrow huh?
ViciousCirce: maybe
```

Failstaff: don't come much bigger
Asmodeus: waddaya mean maybe?
ViciousCirce: big show if OLU shows up
Asmodeus: why wouldn't she?
ViciousCirce: . . .
ViciousCirce: she might not exist? the summoning
    might fail? she might be on the rag? there
    are 10K reasons why not. just saying.
PouncySilverkitten: yes but what about the
    mirror/silver coins/milk/etc???
Asmodeus: and she fixed my scar
ViciousCirce: yeah yeah yeah look I don't want o be
    the asshole. just, I've seen some serious major
    league spellwork. no actual gods yet tho.
PouncySilverkitten: but you do believe that there
    is a higher praxis
ViciousCirce: believe there might be. = why I'm
    still here
ViciousCirce: and anyway
ViciousCirce: what if OLU does come. what if she
    is real. what next. how does it go down. what
    if she won't teach us. I mean do you want to
    just summon a god or do you want to be a god?
PouncySilverkitten: be. but this = necessary
    first step
Failstaff: but OK good point VC. maybe OLU isn't
    looking for interns
ViciousCirce: seriously say she manifests
    tomorrow. how does the conversation go
    pouncy?

It was weird that they hadn't talked about this stuff openly before: what they would actually say and do if she came. Maybe it was easier to do it online than face-to-face. There was less pressure. The stakes seemed lower. Keep it casual.

PouncySilverkitten: since you ask I've thought a
    lot about this

Asmodeus: you better have

PouncySilverkitten: so. ahem. yr standard issue
god follows one of two protocols, right?

Failstaff: uh. splain.

PouncySilverkitten: protocol #1 = prayer. this is
more yr modern christian deity. you pray for
X. god listens then judges you. if you're
deemed worthy/good/whatever you get what you
prayed for. you get X. if not then not.

Asmodeus: OOOOOPS I forgot to be good

PouncySilverkitten: now yr ancient pagan deity
follows protocol #2. more a basic
transactional kinda deal. demands a
sacrifice in return for goods and services.

Failstaff: those were the days

PouncySilverkitten: and then the nature of the
sacrifice itself follows one of two
protocols. symbolic or real.

Asmodeus: testify my bruthaaaaa

PouncySilverkitten: #1 symbolic = something
you don't really need but that signifies
yr devotion to the deity. a fatted calf
or whatever etc. #2 real = something
you do need, that proves yr devotion
to the deity. ie your hand, foot, blood,
child, etc

ViciousCirce: like abraham & isaac. sometimes
God wants your son. sometimes He'll settle
for a ram.

PouncySilverkitten: exactly. that's my rough n
ready take

ViciousCirce: fine so run the numbers gents and
you get three different scenarios and we're
screwed 2 out of 3.

ViciousCirce: modern deity: we're screwed because
we are presumably unworthy hence our prayers
go unanswered

ViciousCirce: pagan deity #2: if she demands

    a real sacrifice we're screwed because
    hello pouncy I need my foot or whatever
ViciousCirce: pagan deity #1 is our only shot.
    symbolic sacrifice. fatted calf in exchange
    for the divine praxis. one in three. that's
    my take. rough n ready
Failstaff: AND SORRY BUT WHAT IF I REALLY
    NEED MY FATTED CALF WHAT THEN P
    WHAT THEN
Asmodeus: sorry pouncy but do I really have to be
    the one to say that you have no FUCKEN idea
    what you're talking about
Asmodeus: literally none
PouncySilverkitten: o rly?
Failstaff: ?
ViciousCirce: . . .
Asmodeus: you think this is a male god you are
    dealing with ie you writ large. wrong. OLU is
    a godDESS. a lady god. this is NOT about
    PROTOCOLS
Asmodeus: I believe in Our Lady Underground
    and I believe that she will help us not
    because it is in her interest to do so or
    because she wants to eat your fucking foot
    or whatever but because she is KIND.
    pouncy u twat
Asmodeus: this is not a transaction bitches this
    is about mercy. this is about forgiveness.
    this is about divine grace. if Our Lady
    comes, that is what will save us.

   Long silence. Dead air. The next message was time-stamped a full
two minutes later.

PouncySilverkitten: so how about it VC. r you in
    or r you out or what r u?
[ViciousCirce has left this thread]

They did it in the Library. It was the only room big enough. They'd had to pack up all the books and stack them in the Long Study and elsewhere—the halls were overflowing with them—and dismantle those beautiful floating shelves. The walls were bare, the way they would have been when this was a farmhouse. The windows were flung open to the cold, quiet late-autumn air. The early evening sky was an unnaturally amazing blue, almost a royal blue.

It was all arranged very precisely according to ex-Saint Amadour's Phoenician invocation, down to the letter. The floor was a maze of chalk runes and patterns. Gummidgy would take the role of mistress of ceremonies and high priestess. Any of them could have handled the technicalities, but it had to be a woman, and of the women, dour, towering Gummidgy was the player deemed least likely to crack up at a crucial moment. She wore a simple flowing white gown. So did everybody else. Gummidgy also wore a crown of mistletoe.

So your basic Golden Bough deal, Julia thought. Fucking mistletoe. She never saw what all the fuss was about. Sure, it's pretty enough, but at the end of the day it's still a botanical parasite that strangles its host.

All the old furniture had been exiled from the room. In its place there was only a thick yew table, constructed to exacting specifications, and a huge hewn stone altar that would have cracked the floor if they hadn't braced it up from below and put some structural spells on the brace. The entire place had been purified in half a dozen ways, as had they—they'd fasted, and then drunk some nasty teas that made their pee change color and smell weird, and burned herbs in clay pots.

They'd done just about everything but actually bathe. The purification was symbolic, not hygienic. Actual medical hygiene didn't seem to be of great interest to the goddess.

"This isn't a patriarchal, Old Testament show," Asmodeus said sharply, when people complained. "Get it? Dirt does not contaminate, it generates. O.L.U. doesn't care if we're menstruating. She embraces the body."

This was followed by ribald witticisms from the menfolk signifying their willingness to offer themselves as symbolic husbands to the goddess. I got yer chthonic sacrifice right here in my pants, etc. etc. But Asmodeus's famous sense of humor was temporarily in remission for the occasion. Maybe it was nerves. Asmodeus wasn't high priestess material, but she seemed to have appointed herself the goddess's chief political compliance officer. She'd even argued that they should all go off their various medications for the occasion too, a suggestion that was universally ridiculed.

The yew table supported three beeswax candles and a big silver bowl full of rainwater; the bowl had cost about as much as the entire swimming pool had. The stone, a massive block of local marble, supported nothing. To be honest they weren't totally sure what it was for. Gummidgy took her place before the table while the others stood along the walls on either side, four and five. It was asymmetrical, but there was nothing specifically against it in Amadour's palimpsest, which was otherwise pretty lucid for a document prepared by a guy who lived in a cave and was pushing two millennia at least.

Julia's mind was a hot, churning mix of excitement and nerves, which she kept from boiling over with lashings of cool skepticism. But she remembered the rough, stiff feel of the statue's kiss in her dream. As creepy and Freudian as it sounded, she had felt so loved. She'd hoped she'd dream it again last night, but there had been nothing. Just dead air.

Pouncy was to her left. Asmodeus and Failstaff were opposite her so she could see them, but she avoided their eyes. They needed a full hour of silence before the summoning could begin, and tittering had to be kept to an absolute minimum. From outside they could hear the lowing and bleating of the sacrificial animals they'd brought in for the occasion: two sheep, two goats, and two calves, one of each pure black and all white, all shampooed within an inch of their imminently endangered lives. Should a symbolic sacrifice be required, they wanted to make sure the cupboard wasn't bare.

By seven o'clock the sun was down and the moon was on the rise, lipping up over the hills and fields behind Murs. Once it cleared the trees, a huge white arc light that seemed to be trained on their house alone, Gummidgy moved from her station in the center of the room and lit their candles one by one with the tip of her finger. Julia angled her candle so the wax wouldn't run down it and onto her hand. A hot droplet pricked her bare foot.

Gummidgy returned to the table and began the invocation. Somehow the candles on the table had been lit in the meantime, without anybody noticing.

Julia was glad it wasn't her in the hot seat. For one thing the invocation was long, and who knew what would happen if you munged it. Maybe it would just fizzle, but maybe it would snap back at you. Some spells did that.

For another it wasn't a spell, exactly. There was a lot of beseeching in it, and in Julia's opinion a magician did not beseech, she commanded. The grammar of it was all weird too. It kept repeating and circling back on itself, working through the same phrases over and over again. Frankly it sounded like junk to Julia. There was no proper structure to it, just a lot of talk about mothers and daughters and grain and earth and honey and wine, all that Song of Solomon stuff.

But it wasn't bullshit, that was the really crazy thing. Gummidgy was getting traction with this crap. Julia couldn't see anything, there were no visual phenomena, but she didn't have to. It was blindingly obvious that magic was happening. Gummidgy's voice was getting deeper and more echoey. Certain words made the air vibrate, or caused sudden rushes of wind.

Julia's candle started flaring up like a torch. She wished it wouldn't— she had to hold it at arm's length to keep it from singeing her hair, which she had left loose, because it had seemed more feminine and O.L.U.-like. Something was happening. Something was on its way. She could feel it coming like a freight train.

It was only then that Julia realized something, something absolutely terrible, that it would have been hard to admit to Pouncy or the others even if it weren't too late: she didn't want it to work. She wanted the spell to fail. She had made a grave mistake—she had misunderstood something about herself, something so basic she couldn't understand how she'd missed it until now. She didn't need this, and she didn't want it. She didn't want the goddess to come.

Pouncy had told her when she first got to Murs that it wasn't enough for her to love him and the others, she had to love magic more. But she didn't. She came to Murs looking for magic, but she was also looking for a new home, and a new family, and she'd found them all, all three, and it was enough. She was content; she didn't need anything else, least of all more power. Her quest had ended and she hadn't even known it till this moment. She didn't want to become a goddess. All she'd wanted was to become human, and here at Murs it had finally happened.

Now it was too late. She couldn't stop what was happening. The goddess was coming. She wanted to throw down her candle and run around the room shouting at them, breaking up the flow, telling them it was okay, they didn't have to do this, they had all they needed right there all around them if they could only see it. Our Lady Underground would understand that—O.L.U., goddess of mercy and fruitfulness, she above all would understand what Julia had only just figured out.

But there was no way Julia could make the others understand. And there were titanic energies in the room with them now, giant forces, and there was no telling what would happen if she tried to disrupt the casting. Julia's whole body was goose bumps. Gummidgy's voice was getting louder. She was building up to the big finish. Her eyes were closed, and she was swaying from side to side and singing—it wasn't in the invocation, the melody must have come to her straight over the transom, out of the ether, via the heavenly wireless. The windows on one side of the room were solid moonlight now, as if the moon had come down from its orbit and was hovering right outside, peering in at them.

It was hard to tear her eyes away from Gummidgy, but Julia risked a glance to her left, at Pouncy. He looked back at her and smiled. He wasn't nervous. He looked calm. He looked happy. Please, if nothing else, please let her give him what he needs, she thought. Julia clung to this truth: that O.L.U. would never ask them for something they couldn't give. Julia knew her, and she would never do that.

One of the candles on the table had started to spit and crackle and flare. It produced a gout of flame, a big one that went halfway up to the ceiling and made a deep guttural *woof,* and then it spat out something huge and red that landed standing on the table. Gummidgy gave a choking cough and dropped to the floor like she'd been shot—Julia could hear the crack as her head hit.

In the sudden silence the god struck a triumphant pose, arms wide, and held it. It was a giant, twelve feet tall and lithe and covered with red hair. It had the shape of a man and the head of a fox. It was not Our Lady Underground.

It was Reynard the Fox. They'd been tricked, but good.

"Shit!"

It was Asmodeus's voice. Always quick, was Asmo. In the same moment came the rifle shot of all the windows slamming shut at once, and the door, as if something invisible had just left in an almighty huff. The moonlight went out like a switch had been flipped.

Oh God oh God oh God. The fear was instant and electric, her whole body was almost spasming with it. They'd stuck out their thumbs and they had gotten into the wrong car. They'd been tricked, just the way O.L.U. had been in the story, tricked and sent to the underworld, if She even existed at all. Maybe She didn't. Maybe it was all just a joke. Julia threw her candle at the fox. It bounced off His leg and went out. She'd pictured Reynard the Fox as a playful, spritely figure. He was not that. He was a monster, and they were shut in here with Him.

Reynard jumped lightly down from the table, a carnival showman. Now that He had moved she found she could move too. She was crap at offensive magic, but she knew her shields, and she knew some sledgehammer dismissals and banishments. Just in case, she began piling up wards and shields between herself and the god, so thick that the air turned amber and wavy, tinted glass and heat ripples. Next to her she could hear Pouncy, still calm, preparing a banishment. The situation was salvageable. It didn't work, so let's get rid of this shithead and get out of here. Let's go to Greece.

There was hardly any time. Reynard's mouth was a nest of pointy teeth. That's the thing about those tricksters, isn't it: they're never really all that fucking funny. She knew if He went for her, if He even looked at her, she would drop whatever she was casting and run, even though there was nowhere to run to. She stuttered twice, her voice broke, and she had to start a spell over. It must have been a trick all along. It was sinking in.

There never was an Our Lady Underground at all. Was there. She didn't exist. It made Julia want to weep with terror and sorrow.

The fox was looking around Him, counting His winnings. Failstaff—oh, Failstaff—made the first move, advancing on Him from behind, soft-footed for a big man. He'd amped up his candle into something like a flamethrower and was aiming it two-handed. Big as he was, he looked tiny next to a real giant. He'd barely got the thing flaming when Reynard turned suddenly, grabbed his robe, and pulled him over with one huge hand and put him in the crook of His arm, like He was going to give him a Dutch rub. But He didn't give him a Dutch rub. He broke Failstaff's neck like a farmer killing a hen and dropped him on the floor.

He lay on top of Gummidgy, who still hadn't moved. His legs shook like he was being electrocuted. All the breath went out of Julia's chest and got stuck there. She couldn't inhale. She was going to pass out. At the other end of the room a party of three was already going at the door, trying to unseal it. They were working together, Iris in the middle: big magic, six-handed. Warming to His task, humming what might have been a jolly Provençal folk song, Reynard hefted the big block of stone with both hands and heaved it into them. Two of them went down hard under it. The third—it was Fiberpunk the Metamagician, him of the four-dimensional shapes—kept gamely at it, ice-cold under fire, taking all three parts himself without dropping a stitch. Julia always thought he must be a bit of a fraud, with all that shit he talked, but he had chops. He was rattling off some sick self-reflexive unlocking sequence like it was no big thing.

Reynard took him with His two big hands, around the chest, like a doll, and threw him up against the ceiling, thirty feet up. He hit hard—maybe Reynard was trying to make him stick—but he was probably still alive when his head clipped the table on the way down. His skull burst like a cantaloupe, spilling a fan of bloody slurry across the smooth parquet. Julia thought of all the metamagical secrets that must have been locked in that orderly brain, now catastrophically, irreversibly disordered.

It was all over now. All ruined. Julia was ready to die now, she just hoped it wouldn't hurt too much. Reynard squatted and put His hands in the blood and whatever else and smeared it sensually on His luxurious fox-fur chest, matting it. You couldn't tell if He was grinning like a mad thing or if that's just how foxes' mouths looked.

Two minutes after the fox-god arrived Pouncy, Asmodeus, and Julia were the last of the Murs magicians, the cream of the safe-house scene, left alive on the planet. For a moment Julia felt her feet leave the floor— it must have been Pouncy, trying to buy them a minute by taking them up to that high ceiling, but Reynard cut the spell off when they were only a couple of feet off the floor, and they dropped back down hard. He picked up the heavy silver bowl, dumping out the rainwater, and threw it at Pouncy like a discus. Just as He did, Asmodeus finished up something she'd been working on since the god arrived, a Maximal Dismissal maybe, with a little something extra on it, something sharp that actually tweaked Reynard's attention.

It didn't hurt Him, but He felt it. You could see His big pointy ears twitch with annoyance. The cup struck Pouncy hard, but off-center. It crunched his left hip and went rocketing away. Pouncy groaned and folded in two.

"Stop!" Julia said. "Stop it!"

Fear: Julia was all out of it. A dead woman didn't feel fear. And she was all out of magic too. She was going to say some regular words for a change, non-magic words. She was going to talk to this asshole.

"You took our sacrifice," she said. She swallowed. "Now give us what we paid for."

It felt like she was trying to breathe at thirty thousand feet. The fox looked down His narrow muzzle at her. With His doggy head and human body He looked like the Egyptian death-god Anubis.

"Give it to us!" Julia shouted. "You owe it to us!"

Asmo watched her from the other side of the room, frozen. All her knowing, savvy Asmo attitude had fallen away. She looked about ten years old.

Reynard gave a loud bark before He spoke.

"A sacrifice is not to be taken," He said, in a deep, reasonable voice, with only a very slight French accent. "A sacrifice is to be freely given. I took their lives. They did not offer them to me." It was like He couldn't believe the rudeness of it. "I had to *take* them."

Pouncy had pushed himself up into a sitting position against the wall. The pain must have been appalling. Sweat stood out all over his face.

"Take my life. I'm giving it to you. Take it."

Reynard cocked His head. Fantastic Mr. Fox. He fingered His whiskers.

"You are dying. You will be dead soon. It is not the same."

"You can have mine," Julia said. "I'm giving it to you. If you let the others live."

Reynard groomed Himself, licking blood and brains off the back of His paw-hand.

"Do you know what you have done here?" He said. "I am just the beginning. When you call on a god, all gods hear. Did you know that? And no human has called down a god in two thousand years. The old gods will have heard too, you know. Better to be dead when they come back. Better never to have lived, when the old gods return."

"Take me!" Pouncy moaned. He gasped as something inside him gave way, and he whispered the rest. "Take me. I'm giving you my life."

"You are dying," Reynard said again, dismissively.

He paused. Pouncy said nothing.

"He has died," Reynard announced.

The fox-god turned to Julia and raised His eyebrows, studying her. A real fox wouldn't have those, Julia thought meaninglessly.

"I accept," He said. "The other one can live, if you give yourself to me. And I will give you something more. I will give you what you wanted, what you summoned me for."

"We didn't summon you," Asmo said in a small voice. "We summoned Our Lady." Then she bit her lip and fell silent.

Reynard regarded Julia critically, and then He went for her. He went right through her wards like they weren't there. Julia was ready to die—she closed her eyes and let her head fall back, baring her throat for Him to rip it out. But He didn't. His hairy hands were on her, He dragged her across the room and forced her upper body down so she was bent over the yew table. Julia didn't understand, and then she did and she wished she hadn't.

She fought Him. He pinned her torso down on the wood with

one hard, heavy hand, and she tore at his fingers but they were like stone. She had agreed, but she hadn't agreed to this. Let Him kill her if He wanted. It hurt when He tore her robe off—the fabric burned against her skin. She tried to look behind her at what was happening, and she saw—no, no, she didn't see that, she saw nothing—the god's big hand working casually between His legs as He positioned Himself behind her. He kicked her bare feet apart with a practiced kick. This wasn't His first time at the rodeo.

Then He pushed Himself inside her. She had wondered if He would be too big, if He would tear her open and leave her gutted and flopping like a fish. She strained against Him. Exhausted, she rested her hot forehead on her arm in what she supposed was the manner of rape victims since the beginning of time. Her own hoarse panting was the only sound.

It took a long time. It was not a timeless period; she didn't pass out or lose track of time. She would have said it took between seven and ten minutes for the god to finish raping her, and she was there for every second of it. From her vantage point she could see Failstaff's thick legs on the floor, not moving anymore, overlapping Gummidgy's long brown ones, and she could see where the two who had died by the door lay, a huge continent of blood having flowed out from under the stone block and joined into one shape.

Better me than Asmo. She couldn't see Asmodeus, because she couldn't look at her, but she could hear her. She was crying loudly. She sounded like the little girl she still essentially was, a little girl who had lost her way. Where was home for her? Who were her parents? Julia didn't even know. Hot tears flowed down Julia's cheeks too, and slicked her arm, and wet the brown wood.

The only other noises were those made by Reynard the Fox, the trickster-god, grunting softly and hoarsely behind her. At one point a couple of rebel nerve endings attempted to send pleasure signals to her brain, whereupon her brain burned them out with a pulse of neurochemical electricity, never to feel again.

Before He was done with Julia, Asmodeus doubled over and threw up, splat, on the floor. Then she ran, slipping once on vomit, once again on blood. She reached the door, and it opened for her. It took a long time to close behind her. Through it, and through a window across the hall, Julia caught a glimpse of the innocent green-black world outside, impossibly far away.

The fox-god barked loudly when He came. She felt it. The terrible, unspeakable thing, which she would never tell anybody, not even herself, was that it felt wonderful. Not in a sexual way—God no. But it filled her up with power. It flowed into every part of her, up through her trunk, down her legs, and out through her arms. She clenched her teeth and shut her eyes to try and stop it, but it even reached her brain, lighting her up from within with divine energy. She opened her eyes and watched it fill her hands. When it reached the tips of her fingers her fingernails glowed.

And then He took something from her. As He withdrew His penis from her, something came out with it. It was like it caught on some-thing—a transparent film, it felt like, something inside her, the same shape as her. It was something invisible that had been with her always, and Reynard ripped it away. She didn't know what it was, but she felt it go, and she shuddered when she felt it. Without it she was something different, something other than what she had been before. Reynard had given her power, and taken something in payment that she would have died rather than give up. But she didn't get to choose.

Finally, it might have been ten minutes later, she raised her head. The moon was back up in the sky where it belonged, as if it were blameless, and had taken no part in this. It was just a regular moon now, a sterile rock, frozen and suffocated to death in the vacuum, that was all.

Julia stood up and turned around. She looked at Pouncy. He was still sitting up against the wall, steely eyes still open, but very definitely dead. Maybe he was in heaven now. She knew she should feel something, but she felt nothing, and that in itself was horrifying. She walked to the door and out through it, her bare feet splatting lightly in the cool blood. She didn't look back. All the lights were off. The house was empty. Nobody home.

Thinking and feeling nothing, because there was nothing left to think or feel except the unpleasant stickiness of blood and God knew what else on her feet, and between her toes, she stepped out onto the lawn. Something terrible has happened, she thought, but no emotions attached to those words. The sacrificial animals were all gone, escaped somehow and fled, except for the two sheep, who wouldn't meet her eyes. For some reason the sun was coming up. They must have been in there all night. She rubbed her feet in the cold dew, then bent down and put her hands in it and rubbed them on her face.

Then she uttered a word she had never heard before and flew, naked and bloody as a newborn baby, up into the lightening sky.

CHAPTER 26

The others had stayed out on the beach until dawn, waiting for Quentin and Julia to come back up from the underworld. Finally they'd given up and gone back to their berths aboard the *Muntjac*, chilled and exhausted, to sleep. When they woke up a few hours later they were relieved, and then overjoyed, to find Quentin and Julia waiting for them on deck.

Though the scene they woke up to was a weird one. Julia stood there transformed, newly beautiful and powerful. She radiated an air of peace and triumph. Quentin wasn't transformed, but something else was going on with him: he was down on his hands and knees for some reason, just staring at the wooden planks of the deck.

They had flown up and up and up, until gradually Quentin realized that the weightless feeling he had was of them descending instead, but not the way they had come: they dropped down through wet clinging clouds, and then he saw a little chip of wood below them in the ocean that turned out to be the *Muntjac*, the water around it glittering with dawn light. The goddess placed them on the deck, kissed Julia on the cheek, and vanished.

Quentin found that he couldn't stand on his own; or he could, but he didn't want to. He got down on all fours and put the key down in front of him. He looked at the good wooden planks the *Muntjac* was made of, really looked at them: after a night spent in hell everything was real and vivid and impossibly detailed. Colors looked superbright, even the grays and browns and blacks and the other undistinguished, intermediate noncolors that he ordinarily would have skipped over and ignored. He followed the lines and striations and tiger stripes of the wood, drawn and arranged with careless perfection, dark and light, order and chaos, all mingled together with little splinters along the edges of the boards that had been scuffed up and set at different angles, each one, by the passage of careless feet.

He absolutely understood how weird and high-seeming he looked, but he didn't care. He felt like he could stare at the wood forever. Just this: the good, hardy, noble wood. He was never going to lose this, he thought. He was going to enjoy everything exactly as much, to the atom, as Benedict would have enjoyed it if he could have come back from the underworld. And Alice, and all the rest of them. It was all he could do for them. Earth or Fillory, did it even matter? What was the huge conundrum? Everywhere you looked there was so much richness, you could never exhaust it. Maybe it was all a game, that got crumpled up and thrown away at the end, but while you were here it was real.

He pressed his forehead against the deck, hard, like a penitent pilgrim, and felt the beat of the waves transmitted through it from below like a pulse, and the heat of the sun. He smelled the sour salt smell of seawater, and he heard the hesitant footsteps of baffled people gathering around him, unsure of what to do. He heard all the other meaningless noises reality was always cheerfully making to itself, the squeaks and scrapes and thumps and drones, on and on, world without end.

He took a deep breath and sat up. Away from the warmth of the goddess's body he shivered in the early morning ocean air. But even the cold felt good to him. This is life, he kept saying to himself. That was being dead, and this is being alive. That was death, this is life. I will never confuse them again.

Then people were hauling him to his feet and guiding him down below to his cabin. He was pretty sure he could have walked on his own, but he let them half carry him—they seemed to want to do it, and who was he to stand in their way? Then he was lying on his side on his bed. He was dead tired, but he didn't want to close his eyes, not with everything that was going on all around him.

Some time later he felt someone sit down on the edge of the bed. Julia.

"Thank you, Julia," he said after a while. His lips and tongue felt thick and clumsy. "You saved me. You saved everything. Thank you."

"The goddess saved us."

"I'm grateful to Her too."

"I'll tell Her."

"How do you feel?"

"I feel finished," she said simply. "I feel like I am finally finished. I became who I was becoming."

"Oh," he said, and he had to laugh at how completely stupid he sounded. "I'm just glad you're all right. Are you all right?"

"I was stuck in between for so long," she said, instead of answering his question. "I couldn't go back—I wanted to, for a long time. A long time. I wanted to go back to before what happened, when I was still human. But I couldn't, and I couldn't go forward either. Then somehow in the underworld I realized for the first time, really understood, that I was never going back. So I let go. And that's when it happened."

He felt tongue-tied. What did you say to a newly minted supernatural being? He wanted to just stare at her. He'd never been in such close quarters with a spirit before.

"You said you were a dryad."

"I am. We're the daughters of the goddess. That makes me a demigoddess," she added, by way of clarification. "I'm not literally her daughter of course. It's more of a spiritual thing."

Julia was still Julia, but the anger, the sense that she was violently at odds with the world over some crucial point, was gone. And she'd gotten her contractions back.

"So you take care of trees?"

"We take care of the trees, and the goddess takes care of us. There's a tree that belongs to me, though I'm not sure where it is. I can feel it though. I'll go there as soon as we're done." She laughed. It was good to know she still could. "I know so much about oak trees. I could bore you to death with it.

"Do you know, I had almost lost faith in the goddess? I almost stopped believing in Her. But I realized I had to become something. I had to take what was done to me and use it to make myself into what I wanted to be. And I wanted this. And when I called Her, the goddess came.

"I feel so powerful, Quentin. It's like there's a sun inside me, or a star, that will burn forever."

"Does that mean—are you immortal?"

"I don't know." And here a cloud passed over her face. "In a way, I've already died. Julia is dead, Quentin. I'm alive, and I may be alive forever, but the girl I was is dead."

Sitting this close to Julia, he could see how inhuman she was now. Her flesh was like pale wood. The girl he'd known in high school, with her freckles and her oboe, was gone forever—she'd been destroyed and discarded in the making of this being. Julia would never be mortal again. The Julia sitting next to him on his bed was like a magnificent memorial to the girl she used to be.

At least this Julia was beyond all that. She was out of the game, the living and dying game, that the rest of them were trapped in. She was different. She wasn't kludgy, rickety flesh and blood anymore. She was magic.

"There are things you should know," she said. "I can tell you now, how this all began. Why I changed, and why the old gods came back."

"Really?" Quentin propped himself up on one elbow. "You know?"

"I know," she said. "I'm going to tell you everything."

"I want to know."

"It's not a happy story."

"I think I'm ready," he said.

"I know you think that. But it's sadder than you think."

There were no more islands. They were past that now. The *Muntjac* slit its way through calm empty ocean, day after day, farther and farther east, the sun rising in front of them, roaring by overhead, and then extinguishing itself nightly in the water behind them. It was visibly larger in the mornings—they could almost hear the muffled rumble of its burning, like a distant blast furnace.

After a week the wind died, but the sky was clear, and in the afternoons and evenings Admiral Lacker raised the light-sail, and they ran along on the strength of a storm of sunshine. Quentin had been to the far west of Fillory, when he hunted the White Stag over the Western Sea, but the far east was a very different place. It had a polar quality. The sun was bright and hot here, but the air was getting colder. Even in the mornings, when the sun seemed dangerously close, like it was going to light the mast on fire, they could see their breath. The blue of the sky was deep and vivid. It felt like Quentin could fall up into it if he wasn't careful.

The water was an icy aquamarine, and the *Muntjac* slipped through it almost frictionlessly, barely leaving a ripple. It was different stuff from ordinary seawater—silkier and less dense, with almost no surface tension, more like rubbing alcohol. Only one kind of fish lived in it, long silvery bullets that flashed and dashed through the water in diamond-shaped schools. They caught a few, but they didn't look edible. They had huge eyes, and no mouths, and their flesh was bright white and smelled like ammonia.

The world around them began to feel thin. It was nothing Quentin could put his finger on, but the material of reality itself seemed to be getting sheer and fragile, stretched taut over its frame. You could feel the chill of the outer dark right through it. They all caught themselves moving slowly and gently, as if they might put a foot through the fabric of space-time by accident.

The sea was getting shallower too. You could see the bottom through the glassy water, and every morning when Quentin checked it, it was closer. This was an interesting phenomenon from an oceanographic point of view, but more to the point it was a problem. The *Muntjac* wasn't a big ship, but it still drew twenty feet or so, and at this rate they were going to run aground long before they got to wherever the hell they were going.

"Maybe Fillory doesn't have an End," Quentin said one night, as they were tucking into their increasingly meager and unappetizing rations.

"What, like it's infinite?" Josh said. "Or it's a sphere, like Earth? God, I hope it's not that. What if we end up back at Whitespire again? Man, I'll be pissed if all we've done is find the Northwest Passage or whatever after all that."

He licked his fingers, getting the extra salt from a salt biscuit. He was the only one who didn't seem overawed by the situation.

"I meant more like a Möbius strip. What if it's all one side, and no edge?"

"I think you mean a Klein bottle," Poppy said. "A Möbius strip still has edges. Or one edge."

"You mean a Klein bottle," Julia confirmed.

Nothing like having a demi-goddess around to settle an argument. Julia didn't eat anymore, but she still sat at dinner with them.

"Is it a Klein bottle? Do you know?"

Julia shook her head.

"I don't know. I don't think so."

"So you're not omniscient?" Eliot said. "I don't mean that in a bad way. But you don't know for sure?"

"No," Julia said. "But I know this world has an End."

They all woke up early the next morning when the *Muntjac* ran aground.

It wasn't like they hit a wall. It was more gradual: a distant grinding sound, gentle at first, then louder, and then suddenly urgent, bone on bone, ending with everything on board, people included, slewing gently but firmly into the nearest forward wall as the ship came to a complete stop. And then, ringing silence.

They all came up on deck in their robes and pajamas to see what had happened.

The stillness was uncanny. All around them the sea was flat and glassy as a coat of fresh varnish. No wind blew. A fish jumped, maybe a quarter-mile away, and it sounded as loud as if it were right next to them. The sails hung slack. The slightest vibration sent circular ripples gliding away toward the horizon in all directions.

"Well," Eliot said, "that tears it. What do we do now?"

It crossed Quentin's mind, as it had presumably crossed that of the crew, that they had long ago passed the halfway point of their supplies. If they couldn't go forward they would die on the way back. Or just die here, marooned in a desert of water.

"I will speak to the ship," Julia said.

As she had even when she was still human, Julia meant what she said and said what she meant. She went down to the hold, to the heart of the ship, where the clockwork was, knelt down, and began to whisper, stopping now and then to listen. It wasn't a long conversation. After four or five minutes, she patted the thick base of the *Muntjac*'s mast and stood up.

"It is settled."

It wasn't immediately clear what had been settled, or how, but it became apparent. They floated free of the bottom and began gliding forward again as if nothing had happened. Quentin only figured it out when he happened to look back at their wake. Enormous old planks and beams and other assorted carpentry were bobbing and turning in the water behind them. The *Muntjac* was making herself smaller, rebuilding herself from the keel up and discarding the extra wood as she went. She was giving up her body for them.

Quentin's eyes smarted. He didn't know what sort of being the *Muntjac* was, whether it had feelings or whether it was just some kind of mechanism, an artificial intelligence constructed out of rope and wood, but he felt a surge of gratitude and sadness. They'd asked so much of it already.

"Thank you, old girl," he said, just in case it, or she, could hear him. He patted the worn railing. "You've saved us one more time."

The shallower the ocean got the more the *Muntjac* had to alter herself. Quentin told the crew to bring up the sloth, who permitted herself to be slung from a yard, blinking and yawning in the open air. They emptied the cabins and the hold and piled up everything around them on deck.

Banging and groaning sounds came from below, deep in the ship's guts. Quentin watched as first the *Muntjac*'s high, proud stern dropped into the water, then its bowsprit and its entire forecastle. At around four o'clock in the afternoon the mizzenmast toppled over into the water with a huge splash and was lost astern. The foremast went that evening. They slept on deck that night, shivering under blankets in the chill.

In the morning when they woke up the sea was shallow enough to wade in, and the *Muntjac* had become a flat single-masted raft. Its hull was completely gone; only the deck was left. The ocean mirrored the cloudless dawn light, making an infinite plain of smoky rose. When the sun boiled up over the horizon it was immense—you could see its corona curling around its bright, unbearable face.

At noon they ran aground again—the front edge of the raft crunched to a stop on the sandy bottom. That was it; the *Muntjac* was going no farther. She had nothing more to give.

But by now they could see that their journey did in fact have a destination. A low, dark line had materialized out of the distance, running the full width of the horizon. It was impossible to guess how far away it was.

"Looks like we'll have to walk," Quentin said.

One by one Quentin, Eliot, Josh, Julia, and Poppy swung over the side and dropped into the water. It was cold but shallow, not even knee-deep.

They had already set off when they heard a splash behind them. Bingle had climbed over the railing—he was coming too. Evidently he did not consider his bodyguarding duties fully discharged. And Abigail the Sloth: he was carrying her piggyback, her long arms around his neck like a fur wrap, her claws hooked together in front of him.

The loneliness of the scene was beyond anything. After an hour the ship was virtually invisible behind them, and the only sound was the steady soft *slosh-slosh* of their footsteps. Sometimes the mouthless fish came and bumped harmlessly against their ankles. The thin water was easier to walk through than regular seawater would have been; it put up less resistance. Julia walked along on the surface as befitted a demigoddess. No one spoke, not even Abigail, who was almost never at a loss for words. The ocean was smooth as glass to the horizon.

The sun was hot on the tops of their heads. After a while Quentin gave up staring at the horizon and looked only down, at his familiar black boots taking step after step after step. Each step took them closer to the end of the story. They were going to finish this. Something could still go wrong now, probably, but he had no idea what. He could gauge their progress by the gradual shallowing of the water, from his calf down to his ankle and finally to a thin film of water that splatted underfoot. The sun was low in the sky behind them. Far off to their right a single evening star had appeared, with its twin shimmering below it in the water.

"Let's hurry," Julia said. "I can feel the magic going."

By that time the wall in front of them was very clear. It might have been ten feet high and was made from old, thin bricks—it looked like the same bricks they'd used to build the wall in hell. They must have used the same contractor. It stood at the back of a thin gray sandy beach that stretched off to the vanishing point in both directions. A huge old wooden door was set in it, bleached and worn by time and weather. As they came closer they could see that the door had seven keyholes of different sizes.

On either side of the door were two plain wooden chairs, the kind of old chairs that might have gotten exiled to the porch because they were too shabby for the dining room, but were still too good and sturdy to throw away. They didn't match; one of them had a wicker seat. In the chairs sat a man and a woman. The man was tall and thin, fiftyish, with a stern, narrow face. He wore a black dinner suit, complete with tails. He looked a little like Lincoln on his way to the theater.

The woman was younger by a decade or so, pale and lovely. As they stepped onto dry land she raised a hand to greet them. It was Elaine, the Customs Agent from the Outer Island. She looked a lot more serious than she had the last time he'd seen her. She had something in her lap: the Seeing Hare. She was petting it.

She stood up, and the hare jumped down and skittered off down the beach. Quentin watched it go. It made him think of little Eleanor and her winged bunnies. He wondered where she was, and who was taking care of her. Before this was over he would ask.

"Good evening," Elaine said. "Your Majesty. Your Highnesses. Good evening, all of you. I am the Customs Agent. I tend to the borders of Fillory. Borders of all kinds," she added pointedly, to Quentin. "I believe you met my father? I hope he didn't inconvenience you too greatly."

Her father? Ah. More fairy tale. He supposed that fit together neatly.

"Bother, it's almost time," the man said. "The gods are finishing their work. Magic is almost gone, and without it Fillory will fold up like a box with us in it. Do you have the keys?"

Quentin looked to Eliot.

"You do it," the High King said. "It was your adventure first."

Eliot held out the ring with the seven keys, and Quentin took it and walked over to the big wooden door. He kept his back straight and his gut sucked in. This was the moment, he thought. This was the triumph.

People would tell this story forever. Though they might leave out how melancholy the twilit beach seemed, like all beaches in the early evening, when the fun is over. Time to slap the sand off your feet and pile into the station wagon and go home.

"Smallest to largest," said the man in the tuxedo, sternly but not unkindly. "Go ahead. Leave them in the locks as you go."

Quentin slipped each one off the key ring in turn. The first, tiniest lock turned easily—you could feel a mechanism of fine, well-oiled gears meshing and interlocking and turning inside the door. But each successive key put up more resistance. The fourth one was set so high up that he had to stand on his tiptoes to turn it. He could barely budge the sixth, and when he finally got it going, his fingers bending back and his knuckles white with the effort, light flashed inside the keyhole, and it spat out sparks that stung his wrist.

The last one wouldn't turn at all, and in the end Quentin had to ask Bingle for his sword, which he stuck through the metal ring at the end of the key and used as a lever. Even then the man in the formal suit had to get up from his chair and help him.

When it finally gave and began to move, it was like he'd fitted a key into a hole in the hub at the center of the universe. Together he and the man put their backs into it—Quentin's face was crushed into his shoulder. His suit smelled faintly of mothballs. As the key turned, the stars turned overhead. The whole cosmos was rotating around them, or maybe it was Fillory that was turning, or maybe there was no difference. The night sky spun above them until the day sky replaced it overhead. They kept turning, and the day sky sank below the horizon again, and the stars rushed back out.

Full circle. They were back where they started. There was a deep click that seemed to echo forever, the sound bouncing off the outer walls of the world, a bank vault opening in a cathedral. The door swung slowly inward. Behind it, through the doorway, was empty space, black sky, stars. Quentin took an involuntary step back. Everybody on the beach, even Bingle, even the sloth, let out a breath they didn't know they'd been holding.

"Well," Elaine said shakily. She was flushed, and she even laughed a little. "I have to admit, I wasn't sure that would work."

"Did it work?" Quentin said. He looked around for a sign that things were different. "I can't tell."

"It worked."

"It worked," Julia said.

Somebody caught Quentin from behind in a huge bear hug. It was Josh. They fell down on the chilly sand together, Josh on top.

"Dude!" Josh yelled. "Look at you! We just saved magic!"

"I guess we did." Quentin started laughing, and then he couldn't stop. It was all over. Magic wasn't going to leave them after all. They had their own magic now, and it was safe. Not just in Fillory but everywhere. Nobody could take it away from them. Probably a little more dignity befitted the Saviors of All Magic, but fuck it. Poppy whooped and piled onto them too.

"You losers," Eliot said, but he was grinning his crazed, jagged grin. "We should have brought champagne."

Quentin lay back on the sand and looked up at the darkening sky. He could have fallen asleep right then and there on the sand, and slept all the way back to Whitespire. He closed his eyes. He heard Elaine's voice.

"If you like," she said, "you can go through it."

Quentin opened his eyes again. He sat up.

"Wait," he said. "Really? Through the door? What's back there?"

"The Far Side of the World," the Customs Agent said simply.

"The Far Side," Eliot said. "We don't know what that means."

"I should explain," she said. She settled herself back on her chair. "Fillory is not a sphere, like the world where you were born. Fillory is flat."

"So not a Klein bottle?" Josh said.

"I have so many questions," Poppy said. "Like how does gravity work?"

"As such," Elaine went on, ignoring them, "Fillory has another side. A verso, if you will."

"What's on it?" Quentin asked. "What's over there?"

"Nothing. And everything."

When this was over Quentin was ready for a long vacation from gods and demons and all their cryptic utterances.

"There is another world there, waiting to be born. A world for which Fillory was in a sense merely a rough draft. You might make an analogy: the Far Side is to Fillory as Fillory is to your Earth. A greener place. A realer, more magical place."

This was a new wrinkle. He and Poppy and Josh got up from the sand, feeling a little silly. They brushed themselves off and stood at attention.

"Each of you has a choice, whether to go or to stay. I cannot guarantee that anyone who passes through the door will be able to return here. But if you do not go now, there will never be another chance."

"But what's really there?" Quentin said. "What's it like?"

She looked at Quentin, calmly and directly.

"It's what you want, Quentin. It's everything you're looking for. It is the adventure of all adventures."

There it was. The real end of the story, the happy ending. All he could think was: Alice. She could be waiting for him there. Elaine surveyed the group, where they stood in a loose half circle in front of the door. Her eyes met Eliot's first. He shook his head slowly.

"I'm High King." His voice was as serious as Quentin had ever heard it. "I can't go. I'm not going to leave Fillory."

She turned to Bingle, who still had the sloth on his back, peeking over his shoulder like a baby koala. Bingle closed his hooded eyes.

"It was never my destiny to return," he said. He stepped forward. So he was right after all. Quentin supposed that by now Bingle had earned a free pass on the dramatics.

"I also will go," the sloth said over his shoulder, in case anybody had forgotten about her.

Elaine stood aside and indicated that they should proceed. Without hesitating Bingle walked up to the doorway and opened it all the way.

He was silhouetted against the immense twinkling emptiness. In the night sky beyond him a comet rocketed past, sparking and sputtering merrily like a cheap firework. This was what passed for outer space in Fillory, Quentin supposed. At the bottom of the doorway he could see just the tip of one of the silver moon's horns. It was rising, on its way to its regular appearance in the night sky of Fillory.

It felt like you could be sucked out through the doorway if you got too close, like through an air lock. But Bingle just stood there, looking around.

"It's down," Elaine said. "You have to climb."

There must have been a ladder. Bingle turned to face them, got to his knees, moving slowly to avoid dislodging the sloth, and felt around with his foot till he evidently got it on a rung. He nodded goodbye to Quentin and began to climb down, step by step. His narrow olive face disappeared below the edge.

"Once you get halfway gravity turns around," Elaine called after him. "And you start climbing up. It's not as tricky as it sounds," she added to the rest of them.

She turned to Quentin.

Two times before Quentin had made this same decision. He'd stood on the threshold of a new world and then stepped over it. When he'd arrived at Brakebills he'd thrown his whole life away, his whole world and everyone he knew, in exchange for a shiny magical new one. It had been easy, he'd had nothing worth keeping. He'd done it again when he came to Fillory, and it wasn't much harder the second time. But it was harder now, the third time, very hard. Now he had something to lose.

But he was stronger now too. He knew himself better. It turned out his journey wasn't over after all. He wasn't going to go back. He looked at Eliot.

"Go," Eliot said. "One of us should."

God, was he that easy to read?

"Go," Poppy said. "This is for you, Quentin."

He put his arms around her.

"Thank you, Poppy," he whispered. Then he said it to all of them: "Thank you."

His voice caught on the phrase. He didn't care.

Standing in the doorway, he took a deep breath as if he were about to climb down into a pool. He could look out and survey it all: he was backstage at the cosmos. Far below he could see Bingle and the sloth, tiny, still climbing down what looked like an endless column of iron rungs. The entirety of the moon was hanging right there in front of him, bright and glorious in the abyss, glowing with its own light. It looked like he could jump to it. It was smooth and white, no craters. He hadn't realized the tips of the horns were so sharp.

He knelt down to start his climb.

"That's odd." The Customs Agent frowned. "Wait a moment. Where's your passport?"

Quentin stopped, on one knee.

"My passport?" he said. This again. "I don't have it. I gave it to the kid in hell."

"In hell? The underworld?"

"Well, yes. I had to go there. That's where the last key was."

"Oh." She pursed her lips. "I'm sorry, but you can't go through without a passport."

She couldn't be serious.

"Well, but hang on," Quentin said. "I have a passport. Eleanor made it for me. I just don't have it on me. They have it in the underworld."

Elaine smiled, a tired smile that wasn't completely devoid of sympathy, but wasn't exactly brimming over with it either.

"Eleanor can only make you one passport, Quentin. You've used yours. I'm sorry. I can't let you through."

This couldn't be happening. He looked past her to the others, who were standing watching him blankly, the way the passengers in a car look at the driver when he's been pulled over for speeding. He tried to make his face communicate something, something on the order of, can you believe this shit? But it wasn't easy. He was being asked to be a good sport, but this cut deeper than that. This was his destiny here, and she wasn't going to take it away on a technicality.

"There has to be a loophole." He was still kneeling on the threshold, looking up at her, halfway out the door. He could feel the Far Side pulling at him, bright and joyful, with its own gravity. This was where his story led. "Something. I had no choice, I had to go to the underworld. And not to put too fine a point on it, but if I hadn't we never would have opened the door. We wouldn't be here. The world would've ended—"

"That is what makes this all the harder."

"—so you know," Quentin kept talking, louder, "if I hadn't gone to the underworld there wouldn't *be* any going to the Far Side of the

World." He knew if he stood up it would be over. "There wouldn't be any Far Side left. All of this would be gone."

Her expression didn't change. The woman was psychotic. She wasn't going to give in, no matter what he said.

"All right," he said. He waited as long as he could, then he stood up. He held up his hands. "All right."

If there was one thing he'd learned on this fucking quest it was how to take a punch. He dropped his hands. He was still a king, for Christ's sake. That would do for a destiny. He had no complaining to do. He'd had more than his fair share of adventures. He knew that. Quentin went over and stood next to Poppy, the woman he'd just tried to abandon. She put her arm around his waist and kissed him on the cheek.

"You'll be okay," she said. Her hands felt cool on his. Elaine was closing the door.

"Wait," Julia said. "I want to go through."

The agent stopped, but she didn't look as if she thought she'd made a mistake.

"I'm going through," Julia said. "My tree is waiting for me there. I can feel it."

Elaine conferred with her partner quietly, but when they were done they both shook their heads.

"Julia, you must take some blame for the catastrophe that nearly occurred. You and your friends invoked the gods, and drew their attention to us, and brought them back. You betrayed this world, however unknowingly, in order to increase your own power. There must be consequences."

For a long moment Julia stood perfectly still, staring not at the Customs Agent but at the half-open door. Her skin began to glow, and her hair crackled. The signs weren't hard to read. She was prepared to fight her way through if necessary.

"Wait." Quentin said. "Hang on a minute. I think you're missing something." It was almost dark out now, and the sky was a riot of stars. "Do you two have any idea what she's been through? What she lost? And you're talking about consequences? She's had plenty of consequences. And oh, by the way, not that it counts for much apparently, but she saved the world too. You'd think she was due a bit of a reward."

"She made her own decisions," the man who sat by the door said. "All is in balance."

"You know, I've noticed that you people, or whatever you are, are pretty free with assigning that kind of responsibility. Well, Julia wouldn't have done what she did if I'd helped her learn magic."

"Quentin," Julia said. "Cease." She was still powered up, ready to make her move.

"If you want to play that game, let's play it. Julia did what she did because of me. So if you want to blame somebody, blame me. Put that wrong on me where it belongs and let her go through to the Far Side. Where she belongs."

The silence of the beach at the end of the world descended again. They saw by starlight now, and by the light of the impending moon, leaking through the half-open door, and by Julia-light: she was glowing softly, with a warm white light that threw their shadows behind them on the sand and glimmered on the water.

Elaine and the well-dressed man conferred again for a long minute. At least they weren't quibbling about passports. Probably Julia hadn't needed hers to get into the underworld. She slipped in under the radar.

"All right," the man said, when they were finished. "We agree. Julia's fault will be upon you, and she will pass through."

"All right," Quentin said. Sometimes you win one when you least expect it. He felt strangely light. Buoyant. "Great. Thank you."

Julia turned her head and smiled at him, her beautiful unearthly smile. He felt free. He'd thought he would carry his share of that unhappiness for the rest of his life. Now, suddenly, he had shed it when he least expected it, and he felt like he was going to float up into the air. He had atoned, that was the word for it.

Julia took both his hands in hers and kissed him on the mouth, a long kiss, full at last of something like real love. Demi-goddess or no, at that moment she seemed fully herself to him in a way she hadn't for years, not since their last day together in Brooklyn, when both their lives had been changed beyond recognition. Whatever losses she'd suffered, this was Julia, all of her. And Quentin felt pretty whole now too.

She stepped up to the doorway, but she didn't kneel. She straightened and squared herself like an Olympic diver and then, disdaining the ladder, she dove off the edge, straight down, and disappeared.

When she was gone the beach was a little darker.

It was over and done with at last. He was ready for the curtain to come down. He wasn't looking forward to the all-night slog back to the *Muntjac,* and God knew how they were going to get home from there. Surely there must be some trick, some more magic lying around somewhere that would enable them to skip over that part. Maybe Ember would come.

"Where's the damn Cozy Horse when you need it?" Josh must have been thinking the same thing.

"And how should Quentin pay?" the Customs Agent said. She was speaking to the man in the black suit.

Suddenly Quentin felt less tired.

"What do you mean?" he said. They were whispering again.

"Hang on," Eliot said. "That's not how it works."

"It is," said the man, "how it works. Julia's debt is now upon Quentin, and he must settle it. What is it that Quentin holds most dear?"

"Well," Quentin said, "I'm already not going to the Far Side."

Brilliant. He should have been a lawyer. A thought froze him: they were going to take Poppy. Or do something to her. He was afraid to even look at her in case it gave them ideas.

"His crown," Elaine announced. "I am sorry, Quentin. As of this moment you are no longer a king of Fillory."

"You exceed your authority," Eliot said hotly.

Quentin had been braced for devastation, but when it came he didn't feel anything at all. That was what they were taking, and they would take it. Had taken it. He didn't feel any different. It was all very abstract, kingliness, in the end. He supposed what he would miss most was his big, quiet bedroom at Castle Whitespire. He faced the others, but none of them looked at him any differently. He took a deep breath.

"Well," he said stupidly. "Easy come."

That was the end of Quentin the Magician King, just like that. He was somebody else now. It was a silly thing to be sad about, really. For God's sake they'd just saved magic, saved all their lives. Julia had found her peace. They had finished the quest. He hadn't lost, he'd won.

Elaine and the man in the suit had resumed their stations, on their chairs, like a pair of seated caryatids. Job well done. God, he couldn't believe he'd flirted with her back on the Outer Island. She wasn't so different from her father, in the end.

He had high hopes for her daughter, anyway.

"Give my best to Eleanor," he said.

"Oh, Eleanor," Elaine said in the dismissive tone she reserved for her daughter. "She still talks about the time you picked her up, how far she could see. You made quite an impression on her."

"She's a sweet girl."

"Can't tell time yet. Do you know, she's absolutely obsessed with Earth now? She asked me to send her away to school there, and I'm sorely tempted to do it, I can tell you. I'm counting the days."

Good for Eleanor, Quentin thought. She was getting off the Outer Island. She would be all right.

"Imagine that," he said. "When she's old enough for college, drop me a line. I might be able to recommend one."

It was time to go.

The sea was no longer empty. Something was coming toward them across it: it was Ember, late as usual, trotting neatly across the skim of water. Wouldn't be like Him to miss a good dethroning.

"So," Quentin said. "Back to the *Muntjac?* Or?" Maybe the magic sheep would be good for a ride home. He really did hope so. Ember took His place by Eliot's side.

"Not for you, Quentin," He said.

And then Eliot did something Quentin had never seen him do before, even after everything they'd been through together. He sobbed. He turned away and walked a few steps down the beach with his back to them, arms crossed, head down.

"It is a dark day for Fillory," Ember said, "but you will always be remembered here. And all good things must come to an end."

"Wait a minute."

Quentin recognized this little speech. It was the canned farewell that Ember delivered in the books, every time He did what He did best, which was to kick visitors out of Fillory at the end.

"I don't understand. Look, enough is enough."

"Yes, Quentin, enough is enough. It is exactly that."

"I'm sorry, Quentin." Eliot couldn't look at him. He took a rattling breath. "There's nothing I can do. It's always been the rule."

Fortunately Eliot had a gorgeous embroidered handkerchief to blot his eyes with. He'd probably never had to use it before.

"For God's sake!" Quentin might as well get angry, there was nothing else left to do. "You can't send me back to Earth, I live here now! I'm not some schoolkid who has to get back in time for curfew or fifth form or whatever, I'm a fucking grown-up. This is my home! I'm not from Earth anymore, I'm a Fillorian!"

Ember's face was impassive beneath His massive stony horns. They curled back from His woolly forehead, ribbed like ancient seashells.

"No."

"This isn't how it ends!" Quentin said. "I am the hero of this goddamned story, Ember! Remember? And the hero gets the reward!"

"No, Quentin," the ram said. "The hero pays the price."

Eliot put a hand on Quentin's shoulder.

"You know what they say," Eliot said. "Once a king in Fillory, always—"

"Save it." Quentin shook him off. "Save it. That's bullshit and you know it."

He sighed. "I guess I do."

Eliot had himself back under control now. He held something out, small and pearly, pinched in his handkerchief.

"It's a magic button. Ember brought it. It will take you to the Neitherlands. You can travel back to Earth from there, or wherever you want to go. It just won't take you back here."

"I can hook you up, Quentin!" Josh said, trying to sound cheerful. "Seriously, I practically own the Neitherlands now. You want Teletubbies? I'll draw you a map!"

"Oh, forget it." He still felt angry. "Come on. Let's go back to our home fucking planet."

It was all over. He always hated these parts, even when they were just stories, even when they weren't about him. He would think about the future soon. It wouldn't be that bad. He and Josh could live in Venice. And Poppy. It wouldn't be bad at all. It was just that he felt like he'd just had a limb severed, and he was looking down at the stump waiting to start bleeding to death.

"We aren't coming, Quentin," Poppy said. She was standing by Eliot.

"We're staying," Josh said. Even in the cold and the darkness, Quentin could see him blushing furiously. "We're not going back."

"Oh, Quentin!" He'd never seen Poppy look so upset, not even when they were freezing to death. "We can't go! Fillory needs us. With you and Julia gone there are two empty thrones. One king, one queen. We have to take them."

Of course. A king and a queen. King Josh. Queen Poppy. Long live. He was going back alone.

This, now, this stopped him. He'd known that adventures were supposed to be hard. He'd understood that he would have to go a long way and solve difficult problems and fight foes and be brave and whatever else. But this was hard in a way he hadn't counted on. You couldn't kill it with a sword or fix it with a spell. You couldn't fight it. You just had to endure it, and you didn't look good or noble or heroic doing it. You were just the guy people felt sorry for, that was all. It didn't make a good story—in fact he saw now that the stories had it all wrong, about what you got, and what you gave. It's not that he wasn't willing. He just hadn't understood. He wasn't ready for it.

"I feel like an asshole, Quentin," Josh said.

"No, listen, you're totally right." Quentin's lips were numb. He kept talking. "I should have thought of it. Listen, you're going to love it."

"You can have the palazzo."

"Great, man, thanks, that'll be great."

"I'm sorry, Quentin!" Poppy threw her arms around him. "I had to say yes!"

"It's okay! Jesus!"

You didn't want to be a grown man saying come on, it isn't fair. But it didn't feel all that fair.

"It is time," Ember said, standing there on His stupid little ballerina hoofs.

"Listen, we have to do this now," Eliot said. His face was white. This was costing him too.

"Fine. Okay. Give me the button."

Josh hugged him fiercely, and then Poppy. She kissed him too, but he could hardly feel it. He knew he would be sorry later, but it was just too much. He had to do this right now or he was going to implode.

"I'll miss you," he said. "Be a good queen."

"I have something for you," Eliot said. "I was saving it for when this was all over, but . . . well, I guess it's all over."

From inside his jacket Eliot brought out a silver pocket watch. Quentin would have known it anywhere: it was from the little clock-tree that had been growing in the magic clearing in the Queenswood, where all this began. Eliot must have harvested it when he went back there. It ticked away merrily, as if it were happy to see him again.

He put it in his pocket. He wasn't in the mood for merriness. Too bad it wasn't a gold watch: the classic retirement present.

"Thank you. It's beautiful." It was.

The huge horned moon of Fillory was up now, clearing the wall at the edge of the world with its nightly leap. It didn't rumble, like the sun, but this close it rang faintly, like a struck tuning fork. Quentin looked at it long and hard. Probably he would never see it again.

Then Eliot hugged him, a long hug, and when he was done he kissed Quentin on the mouth. That Quentin felt.

"Sorry," Eliot said. "But you were kissing everybody else."

He held out the button. Quentin's hand shook. Even as he took it, almost before he touched it, he was floating up through cold water.

It had always been cold, going to the Neitherlands, but he never remembered it being this cold. The water burned against his skin—it was Antarctic cold, like when he'd had to run to the South Pole from Brakebills South, years ago. The wound in his side ached. Hot tears leaked out from under his eyelids and mingled with the frigid water. For a long second he hung there, weightless. It felt like he was motionless, but he must have been rising up through the water because with no warning something rough clonked him on the top of his head, hard enough that he saw silver sparkles.

Insult to injury: the fountain was frozen over. Quentin groped frantically at the ice above him, almost losing the button in the process.

Nobody thought of this? Could you drown in magic water? Then his fingers found an edge. They'd cut a hole in the ice, he'd just missed it.

The hole was frozen over too, but only lightly. He cracked it satisfyingly with his fist. It was good to punch something and feel it break. He wanted to break it again. He wriggled up and out—he had to sprawl awkwardly on the slick ice with his upper body, like a seal, and then grab the stone rim of the basin and pull himself the rest of the way out of the hole. He lay there for a minute, gasping and shivering.

For a second he'd forgotten everything that had just happened. Nothing like a brush with death to take your mind off your troubles. The magic water was already evaporating. His hair was dry before his feet were even out of the water.

He was alone. The stone square was silent. He felt dizzy, and not just because he'd hit his head. It was all crashing in on him now. He'd thought he'd known what his future looked like, but he'd been mistaken. His life would be something else now. He was starting over, only he didn't think he had the strength to start over. He didn't know if he could stand up.

Feeling like an old man, he boosted himself down off the edge of the fountain and leaned back against it. He'd always liked the Neitherlands—there was something comforting about their in-between-ness. They were nowhere, and as such they relieved you of the burden of being anywhere in particular. They were a good place to be miserable in. Though God help him, Penny would probably come floating by in a minute.

The Neitherlands had changed since he and Poppy had been there last. The buildings were still broken, and there was still a little snow in the corners of the square, in the shadows, but it wasn't coming down anymore. It wasn't freezing. Magic really was flowing again: you could see it here. The ruins were coming back to life.

Though they weren't going back to normal. A warm breeze blew. He'd never felt that in the Neitherlands before. They'd always been asleep, but now they were waking up.

Quentin felt ruined too. He had that in common with the Neitherlands. He felt like a frozen tundra where nothing grew and nothing would ever grow again. He had finished his quest, and it had cost him everything and everyone he'd done it for. The equation balanced perfectly: all canceled out. And without his crown, or his throne, or Fillory, or even his friends, he had no idea who he was.

But something had changed inside him too. He didn't understand it yet, but he felt it. Somehow, even though he'd lost everything, he felt more like a king now than he ever did when he was one. Not like a toy king. He felt real. He waved to the empty square the way he used to wave to the people from the balcony in Fillory.

Overhead the clouds were breaking apart. He could see a pale sky, and the sun was pushing through. He hadn't even known there was a sun here. The silver watch Eliot gave him was ticking along in an inside pocket of his best topcoat, the one with the seed pearls and the silver thread, like a cat purring, or a second heart. The air was chilly but it was warming up, and the ground was littered with puddles of meltwater. Stubborn green shoots were forcing themselves up between the paving stones, cracking the old rock, in spite of everything.